MURDER,
A RANDOM ACT

ROCKY W. DORCY

MURDER,
A RANDOM ACT

Rocky W. Dorcy

Published by:
Gray Door Books, LLC
P.O. Box 363
Edgewater, FL 32132
Email: graydoorbooks@aol.com
Web: http://www.graydoorbooks.com

Cover photo credit: Jason Peterson
Special thanks to Harry H. Dorcy, Jr. for assisting in final editing

ISBN: 0996050108
ISBN 13: 9780996050104
Library of Congress Control Number: 2014936365
Gray Door Books, LLC, Edgewater, FL

For my mother, Elizabeth June Dorcy, who taught me the importance of being a good, kind, and fair person.

For William Vincent Dorcy, the stepfather whose name I proudly bear. My most profound regret is that I never showed this incredible man how much he meant to me.

For Harvey Cohen, who late in both of our lives, honored me by treating me like a son, and by letting me treat him like the father I never met.

My mother and stepfather died of natural causes. Harvey Cohen however, was murdered in his home on September 19, 2013, in Encino, California. The murderer or murderers are still at large. There is a substantial reward for information leading to the arrest and conviction of the perpetrators of this senseless and apparently random act.

If anyone reading this book has any information regarding the identity of those involved, please contact the Los Angeles Police Department.

PROLOGUE

LUCIA CABELLA

CHAPTER 1

SIXTEEN YEAR-OLD Duncan Cabella was flipping through the pages of his algebra book, desperately trying to fight off boredom, when he noticed a shadow creeping across the wall of his bedroom.

The only window in his room faced the fenced-in backyard of the modest two-bedroom stucco home in Tarzana, California, where he lived with his widowed mother.

Welcoming the distraction, Duncan lifted the corner of the opaque shade and peeked outside. To his surprise, a rather large man, clad in black, was standing motionless at the back door.

What's he doing back there?

Poking his head out of his bedroom door, he looked down the hallway toward the front of the house as he softly called out, "Mom?" Even as the word was coming out of his mouth, he heard a knock at the front door.

"I'll get it," his mother said, running her fingers through his thick, black hair as she whisked past.

Duncan hadn't noticed her coming up from behind and was startled by her touch. Or maybe it was the mysterious man in the backyard. Whatever the reason, he flinched and a chill ran up his spine.

"Mom! Don't do that! You scared the crap out of me."

She let out a little chuckle. "You're such a scaredy-cat. And don't say that word. You know I don't like it when you say bad words."

Catching his breath, he said, "There's someone at the back door, too. I'm going to go check it out."

"Oh no you don't! I know you. You're just looking for an excuse to get out of your room. Get back to your studies. Remember your promise?"

"Yes, Mother. I'm going to law school, even if it kills me," Duncan muttered in the same playfully mocking cadence he had used in response to that question at least a million times.

"No, you're going to law school, or *I'll* kill you," she said in a loving but emphatic tone. "Now, don't make me tie you to your desk." The thought of tying her son to his desk made her let out another little giggle.

Using guilt as only a Catholic mother can, she'd extracted the promise that he'd become a lawyer. A promise that she never grew tired of reminding him of, and one that he was determined to keep.

"What about the man in the backyard?"

"I'll take a look after I get the front door. Back to work!" She looked over her shoulder just in time to see Duncan's head disappear back into his bedroom.

"Good boy," she whispered as she headed for the front door.

Lucia Cabella was a loving mother and a devout Catholic. Duncan was a devoted son and a mama's boy in every sense of the term.

Just as Duncan sat back down at his desk, he heard glass breaking and his mother scream.

"No, no!" He heard a struggle and then, "Don't hurt my boy. Run, Duncan! Run!"

His first thought was to run toward the sound of his mother's voice, but before he could move, someone came crashing through the back door.

A lifetime of obeying his mother, mixed with more than a little fear, triumphed over his instinct to run to her aid. Duncan dove head-first through the open bedroom window into the backyard, tearing the shade from the wall, dragging it through the window with him.

Shrubs broke his fall, the branches carving long, deep scratches down his arms and across his face. Disoriented and afraid, he didn't know what to do. Hearing footsteps running both inside and outside the house, he thought, *If I run they'll catch me for sure.*

The house was on a raised foundation with a crawl space below the hardwood floors. Luckily, he was lying directly in front of the opening. Quickly removing the wood-framed wire-mesh screen that covered the entry, he slid under the house, replacing the screen behind him.

There was no more than twelve inches of clearance between the bottom of the floor joists and the dirt beneath him. *Enough room for me, but not for that fat man. He'll never be able to get in here,* he thought, praying he was right.

Duncan managed to slither under and around the plumbing until he was directly under the kitchen. He could hear several voices, including his mother's. The voices were of men with thick Italian accents and harsh tones.

Then Duncan heard another set of footsteps walk into the kitchen. The room fell silent until a new voice filled the air. Unlike the other men, this man spoke impeccable English without a trace of an accent. However, the cadence of his speech, and the clear and refined enunciation of each word, made his voice as memorable as any Duncan had ever heard.

After speaking to the other men in the room for just a brief moment, the man turned his attention to Lucia, asking in a calm, deliberate tone, "Where can we find your son? Where would he go?"

"You'll never find him. He's far too smart for the likes of you," she said with strength and conviction in her voice.

A short silence was broken by another man's voice. "Sir, we gotta get you out of here. Dat kid mighta already called the cops."

"Yes. You are right. I should be going. As you can see madam, I must keep this short."

Still speaking in a perfectly calm tone, he continued his questioning. "I am going to ask you one last time. Where is your son? You will tell me where your son is, or I will have one of these nice gentlemen place a gun to your head and pull the trigger."

Almost before he could complete his sentence, Lucia responded defiantly, "You missed your chance. No matter what you do to me, you're dead. Vinnie will come after you."

Who'll come after them? Vinnie? Vinnie who? What is happening? Duncan whispered to himself.

"You may be right, my dear. God knows, you may be right. But let us talk about *your* life for a moment. It will end in precisely ten seconds if you do not answer my question. Where is your son? Ten, nine, eight..."

Faintly, in a prayerful tone, he heard his mother's voice. "God, please protect my son."

"...three, two, one." And then, a muffled gunshot.

Until that very second, Duncan had not even considered the possibility that they would really shoot his mother. Nothing was making any sense. But with the sound of the gunshot still echoing in his ears, the reality of the moment came crashing down upon him.

It took every fiber of Duncan's will to keep from sobbing hysterically. When he could no longer physically control his sorrow, he filled his mouth with dirt to muffle the involuntary sounds of pain that tried to escape from his lips. His chest was heaving, and every muscle in his body began to twitch uncontrollably.

Hearing footsteps moving from the kitchen toward the front of the house, he fought to control his fear as he made his way over to a second opening, this one facing the front, in the crawl space. As he peered through the wire-mesh screen, he saw five men walking down the driveway. At first he could only see their backs; even so, it was clear that the silver-haired man in the middle was in charge. Walking erect, he took the long, loping strides of a confident man. He had the lean athletic frame of a much younger man than his face revealed him to be when he turned momentarily to speak to the other men.

"Find that boy before he does!" the silver-haired man demanded.

Who is 'he'? Is that the same person Mom said was going to get them? Denny? No. Vinnie? Duncan's mind was racing.

"Yes, sir," a short, stout man replied.

"Take two men and find that boy! If he gets away, I'm going to hold you personally responsible. Do you understand me, Paulie?"

"Yes, sir."

The man named Paulie opened the door of a black Cadillac, and the silver-haired man slid inside. As he did, Duncan stared hard at his profile. He tried to burn that image into his mind, but he had only a split second before the face disappeared behind the Cadillac's tinted windows. However, there was no doubt in his mind that it was the silver-haired man's voice he'd heard in the kitchen. That voice would haunt him for the rest of his life.

Twisting his body around just enough to free his right arm, Duncan reached back and removed his wallet from his rear pocket. Folding it open, he gently slid out an old photo of his mother.

Duncan lay motionless for hours, tears streaming down his face, staring at the picture of his mother in the dim light that seeped through the wire-mesh screen.

On the back of the picture was a telephone number. There wasn't enough light to read it, but he knew it by heart. For as long as he could remember, his mother had made him promise to call that number if anything bad should ever happen to her. She would never explain to whom the number belonged, or why he should call. Thinking that she was being rather melodramatic, he had on occasion contemplated calling the number just to see who would answer. But his strict Catholic upbringing wouldn't allow him to defy his mother.

It was getting dark outside. Over three hours had passed, and he had not heard a single sound.

They're gone, but they might be watching the front of the house. I should go out the back way just in case.

Duncan crawled out from under the house, still spitting out the dirt now caked on his dry tongue.

Cautiously, he entered the house through the fragments of wood and glass—all that was left of the back door.

The entry led directly into the kitchen. The shock of seeing his mother lying dead, face down on the white tile kitchen floor, froze him in his tracks. A single gunshot wound in the back of her head had caused a puddle of dark red blood to form an almost perfect halo around her sprawling black hair.

Just like the angels in the stained-glass windows at church, he thought, hanging his head.

He felt like crying, but he'd left all his tears under the house. On tiptoes, he carefully stepped around her body, as if a misstep might wake her from a deep sleep. Picking up the telephone, he dialed the mysterious telephone number on the back of his mother's photo. It rang only once. A man's voice answered.

"Lucia?"

Duncan was caught off guard at hearing his mother's name. "No, no, sir. This is her son, Duncan." He did not know whom he was talking to or what he should say. The words escaped his lips almost involuntarily. "Someone killed my mom."

Saying it out loud made it feel real for the first time. A pain formed in his chest, making it impossible to breathe.

"Are you there? Are you there, Duncan? Are you there?"

It took a moment for Duncan to regain enough composure to respond. "Yes, sir, I'm still here."

"Where are you, Duncan? Where are you right now?"

Dazed, he couldn't focus on the question. "Mom told me to call this number if anything ever happened to her. What should I do?"

In a stunned but deliberate voice, the man repeated his question. "Where are you?"

"I'm in my house with Mommy." Duncan hadn't called her *Mommy* for many years. "She's dead. They broke in and killed her. She's dead."

"Who broke in? Who killed your mother?"

"I don't know. I don't know. A bunch of men, I don't know who they were. I don't know! They just kept asking her where I was. When she wouldn't tell them, they shot her."

Duncan looked down at his mother's lifeless body. A single tear began to roll down his cheek.

"Hold on, Duncan. Help is on its way. Don't hang up the phone."

Duncan could hear the man barking out orders in the background. Seconds later the man was back on the line.

"Duncan, you said 'a bunch of men.' How do you know your mother was killed by a bunch of men?"

"I was here. I saw it."

"You saw them kill your mother?" the voice said, astonished.

"No, that's not right. I didn't see them. I heard them."

"You heard them kill her?"

"Yes, sir, I was hiding under the house. They couldn't find me."

"Are you hurt?"

"No." Just then, Duncan noticed the dried blood that had mixed with dirt to form a red plaster cast on his arms.

"No, not really. I hurt myself jumping out the window, but I'm okay."

"I want you to go back under the house until my men get there. Do you understand?"

"No, sir. I don't understand anything." Duncan screamed into the phone at the top of his voice. "I'm going to stay with my mom."

"Son, I don't have the time or the patience to be sweet and kind. Your mother is dead. I promised her I'd protect you. I can't do that if you won't listen to me. Now, get your ass under that house right now!" the voice bellowed.

Ignoring the stern command, Duncan felt an inexplicable calm sweep over him. "Should I call the police?"

"No! Absolutely not! Under no circumstances are you to call the police. Just get under the fucking house," the voice demanded, sounding more frantic than commanding. There was a moment of silence. "Duncan, did you hear me?"

"Yes, sir. I heard you. But I'll be in the kitchen with my mom. Please get here as fast as you can."

Duncan dropped the receiver from his hand and looked down at his mother. Kneeling to the floor beside her, he clutched her limp cold hand tightly in his and began reciting the Lord's Prayer.

PART I

THE MURDER OF DEBRA BARNS

CHAPTER 2

Thirty-four years after the murder of Lucia Cabella.

DUNCAN BENT DOWN to pick up the round-back wooden chair that had been knocked over during the struggle. He displayed no sense of urgency as he slowly lifted the chair from the kitchen floor and gently placed it back on its four spindly legs.

His heartbeat was returning to normal, and the beads of sweat that had formed on his forehead were quickly evaporating away. Still, he was emotionally exhausted.

I need to rest a moment before I get out of here, he thought, sitting on the edge of the small white chair.

He had been staring at her lifeless body for what felt like a lifetime. But the girl had been dead for less than five minutes. The echoes of her moans had already begun to subside inside Duncan's head. They too were evaporating into the near silence of the room. The only sound came from drops of blood that fell heavily onto the white tile floor. Blood was oozing down the back of her neck. It drained from the wound at the base of her skull to form a large pool on the table. The blood had taken on the mood of the room, turning a dark maroon. A narrow stream had broken away from the main pool, winding its way to the table's edge.

Spellbound, Duncan watched as droplets formed, each expanding until its weight caused it to plummet to the floor. When they hit, they exploded like miniature bombs, sending bloody shrapnel in every direction.

His victim lay face down sprawled across the kitchen table, legs draped over the edge, feet resting lifelessly on the floor. She was naked except for the left sleeve of her blouse, which hadn't been torn away in the violence that preceded her death.

He couldn't help but admire her features. *Maybe five foot five. Twenty-five, maybe twenty-six,* he thought to himself.

Her firm, voluptuous breasts were made to appear even larger by her tiny waist. The arch in her back was slightly exaggerated as it descended beautifully into a perfectly round ass.

Young and very pretty—not Duncan's typical victim, but then he had no "typical" victim.

She hadn't been selected because of her looks. In fact, she hadn't been selected at all. It would be far more accurate to say Duncan selected opportune *places* rather than opportune *victims*. It was simply the young woman's misfortune to be in the wrong place at the wrong time.

CHAPTER 3

DUNCAN HADN'T NOTICED the similarities at first, but in the still of the moment, he was transported back thirty-four years, back to the time of his mother's murder. The white tile kitchen floor, the antique green cabinets, the innocent victim lying lifelessly in a puddle of her own blood; it could just as easily have been his mother.

His mind began to wander as the rhythmic sounds of the drops of blood dripping on the floor played their mesmerizing tune. The events that led to this young girl's demise began to replay in his head.

Duncan had flown into Boston's Logan Airport earlier that morning. It just happened to be his birthday, January 28. On that cold January day, he'd met with the CFO of Varatex, a Fortune 500 company, who'd been accused of conspiring to have his wife killed.

Duncan's reputation as a criminal attorney ranked him among the best in the country. The rumors that he'd once been lead counsel for the most powerful criminal syndicate in the country—and possibly the world—only served to enhance his reputation.

Having enough money to afford his hefty fees was no guarantee that Duncan would take your case. Over the years, he'd grown very particular about the type of case—or more to the point, the type of *client*—he'd represent. He had developed a reputation of turning down clients with inexhaustible resources for no discernable reason.

His record of obtaining acquittals or favorable plea bargains in high-profile criminal cases kept his services in demand. Even his conspicuous lack of interest in the practice of law over the last year hadn't reduced his popularity. Prospective clients were always clamoring for his services.

Duncan had spent three hours with his new client, completing his business by two o'clock that afternoon. After his meeting, he caught a cab back to his hotel, taking the elevator to his penthouse suite perched high above the Boston skyline.

Scheduled to fly back to Los Angeles the next morning on a nine fifteen flight, he'd factored in more than enough time to commit his crime.

He took only a few minutes to freshen up, washing his hands and splashing water on his face. At three o'clock, he grabbed from the foot of the bed the large bag that he'd packed earlier that day and headed for the elevator. In his bag was a change of clothes and an empty pre-paid FedEx container.

Leaving the hotel by taxi, he headed for the public library in downtown Boston. Once there, he accessed several websites, including the public transportation websites, where he confirmed bus routes and schedules for a variety of business and residential areas.

It still amazed him how much easier the Internet had made obtaining all sorts of information. It hadn't been that many years ago that, to cover his tracks, he'd been forced to use a maze of corporate shells to clandestinely obtain the same information. Now he could anonymously find anything he wanted with just the click of a mouse.

Technology had come a long way since his first purchase of an IBM 386 computer, whose only practical function was word processing. He loved technology, considering himself something of a techie (not to be confused with a *Star Trek* aficionado). He was one of those guys who couldn't wait to purchase the latest gadget. If it was newer, faster, smaller, or had more memory, he just had to have it.

The week before his trip, Duncan read the local Boston papers, familiarizing himself with local bars and clubs. He even read the local news sections that usually end up in the recycle bins unread. Only the die-hard Bostonians—and Duncan—took the time to read about those poor unfortunates who spend their lives catering to the Boston elite. Wedding announcements, yard sales, grand openings, local events, arrest reports; no section of the paper went unread. Each seemingly insignificant piece of information gave Duncan insight into the personality of the community in which he had chosen to commit his dastardly crimes.

He paid special attention to the weather reports and local fashions to make sure that he was properly dressed. His attire was the most important element in becoming just another face in the crowd. For his plan to succeed, he couldn't afford to look like a tourist.

Two hours later, Duncan left the library on foot. He walked only two blocks and then slipped into the restroom of a Shell gas station. When he entered, he looked like an attorney needing to take a leak. When he emerged, he was indistinguishable from any other lower-middle-class Bostonian (with the exception of the boorish accent, of course). The attendant paid scant attention to the transformation as Duncan casually strolled away from the station.

At a nearby FedEx drop-off he deposited his box, which now contained his business suit, shirt, tie, and shoes.

Confident he could pass for a local, he hopped on a bus and headed toward a suburb twenty miles outside of Boston proper.

CHAPTER 4

THE WEATHER WAS just as had been forecast in the newspapers he'd read a week ago and again that afternoon at the library. As late afternoon faded to dusk, a chilling breeze swept in, dropping the temperature to a skin-tingling forty degrees.

As he rode buses through a variety of neighborhoods, he noticed that people had begun to bundle themselves up against the cold; hats and scarves obscured their faces. Each pedestrian began to look indistinguishable from the next. Wrapping his scarf loosely around his neck, he admired his reflection in the window. *Do they all look like me, or do I look like them?*

The thought made him smile.

While on the bus, he avoided eye contact with fellow riders, not looking away, but never encouraging eye contact. He read nondescript newspapers, avoiding popular books and magazines that some lonely, pain-in-the-ass Chatty-Cathy type of person might consider an invitation for conversation.

Changing buses several times, he was careful not to spend too much time on any one bus. Before each transfer, he slightly modified articles of clothing to make his appearance a little different while still maintaining the look of a local. Raising or lowering a scarf, turning reversible gloves inside out, changing glasses—all of these added to the deception.

When the bus turned at the corner of Staton Avenue and Borrows Road, he spotted what he'd been searching for. Just behind a strip mall filled with no-name businesses struggling to survive, was a lone row of old, run-down apartment buildings.

That's the place. Time to take a walk.

It was almost six thirty when Duncan exited the bus.

Having braved the heavy traffic, cars and buses were just completing their daily mission of transporting the town's tired residents back to their working-class neighborhoods. There were still a good number of people shuffling along the sidewalks. One more body bundled against the biting evening air would go unnoticed.

His timing was fortuitous. Just as he stepped onto the sidewalk, he noticed a lovely young woman heading toward him.

She cast a friendly smile at Duncan as she passed, the kind of smile that says hello or how are you? without saying the words. He acknowledged the smile with a quick nod.

She was rubbing her hands together to keep them warm. A smile crossed his face as he watched. *No wedding ring!*

She was walking in the direction of the apartments behind the strip mall. *Be the one,* he thought, as he pulled his scarf up over his chin.

Duncan glanced upward toward the sky. *Still enough daylight peeking through to get a better look at those apartments before the sun sets. Let's just hope that's where you're going, young lady.*

He waited a moment at the bus stop before following some thirty yards behind. He watched her turn down the street directly behind the strip mall.

As they drew nearer to the apartments, he could see that it was a two-story structure. *The doors are too close together to be large units. Probably studios, maybe one-bedrooms,* he thought.

The entrances were poorly lit, with the doors inset three or four feet from the front wall of the building. *It'd be damn near impossible for anyone to see me in the doorway unless they were standing directly in front of me.*

She turned up the walk to a dark corner unit. *Good, good, that works,* Duncan thought.

She turned on the light in the front room as she entered. For a brief moment he could see inside. The front room was small and sparsely furnished. *One bedroom. Thought so.*

When they arrived, the apartments above and beside hers were dark, as was the one she entered. *She is alone, at least for now.*

As he inconspicuously strolled by, he immediately recognized it as the right location. *Yes. She'll do just fine.*

His mind went to work calculating his next move. Over two decades of practice had etched the outline of a plan in his mind. However, each place and each victim was unique.

Because his murders were completely random, he needed to make important decisions on the spot. *How will I enter this apartment? When will I enter the apartment?* were the first two questions that popped into his head.

He'd noticed that the locks on the front door were old and cheap-looking. *If there is enough time, I could wait until she goes to sleep. I can pick those locks easily.*

He glanced down at his watch. *No, there won't be enough time for that. Hell, she's small; I could overpower her if I had to. If I can draw her to the door, I can force my way in.*

When to enter the apartment would be more problematic. He was mindful that the buses ran on the half-hour, with the last bus leaving the area at nine thirty. Taking into account bus changes and connections, he had to be on the bus by nine. That gave him just over two hours to get back on a bus.

Duncan was fully aware that taxi drivers keep logs of their fares. The only way back to his hotel that night would be by bus. *If I miss the last bus, I'm screwed.* That knowledge would be his guide for making all other decisions that night.

He continued to walk slowly down the street as he mulled over his options. From his glimpse into the apartment, he noticed that there wasn't a television in the front room. *She must have a TV. Maybe I'll get lucky. If she goes to her bedroom to watch it, I could get in there unnoticed.*

But it was Friday night. Such a pleasant-looking girl might be going out on a date or expecting company. *I'd better wait until at least seven thirty before trying to break in, just in case she's expecting company.*

CHAPTER 5

DUNCAN COULDN'T JUST aimlessly wander the streets and wait to make his move, so he headed back toward the bus stop. On his way, he would pass directly in front of her apartment a second time. It would give him a chance to take a better look at the front entry. As he approached, his prey unexpectedly emerged from her apartment.

Walking less than ten yards behind her, he began to curse under his breath. *Shit! That's just bad luck. Is there time to find another victim? I don't want to leave this place without a kill.*

"Goddamn it," he mumbled quietly to himself, "I owned this bitch. Fuck!"

He'd been forced by unforeseen events to abandon his murderous plans on numerous occasions. That didn't change the fact that he hated losing a chance to get away with murder.

His frustration quickly turned to elation when he noticed that she'd changed into comfortable-looking sweat pants. Her black galoshes and old jacket, neither of which had probably ever been in style, restored his hope.

Wherever she's going, she's not dressed to impress. A real sense of excitement filled his chest as he watched her turn the corner ahead of him. Slowing his pace, he watched from a distance until she entered a small convenience store.

He mouthed, "In that getup, she'll be back."

There's no time to waste. I need to get in that apartment now, before she gets back.

Once she was completely out of sight, he reversed direction again, casually sauntering up the walkway to her unit.

The door had a lock in the handle and a separate dead bolt. Removing the waterproof leather gloves, he revealed the thin rubber gloves beneath. Grabbing the doorknob, he twisted it back and forth, just to make sure that it was locked. It was. Holding the knob with his left hand, he slowly but firmly pushed and pulled the door in and out as far as it would move.

From the play in the door, he discovered that in her haste, or maybe just out of habit, she hadn't locked the dead bolt.

You're making this too easy, girl.

Years earlier, Duncan had been invited to watch a Los Angeles Kings hockey game in a luxury box owned by a large lock manufacturer. One of the executives jokingly told him, "In Europe, locks are meant to keep people out. But in America, locks only keep people in."

Duncan came to learn that the executive's words, while spoken in jest, were true. In Europe, dead bolts are set into steel frames. In the United States, doorjambs are almost always cut from thin pine.

As he looked at the door, he thought, *Pine doorjamb. I could pop this door open with one good shove. Doesn't anyone in this country understand that locks are only as good as the door casing? Cheap-ass landlords! No. I can't just break it open. If she sees a broken door, she'll bolt. I'd better use a little finesse.*

Having made a study of the techniques and tools used by locksmiths, he'd taught himself how to pick almost every brand of lock. He opened a small leather case that contained an array of metal picks resembling miniature dental instruments.

While jimmying locks wasn't a particularly complicated procedure, he learned that it was easier to just bypass them. Taking a credit-card-size piece of plastic from the case, he slid it between the door and the frame, dislodging the bolt and causing the door to swing open.

He had the tools and expertise to pick the lock; he just didn't need the knowledge that night.

Sometimes low tech works best, he thought with a smile on his face.

CHAPTER 6

ONCE INSIDE THE apartment, he checked to make sure he hadn't inadvertently left the door unlocked. Using a penlight, he made a quick scan of the front room. *No signs of roommates in this room.* A telephone bill sitting on a coffee table was addressed to Debra Barns.

Debra? Debra? Just doesn't look like a Debra—Charlotte, maybe Vanessa. Definitely not a Debra.

Continuing his search, he found nothing in the closet or bathroom indicating that more than one person lived there.

It was, as he'd surmised, a one-bedroom apartment with a small separate kitchen. While the building was old, Debra's unit was immaculate. It bore the evidence of a woman's touch, everything from little knickknacks to linen tablecloths. The white tile floor in the kitchen was so clean, it looked wet in the glow of his penlight. Across from an avocado-green refrigerator sat a small wooden table and two wooden chairs with rounded tops. They had been painted white to match the table.

Duncan moved on to the bedroom. Opening the drawer of the nightstand, he laughed. *Does every woman in America now own one of these?* He picked up the pretty pink five-inch dildo with a little anal stimulator attached. Wrapping it neatly in a tissue he'd taken from a dispenser on top of the nightstand, he walked back to the kitchen to find a few additional items he'd need.

Even before finding her sex toy, he'd decided to make this murder appear sexually motivated. *Using her own dildo will add to the illusion.*

Whenever possible, he used items found in the victim's home to assist in perpetrating the crime. As he became more proficient at committing murder, he learned to bring as little as possible to a crime scene.

The average person had no idea how adept the police were at tracing even common household items back to their owners (or at least back to the point of sale). By using the victim's items, any trace would lead right back to the victim.

Rummaging through the drawers in the kitchen, he found the two other items he'd been looking for, a four-inch steak knife and a pair of scissors. Experience had taught him that these were the types of items that he was sure to find in almost every home.

He put the scissors, together with the tissue containing the dildo, on top of a small shelf attached to the wall directly above the kitchen table.

It might have been easier to place the scissors in his pocket, just in case he wasn't able to drag his victim into the kitchen. However, he never placed the victim's property in his pockets, for fear that he might forget to remove them.

Unless it was completely unavoidable, he made it a rule not to take anything from a crime scene, and never to leave anything he brought with him behind.

Ripping the cords off a toaster and a hand mixer, he stood in the dark kitchen, with knife in hand, waiting for Debra to return. He didn't have to wait long. Ten minutes later, a key turned in the front door.

Setting down her bag of groceries, she clicked on the light in the front room, this time double-locking the door behind her. After slipping her bare feet out of the oversize galoshes, she removed the unattractive wool coat, laying it over the back of an overstuffed chair.

Carrying her bag with both hands, she hit the light switch on the wall with her elbow as she entered the kitchen. Like a floodlight, the bulb behind Duncan illuminated the small room.

She didn't notice his long shadow stretched across the white tile floor until it was too late.

CHAPTER 7

DUNCAN CAME UP behind Debra quickly and with great force, pushing her body hard against the sink. The impact sent the bag flying across the room. As it crashed to the floor, the sound of breaking glass rang out.

Placing his left hand firmly over her mouth, he put the knife to her throat. The suddenness of the assault caused her to panic. She struggled to free herself from her attacker.

When the initial shock passed, she could hear Duncan whispering in her ear. "Don't scream! I don't want to hurt you."

While technically he wasn't lying (deep down inside, he really didn't want to hurt her), his statement was more than a little bit misleading. There was no question that he had every intention of killing her, even if he didn't want to *hurt* her.

There was something disarming in his tone. She became unexpectedly calm and stopped resisting.

Keeping his left hand firmly clamped over her mouth, he continued to whisper in her ear. "When I remove my hand, don't scream, or you will force me to hurt you. Do you understand?"

She nodded, and he slowly removed the hand covering her mouth. Keeping the knife to her throat, he guided her backward toward one of the kitchen chairs. Using only a modest amount of force, he pushed her down into the chair.

Using the toaster cord to tie her hands behind her back, he laced the ends of the cord around the chair.

Always the cautious one, he took a small dish towel off the counter and forced it into her mouth. "Don't try to scream and don't move. This will be over before you know it."

Ever the attorney, he twisted his words to disguise their meaning. While she may have found comfort in them, what he really meant was that she only had a few precious minutes to live.

Looking directly into her eyes, he gauged the reaction to his words. The terror she was experiencing was reflected in her dilated pupils, but she again nodded cooperatively.

"There are some simple rules. If you lie to me you'll regret it, make no mistake about that. Nod if you understand."

She did as he asked.

"Good, let us begin. Do you live alone?" He already knew she did, only asking the question to test her veracity.

She immediately nodded.

"Good, you're doing fine," he said, trying to ease her fear with a comforting smile.

He bent over to pick up the bag of groceries she dropped during their brief struggle. Looking inside the bag, he found a pint of ice cream, a *Redbook* magazine, Oreo cookies, and the remains of a small jar of olives.

Comfort food, the kind you eat alone.

The olive juice had soaked through the paper, filling the air with its pungent aroma. Turning his back to her to place the bag in the sink, he could see her staring at him in a small mirror that hung directly behind the faucet.

Keeping a watchful eye on her in the mirror, he asked, "Are you expecting anyone to come over tonight?"

Their eyes met briefly in the reflection of the mirror. Upon discovering that he had been watching her the whole time, her head drooped down slightly, and there was a noticeable delay in her response.

Duncan could almost see the thoughts racing through her mind. *Should I tell him I'm expecting company? Who should I say is coming? What time? What if he thinks I'm lying? God, please don't let him hurt me. He hasn't hurt me so far. Maybe he will just leave. God, please, please don't let him hurt me.*

Knowing what was going through her mind, he turned to face her, almost challenging her to lie.

"Here, maybe this will help," he pulled the towel from her mouth.

A few seconds passed in silence. "And we were doing so well," Duncan said menacingly. Not knowing what to do, and with precious little time to consider her options, she chose to take the path of cooperation. "No, I'm not expecting company."

"You see, that wasn't so hard. Now, was it?" The feeling of complete domination sent a rush of adrenaline coursing through his body.

Tragically, it didn't matter how she answered. She wasn't going to live through the night.

"Now, if I leave that towel out, can I trust you to keep quiet?"

"Yes, sir. I won't scream. Please take whatever you want. I won't tell anyone you were here. I promise."

Duncan pressed his finger to his lips. "Shhhh."

He walked into the living room and turned off the light, never letting her completely out of his sight.

She began to pray. If she wasn't a religious person before, she'd become one now. With chin quivering, she whispered, "Our Father, who art in heaven..." Stepping back into the kitchen, he noticed the tears running down her smooth, pale cheeks.

Tears had a strange effect on him. They didn't make him mad, angry, or sympathetic. Seeing them just made him more determined to complete the task he came to this sleepy Boston suburb to do.

He knelt down behind Debra to untie the cord wrapped around her wrists. "Now I'm going to untie you, but I need you to put the towel back in your mouth, okay?"

"Yes, sir," she said, fighting back the tears.

Once freed from the cord, she picked up the dishtowel and shoved it back into her mouth.

"Good girl."

"Here, let me help you up."

She tried to say thank you, but the muffled noise sounded more like "hank hue."

She was trembling uncontrollably. Duncan attempted to calm her. "Don't be afraid." But his voice had changed; it had lost its soothing tone.

In that moment Debra began to consider just why he was there. *He hasn't even attempted to take my money. Why would he think I have money? Why is he taking his time? Why isn't he in a bigger hurry?*

Seeing the wheels turning behind her deep blue eyes, Duncan quickly retied her hands, in front of her this time.

Oh my God, he's going to rape me. With that thought her legs felt weak, and her knees started to buckle. Duncan caught her just before she collapsed.

As her mind filled with the images of being violated, Debra tried in vain to plead with him.

"Hees ont ape heee! Hees ont ape heee!" Tears were now flowing from her eyes.

Ignoring her muffled pleas, he spun her around until she faced the kitchen table. Standing directly behind her, he reached around her slender waist with one hand. Fumbling with the drawstring that held up her sweat pants, he accidently pulled the string through one of the loops of the bow, causing the string to knot.

She began to twist and squirm, frustrating Duncan's efforts to untie the knot. As he fought to control her movement, she began to resist with ever-greater intensity. The cord around her hands didn't prevent her from swinging her arms wildly from side to side, striking Duncan with her elbows.

"You little shit. You think you can hit me?" His response was quick and violent. Grabbing a clump of hair, he slammed her face down hard against the table, causing both her nose and upper lip to bleed slightly. "Don't make me hurt you again," he growled.

She was stunned momentarily as he continued working to unfasten the drawstring. Finally giving up, he jerked it hard, breaking the string instantly. The loose-fitting sweats slid over her hips and dropped to the floor. Only the elastic bands at the ankles kept them from falling completely off.

With one hand against her back holding her firmly against the table, he reached up and retrieved the scissors from the shelf. With the precision of a surgeon it took only two cuts to remove her lace panties.

Debra had stopped struggling and lay motionless, sobbing, tears rolling down her cheeks, still trying to verbalize pleas through the towel jammed in her mouth.

"Heees, hees, ont urt mee, heees heees."

He released the pressure on her back and leaned over her until his lips were close enough for her to hear his soft-spoken words. "I'm not going to rape you. You need to trust me. I'm not going to rape you. Just relax, and I'll be out of here before you know it." Again, he was telling a lawyer's truth. He had no intention of raping her—at least not in the traditional meaning of the word.

It was either a tribute to his communicative powers or evidence of how desperately she must have wanted to believe him, but somehow she found solace in his words. Even as she lay half-naked and bent over the kitchen table, pants around her ankles, she needed to believe.

With his victim in a momentary state of capitulation, Duncan seized the opportunity to slip the sweats off over her feet; placing her clothes neatly on the chair he'd tied her to only moments earlier.

Using the scissors, he began to cut a straight line up the center of the back of her blouse, cutting the bra strap along the way. When the cut was complete, he gently folded back the two sides of the blouse, exposing the entirety of her nude body.

He stepped back a second time to admire her splendid form.

She's exquisite! Her muscle tone, her milky white skin, her satiny hair. My God, what a lovely creature.

He felt an erection forming. He wanted her, wanted to be inside her. While he had no compunction about killing her, he'd given his word not to rape her, and he'd not break that promise. In his twisted mind, he could find no moral inconsistency in his logic.

Naked and shivering, she was completely vulnerable, and yet she found the inner strength to stay motionless, still hoping against hope that her deranged attacker would simply leave.

He'd been so engrossed in his visual rape of her body that he hadn't noticed that she'd stopped crying. Taking one last long look, Duncan stepped up behind her again. As he did, he reached for the dildo, setting it down on the table in front of her face.

Debra had been crying so hard that the tears initially obscured her vision. But the tissue wrapping did nothing to conceal its contents.

The expression on her face transformed to that of a teenager who'd been caught masturbating for the first time by her parents. She felt embarrassed and confused.

Thoughts raced through her mind. *Why does he have my dildo? Why does he care if I have a dildo? Please, you promised, don't do this, please no, don't do this.*

All of her questions were answered in an instant. With one hand, he removed the tissue and rammed the dildo into her vagina, making sure that the stimulator found its home.

The insertion was unexpected and painful. The surprise and pain caused her to lurch up hard from the table, kicking one of the chairs over as she fought to stand up. It was all he could do to hold her down. In the struggle, the remainder of her clothes were ripped away, with the exception of the one sleeve of her blouse.

The battle did not last long. Duncan drove the four-inch knife into her neck just below the skull. There was a moan, and then the room filled with the sound of air escaping from her lungs.

The knife had severed part of her spinal cord, entering the lower portion of her brain. Debra Barns died almost instantly.

CHAPTER 8

DUNCAN HAD SEEN so much death that the sight of Debra's lifeless body left him hollow. Not sad, not happy, not anything in between. He felt nothing for her, nothing about her, nothing about anyone he'd ever killed. Nothing at all.

There was a time when Duncan thought that he knew why he killed. But now he was far beyond all that self-rationalization bullshit. *I'm insane, a fucking insane man living behind the mask of a normal man's life.*

His life had come full circle. The murders that had once brought him such pleasure were now the bane of his existence. Instead of wanting to take the lives of others, he oftentimes considered taking his own.

And why not, with all the evil I've done? The powers that be are no closer to catching me now than they were twenty years ago when the killing began. If I don't stop myself, who will? How many people have I killed—seventy-five? One hundred? More?

He couldn't recall, or maybe he didn't want to recall.

Am I going to be able to keep the promise this time? Is this going to be the last time I feed my appetite for murder? Having broken that promise so many times in the past, it was difficult to convince himself that he'd *ever* find the morality that he'd abandoned so many years earlier. Without it he wouldn't stop, he couldn't stop.

This is it. It ends tonight. I will kill myself before I murder another innocent person. As if talking directly to his inner demons, he said aloud, "I'm keeping my promise this time. I swear it."

With those words, he realized that the sight and sounds of the drops of blood beating onto the tile floor had lulled him into a trance. *I've been here too long. My God, what time is it?*

Instantly he was back, his mind no longer wandering. He was alert. Taking only a moment to steal one last look at her beauty, he prepared himself to leave.

It was as if time had stood still. Looking at the clock on the wall, he said aloud, "It's not even eight o'clock. Calm down. You're okay."

Pushing in the button in the center of the doorknob he engaged the lock before closing the door behind him. He casually made his way down the street. He had turned his reversible overcoat inside out before leaving the apartment. He looked like a different man by the time he reached the bus stop.

The cold breeze made him shiver as he walked several blocks past the bus stop where he had exited the bus earlier that evening. When he reached the next stop, he sat on the bench and waited.

Several teenagers were milling around waiting for a ride into town. However, they paid little attention to the man in the full-length overcoat, wearing his hat pulled down low over his face and reading a nondescript paper.

Within fifteen minutes Duncan was on his way back to downtown Boston. On his walk from the bus stop to the hotel, he placed his hat and gloves in his pockets.

It was nearly nine when he reached the Ritz Carlton. By the time he entered the hotel lobby, the murderer had disappeared.

He took the private elevator directly to his penthouse suite, where he removed the overcoat and admired his Bostonian attire in the full-length mirror one last time before changing back into a suit and tie.

The thoughts of killing himself and wresting control from his compulsion were gone. Even the thoughts of that night's murderous acts had been subconsciously tucked neatly away into the darkest recesses of his memory. The self-absorbed attorney was back. He was now more focused on the fact that the events of the evening had left him with a considerable appetite. He hadn't eaten since noon and his stomach was letting him know it.

Duncan picked up the phone and pushed seven. "Good evening. You have reached the concierge's desk, how may I be of service, Mr. Gabrelli?"

"Dinner reservations. Do you have any recommendations?"

"Certainly, sir. Were you looking for any particular menu, sir?"

"A nice prime rib sounds wonderful."

"May I recommend Stanley's? It has the best prime rib in the city, slow roasted to perfection. It is just a few blocks away. Shall I make a reservation?"

"Yes, please. Would you make a reservation for nine thirty?"

"Consider it done. Shall I arrange for a driver?"

"No. Just the reservation, if you please. I think I would rather walk. It is a beautiful night, and I could use the fresh air."

"Excuse me, Mr. Gabrelli, but if you have your heart set on prime rib, might I suggest that I call ahead and have them hold a nice cut for you? This late in the dinner hour, they might be running low on some cuts and temperatures. If you like your prime rib rare, I would suggest that I call ahead for you."

"Yes. Please do that."

"Prime rib rare then, Mr. Gabrelli?"

"Yes. Rare, the bloodier the better," Duncan replied staring at his own sadistic grin in the mirror.

"Is there anything else I can do for you, Mr. Gabrelli?"

"No. Thank you."

"Have a pleasant evening then, and enjoy your dinner."

PART II

IN THE BEGINNING

CHAPTER 9

THE NIGHT HIS mother was murdered, Duncan's life started anew.

Less than ten minutes after hanging up the telephone with his still-unknown protector, two very large men burst into his home, guns drawn. They found Duncan still sitting on the kitchen floor, holding his mother's hand.

There was no way for Duncan to know if they were the men who killed his mother or the men sent to help him, but either way, their entry into the house had no visible effect on him. It was as if Duncan was in a trance.

One of the men placed his hand on Duncan's shoulder. "Duncan, we have to go now, son," he said in a rough but compassionate tone.

Duncan didn't respond.

After making a quick sweep of the house, the other man picked up the telephone receiver, which was still dangling from the wall where Duncan had dropped it, and dialed a number. "Sir, the home is secured."

A pause, then, "Yes, sir, I'm looking at him right now, he's shaken up but seems to be okay."

Another pause, then, "Yes, sir, I understand. Certainly, right away, sir."

Duncan could only hear one side of the telephone conversation, but it was clear that his anonymous protector was on the other end of the line.

The man turned to the boy and said, "Duncan, my boss would like to speak to you."

For the first time since the men had entered the house Duncan looked up and acknowledged their existence. Looking up at the man holding the phone, with a face completely devoid of emotion, Duncan slowly reached out for the receiver.

"Sir, what's going to happen to me?"

"Duncan, my man is going to give you a letter to read." Even as the words were coming through the receiver, Duncan was handed a sealed envelope.

"It's from your mother. She'd always hoped you'd never have to read it. I know that she raised you to be a good boy, but now she needs for you to also be strong; strong for her and strong for yourself."

Staring at the envelope, Duncan tried to get his mind around the events of the past several hours. "Who are you? Who killed my mom? What—what's happened? Why? Please, just tell me why?"

"Son, everything you need to know is in the letter. My men are going to take you to a place where you'll be safe. I want you to read the letter on the way. When you're done reading it, my man is going to destroy the letter."

"Who are you?" Duncan asked almost pleading.

In a stoic, almost emotionless tone, the voice said, "I'm sorry for your loss. Be brave." With that, the voice was replaced with a dial tone.

Duncan was escorted to a black Cadillac where he intently read every word of the six-page letter. The voice on the telephone had lied; it didn't begin to explain everything. The letter read like a bad novel. For the most part, the letter was a rambling expression of the love she felt for her son.

> *If you are reading this letter, son, you made the telephone call, and I am no longer alive. I am sorry that I couldn't protect you from this. Please believe me when I say that I did the best I could. It just wasn't good enough.*

There was scant detail about why their lives had been in danger.

Duncan had no idea that they'd lived under the shadow of such impending doom. *How could I have known? Everything appeared so normal.* The whole idea seemed inconceivable.

When all was said and done, the letter was a mother's sorrowful goodbye. In life she was famous for extracting promises, and would now ask for three more.

I know how scared and confused you must be. But your safety depends on you doing exactly as I now ask. I need you to keep my passing a secret. You must never speak of it to anyone. For reasons far too complicated to explain, you'll not be told the name of your benefactor. I trust him with my most prized possession, YOU. He will look after you. Listen well. Trust him. Most important of all, never try to avenge my death. It's God's will. I leave judgment in his hands, I ask you to do the same. I love you with all my heart. Mom

Tears were running down Duncan's cheeks. When Duncan was done reading, one of the men reached over and took hold of the letter. At first Duncan didn't want to let go. Prying the letter out of Duncan's hand, the man began tearing the letter into small pieces. Seeing the distressed look on Duncan's face, the man apologized. "I'm sorry, Duncan. I'm under orders."

Duncan had no idea where he was headed. They drove for almost an hour before anyone in the car spoke a single word.

"Where are you taking me?" Duncan asked, breaking the deafening silence.

"Somewhere where you will be safe," one of the men replied.

"Safe from who? Who would want to hurt me? Why?! Just tell me why someone wants to hurt me," Duncan demanded.

"I am sorry, young man, I couldn't tell ya even if I knew. I am just following orders." Those were the last words spoken during the three-hour drive. Finally, the Cadillac pulled up in front of the private boarding school, where the dean, together with his new guardian, a middle-aged, slightly balding, pot-bellied, banker-type looking fellow named Mr. Fender stood waiting for Duncan's arrival.

Duncan was staring out of the tinted window of the Cadillac at the spires that jutted up from the roofs of the massive, almost gothic-looking buildings that made up the campus. Etched in the stones that arched over the large wooden doors to the main building were the words, "Kingstone Academy."

The two men stepped out of the car, and Mr. Fender slid in and sat beside Duncan. "Your world is about to change very dramatically," Mr. Fender said in a thick English accent. "Young master, I know you must have a thousand questions, so let me make this perfectly clear. I have no answers!" Duncan did not seem surprised by his words. *Nothing makes any sense, why should that change now?*

"My name is Mr. Fender. I have been retained by your benefactor to care for you. All your needs will be met. But there are rules. Rules you must follow to the letter. The most important of which is that you may never speak of the events of this day to anyone, ever. You may never speak to anyone of your family or of your past, ever. And you must follow my every instruction." Mr. Fender let a second pass to let his words sink in. "Is that understood, young master?"

Duncan found some irony in Mr. Fender's calling him "young master" when it appeared quite obvious that he was not the master, but the servant.

"One last thing. You have a new last name. It is now 'Gabrelli.'"

"No! That is where I draw the line," Duncan replied.

"Good. Yes! It is good that we address this right away. You neither have anything with which to draw a line, nor any sand to draw it in. You will follow my every command. There will not be many demands made upon you, but those that are made will be followed to the letter. Now, young Master Gabrelli," Mr. Fender emphasized the name, "let us retire to your new accommodations. We have much to discuss." Mr. Fender did not wait for a response. He opened the car door and held it open for Duncan.

Mr. Fender, in a voice just loud enough for the dean of the school to hear, told Duncan, "There is no better preparatory school in this godforsaken country. God save you! If it were up to me, you would attend a proper school in England, but this will have to do for now."

Duncan was emotionally, physically, and mentally spent. He had no will to argue the point with Mr. Fender or anyone else for that matter. He quietly slipped out of the car and was escorted by Mr. Fender to his lavish accommodations.

In the blink of an eye his old life was gone, and a new life had begun. His life had been fully funded. Someone cared enough about him to make sure that he wanted for nothing. Even so, he felt empty inside and completely alone. He missed his mother, his friends, and his old life.

He had a million questions. But he knew that his questions would go unanswered, so he never again asked why his old life was gone.

He'd not been a particularly outgoing boy. With the loss of his mother, he withdrew ever inward. He escaped into his studies. His absolute and complete dedication to excellence was perhaps the first evidence of his obsessive personality. Being a brilliant young man with a near photographic memory, he was the perfect student. Other students came to envy and dislike him in equal portions as he pushed the grade curve ever higher.

It was not until he entered college that he was able to form anything resembling a normal relationship with another human being. Up until that time, his best friends had been goldfish that died every two months and were replaced with his new aquatic best friend. While Mr. Fender was always at Duncan's side, he never displayed any emotional connection to Duncan. Mr. Fender undoubtedly cared deeply for Duncan; however, his breeding, his upbringing, and his many years of training as an English servant compelled him to mask his personal feelings for Duncan.

Mr. Fender eventually got his wish, as Duncan attended Cambridge and graduated with the highest honors. After completing his undergraduate studies, Duncan kept the first promise that he'd ever made to his mother. With his grades, LSAT score, and connections, Duncan could have attended any law school—Harvard, Yale, *any* law school he wanted. But he chose the University of California at Los Angeles, School of Law (UCLA), because being in Los Angeles made him feel closer to his mother's memory.

In 1973, Duncan graduated *magna cum laude* from the UCLA. He was the editor-in-chief of the law review, published articles, won eight CalJur awards (for having received the highest grade in a bar-required course), and accumulated countless other distinctions during his three years at UCLA.

During the last two years of law school, he apprenticed as a law clerk at Weiss, Barron & Helms. The firm's letterhead bore only the three founding partners' initials, WB&H. It was the most prestigious criminal law firm in the United States, with offices in New York, Philadelphia, Boston, Los Angeles, Paris, and Germany. Its client list read like a *Who's Who*, including the names of the rich and famous as well as the infamous and notorious.

WB&H had vigorously recruited Duncan after his first-year exams, and he accepted a clerking position in his second year of law school. While he'd distinguished himself as a masterful writer and a creative advocate, it appeared, even to Duncan, that the senior partners were making special efforts to ensure his advancement.

Equally qualified law clerks, from law schools with names like Harvard, Yale, and Penn, could see that the senior partners had taken Duncan under their wing. It was a source of considerable animosity.

The firm was eager to convince Duncan to accept a position with WB&H after graduation. To that end, they made him the most lucrative offer ever presented to a first-year lawyer. In addition to his substantial salary, the package included a new 450 Mercedes Benz SL convertible, club memberships at the Riviera Country Club and Pinehurst, use of the firm's twelve vacation homes, and most important, the key to the executive washroom. It had been a standing joke among the associates that once you received a key to the executive washroom you were a lock to make partner. Some of these perks had previously been reserved only for senior partners.

While Duncan had received a number of offers from law firms across the country, none came close to the one from WB&H. But it was more than just the money. His love, his heart and soul, was rooted in defending those he believed were poor, innocent individuals who had been falsely accused of crimes. Brilliant as he was, he'd not yet realized how the criminal justice system really worked. Despite all that he had gone through, Duncan fought to maintain his belief in the basic goodness of human nature. That belief made him want to believe that his clients were, as they vigorously professed, innocent.

However, his naiveté was short-lived. He may have been naïve, but he was not stupid. He began to observe that in case after case, those who needed the services of his firm were actually high-powered criminals, or at least rich small-time criminals.

It became clear that his wide-eyed innocence had blinded him to the reality of human nature. To his credit, rather than becoming disillusioned with the criminal justice system altogether, he was that much more intrigued by the process.

It was as if a switch had been turned on inside his head. He stopped seeing crime as an issue of right and wrong; the only thing that mattered was defending his client. He began to understand something about his own nature as a result of this revelation.

There was no way of reconciling his Catholic upbringing with his firm's defense of those he now knew to be guilty of the most heinous of crimes. There was a battle of sorts, albeit brief, inside of Duncan between the forces of good and evil. It seemed strange to Duncan that, despite his mother's best efforts, he could so easily ignore the better side of his nature. The real revelation was not just that he was indifferent to his firm's representation of the vilest of the human species, but that he enjoyed being a part of it. His lack of conscience would ultimately serve his clients well.

As a rule, for years after joining a large firm, young attorneys never even *see* the inside of a courtroom. They work behind the scenes, researching legal issues and writing briefs, churning out thousands of billable hours to line the pockets of the partners. But they never directly represent clients.

The partners of the firm interact with clients, taking credit for the younger attorneys' hard work and creativity. It was virtually unheard of for young attorneys at any large firm to have their own clients until their third or fourth year of practice. Even then, the cases assigned to those younger attorneys were strictly scrutinized by senior attorneys of the firm.

Such was not Duncan's fate. Partners of WB&H were compelled to recognize that he was an exception to the rule.

His true talent lay in his ability to communicate and negotiate with the prosecution. He had an uncanny ability to create doubt in the minds of prosecutors and to convince otherwise hard-ass prosecutors to agree to extraordinarily lenient plea bargains.

In only his second year as an attorney at WB&H, Duncan began to be assigned his own clients. At first, he was assigned smaller cases, but they were his own clients nonetheless.

Most of his early cases involved defending the sons and daughters of the rich-and-not-so-famous: clients rich enough to afford the firm, but whose cases were not high profile enough to warrant even a junior partner's attention.

His clients had been accused of everything from shoplifting to burglary. Based on his conversations with his younger clients, he concluded that most were either trying to get back at their absentee parents for making their life too easy, or they felt that their birthright placed them above the law.

In either event, his clients were almost always guilty. It was his job to keep their parents' names out of the local papers and to keep his clients from being punished for their crimes.

Not all of his clients were poor little rich kids. In an effort to impress the local citizenry with its concern for the poor unwashed who dwelled among the more fortunate, WB&H required all of its young attorneys to perform a small amount of *pro bono* work. However, WB&H was not in the business of giving away its time—the indigent had a better chance of winning the lottery than of having the firm represent them for free.

His pro bono work exposed him to a wider variety of criminal cases. Most of his indigent clients were habitual small-time criminals. However, every now and again he would get to represent someone accused of a more serious crime such as rape, assault, drug offenses, or robbery. These cases proved far more interesting to Duncan.

With each new case, he began to understand the true nature of his clients. Rich or poor, they had one thing in common. They were criminals—plain and simple. If they were not guilty of the current charges, then they had almost certainly committed a dozen other crimes for which they hadn't been caught.

What baffled him even more was the reality that they always left evidence of their involvement behind for the authorities to find. The rule appeared to be the more serious the crime, the more careless the criminal.

While most criminals were just careless, there were those who were convinced they could outsmart the police. Frequently they would go so far as to intentionally leave evidence in an effort to prove just how much smarter they were.

Whether they left evidence intentionally or not, the result was the same. They were going to end up in the criminal-justice system. Because the simple truth was that people who committed serious felonies were caught before they left the crime scene. They just didn't know it yet.

If they were lucky—lucky meaning very rich—they were able to afford Duncan. Otherwise, they were in deep shit.

CHAPTER 10

DUNCAN'S UNDERSTANDING OF how to play the criminal *in*justice game grew with each case he handled. Innocence and guilt became irrelevant concepts. Prosecutors and the defense attorneys knew that the innocent client was the exception rather than the rule. The district attorney's office had but one goal: prosecute as many criminals as possible, as economically as possible.

With limited staff and budget, the DA's office was forced to pick its battles wisely. If a defense attorney could force the prosecution to dedicate a disproportionate amount of time and energy prosecuting the case, he'd get a better plea bargain for his client.

Duncan quickly learned that publicity and public opinion were useful tools for overpowering the DA's office. Prosecutors across the country were extraordinarily protective of their reputations in the community. Their internal policy decisions were frequently molded by the ebb and flow of public opinion.

However, publicity could be a client's best friend or his worst enemy. Duncan was becoming a master at manipulating the press, using it as both a sword and a shield. Frequently he would portray the district attorney's office as a group of incompetents in an effort to sell the press (and ultimately the public) on the idea that his client was being prosecuted to further the DA's political or professional aspirations. Conversely (but decidedly less frequently), he'd call press conferences to publicly foist praise on the DA.

Duncan thought that his praise-the-DA speeches sounded more than a little cheesy. At times it was hard to keep a straight face as he forced the insincere words from his mouth. "The DA's office has proved itself to be a bastion of compassion with an unparalleled sense of justice in this case." He was always careful to limit his praise to the case at hand. No matter how corny, the media always loved speeches that said anything flattering about the DA's office. Invariably the speech would show up on the front page of the local newspaper.

The no-holds-barred approach Duncan employed in defending his clients made him disliked and feared—but mostly respected—by prosecutors.

Most of his firm's paying clients had three things in common. They were well educated, Caucasian, and very rich. Despite this, he found his clients as a group to lack both wisdom and intellect.

Unlike most people, he was not one to fall into the trap of confusing knowledge with wisdom. Duncan knew many knowledgeable people, well educated and well read. But Duncan also knew that wisdom could not be found in a book. While he was not able to articulate its source, he seldom found wisdom in people who lacked a keen sense of observation and superior listening skills, two skills Duncan prided himself on possessing. To his mind, most problems in life were caused by those attempting to employ knowledge absent the required intellect and wisdom. *Such people are a danger to everyone, including themselves*, he often thought.

His mother, while not particularly well educated, was a very wise woman. She loved to use little sayings and stories to help him understand everything from human nature to the difference between right and wrong.

As he was growing up, one of her favorite little sayings was, "An ignorant man lacks information, not intellect. A stupid man lacks intellect and therefore can't be taught. You can always educate an ignorant man, but a stupid man is destined to remain stupid. You simply can't change that."

His mother's words could not have better described his clients—in a word, they were stupid.

He began to measure his chances of success in any particular case by gauging the level of his client's stupidity. He jokingly called it the "S factor." The higher the S factor, the more difficult the case would be to win. It became an inside joke between him and his secretary.

Sometimes she would interrupt one of Duncan's client meetings, "Pardon the interruption, but Mr. Helms sent me down to find out what the S factor is." Fighting back a smile, he'd respond, "You can tell Mr. Helms that it's at least ninety percent."

It was mildly depressing to discover that most of his clients turned out to be ridiculously stupid people; on the other hand, the more fatuous clients yielded greater challenges and sweeter victories.

In addition to being stupid (or maybe just another measure of it), the simple truth was that the rich and famous believed they were above the law. To their credit, they were at least half-right. If they had enough money to spend on the right lawyer, they were much more likely to evade justice. However, having loads of money was not a guarantee that they would find the right attorney.

There were plenty of large and well-respected law firms willing to spend considerable sums of their clients' money only to obtain a guilty verdict.

Most people did not understand that, unlike other areas of the law that primarily require superior writing and analytical skills, criminal law requires the additional element of court presence. Without that presence, the best legal minds in the country make mediocre criminal attorneys. Court presence is a gift from the gods. You either have it or you don't; it simply can't be taught. Only a handful of attorneys have it; Duncan had it in spades. Working seven days a week, usually into the wee hours of the morning, he made sure that his clients were above the law. Duncan thought of it as playing Monopoly. He was the real-world Get Out of Jail Free Card.

CHAPTER 11

DUNCAN WAS HONING his skills, waiting for his first big break. From his earliest days with the firm, he obsessed over the smallest details of a client's case. Analyzing files long after the cases had been resolved, he studied the methods authorities used to apprehend his clients, as well as the errors made by both the prosecution and the defense. It became a tantalizing game of what-if. The insight he derived helped him avoid the mistakes of the past and made him an even better attorney. Winning acquittal after acquittal, his name began to appear in the local papers on a regular basis. More important, the senior partners were taking notice of his successes.

From the most unlikely of places, a case that would bring him national notoriety fell into his lap. Late one Friday afternoon, Duncan was working at his desk when he looked up to see Bernard Bentworth standing in his office doorway. "I may have a case for you," Bentworth announced, as if he had been waiting to be recognized before speaking.

Bentworth was a senior partner and a snob of the first order. He seldom lowered himself to speak directly to associates, choosing to communicate via memos or using his secretary, Marla Jones, as a buffer between him and those he deemed beneath him.

Duncan held him in low regard, not because he treated others like peons, but because he was at best an average attorney. Bentworth was, however, one of the guys who signed his checks, so painting on a smile, Duncan invited him in.

Bentworth remained standing in the doorway. He got right down to business. "I need you to fly to Georgia on Monday. There is a young man there I want you to interview for me. I'm not sure we want to get involved in this case. I just want to find out what is going on down there."

Duncan was a little surprised by the visit. "Sir, I have an evidence suppression motion in the Katz matter on Monday morning."

Dismissing Duncan's retort, Bentworth responded in a commanding tone as he turned to walk away, "Get someone to cover for you. You'll be on a plane to Georgia. Stop by Marla's desk before you leave tonight. She'll have your tickets in the file."

Irritated by Bentworth's condescending manner, Duncan responded in kind, "Would it be too much to ask why I'm going to Georgia?"

Bentworth spun on his heels back toward Duncan. The look on his face made it clear that it was indeed too much to ask. "You're going because I'm your boss, and I told you you're going. Is that clear?"

Seeing no advantage in pissing off Mr. Bentworth any further, Duncan responded, "Yes, sir."

Hearing Duncan's capitulation, Bentworth continued, trying to sound magnanimous, "If you must know, my wife asked me to find out why a relative of hers is being charged with murder. I'm not sure how she is related to this hillbilly. It's her cousin's uncle's brother's something. Frankly, I don't care. I just want to be able to tell her that I checked into it. So go check into it! And the next time you question me, you might want to think about looking for other employment." Bentworth didn't wait for a response before he turned and marched back to his office.

The word *murder* had sent a rush of adrenaline through Duncan's body, causing him to completely ignore his boss's crass words. *Holy shit! I can get a murder case!* Duncan wanted to scream with excitement.

Jogging down the hall, he almost beat Bentworth back to his office. Out of breath, he leaned over Marla's desk. "Hello, sweetheart. You've done something with your hair. You look absolutely radiant."

Marla had been Bentworth's secretary for thirty-five years. She was nearly sixty and decidedly unattractive. "Save your flattery, young man. I've seen that look on an associate's face before. Trying to land our first murder case, are we? Careful what you ask for. You just might get it."

Duncan smiled a confused smile. He continued to profess his sincerity. "Marla, you know I adore you. You look great."

With a sweet but disbelieving smile she replied, "Well, it's sweet of you, anyway. Now here is the file and your tickets." As Duncan turned to walk away, Marla called out, "Good luck."

There wasn't much in the file—some handwritten notes and contact information. The only thing he knew for sure was that he was going to interview a young man named Jasper Johnson who had been accused of killing a black teenager. It was not until he arrived in Georgia that he obtained a copy of the charge sheet setting forth the detailed allegations against his client.

Jasper was being accused of tying a teenage boy to the back of his pickup truck and dragging him down country roads until the body was unrecognizable. The criminal counts alleged that Jasper was a member of the National Nazi Party and the Ku Klux Klan. *Yeah, I can see how this kid could be related to that fuckwad Bentworth.* The thought made him smile.

In what seemed a cosmic irony, Duncan initially interviewed Jasper at the jailhouse in Jasper County, Georgia. The surroundings were a far cry from what Duncan had become used to in California. The jailhouse had four cells, one of which was being used to store Sheriff Junior Buford's fishing gear.

Duncan found himself sitting in the sheriff's office staring at no fewer than twenty bass mounted on wooden planks. Buford noticed the interest that Duncan appeared to have in the fish. "Caught every one of those babies, right down da road in Paster's crick. See this one ri'cheer?" the sheriff said, pointing to the largest plank on the wall right behind his head. "Biggest one ever caught roun' these here parts. Put up quite a fight," Sheriff Buford said with great pride.

I am in Hee Haw hell, Duncan thought.

The sheriff had misinterpreted Duncan's look of disdain as one of interest, but Duncan played along anyway. "You must be very proud."

"You betcha sweet ass. We love our fishin' down in this neck of the woods."

Duncan didn't respond, hoping that the fish stories would stop.

"So you're that big city attorney they sent out to represent the kid that done killed that nigra boy?" he inquired, more to make small talk than questioning who Duncan was. The Armani suit and Rolex watch made it apparent that Duncan wasn't from Jasper County, or anywhere else in the South, for that matter.

"Sheriff, to be honest, I'm not sure what the nature of our involvement will be in this matter. I'll know better after I have a chance to talk to Mr. Johnson. If you could show me to the interview room, I'd like to get started."

"Well, son, there ain't no meetin' room, but ya welcome to use my office."

"Thank you, Sheriff Buford. That would be most helpful."

"Hell, boy, no need to be so formal, just call me Bubba. All my friends do."

"Why, thank you, Bubba." Just saying his name made Duncan feel as if he had traveled back to the Old South, and perhaps he had. *Why is this guy being so friendly? Aren't we on different sides?*

"I'll go get ya boy." Leaning across his desk as he stood, Bubba lowered his voice. "You know, just between us, I hope you get that boy off. But it don't look good. No, sir, it damn sure don't look good. The dumb ass confessed. Yup, those federal boys kept him in this room for two days until he confessed."

Duncan was shocked both by the sheriff's apparent sympathy for Jasper and by the disclosure that the feds were already involved, and he was not one to shock easily.

Jasper was brought into the room in handcuffs and leg irons. Duncan reached deep for his most pleasant southern drawl. "Bubba, do you think we can get those removed during the interview?"

"I'd like to help ya, son, truly I would. But if this boy gets away, it'll be my badge. He's big news around dese parts."

"Just the handcuffs, then? I'm going to need him to write down some information for me," Duncan thickened the accent for effect.

Bubba looked from side to side as if someone might be watching, even though they were the only three people in the room. "I guess I can do that. Just don't you get any ideas, you get me, boy?" Bubba looked hard at Jasper, who didn't respond, as he reached over and removed the handcuffs.

Jasper had awkward-looking facial features: beady eyes that were spaced too far apart, a long narrow forehead that dominated his face, oversize ears made to look even larger by his shaved head, and a leering smile that cried out for a good dentist. *Probably the result of allowing cousins to marry*, Duncan thought upon first observing Jasper.

"Good morning, Mr. Johnson. My name is Duncan Gabrelli. I've been sent down here by my firm to interview you. Apparently you have friends in high places."

"Yeah, my momma says she knows folks out there in Californy."

"Well, let's talk about your case for a moment," Duncan suggested, still unable to figure why Bentworth would let anyone know that he had any family connections to this kid.

In the first ten seconds Duncan discovered exactly who Jasper was.

"I hate those fucking niggers," Jasper said, leaving no room for doubt as to his unbridled hatred for all people of color. He saw the world in two colors. Anyone not white was black, and if you were black you were just another nigger. So he pretty much hated 80 percent of the world's population.

"Those bastards are tryin'a railroad my ass. Man, you gotsta get me off. Us white boys gotsta stick together, ya know."

The idea that this subhuman thought that they had anything in common made Duncan feel nauseous. He did, however, find comfort in the fact that he was Italian, a fact which, if known to his client, would have made Duncan just another nigger in Jasper's eyes. Never in the history of the world had a white man found so much comfort in the thought of being considered a nigger.

At first blush, it was easy not to like Jasper Johnson. He was uneducated, vile, and full of hatred. But Duncan could see he was nothing more than the product of his upbringing. His brothers were members of the KKK, as was his father, and his father before him. He only knew prejudice—it was all he'd been taught since birth. It was not that he felt sorry for Jasper; Duncan simply understood him.

There was little doubt in Duncan's mind that his client was guilty as sin. Even so, what made the case interesting to Duncan was its potential to attract national attention. Win or lose, he knew the case was going to get press coverage, and lots of it.

"Hey, you ain't one of those Jew lawyers, are ya? Cuz I don't want no Jew representin' me."

Duncan shook his head in disbelief. "No, I'm not Jewish. But let me help you out here. I don't give a rat's ass whom you hate. So, unless you want to fry in some goddamn electric chair, you'll keep that racist crap to yourself."

Jasper threw a fuck-you stare at Duncan.

"And you can keep that bullshit look, too. Listen up, country boy. I represent bad men for a living, and you're not even in their league. If you want a public defender who couldn't care less if you live or die, just say the word, and I'm out of here. Otherwise, just sit there and answer my questions. If you're lucky, maybe I can find a way to save you from yourself. Do we understand each other?"

"Hey, man, I just wanna get out of here," Jasper muttered in a more humble tone.

"Good. Me, too. So let's get to work."

The interview lasted almost an hour, which was about as long as Duncan could stomach. "Okay, Mr. Johnson, I need to report back to my firm. Someone should be in touch with you in the next few days regarding your case."

"Whatcha mean, 'git back to me'? Ain'tcha gonna take my case?"

"It's not up to me. But it will be my recommendation that we represent you."

Just being around Jasper made Duncan feel dirty; he took the longest shower of his life that night.

Upon his return to California, Duncan went directly to Bentworth's office. Bentworth was sitting behind his massive cherrywood desk reading a newspaper. Duncan made a courtesy knock on the open office door before walking in without waiting for an invitation.

"I met your wife's..." Duncan paused. Thinking better of making the family connection, Duncan continued, "Well, I met with Mr. Johnson. Quite a personality!"

Without lifting his gaze from the paper he was reading, Bentworth responded, "Yes, I've been reading about him. I don't care how mad my wife gets; we won't be representing this...this...this...gentleman. Sorry for wasting your time."

"That's too bad. I think that there's a chance we could win." Duncan hoped Bentworth would take the bait.

"No, I don't want my firm associated with this case."

Duncan was pretty sure what he really meant was that he didn't want his family name connected to the kid. "Sir, I'd really like the opportunity to represent Mr. Johnson."

Bentworth looked up at Duncan for the first time since he walked in the room. "Did I not make myself clear? No. I already said I'm sorry for wasting your time. Now let me get back to work. I assume that you also have work to do?"

Duncan felt dejected; he could feel his first murder case slipping through his hands. "Yes, sir."

I could get that kid off. The confession was coerced, the evidence is a mess. I could win this thing. He wasn't about to give up quite that easily.

That afternoon, Duncan stopped by Mr. Helms's office. "Sorry to interrupt, sir. Can I have a minute of your time?" Mr. Helms was the most senior partner of the firm.

"Sure, come in, Duncan. What's on your mind?"

"Well, sir, it's a little difficult to say. I don't want it to seem like I'm going behind Mr. Bentworth's back."

Helms interrupted, "But you're going to do it anyway?"

Duncan didn't hesitate. "Yes, sir, I am."

"Okay, what's so important?"

Duncan detailed the facts of the Johnson case and his conversations with Mr. Bentworth.

"So let me get this straight. You're asking me to let you represent this piece of scum, at the firm's expense, over the objection of a senior partner, who is, just to make this even more absurd, related to this accused murderer. Have I got this about right?" Mr. Helms asked sarcastically, while simultaneously tapping a Montblanc pen on the desk to the tempo of his words.

"Well, I must admit that it sounded better in my head, but that does pretty much cover it," Duncan responded, trying not to sound too flippant.

Helms thought for at least a full minute before speaking. "Let me talk to Mr. Bentworth. I'll let you know later today."

"Thank you, Mr. Helms." Duncan turned to leave.

"And Duncan, while I appreciate your enthusiasm, in the future, this is not the way these matters are handled."

"I understand, sir. Thank you for your time."

At five that afternoon, Bentworth stormed into Duncan's office unannounced. "You want the case, you got it. But don't think I'm ever going to forget how you got it."

"Mr. Bentworth, it wasn't my intention to offend you. I just think I can win this thing. Even if I don't win, won't your wife be happy we tried?"

"This is not about my wife's happiness. It's about you going behind my back to Mr. Helms after I told you no." Bentworth, fuming, stomped out of the room.

CHAPTER 12

BY THE TIME Duncan and his team returned to Georgia, all the major news organizations were following the case. The brutality of the crime, combined with the backwoods southern setting, made the case perfect fodder for the media machine.

Duncan brought his secretary, Stella Campbell, and a junior associate, Stephen Crocker, to assist him in the defense.

Stephen looked out the window as the plane landed, and then over at Duncan. "Wow, look at all those reporters. Why all this coverage for a small-town murder case?"

Duncan gave Stephen an incredulous glare. "Are you kidding me? It's the type of story the liberal media loves. A story that increases the fear in the minority communities and heightens the general level of tension between the races. Most important, it's a story that sells newspapers."

The three pushed their way through the mob of reporters to a waiting rental car. The town was too small to even have its own rental car agency, so Stella had arranged to have one delivered to the airport from a nearby city.

When they pulled up in front of the Starlight Motel, Duncan looked at Stella like she'd lost her mind. "Are you telling me that these are the best accommodations available?"

"I'm telling you that these are the *only* ones available," Stella replied adamantly.

Duncan was even less pleased when Rose, the little gray-haired lady who owned the establishment, opened the door to his small, musty-smelling room. "Stella, you've got to be kidding me. I can't stay here."

"Do you think I'd stay in this shit hole if there were something better?" Stella said, gritting her teeth.

She hadn't so much as raised her voice to Duncan in the almost four years she'd worked for him, and he'd never heard her curse.

"Okay, okay. It will have to do, for now! Where are we supposed to work? There isn't enough room in here to think."

"Well, sir. I took the liberty of renting all six rooms. We can use some of them to work in and conduct interviews," Stella replied in a more submissive tone.

"If we're really staying in this rat trap, I'm going to need a dedicated fax line installed. God knows I'm going to need to stay in touch with the civilized world."

"I had it installed yesterday, sir. I had it put in the room between yours and Stephen's rooms. All the rooms have adjoining doors so you can both get to it anytime you want."

"So does that mean I can come visit your room whenever I want?" Duncan was trying to be funny and lighten the mood. He had no romantic interest in Stella, even though she was only three years younger than him and not altogether unattractive. While Duncan was a bit flirtatious by nature, he had never given Stella any real reason to believe that he was romantically interested in her. She knew he didn't have those feelings for her, but she secretly wished he had.

"No. You big lech, I'm in room six, all the way over there." She pointed to the room farthest away from Duncan's. "I figured you'd try something like that, so I got as far away as possible."

Duncan feigned being hurt by the rejection. "Stella, I thought you loved me."

Stella noticed an uncomfortable look on Stephen's face as he listened to the sexual banter. "I wouldn't worry about me, Stephen. I've worked for Duncan for four years, and I've yet to see him take a girl out. If I were you, I'd keep my door locked," Stella said laughing.

Stephen nervously waited for Duncan to start laughing before joining in. Stella laughed so hard that tears came rolling down her cheeks. Finally regaining her composure, she continued, "I almost forgot. I arranged for the use of a local firm's library, but it's pitifully small, so

I called Mr. Helms. He assigned Bob Taylor from the New York office to be available should you need him for research or support."

Despite his general feeling of irritation over the accommodations, her thoroughness made him release a pleased smile.

They'd completely forgotten about Rose, who was by this point mad as a nest of hornets. "You city folk. Why don't you just stay in your gosh darn big city if you don't like it round here? Just take the dang keys, and if you getta needin' anythin', don't ask. The answer is no!" Slamming the keys down on a nightstand, Rose scampered away as fast as her rickety old legs would take her. "Well, I never."

As was typical of Duncan, he completely ignored Rose's outburst and got down to business. "Stella, how long do we have this place for?"

"I locked us in for three months."

"Better get another two, just in case."

"From whom? Our new best friend Rose?" Stella replied sarcastically.

Duncan cast a displeased look her way.

"Don't look at me that way. You don't finish this case in ninety days, you won't need a place to sleep, because there'll be two murder trials in this town."

"Why Stella, this small-town life doesn't suit you at all," Duncan said, shaking his index finger at her in a comically exaggerated fashion.

"Very funny, sir, let's just win and go home."

Both Stella and Duncan stopped talking simultaneously and looked at Stephen, who hadn't said a word since leaving the airfield. "Don't look at me. I grew up in a small town just like this. Hell, it ain't that bad."

"Stephen, when the best restaurant in town has a little boy holding a hamburger in front of it, it's 'that bad.' Believe me, it's bad. Now we need to get organized. The two of you get some help turning two of these cracker boxes into offices. I'm going down to the jail to talk to our little angel. Let's get this defense rolling, shall we?"

A deputy led Duncan back to the holding area of the jail. Duncan was careful not to show it, but he was dumfounded to find Jasper sitting on a stool near the edge of his cell, playing checkers through the bars with Sheriff Buford.

"Howdy, Counselor. Your client plays a mean game of checkers," Bubba said as if he'd known Duncan all his life. "Musta beaten me four times in a row."

"More like five, but who's countin'," Jasper bragged.

Jasper was also happy to see his new best buddy. "I know'd you'd take my case. I just know'd it."

The whole scene seemed surreal to Duncan. *Tell me that you haven't been talking to the sheriff about your case. Please just tell me you're not that dumb.*

Looking around at the empty cells, the sheriff said, "Well, son, don't look like you'll be a needin' my office. I'll just leave you boys to talk."

"How they been treating you?" Duncan asked with a tinge of sarcasm in his voice as he watched Buford close the door behind him.

Once they were alone, Duncan grabbed the bars of Jasper's cell and started shaking them. "Are you out of your mind? I thought I told you not to talk to anyone about anything. And you decide to get chummy with Bubba?"

"Hell, you don't have to worry about old Bubba. He's been a friend of my family for a coon's age."

"I can't help you if you don't listen. I'm the only friend you have right now. Me. That's all." Duncan didn't mean to make their relationship sound that personal.

"Why that's pretty nice of you to say."

That was not what Duncan meant when he said 'friend,' but he was too exasperated to explain himself. "He's not your friend. He arrested you, remember? Now, what did you tell him? I want to know every word you said to the sheriff."

"Now don't get so excited. I didn't say much. Besides he had some stuff to tell me. I'm tellin' ya. He's a friend. He was just doin' his job," Jasper insisted.

"Yes. And his job is to keep your dumb ass in jail. Don't tell me— you think he is going to help get you out of this mess?"

"Hell, yeah! Hey, I almost forgot. Bubba said you should ask me about my right to have an attorney. Some type of warnin'. I forgot the name; it started with an M."

"Do you mean the Miranda warnings?"

"Yup, that's it. Hey yore good. You know'd it right off, didn't need to look at no book or nothin'. Any-aways, Bubba said it was very important."

Okay, I'll play along, Duncan thought. "When you were arrested, did someone read you your rights?"

"Sure enough did. Bubba did it himself the night he picked me up."

"And did you understand those rights?"

"Hey, I may not remember what you call 'em, but I know'd what they mean. This ain't the first time I had a run-in with da law. Sure, I know'd 'em."

"Did he tell you that you had the right to an attorney before being questioned?"

"Sure enough did. In fact, just between you and me, he told me not to talk to anyone until I talked to my attorney. So, I said sure, I want to talk to an attorney. I told Bubba that, straight up."

"Well, according to your good friend Bubba, the feds interrogated you for two days before you confessed. They must think you waived your right to an attorney. Did the feds tell you that you had the right to an attorney?"

"No, sir. They never even asked me about it. They just kept askin' me questions and telling me that they know'd I done it. Tellin' me that it would be easier on me if I just confessed. Yup, they kept me in here for two days. Man, was I tired."

Duncan leaned back in his chair. "That's all fine and good, but you know that there are going to be half a dozen FBI guys swearing that you waived that right. Is there anyone that can prove that you didn't waive your right to an attorney?" Duncan paused, "No. No, let me guess. Good old Bubba?"

"Sure enough, he was there the whole time. He told me he'd swear to it. Tell ya the truth, I don't think those federal boys liked Bubba.

They kept tellin' him that they were in charge. I think Bubba tried to tell 'em, but they just won't listen to him."

Duncan laughed. "You just got to love these small towns. Okay, let's get a sworn statement from Bubba before he realizes just how pissed off those federal boys are going to be."

Jasper smiled. "You're in the South now, Mr. Gabrelli. We don't care how pissed off federal boys get."

Duncan could hardly believe what he had just heard. *The law could not be more clear*, Duncan thought. Once Jasper asserted his right to speak to an attorney before questioning, the interrogation had to stop. When the FBI continued to question Jasper, they violated his constitutional right to have an attorney present during questioning. Any statements made by Jasper to the FBI, including Jasper's confession, would be inadmissible in court.

What a colossal fuck up, Duncan thought.

With the testimony of Sheriff Buford, the defense's motion to suppress the confession was granted, and the confession was thrown out. Before the prosecution knew what hit it, the entire tide of the case had turned. Duncan didn't know and frankly didn't care if Sheriff Buford was telling the truth or was just coming to the aid of a good ole boy; he only cared about winning.

Even without the confession, the evidence appeared to be so overwhelmingly in favor of conviction that everyone (including the small-town DA) took little notice of the young, brash attorney defending the case, even if he was from the high-powered firm of Weiss, Barron & Helms. It would be a mistake that they would soon regret.

Duncan knew that the prosecution's case was in disarray, even if the prosecutor didn't. To the surprise of everyone, including the judge, Duncan insisted on an early trial date. He wanted to force the prosecution's hand and not give it time to regroup. Sixty days after Duncan first interviewed Jasper, the case went to trial.

WB&H threw its full weight behind the defense. Using the vast resources of his firm, Duncan simply overwhelmed the prosecution. By the time they recognized just how much trouble they were in, it was too late for the prosecution to salvage its case.

Its confidence in a quick conviction had lulled the prosecution into a false sense of security. However, the police and coroner had done such a shoddy job of collecting and preserving evidence that their confidence only proved to further undermine the state's case.

A small-town DA with a small-town budget was not prepared to confront the parade of expensive and credentialed defense experts whom Duncan called into court. The defense had a field day discrediting the prosecution's evidence, casting doubt into the minds of the jurors.

Inexplicably, even some of the prosecution's witnesses seemed to have lapses in memory, turning them into better witnesses for the defense than for the prosecution. Duncan wasn't sure what made the witnesses change their stories, but he had a sneaking suspicion that some of his client's friends in the KKK might have played a role in the matter.

What should have been a six-month trial ended in just thirty-seven days. The jury deliberated for under three hours before returning the not-guilty verdict. Most of the press had given Duncan little chance of winning. In fact, the acquittal surprised everyone who followed the case, with the sole exception of Duncan, who by his very nature expected to win every one of his cases. Even his client looked a little surprised when the verdict was read by the jury foreman.

Jasper jumped at Duncan, trying to wrap his arms around him, but Duncan pushed him away. "No need for that. I was just doing my job." Even before the court finished thanking the jury, Duncan whispered into Stephen's ear, "Tell Stella to get us out of here tonight. Have her start packing up right away."

Jasper caught up with Duncan at the hotel before he could make his getaway. "Well, buddy, looks like we done it. You left so quick I didn't get a chance to properly thank ya," Jasper said reaching out to shake Duncan's hand.

Duncan did not reciprocate. Shaking his head, he responded, "No. *We* didn't do anything. *I* did it." Jasper was a free man and feeling a little cocky.

"Hell, Mr. Gabrelli, you're not so dumb as to think that you didn't get a little hometown help, if you know'd what I mean?"

"Yes, I 'know'd' what you mean. But let me assure you that all the white-hooded boys in this backwoods state couldn't have kept you out of the chair if I didn't take this case. You 'know'd' what I mean?" Duncan said, mocking him again.

"Okay, you think it was you that got me off? So tell me this, city boy. How do it feel to set a murderer free?" Jasper sniped.

Duncan had been asking himself that very question since the verdict was announced. The truth was it made him feel strong and all-powerful. It was as if he stepped into Jasper's shoes, as if he were the killer. He wanted to suppress the sensation but he couldn't, for a moment he was a god, all-powerful, the master of his universe.

"Jasper, you're a fool. You know why I took this case?" Jasper looked up but didn't answer. "I took this case because I wanted to get away with murder. You didn't get away with killing anyone. I did!"

Jasper looked confused. "You're crazy out of your mind. You didn't even know that nigger."

"Jasper, every morning during this trial I woke up and asked myself, 'Do I want to save Jasper's life today?' And you are goddamned lucky that the answer was yes, or else you would be swinging from one of these oak trees. You see, I *like* the idea of people getting away with murder. So the answer to your question is, it feels great. So go climb back under your rock before I decide to get away with killing you."

The smirk disappeared from Jasper's face. "You're crazy, man."

"Yes. I am. So off with you, and take your little dog with you, before a house falls on you, too," Duncan said, again mocking his client, this time with a line from *The Wizard of Oz*.

Jasper hollered, "Fuck you, man. Yore crazy," as he sped away in his rusty '65 Chevy pickup.

Stella heard the commotion and came running. "Is everything okay, Mr. Gabrelli?"

"Yup, just talking shop with Jasper." He smiled at Stella. "I guess there will be only one murder trial after all."

"Three months and five days. It was close, very close." Stella smiled and went back to the business of packing up the office.

Jasper's acquittal triggered the seething volcano of emotion that had been lying dormant deep within Duncan's soul to erupt and roar to life. As hard as he tried to forget that horrible day, the voice of his mother's murderer was always lurking somewhere in the recesses of his mind. Immersing himself in work kept him from reliving her death, but it was deeper than that. He was trying to suppress the voices in his head. They called to him. At first the words were too faint to make out, but now, in that moment, they were crystal clear. They were loud and strong. "You are the murderer. You are the murderer."

For years the ramparts he had built around his heart had protected him from the voices, but they had now found the back door. The first night after the Georgia verdict, in his dreams he became the killer, pulling the trigger, watching his mother's head jerk forward violently as she slumped to the floor. What was worse, he quickly began to welcome their nightly visits. The victim was no longer his mother. It was someone, anyone, no one.

His growing obsession with reviewing criminal case files was spiraling into a full-on addiction. He was developing an unhealthy fascination with murder cases that transcended his mother's death. Perhaps it was the guilt he felt for not having run to her aid, or perhaps it was just having survived. Whatever the reason, freeing a poor racist from Georgia had opened the cage. The beast within Duncan was eager to run free.

CHAPTER 13

J ASPER'S ACQUITTAL HEADLINED the evening news programs across the country. The press had long ago crossed the line between creating the news and reporting it. It had now painted itself into a corner. Having predicted that a guilty verdict was inevitable for the past three months, the press was in the unenviable position of either admitting they had misjudged the strength of the defense or declaring that the verdict was a miscarriage of justice.

It didn't take a genius to figure out which route the press would choose. Newspapers and newscasters across the country promptly lampooned the members of the jury for acquitting Jasper, in what they called "a clear miscarriage of justice." Even the radical right chimed in, screaming that it was just another example of how judges are letting criminals go free, an argument that was absurd in light of the fact that this was a jury trial. *Absurdity is the bread and butter of the radical right,* Duncan thought as he read his paper during breakfast.

Duncan's contributions in obtaining the acquittal were not overlooked by the press, who were frantically searching for scapegoats to justify their own biased reporting. They questioned everything from his morality to his humanity for even accepting the case.

Most of the print and television media vilified Duncan, but there was a small but vocal faction who chose to admit they underestimated the true strength of the defense. While disagreeing with the verdict, they attributed the victory to Duncan's superior lawyering skills.

Duncan was fond of using the well-worn maxim used by criminal defense attorneys: "Even bad press is better than no press at all." He may have thought it comical, but the publicity he'd been receiving was starting to instill at least a modest amount of fear into prosecutors throughout Los Angeles.

Prosecutors live or die on their percentage of convictions. The better the conviction rate, the faster they're promoted. More important, prosecutors with high conviction rates are able to command higher salaries when they leave the DA's office for private practice (as almost all prosecutors do). The last thing a prosecutor wants is to go head-to-head against a proven winner, and Duncan had become just that.

As his reputation grew, the firm started to assign him more high-profile cases. He was made a junior partner in early 1977. From that point forward, there were no cases too big or too high profile.

Clients who had employed the services of the firm for many years began to insist that Duncan handle their cases. His firm was reaping the rewards of Duncan's fame, in the form of new clients, too.

He began to find it difficult to keep up with his workload. Notwithstanding his heavy load, he continued to accept a small number of pro bono clients. However, within two years of becoming an junior partner, he was forced to stop taking pro bono cases altogether.

The few pro bono cases that he did take were cases that most attorneys would not have chosen even if they were being paid. The clients were mostly indigent, who had been accused of such unpopular crimes as illicit drug use, child molestation, and murder. He thrived on the publicity he received from these cases.

With more work than there were hours in the day, he soon had neither the time nor the desire to supplement his caseload with any matter that did not put his name on the evening news.

CHAPTER 14

DUNCAN COULD NO longer close his eyes to the fact that his fixation with the analysis of case files had metamorphosed into an unhealthy compulsion. It was as if some invisible force was compelling him to delve ever deeper in the minutiae of the files. He began to obsess over the details of his clients' crimes long after the cases were resolved. He would forego virtually all other forms of entertainment; opting instead to stay up until all hours of the night analyzing criminals' motives, methods, and mistakes.

The obsession expanded beyond analysis of his own case files, eventually growing into the review of virtually every case his firm handled. With each case file he dissected, he honed his ability to unmask the mistakes the criminal had made. As a byproduct of that knowledge, he was developing an outline for what a criminal would have to do to commit a crime without getting caught.

He found his "hobby," as he called it, to be as perplexing as it was titillating. Each time he thought that he was getting close to finding a prototype for the perfect crime, he discovered that there were ten new variables that he hadn't considered.

Because there were unpredictable and sometimes arbitrary factors that frequently came into play, he was forced to conclude that on a strictly technical basis, the perfect crime would never be achievable. Even so, he was still extraordinarily fascinated by the number of cases that involved predictable—and yet unaccounted-for—factors. By failing to anticipate even the most obvious facets of their crimes, criminals all but assured their apprehension.

Because Duncan was a practical person, his definition of the perfect crime was result-oriented. The perfect crime, to Duncan's mind, was a crime where the criminal did not get caught. The criminal case files he had studied revealed that there was seldom even a legitimate attempt to commit the perfect crime. What the files did reveal, however, was that criminals were, as he had concluded years earlier, not a very intelligent collection of individuals. Having reached this somewhat obvious conclusion, he marveled at his clients' poor career choice.

He knew that not all the variables that might arise during the commission of a crime could be controlled, or even accounted for. But deep down inside he still believed that if a crime were meticulously designed and planned, a person could virtually guarantee that he would not be apprehended. *It would take a brilliant mind to design such a perfect crime.*

Being neither shy nor humble, he believed that only a man of his superior knowledge and intellect could devise such a crime. That belief evolved into an intellectual quest, a quest to design the perfect crime. But not just any crime; while he may not have realized it at the time, he was a man with murder on his mind.

At first it was just a game to Duncan, something to feed his thirst for cerebral stimulation. During conversations with his less sophisticated clients, some would brag about the crimes they had gotten away with. He secretly made detailed notes of the stories to use in his research and planning. Taking into account the natural tendencies of his clients to exaggerate, embellish, and lie, he began to see a pattern forming regarding crimes for which his clients hadn't (as yet) been caught.

Unfortunately, even discounting his clients' propensity for deceit, the overriding theme appeared to be that the successful criminal had just gotten lucky. They just seemed to be in the right place at the right time to avoid apprehension. Frequently, there was little—or no—planning for the crime. More often than not, the crimes were spontaneous or crimes of opportunity. In those cases, the criminals appeared to be relying purely on chance, rather than strategy.

He just couldn't bring himself to believe that the only way to commit a crime and not get caught was to cast your lot completely to fate.

As he saw it, depending on kismet to avoid getting caught was even more dangerous than having a bad plan. Counting on providence was like rolling the dice. While you might get away with one, two, or even a dozen lucky rolls, the odds were sure to catch up with you sooner or later. Besides, he knew that luck, good or bad, was a variable neither he nor anyone else could control.

As weeks of research turned into months, and months into years, his intellectual exercise was now a way of life. After years of playing the game of "What if the client had done this?" or "What if the client had done that?" he was still struck with the undeniable conclusion that he was far from his goal of formulating the perfect crime.

Something was missing. There had to be something he was overlooking. As hard as he tried, he just couldn't find the missing pieces of the puzzle. His belief that the answer was out there in the abyss—waiting for him to find it—only made the search that much more frustrating.

PART III

THE DEATH OF JESSICA LOPEZ

CHAPTER 15

THE CHAIN OF events that began in January 1979 would forever alter the course of Duncan's life. He had been made a junior partner two years earlier and had moved to a large corner office of the firm's penthouse suite. The office had windows on two sides that overlooked downtown Los Angeles.

That Monday started with an early morning appearance in federal court. Finding his case last on the calendar, he spent most of that morning cooling his heels on the uncomfortable wooden benches inside the courtroom waiting for his case to be called. It was almost eleven o'clock when he returned from court, a little distracted and behind schedule.

He hurried down the hall, past Stella's desk. She waved her arms, frantically trying to get his attention as he rushed by, but he was in a near run and deep in thought as he blew by her without notice. She was trying to alert him to the fact that he had guests waiting for him in his office. And not just *any* guests.

As he stepped inside the office, he found three of the most senior partners—Sandler Helms, Bernard Bentworth and Samuel Kenderman—not so patiently waiting for him. As if the move had been choreographed in advance, each partner simultaneously glanced down at his watch as Duncan strolled in.

Duncan managed to conceal his surprise and simply said, "Good morning, gentlemen." He shook hands with each of them before taking his seat behind his large mahogany desk.

"What can I help you gentlemen with this fine morning?" he said, slightly exaggerating his southern drawl.

The stone-faced men did not respond to his query.

There was a moment of awkward silence before Sandler Helms asked him, "How would you like to become a full partner of this firm?"

Duncan's chest tightened, and his mouth became instantly dry.

The question caught him by complete surprise. Only in his most exaggerated and fanciful dreams could he have imagined becoming a full partner in less than a decade. Instinctively he knew that these three men were about to exact a hefty price for bestowing upon him this unexpected honor—not to mention the substantial increase in salary.

After a short but palpable silence, Duncan responded, "So whom do I have to kill?" There was a lilt in his voice as he tried to hide the uncomfortable feeling buried deep in the pit of his stomach. It was almost as if, in some comical way, he half expected Mr. Helms to hand him a dossier of a rival lawyer they wanted murdered.

"Nothing quite as sinister as all that," Mr. Helms replied with a slight chuckle. The comic relief noticeably reduced the tension that had filled his office. "But you may someday wish that we had asked you to perform such a simple task." Mr. Helms continued in a more somber tone, "I assume that you have heard the name Vincenzo Bartelli?"

"Why, yes—of course I have," Duncan replied, still trying to get his bearings. "He kills people for a living, right? At least that is the vicious rumor going around town. Or should I say, around the country? And, oh yes, he and his associates are also some of this firm's most lucrative clients."

Mr. Helms was not amused by his flippant reply. He looked Duncan directly in the eyes. "Yes, Mr. Bartelli has been my client for many years. I daresay that this firm was built on funds received defending him and his associates." His rather stern reply left Duncan wondering whether he had inadvertently insulted Mr. Helms.

The sound of Mr. Helms's voice softened as he continued, "So, Duncan, my boy, let me tell you about my client and good friend, Vincenzo Bartelli. The FBI and various other state and federal agencies have been trying to convict Mr. Bartelli for crimes ranging from murder to jaywalking for many years without much success, thanks in no small part to the efforts of this firm. Some of these government agencies are more than a little pissed off at my friend. Well, yesterday Christmas came early for the Feds. Mr. Bartelli's son, Santino, was arrested and charged for the murder of a fourteen-year-old girl. While all the facts are not clear, Mr. Bartelli believes that his son is being framed by the government to get back at him personally. He wants this firm to represent his son. More to the point, Duncan, he's asked that you handle the case."

Duncan hadn't realized that Mr. Bartelli was a personal friend of Mr. Helms. He was now fairly certain that he had offended Mr. Helms with the "he kills people" comment. Even so, Mr. Bartelli's reputation was well known to the world, and Duncan was hopeful that his boss would understand that the comment was meant in jest.

While this was just the kind of case that Duncan lived for, he knew that there was more to this story than met the eye.

When Mr. Helms stopped talking, a hard silence fell over the room. Leaning back in his chair, Duncan just sat there staring at the three men.

"What, nothing to say? Can it be that the famous Duncan Gabrelli's tongue is tied?" Mr. Bentworth declared, sounding almost pleased with himself. Mr. Bentworth was still harboring considerable enmity toward Duncan over the Jasper Johnson affair.

"No sir, I'm not tongue-tied," Duncan instantly replied. "I'm just waiting for Mr. Helms to complete his thought. I'm waiting for one of you to tell me why in God's name the three of you are in my office this morning. I'm waiting to hear how bad I'm going to get fucked if this case goes wrong." Duncan's voice grew louder and sounded more aggravated with each word.

What the hell, I have already offended Mr. Helms once this morning. Why stop when I'm on such a roll? Besides, if Mr. Bartelli wants me to handle the case, it's not very likely that they were going to fire me. At least not today, Duncan thought.

Bernard Bentworth found no humor in Duncan's brash response and seized upon the opportunity to release a little pent-up hostility. "Do you think this is a joke?" The question was clearly intended to be rhetorical. "I was practicing law when you were still in elementary school. If you intend to keep your job with this firm, you will keep your wise-ass mouth shut, and do your fucking job. Does that complete our thought for you, Mr. Gabrelli?"

From the expression on Samuel Kenderman's face, he was champing at the bit, waiting for his turn to verbally lay the leather to Duncan.

Before Duncan had the opportunity to tell Mr. Bentworth to go fuck himself, which was his intended response, and just as Mr. Kenderman found an opening to voice his disdain for Duncan's remarks, Mr. Helm intervened.

"Gentlemen, relax. We can address Duncan's bedside manner another time."

The three partners glanced at each other. If there was any question about who was in charge, it was answered in that moment. "Now I would like to speak to Duncan in private. Gentlemen, would you please excuse us?" Mr. Helms announced in an authoritative tone.

Mr. Helms cast a you're-excused look in the direction of Mr. Bentworth and Mr. Kenderman and, without saying another word, the two senior partners stood up and left the room like two well-behaved little children who had been asked to leave the room while the grownups talked.

This has got to be killing that asswipe. That's right, you can just tuck your tail and leave, Duncan thought as he watched Mr. Bentworth close the door behind him.

While Mr. Helms was taken aback by Duncan's choice of words, he was impressed by both his intuitiveness and directness.

When they had left, Mr. Helms walked over and placed both hands on Duncan's desk. Leaning across the desk he decreed, "You can't lose this case. When I say you can't lose this case, I mean that literally. You cannot lose this case." He paused for a moment for effect then continued, "Mr. Bartelli instructed me to be sure that you understand the importance of this matter. To that end, he has insisted that this firm fire you if you lose. If his son spends so much as one day in prison, you are done with this firm. With any firm."

Duncan let what Helms was saying sink in for a minute before he responded. The problem was painfully clear—he really did not have a choice in the matter. "So let me see if I understand the situation. If I turn down the case, Mr. Bartelli takes his rather substantial business to another firm; I end up fired and on Mr. Bartelli's shit list. If I take the case and lose; I end up fired and on Mr. Bartelli's hit list. If I take the case and win; I save my ass and the firm's ass in the bargain." There was a short pause, "Well, all I can say is that you were right."

Looking puzzled, Mr. Helms questioned, "Right about what?"

"I *would* rather you just asked me to kill someone."

Mr. Helms returned Duncan's grin. "So you will take the case?"

Without skipping a beat, he looked Mr. Helms in the eyes, smiled a big toothy smile, and said, "Hell, I wouldn't give up this opportunity if my life depended on it."

Both men laughed nervously as Mr. Helms shook Duncan's hand and left the room without another word.

CHAPTER 16

AFTER THE MEETING with Helms, Duncan drove to the Los Angeles County Jail to size up his new client. He arrived downtown between Temple and First Street, at twelve thirty.

Notwithstanding the fact that Duncan worked for what the police referred to as the "dark side" (the brotherhood of defense attorneys), for the most part they liked his charismatic personality and respected his professionalism. Duncan's reputation had grown to almost mythical proportion among the inmates, and he had become somewhat of a celebrity at the jail.

By twelve-forty-five he was in a private interview room sitting across a small wooden table from Santino Bartelli. Only the most high-powered attorneys get such fast service. The look on Santino's face when he walked into the meeting room made it clear that he was somewhat impressed with Duncan's pull at the jail.

He looks like a mob boss's son, Duncan thought immediately. *That devilish look will make this case even more difficult to win.* To make matters worse, when Santino opened his mouth, he sounded as if he fell straight out of the pages of *The Godfather*.

It took him a full two minutes to realize that Santino was a prick of the highest order.

His initial interview with criminal clients always consisted of giving one very important admonition. *Keep your case to yourself. Do not discuss your case with anyone except your attorney.* "I don't want you making friends in here. I don't want you to confide anything to anyone, except me. Do you understand?"

Santino was not even pretending to listen. "So my dad must be paying you a pretty penny to defend me. Better win. Daddy does not like to be disappointed."

Duncan ignored the query and continued to give his stock speech. "The old cliché 'the walls have ears' couldn't better describe jails. I don't want you to discuss anything with the other inmates, not your name, not your age, not even your shoe size. Do you understand me?"

Santino was not used to being ignored. "Look, legal-boy, if my dad thinks you can get the job done, fine, but this is not my first stay at the gray walls hotel. I know what to do, and I don't need a suit to tell me what I know."

Santino's responses to Duncan's inquiries thus far had been laced with a smug confidence that he would evade justice. It was clear that he was used to his father bailing him out of trouble. It was also clear that there was no doubt in Santino's mind that his father would come through again.

Duncan had had enough of Santino's wise-ass remarks. "Look you jerk-off, out there in your world you're a tough guy, and I get it. If we were out there, I would not be saying what I'm about to say. But, in here, I am God. Not a god, I'm *the* God. Out there, your daddy can help you. But he is not going to get you out of here. If you walk from this, it will be me saving your ass. So unless you want to spend the rest of your fucking life in prison, I'm going to respectfully suggest that you shut your mouth and pay attention."

Santino sat stunned in his seat. No one had ever talked to him that way, at least not without getting beaten half to death. Santino was not smart enough to know that his confidence in his father was misplaced.

"Do you know who I am? Who my father—"

Before Santino could finish his sentence, Duncan cut him off. "I can see that you're a slow learner. Out of respect for your father, I'm going to give you one more chance. However, if I hear one more word from you, I'm out of here."

The two men stared intensely at each other. After a full minute of a hard silence, Duncan said, "Good, now let's get to work."

It took every ounce of what little self-control Santino possessed to stop himself from slugging Duncan in the face. But something inside him told him to wait—at least until he spoke to his dad—before he did anything else stupid. In truth, it was fear more than self-control that held Santino back that day. He could not help but think that he might have bitten off more than he could chew this time.

But he vowed to himself not to forget Duncan's disrespect. *I need your help now, you prick. But when I get out of here, I'm going to kick your motherfucking ass,* kept playing in Santino's head during their entire meeting that day.

During their initial meeting, Duncan spent very little time discussing the murdered fourteen-year-old girl.

"You'll be seeing a lot of me. So if you need anything, let me know. Don't ask anyone for anything. Do you understand?"

Santino was finally listening. "Got it, you're the boss as long as I'm in here," Santino responded, emphasizing the latter part of the sentence.

Duncan could only stomach an hour of Santino's bullshit. By the end of the meeting Duncan thought that he should just go ask Mr. Bartelli to shoot him now and get it over with. With Santino as a client, this case appeared to be almost unwinnable, no matter what the evidence might prove.

CHAPTER 17

NOT BEING THE type of person who wasted time, Duncan had made an appointment to meet with Mr. Bartelli before even leaving his office to meet with Santino. Apparently, Mr. Bartelli didn't like to waste time either. He was sitting in Duncan's office, in Duncan's chair, when Duncan returned.

"Why isn't my son out of jail?" Mr. Bartelli asked before Duncan even got both feet into the office.

Duncan had already put Santino in his place earlier that morning, and he was not in the mood to take any shit from Santino's father. "You are in my chair!" Duncan said calmly, ignoring Mr. Bartelli's question altogether. He immediately regretted the brash power grab.

Vincenzo sprang up out of the chair. "Your chair? Do you know who pays for this fucking chair? Me! And I will sit in whatever fucking chair I please."

Before Duncan could respond, Mr. Bartelli leaned his rather large upper torso across his desk. Duncan was now standing directly in front of his desk. The two men were so close that Duncan could feel Mr. Bartelli's hot breath in his face. "Get Santino out on bail, immediately!" The look on his face left little doubt that Mr. Bartelli was not making a request. It was a demand.

Duncan's mind was racing, desperately searching for the right response.

With Mr. Bartelli as his father, combined with the accusations of killing a minor, Duncan knew that the prosecution was going to do everything in its power to convince the judge to deny Santino bail.

Mr. Bartelli had more than just a little knowledge of—and experience in—the criminal courts. It should have come as no surprise that it was going to be difficult to convince the court to set bail in his son's murder case.

Making promises is an anathema for attorneys, and in particular criminal attorneys. However, Mr. Bartelli's penetrating stare moved Duncan to attempt to placate him. "If I can't get your son out on bail, then no one can."

"Who the fuck to do you think you're speaking to? I don't care what other people can do. I only care about what *you* can do, and what I want you to do is get bail set for my son. Are we completely clear on this matter?"

Duncan was not about to let anyone, not even the Great and Powerful Vincenzo Bartelli, berate him in his own office. In an effort to regain the initiative, Duncan calmly folded his arms across his chest and looked directly into Mr. Bartelli's eyes. "Sir, I understand exactly what you want me to do. I assure you that I will do everything possible. But you need to understand *me* now. Only a fool would promise to get bail for your son. I'm no fool, so you'll get no such promise from me. If you're looking for that promise, you're in the wrong office."

He hadn't originally intended to be quite so firm. The words just seemed to form themselves.

Mr. Bartelli's face turned crimson. "You must know that I'm not accustomed to being spoken to in that tone. So you damn well better be as good as Helms says you are, or you and I are going to revisit this conversation."

His words were confrontational and threatening, but he looked impressed, almost proud. The look that followed his words told Duncan that in some strange way Mr. Bartelli was capitulating. Maybe in the only way a man like that could.

Mr. Bartelli slipped out from behind Duncan's desk and moved to the window, where he stared out over the Los Angeles skyline.

As if the meeting had just begun, Mr. Bartelli asked. "So what's the plan?"

"We either push for an immediate bail hearing, or we request more time to prepare. I recommend the latter."

"How much time?"

"Two days, maybe three."

"I leave it in your hands. Get it done and don't fuck it up."

The only good news Mr. Bartelli brought to the office that day (and, as the facts of the case began to come into focus, perhaps the only good news he might expect to receive) was that Duncan would have at his disposal an inexhaustible budget for the defense of Santino.

Duncan looked down at his watch. "Mr. Bartelli, I've scheduled a partnership meeting in fifteen minutes to discuss your son's case. If you'll please excuse me, I need to make a few notes before the meeting."

"Good, I cleared my calendar for the day. I'll sit in."

After a brief pause, Duncan replied, "No! I'm afraid that will not be possible."

"I'm paying the bills, and if I want to be at the meeting then I will be at the meeting, you impertinent little prick. You get my point?"

"Yes, sir, I do. And if you want me to continue to represent your son, you will continue paying those bills. But you cannot attend this meeting. Do you get *my* point?"

The veins in Mr. Bartelli's neck began to throb visibly.

"Look, Mr. Bartelli, I represent your son, not you. There are at least a hundred good reasons why you can't be present. But I don't have the time to explain or debate the issue. You're just going to have to trust me."

Mr. Bartelli was still fuming. "Perhaps I need to take this up with Mr. Helms."

Duncan looked thoughtfully at Mr. Bartelli. *If I don't make it clear who's in control right now, it will be clear who's in control!*

"Perhaps, but I can assure you that only one of us will be at the meeting. Now, please excuse me, I need to prepare for the meeting. Or do I?"

Mr. Bartelli's face looked like a cherry bomb. Just before it exploded, Mr. Bartelli spun on his heels and marched toward the door.

"One more thing, Mr. Bartelli. You hired me to be a 'prick,' so don't think that your little scene from *The Godfather* intimidated me."

Mr. Bartelli heard Duncan but did not acknowledge the comment on his way out the door.

Duncan wiped the sweat from his brow and headed to his meeting.

CHAPTER 18

WHEN DUNCAN ENTERED the conference room, Sandler Helms, Bernard Bentworth, Samuel Kenderman, and seven other partners were already seated. The meeting started without the normal formalities.

"What kind of support staff are you going to need?" asked Helms.

Duncan glanced down at his note pad. "I'll need Stanley, Cohen, Hurey, Dixon, and Thaler."

"You need five of our best junior partners to assist you in this one case? You know they already have heavy case loads?" Bentworth asked rhetorically and in sarcastic disbelief.

"Have you talked to them to check their schedules?" Kenderman chimed in.

"I'm sorry, I did not make myself clear. I'll need them full time. All six of us will have to transfer our case loads," Duncan replied very matter-of-factly. Without skipping a beat he continued, "I will also need six law clerks and at least a dozen secretaries. I've made a list of names."

Duncan passed out copies of the list to everyone in the room and looked down at the end of the table at Samantha, the office manager. "I need you to clear their desks. Get with human resources to arrange for replacements. As of today, they work for me. Can you handle that?"

Samantha had been staring down at the list of names, and was the first to break the uneasy silence that had filled the room, "You have Marla Jones on the list. She is Mr. Bentworth's secretary?" her tone was more of a question than an observation.

"I need this taken care of this afternoon by three o'clock. You're excused, get started." Mr. Bentworth looked to Helms for support, but none was forthcoming.

"What should I tell them? How long will this reassignment last?" Samantha asked.

"I'll talk to each of them later. Just make sure that it's done by three."

Bentworth and Kenderman were still trying to lift their jaws off the table. They looked over at Helms for assistance. "This will only be temporary," Helms said gesturing with his hands for the men to stay calm. The smile that Helms was trying to hide did not escape Duncan's attention.

If Bentworth hadn't hated Duncan before, he did now. The idea that a young, upstart attorney would be given the power to dictate how such an important case would be handled was unfathomable to Bentworth. Reassigning his secretary was the last straw.

"Sandler?" Bentworth rarely referred to Helms by his first name. "This is outrageous!" he yelled almost at the top of his lungs. "Are we really putting the fate of this firm in the hands of this—of this...of this child?"

"Bernard, have a seat. We will discuss this matter, just the two of us, after the meeting," Helms responded, firmly but respectfully.

Bentworth's face was crimson red. "I think I will not 'have a seat.' I have heard just about enough of this nonsense," were his last words before storming out of Helms's office.

Ignoring the palpable tension in the room, Duncan continued as if nothing had happened. "Let's discuss the case, then, for a moment. I met with both Santino and his father today. Based on those interviews and the police report, it's my initial impression that we will be lucky to keep this kid out of the 'chair.'"

Duncan looked around the table at the pained look on the partners' faces. "Why so glum, men? Mr. Bartelli wrote a retainer check in the amount of five million dollars on his way out the door. I told him it should cover the fees through the bail hearing next week."

It's amazing how far a few million dollars will go to cheer up a roomful of attorneys, Duncan thought, noticing the change in mood at the table.

"The bad news is that Mr. Bartelli insists that we get his son released on bail. So we're going to have to earn that money."

"What are the chances of getting bail?" Helms inquired.

"Normally, I would say pretty slim. But the DA's office has assigned Nathan Webb to prosecute the case."

Webb was the attorney at the DA's office with far and away the best trial record, a fact well known to everyone in the room.

"Webb is the best they have, and you see that as a good thing?" Kenderman said, shaking his head.

"With all due respect, it's been a while since you have defended a case." There was no way of saying that respectfully, so Duncan did not even try. "Webb may have the most convictions, but he is far from their best attorney. Hell, Sheila Cross is twice the attorney Webb is. I might be a little more concerned if Sheila were handling the case. Webb only takes sure things. There is no way he accepted this case voluntarily. He must have been ordered to take it by the district attorney himself. I assure you that Webb is shitting his pants right now. He's going to have to do battle against a firm that is actually prepared to litigate. Besides, he is a pontificating jerk. We will use his self-aggrandizing personality against him."

"What can we do to help?" asked one of the junior partners, hoping to sound supportive in front of his bosses. Duncan knew ass-kissing when he heard it. Hell, he was a master at it. Without looking up, he replied, "Keep out of our way!"

"Sorry, gentlemen, but I have work to do." Without as much as an excuse me, Duncan headed for the door.

Helms followed Duncan into the hallway. "I spoke with Mr. Bartelli this morning."

"Let me—" Before Duncan could explain, Mr. Helms cut him off. "You must have made a very good impression. He is a man of few words, but I could tell that he was impressed. Good job. And don't worry about Mr. Bentworth. I will talk to him."

"I wasn't worried," Duncan replied smugly.

At Duncan's direction, Stella had already turned Duncan's office into a war room. "Stella, get Stanley, Cohen, Hurey, Dixon, and Thaler in here right away. Oh, and ask Bender to get in here, too."

Bender was not originally on his list. He was not the best or brightest junior partner with the firm, but he thought he was, and that was exactly what Duncan needed.

"Some of them may be at lunch, sir."

"I said right away! Find them and get them in here now."

Stella was used to seeing the transformation that took place when Duncan went from easy-going guy to defense mode, so she took no offense at his curtness.

"Yes, sir."

All six attorneys were in his office within ten minutes. Only Thaler and Stanley had any idea what was going on. Therefore, there was a strange vibe in the room. Until that moment, each of the six attorneys held approximately the same level of seniority with the firm that Duncan had.

"As you are probably aware, Vincenzo Bartelli's son is being prosecuted for murder. Mr. Bartelli is this firm's largest client. He has chosen me to lead the defense. Let me say that again. Mr. Bartelli has chosen *me* to defend his son. You now work for me, not the firm, until this case is over."

The six attorneys looked around the room at each other without saying a word. Duncan could see a hundred questions forming and floating around in their eyes.

Bender stood up and said, "Who died and made you God? I must have a dozen—"

Duncan cut him off in midsentence. "You're fired. Get out of my office." It played out exactly as he thought it would. He knew that Bender would say something stupid and give him the vehicle to make his point. Point made.

"You can't fire me." Bender looked around the room, but no one would make eye contact.

Duncan picked up the phone and called accounting. "Please cut a check for Steven Bender, this will be his last day with the firm." Before the accounting clerk could question his authority to fire Bender, Duncan slammed down the receiver. Bender's eyes again scanned the room for support. Finding none, he marched to the door and left the room without another word. Later that day, a security guard escorted Bender from the building. Duncan would make sure that the spectacle was observed by everyone on his team.

"So, as I was saying, you were not assigned to this case. I chose each of you based on your individual strengths. There is only one way off this team: prove me wrong about you. Do that, fuck up just once, and you're gone."

"So that we are clear, this is not a democracy. I am in charge—completely in charge. Any questions?"

Duncan was being rhetorical and only let a second pass before continuing with his speech. "This is our war room. Nothing leaves this room. You may not discuss this case with anyone who is not on this team. Is that clear?" Again, he gave no time for objections or responses.

"Let's get started. Stella has given each of you a copy of the charges against Santino. As you will see, the allegations are pretty macabre. To avoid having the charges read in open court I waived Santino's right to an arraignment hearing. So bail is the first issue we need to address. We must win at the bail hearing. No, not must, we will get bail granted in this case."

"When are we going to file a motion for bail?" Cohen asked.

"Immediately. I want to keep the pressure on the prosecution in every aspect of this defense. I want us on the offense during this entire trial. No delays. I want Webb to rue the day he took this case."

Hurey had only read through about half of the charges alleged against Santino, when he mumbled just loud enough for those in the room to hear, "Jesus! Getting bail set in this case is not going to be easy." He had not meant to say that out loud.

"Okay, let's address Mr. Hurey's concern. Don't let the horrific nature of the charges distract you. That is exactly what the prosecution wants you to think. The courts have interpreted the Eighth Amendment to the Constitution to allow for bail provided that the defendant is not a flight risk and does not pose a threat to the community by his release. We need to focus on those too questions. We have all seen judges set astronomically high bail amounts in order to keep a defendant in jail. Remember, we don't care how high the bail is; we only care that bail is granted, at any number. I am sure that Mr. Bartelli will pay whatever is required to get his son out of jail."

"Yes, it's certainly good to have a rich daddy," Hurey said trying to fight back his smile.

"Look, we all know the main factors that make it tough, if not impossible, to get bail: outstanding warrants, arrests while out on bail for another matter, failure to appear in the past, arrests while in possession of a weapon, and last but not least, being arrested for a violent crime." In this case, none of them apply except the violent crime allegations. So, this should be easy, right? I mean, except if you take into consideration that our client is the son of Vincenzo Bartelli."

Duncan's comment was acknowledged with nervous smiles.

"I'm going to divide us into groups. Each of you will be responsible for a specific aspect of the defense. You will be assigned a support staff. If you need more help, ask. If you need more bodies, get them. If you can't get them, ask me, and I will get them. Under no circumstances will it be acceptable for you to blame your failure to complete a task on understaffing. Is that completely understood?"

All five attorneys responded in unison, "Yes, sir" as if they had always referred to Duncan as their boss.

"Good."

"Dixon, I want you to review the transcripts of every bail hearing presided over by Judge Polan in our case files in the past ten years. I want you to call other firms, see what they might have to help. Get your hands on as many of their documents as you can. Research every published case and appeal involving Polan's rulings on bail. I want a report on my desk by the end of business tomorrow. Recruit as many law clerks as you need. See Paul if you need secretarial support."

"Just cases where he granted bail?" Dixon asked making notes on a yellow legal pad.

"When I said every, I meant every. A good attorney should be able to learn as much from why Polan denied bail, as he can from why Polan granted it. You are a good attorney. Aren't you?"

"I am a great attorney. I apologize, my mistake. It won't happen again. I'll get right on it."

"You must be, because that was the only answer that was going to keep me from kicking your ass out of this office."

"Thaler, I want to know everything there is to know about Santino and Vincenzo Bartelli. Criminal records, assets, clubs they attend, charitable donations, medical records, anything, everything."

Duncan could see that Thaler was resisting the temptation to ask a question. He was probably afraid of catching the same hell Dixon had just caught.

"Yes, you can talk to Mr. Bartelli directly. I have already let him know that you will be calling. And don't even ask me why I want to know about Vincenzo. I would rather live under the delusion that I was right about you."

Duncan looked directly at Thaler. "Yes, I can read minds." Based on the look on his face, that must have been exactly what Thaler was thinking.

If Duncan was trying to let everyone in the room know he could be a hard-ass, he was doing a good job at communicating that point.

"Hurey, if we are going to get bail we are going to need strong legal arguments. Start putting together the outline of a brief. Here is a copy of the police report. This is an ugly murder. So don't try to make this crime appear less gruesome than it is. Stick to the law."

"Yes, sir."

"You may think this is an easy job. Don't fool yourself. I don't want one of those boilerplate briefs that this firm pumps out. Look for new law, revisit old law; be creative."

"Yes, sir."

"Stanley, organize the private detective operations and surveil-lance. I want to know everything about Webb from the DA's office, Judge Polan, the victim, her family, witnesses, everyone involved in any way with this case."

Duncan noticed that Stanley had stopped writing when he mentioned Judge Polan's name. "Some of this surveillance may not be ethical. Should I check the law on that issue?" Stanley questioned reluctantly.

"Don't be a fucking Girl Scout. Information is king! I want information on everyone, particularly Judge Polan. Is that clear?"

"Yes, sir."

"Hire two—no, three—separate private detective agencies for each individual being investigated. I want cross-references and verifications. If necessary, get some out-of-state firms involved. But I want that information now. We have deep pockets. You have the authority to pay whatever it takes to get them on the job now, this minute."

"Cohen, you're the heart of this operation. Dixon, Thaler, Stanley, Hurey, I want your reports to go through Cohen.

"Cohen, I want you to review and filter their research. You will be responsible for putting all the pieces together. At first there won't be much for you to do, so be a floater. If you see someone needs help, pitch in."

"I'm on the team."

"Okay, here is a list of the names of law clerks and secretaries. If your initials are beside their name, they are on your team. They are dedicated to this project and at your disposal twenty-four-seven, which means that all of you are also on this case twenty-four–seven. No one has a personal life until the bail hearing is won. I had Stella book the entire twelfth floor of the Bonaventure Hotel. That's forty rooms. Until the bail hearing is over everyone on this team stays downtown. I don't want to waste time, so each of you is authorized to approve payment of any expense incurred by your team. This will be a major inconvenience to some of the secretaries and clerks, so I want you to be generous; if they have any expense related to staying downtown, I don't care what it is, just approve payment. Additionally, each member of your staff will receive a thousand-dollar bonus for this week. I want to be in court in three days, so get to it."

"Before we get down to business, I have one question," Cohen said almost nonchalantly as he rolled up the cuffs on his shirt. "What's with this last name thing? We have worked together for a while now, and we are still on a last name basis?" Cohen was smiling as he asked, but there was a twinge of sincerity in his voice.

Ignoring Cohen's question, Duncan responded, "Let's get to work, gentlemen, the clock is ticking."

Duncan and his crew worked around the clock right up until two hours before the bail hearing.

Santino's bail hearing was big news. The press descended on the courthouse in force. They were looking for a show, and Duncan was not one to disappoint.

Five stretch limousines and a large enclosed truck carrying seventy-two boxes of case files pulled up in front of the courthouse just twenty minutes before the scheduled hearing.

The caravan had actually been parked several blocks from the courthouse for the better part of an hour, but Duncan chose to wait until the last minute for effect.

Three of the limos carried the defense team consisting of six lawyers, five paralegals, and Stella.

The other two limos carried Mr. Bartelli and his entourage of bodyguards.

No one expected Mr. Bartelli to appear, thinking that his presence might weaken his son's chances of getting bail set, but Duncan had a plan, and Mr. Bartelli was the bait.

Two by two, the attorney and their staff made their way up the courthouse steps. The press was getting the spectacle they came for—in spades.

If Webb wasn't intimidated before, he surely is now, Duncan thought as he and his minions marched into the courtroom.

Webb and one assistant were already seated at the prosecution's table. Due to the high-profile nature of the case, this was the only matter on the judge's calendar that morning. The judge hadn't yet taken the bench.

"Good morning, Mr. Webb. It's a fine day for a bail hearing, wouldn't you agree?" Duncan said as he approached the prosecution's table.

Duncan's smug tone was as calculated as the show he had just put on for Webb and the press.

"Good morning, counselor," Webb replied, trying to sound calm and collected.

Duncan stopped suddenly, and his entourages stopped simultaneously, as if the event were choreographed. "The name is Duncan Gabrelli. You'll remember it tonight when you wake up in a cold sweat wondering how you lost this hearing," Duncan said in a faint, condescending tone meant only for Webb's ears.

A buzzer sounded, and the bailiff called out, "All rise and face the flag. This court is now in session, the Honorable Alvin J. Polan presiding.

Judge Polan took the bench at precisely 10:00 a.m. Polan hadn't expected such a full courtroom, and the sound of nearly twenty people rising to their feet caught Judge Polan off guard, causing him to flinch.

"Good morning, counsel."

"Good morning, Your Honor," rose up in loud chorus from the defense side, nearly drowning out the prosecution's meek reply.

"Bailiff, call the first case."

"In the matter of the State of California versus Santino Bartelli, case number LA837654, will counsel come forward and be heard."

The pressure of the moment was already taking its toll on Webb, and his voice cracked as he said, "Your honor, prosecution requests that no bail be set in this matter,"

Judge Polan looked over at the size of the defense and smiled. "It would appear that the defense has not changed its mind and is requesting that bail be set?"

"Yes, Your Honor."

"Okay, Mr. Webb, present your argument."

"As Your Honor is aware, this is a particularly heinous crime. The charges in this case include rape, sodomy, murder, and arson of the victim's body to destroy evidence."

"Yes, I read the briefs in this case. In fact, in many aspects, the papers filed by the defense in this case are more graphic than those of the prosecution. I am fully aware of what can only be called a gruesome crime. Let's get to the issue at hand. Why should this court deny bail in this case?"

Duncan had already scored a small victory, and the prosecution never knew what hit them. By laying out the details of the alleged crime in such detail, the judge was not inclined to spend a lot of time discussing the crime itself.

The crime was so violent that defusing the impact by letting several days pass between the hearing and the day the judge read the pleading could only help the defense.

A better attorney would have forced the issue to keep the crime in the forefront of the judge's mind, but this was Webb.

The prosecution led off with a meticulously detailed report of Vincenzo Bartelli's numerous brushes with the criminal court system.

"Very well, Your Honor, it is important to understand just who the defendant is in this case. He is the son of Vincenzo Bartelli."

Webb paused as if he had just dropped a bombshell in the court. Or maybe he was waiting for Duncan to object.

Webb looked a bit puzzled, glancing over at Duncan before continuing, "Your Honor, Vincenzo Bartelli is reputed to be the head of the largest organized crime family in the United States, maybe the world."

Webb paused again. This time it was clear to everyone in the courtroom that he was expecting Duncan to vigorously object to the use of Santino's father's record at his son's bail hearing. Even the judge threw a confused glance in Duncan's direction.

Duncan remained seated at the defense table pretending to show little interest in what the prosecutor was saying.

The prosecution hadn't expected to get away with tarring Santino with his father's brush. When no objections were forthcoming, Webb wallowed in his perceived advantage.

Webb raved on with accusation after accusation against the character of Vincenzo Bartelli, periodically pointing his finger at Vincenzo, who sat in the audience looking unmoved by the attacks.

Webb was going exactly in the direction Duncan thought he would go. For two days prior to the bail hearing, Mr. Bartelli had been coached on how to remain calm in the face of the anticipated attacks on his character. Duncan set up mock hearings to test Mr. Bartelli's reaction. As the prosecution piled accusation upon accusation, Mr. Bartelli, looked on, expressionless, just as he had been instructed.

Webb introduced evidence of Mr. Bartelli's wealth and ability to help his son leave the jurisdiction if bail was granted.

Duncan was allowing such a wide berth that Webb found himself working off his scripted argument. Thinking on his feet was not Webb's long suit, and it was beginning to show in his often rambling and repetitive diatribe.

Duncan's investigator had discovered that Judge Polan had a slight hearing problem. Therefore, during Webb's entire presentation, you could hear the entire defense team, penciling on yellow legal pads, occasionally pulling files from the stacks of boxes that lined the wall behind the defense table. The noise was not loud, but it provided just enough background noise to make it hard for Judge Polan to hear everything Webb was saying.

The plan was working. Duncan had given Webb enough rope to hang himself, and Webb did just that. He had spent far too much time discussing Vincenzo and far too little time discussing the evidence that supported denying bail.

The prosecution rested, and it was Duncan's turn.

His associates each ripped pages off their note pads and handed them to Duncan. He studied them intently, periodically staring over at Webb. The pages contained pictures they had drawn of the back of Webb's head, rainbows, and kitty cats. The pages were supposed to be blank, but Duncan saw the humor and fought back a smile.

It was all part of Duncan's overall plan to intimidate and confuse the prosecution. He could tell from the look on Webb's face that it was working.

Laying the pages face down on the table, Duncan stood up and walked slowly to the rostrum. He took only a moment to review his own notes, and then he began to make his case.

"I was trying to find the crux of the prosecution's argument, but I must admit that I am at a loss to find it. Perhaps it would be helpful if we addressed the issues before the court today. Simply stated, we respectfully argue that Santino Bartelli is neither a flight risk, nor would he be a threat to society if he were granted bail.

"Why does the prosecution claim he is a flight risk? We endured almost an hour of the prosecution's unsupported allegations. They believe that Santino's father is the head of a crime family. It may come as some surprise to the prosecution, but Vincenzo Bartelli does not stand accused of any crime before this court.

"However, as long as the prosecution is going to make Vincenzo's record an issue in this bail hearing, the court should consider two very salient points that the prosecution omitted. First, Vincenzo Bartelli has never been found guilty of any crime. *Ever.* Let me repeat that: *ever.* Second, Vincenzo Bartelli has never attempted to flee prosecution in any of the dozens of criminal matters that the prosecution has so eloquently detailed for the court today."

"Counsel, let me interrupt you for a moment. I am inclined to agree that Vincenzo Bartelli's alleged criminal activities are not particularly relevant, albeit disturbing if true. But I was surprised to find no evidence of Santino's prior criminal history. What can you tell me about your client?" The judge was clearly hoping to help the prosecution with the question.

"I was just about to get to that, Your Honor. My client has no prior record. He has never been prosecuted for any crime."

Duncan had discovered that Santino had lied during his initial interview. He had never spent any time in the "gray-wall hotel," as he put it. Maybe a few hours in a local jail, but no real time.

Duncan was, however, playing fast and loose with the truth. Santino had been arrested on many occasions, but Vincenzo's connections with certain elements of the police force and influence with public officials had kept his son's official record clean. *It's only a white lie*, Duncan thought.

"Mr. Webb would have this court believe that because the defendant's father is a wealthy man, that the defendant is a greater flight risk. As the court can see from the size and presence of the defense team assembled here today, Mr. Vincenzo Bartelli is committed to use his wealth to provide the best defense possible against these false charges brought against his son, not to aid him in fleeing this jurisdiction. Both the defendant and his father are longtime residents and have considerable family and business ties to this community."

Duncan knew that the prosecution's ineptness was not in and of itself going to win the day. He needed to attack the prosecution's case against Santino if he had any chance of getting bail set. If the court believed that Santino was a threat to the community, bail would not be granted.

"Your Honor, that leaves us with the real question, 'Is Santino a threat to the community?' I am sure that somewhere in the prosecution's rambling statement, they attempted to address this issue. But, for the life of me, I can't tell you what their argument was.

"Generally, I would be inclined to rest, but I believe that there is substantial evidence that Santino is an asset to the community rather than a threat. Santino has made numerous and substantial donations to organizations from the Girl Scouts to AARP. Santino is the chairman of seven philanthropic trusts that contribute to schools, hospitals, and churches across the county."

Of course, these donations were made by Vincenzo in Santino's name, but Duncan didn't share that bit of information.

In addition to Santino's financial contributions, Duncan was also able to produce documents showing that he spent time helping out in soup kitchens and halfway houses. Duncan knew that the documents were forged, but he was confident that Mr. Bartelli made sure there was no way the prosecution could ever prove that fact.

By the time he had finished with his argument, one might have thought that Santino was up for sainthood.

Duncan also made a clear and convincing case that Santino was not a threat to jump bail. It helped his argument that despite Santino's many run-ins with the law, Mr. Bartelli had used his connections at almost every level of law enforcement to keep his son's criminal record clean.

The prosecution had played right into Duncan's hands. By spending so little time setting forth evidence against Santino, Duncan was able to take considerable liberties with the facts.

While the prosecution attempted to overcome its error in rebuttal, it was too late.

In truth, everyone—the judge and prosecution included—knew that Santino was not going to flee prosecution. It was the prosecution's failure to present a strong and coherent argument evidencing that Santino was a threat to the community that tipped the balance in his favor.

His tactically perfect attack on the prosecutor's argument had laid waste to the prosecution's arguments to deny bail.

"Mr. Gabrelli, do you have anything further to add?"

"No, Your Honor."

"Mr. Webb?"

"No, Your Honor."

While the judge was convinced to grant bail, he did not, however, want the media to tear him apart for being soft on such a notorious figure. "I have heard the evidence presented, and it is the ruling of this court that bail should be granted in this case. However, considering the serious nature of the charges and the considerable funds at the defendant's disposal, I am inclined to set the highest bail that this court has ever set. I am granting bail in the amount of ten million dollars. Further, should the defendant post bail, he will be required to surrender his passport and will be confined to his residence, with limited travel allowance until trial. This court now stands adjourned."

If Judge Polan was under the delusion that setting such a high bail was going to keep Santino in jail, it was quickly dispelled. Three hours after the court set the amount, Santino was sitting smugly on his father's sofa, no doubt feeling that he beat the system again.

Duncan couldn't help but think about the mistakes the prosecution had made during the bail hearing. Had the prosecution done its job, Santino might be sitting in jail waiting for trial.

Among lawyers there is a saying, "Tough cases make bad law." In fact, Duncan had seen judges ignore the letter of the law, unable to separate their emotions from their duty. The fact that the judge granted bail told Duncan that he had a judge who was prepared to do his job, even in a tough case—a fact that would be of help in Santino's case. Of course, Duncan and his team already knew that about Judge Polan. They had done their homework, and it was already paying dividends.

After the bail hearing, Santino and members of Duncan's team were dancing around like they had just won an acquittal. Duncan and Mr. Bartelli, on the other hand, knew that the battle had just been joined. The district attorney's office might be licking its wounds now, but it was going to pull out all the stops to get a conviction in this case.

There will be no plea bargain in this case. It's going to be win or lose, Duncan thought.

Later that day, back in the war room, Duncan was addressing the troops.

"Excellent job! But that was a battle—not the war. I can assure you that the DA's office has pictures of each of you hanging on its wall tonight. We are public enemy number one. Make no mistake about it; they'll be ready for us next time. We're going to have to work harder and be smarter than the DA."

"We're already putting in eighteen-hour days," Cohen said what was on everyone's minds.

"I hear you. I've recruited more help. We are adding ten junior attorneys to the defense team. You will each be assigned two for your group."

"It's Thursday, right?" Duncan was so immersed in the case that he had lost track of what day it was.

"Yes, sir," Cohen replied.

"I want all of you to go home and don't come back until Monday."

A look of surprise hung on the faces of the team.

"No, this is not me being nice. Spend this weekend saying good-bye to your girlfriends, wives, and kids. Get laid, go to the zoo, do whatever people like you do. Because starting Monday we go back to having no other lives until we win an acquittal. Now get out of here before I realize that this is a mistake."

"People like you?" Each of them was thinking *fuck you* but no one said a word. They were just happy to get away from Duncan for a few days.

His team was taking a long weekend off, but not Duncan. He spent the rest of Thursday afternoon outlining his battle plan. How to best position his troops, looking for weaknesses in the prosecution's case, and whom to delegate various tasks to.

When Duncan arrived in his office at six thirty Friday morning, Cohen was sitting at the small conference table.

"I thought I gave you the day off, Harvey." That was the first time he had addressed Cohen by his first name, and it took Harvey a moment to realize Duncan was talking to him.

"Do you know many Jews?" Cohen asked.

"A few."

"Well, in a Jewish household, there is a division of labor. The husbands work, and the wives spend. Husbands don't go shopping with their wives, and wives don't go to work with their husbands. It's in the Talmud, so what's a Jew to do?"

Duncan smiled. "She can't go shopping if you're making love to her. I thought saving money appealed to you guys."

"You really need more Jewish friends. Do you know how to get a Jewish girl to stop having sex?"

Duncan shrugged. "No, how?"

"Marry her."

Duncan laughed out loud. "Okay, I still think that you're being a brownnoser, but I could use your help."

CHAPTER 19

THE FACTS OF Santino's case were gruesome. In addition to the charge of murder, the criminal complaint alleged sexual assault, sodomy, use of the date rape drug "roofies," arson, and torture.

The complaint graphically detailed the allegations that Santino had offered a fourteen-year-old girl named Jessica Lopez a ride home from a party. At least a dozen witnesses saw Santino and Jessica get into his Lamborghini and leave the party. He drove her to a motel, where two motel employees would testify that they saw him register for a room and enter the room with Jessica.

The complaint alleged that Santino had put roofies in Jessica's drink shortly before the two left the party. With Jessica under the influence of the drug, he allegedly checked into the motel with the intent of raping her. With his young victim nearly catatonic, he allegedly beat, raped, and sodomized her. High on cocaine, Quaaludes, amphetamines, and alcohol, he allegedly killed her. He was also accused of attempting to cover up the crime by setting the motel room ablaze. The fire had made it difficult to establish with absolute certainty how the murder was committed, but the prosecution surmised from the charred remains that she'd been bludgeoned in the head repeatedly with a blunt instrument.

When the police caught up with Santino the next morning, he was passed out in his Lamborghini in the driveway of his Malibu home approximately forty-five miles from the scene of Jessica's murder.

Upon entering the Malibu property, the police searched Santino and his automobile. His clothes were drenched in blood, booze, and sweat. The blood was later found to be a perfect match with the victim's blood. Scientific analysis of his clothes and interior of the vehicle later revealed that various other bodily fluids were present, including Jessica's oral and vaginal fluids.

As Duncan read the allegations in the complaint, he began to shake his head. One thought kept running through his mind. *This case is a defense attorney's fucking nightmare.*

CHAPTER 20

DUNCAN REMEMBERED WHAT Helms had told him in their initial meeting. Mr. Bartelli believed that his son was being set up by the government. While Duncan understood that a man like Mr. Bartelli had the right to be a little paranoid (after all, he was the head of the largest criminal organization in the world), he was clearly in denial about the crime that his son committed.

Even so, Duncan was sure that the competition between the various state and federal agencies to take credit for the arrest of Vincenzo Bartelli's son would lend itself to mistakes being made.

Duncan and his team spent weeks poring over police reports and witness statements until they found the first big break in the case. The local police, in their rush to prevent others from claiming credit, had neglected to get a warrant before entering Santino's Malibu property.

At precisely the same time the local police were storming the Malibu compound, the chief of police, in an effort to secure his fifteen minutes of fame, held a press conference.

"Santino Bartelli, the son of Vincenzo Bartelli, is being sought for questioning in the murder of a fourteen-year-old girl late last night."

"Due to the victim's age, her name is currently being withheld. I will take a few questions."

The press had gotten wind that Vincenzo Bartelli's son had been implicated in a murder. Stories stretching from Santino having been murdered to Santino being the murderer were grinding their way through the rumor mill.

"Is Santino a suspect in the murder?" one reporter called.

"Yes, from the evidence I've seen, I'm convinced that he committed this horrible crime. He is our prime suspect at this time, and an APB has been sent out for his arrest."

The members of the press were taken aback by the unexpected candor of the chief.

"Did I hear you say that a warrant had been issued for Santino's arrest?"

"Yes, next question," the chief replied emphatically.

"In light of his father's reputed mob connections, is there any evidence to indicate that the crime was mob connected?" another screamed.

"My office is fully aware of Santino's mob connections. Our investigation is focusing on the possible connection. Yes, there is evidence, but I am not at liberty to discuss the specific evidence at this time."

"Has Santino fled the country?"

"We have already notified the appropriate federal agencies; it is unlikely that he has left the country."

The chief's comments had worked the press into a frenzy. Reporters were screaming out questions so loudly and so quickly that they formed an unintelligible garbled noise.

"Chief?"

"Chief?" they cried.

"I'm sorry. That's all the questions for now. I will update you as information becomes available."

What had inspired the chief to hold the press conference was a mystery. Even more mysterious was the fact that he chose to comment on a case that he clearly knew nothing about.

There had been no APB put out on Santino, no federal agencies had been contacted, no warrants had been issued, and no one in his office, or anywhere else, believed that the murder was related to organized crime.

The chief would end up getting more time in the spotlight than he had bargained for. The bad press and public outrage that followed the trial eventually forced the chief into early retirement. He was only the first in a long line of people who would wish that they'd stayed faraway from the firestorm of publicity that raged around the murder case.

When the police arrived at his Malibu home, Santino was asleep in his Lamborghini, still recovering from his excesses of the night before. The Lamborghini was parked in his driveway inside a gated compound.

Officers Stan McLaughlin and Bert Kacy were the first to arrive on the scene. They called immediately for backup and waited outside the compound until three squad cars arrived, carrying the watch commander, Randall Thompson, and five other officers.

Commander Thompson called for Santino to open the gate. But Santino was fast asleep.

Thompson looked over his shoulder and noticed that the press had picked up the story on their police scanners and was out in force.

The commander assigned three of his men to crowd control, which was a euphemism for press control.

"How far back do you want them, Commander?" one officer asked.

"Let them get a good look. Just keep them off the property. This is my chance at stardom. Which is my good side?" the commander jested as he walked away.

Leaning in so that only his men could hear, the commander said, "You're on TV; let's put on a good show."

Looking directly into the cameras, he called out, "Officers McLaughlin and Kacy, get a pry bar and open that gate."

None of the officers questioned the order to break open the gate without first obtaining a warrant.

The five officers entered the Malibu compound with guns drawn.

Officer Kacy opened the car door. The two others dragged the unconscious Santino out, throwing him face down onto the cement driveway.

Hitting the ground did not wake up Santino, but the knee of the 230-pound officer to his spine got Santino's attention.

"What the fuck, man."

"Don't move," Commander Thompson called out loud enough for his adoring press to hear.

"I'm not moving, just get off me. What are you fucking doing? Get off me."

Once the handcuffs were on, Santino was lifted to his feet and read his rights.

"You have the right to remain silent. You have the right to speak to an attorney. If you cannot afford an attorney..."

The officer looked around the multimillion dollar estate and smiled.

"...one will be provided to you at no cost. If you give up these rights, anything you say can and will be used against you in a court of law. Do you understand these rights?"

Even in his nearly comatose condition, he knew to keep his mouth shut. "I want to call my lawyer," Santino slurred just before he passed out.

Once on the Malibu estate, the police searched Santino's personal property and automobile.

Bright and early Monday morning, Duncan and his team began formulating their assault on the evidence seized at Santino's Malibu home.

The defense was gearing up to file pretrial motions that would seek exclusion of all the evidence recovered (based on violations of Santino's Fourth Amendment rights against illegal searches and seizures.)

The most renowned and well-respected constitutional scholars in the country, including professors from both Harvard and Yale, were retained to help prepare the legal arguments. If successful, even the blood and body fluid evidence found in the Lamborghini and on Santino would be excluded.

The prosecution requested three separate continuances of the hearing on Duncan's motion to exclude evidence. The court granted each of the prosecution's requested continuances, over Duncan's well-reasoned objections, in a transparent attempt to give the prosecution additional opportunities to find legal authority (any legal authority) that would give Judge Polan solid legal footing upon which he could rely for not excluding the evidence.

Judge Polan knew that the prosecution was in trouble early in the case, and he was in no hurry to make a ruling on the motion. However, the day of reckoning finally came as the attorneys for both sides filed into the courtroom before Judge Polan.

Scientific advances had made blood and fluid evidence powerful tools in obtaining convictions. The prosecution vigorously opposed the motions to exclude, filing a seventy-five-page brief and two twenty-plus-page supplemental briefs. The district attorney's office logged hundreds of exhibits with the court in support of its opposition.

At the heart of the argument was whether the police had probable cause to enter the Malibu property without a warrant.

"Okay, I've read your briefs and reviewed the exhibits filed with this court. Mr. Gabrelli, it's your motion. Proceed."

"Thank you, Your Honor. The police did not obtain a warrant before they entered my client's estate. That fact is not in dispute.

"Further, it is not disputed that the evidence identified in the motion, including the clothing, blood, and bodily fluid evidence came directly from the warrantless searches made of my client's person and property at the Malibu estate.

"Therefore, the prosecution's burden is to prove to this court that the police had probable cause to enter the estate without first obtaining a warrant.

"As Professor Bickner, senior professor at Harvard Law School and recognized world over as the leading expert in constitutional law, so eloquently states in the declaration attached to our moving papers, there are only two recognized exceptions to the warrant requirement that apply to the facts of this case.

"One, if the police are in what the cases refer to as 'hot pursuit' of an escaping felon, and two, if the police had cause to believe that serious injury might be caused if they waited to obtain a warrant. Now, the state argues that they were in 'hot pursuit' of a felon.

"I would refer this court to the incident report filed by Officers McLaughlin and Kacy, attached as defendant's exhibit T. These were the first officers who arrived at the Malibu property on the day of my client's arrest.

"According to the report, they arrived on the scene over thirty minutes before any other officers arrived. Officer Kacy writes, and I quote, 'Officer McLaughlin and I arrived at 4265 Pacific Palisades Blvd., Malibu, California at 7:13 a.m.' The report goes on to say, 'Through a locked gate, I observed a white male matching the description of the suspect, Santino Bartelli, sitting in a red Lamborghini. Suspect appeared to be asleep. I called for backup at 7:21 a.m. Backup arrived at 7:46 a.m.' Farther down in that same report, Officer Kacy wrote 'flat tire.'

"I would ask the court to look at defendant's exhibit M. This is a blowup of a frame of the video taken by WKTZ News on the day of my client's arrest. It is the driver's side rear tire of the defendant's car visible from the street and reported by Officer Kacy. The tire is not just flat, it is ripped to shreds.

"Our expert has testified that 'based on the low profile of the Lamborghini, there is no way this car could have been driven faster than ten miles per hour, if it could be driven at all.'

"Now I would direct the court's attention to defense exhibits D, E, F, G, and H. These are the incident reports filed by other officers at the scene on the day of my client's arrest. While they have some glaring inaccuracies and contradict each other, what is clear from all the reports is that the defendant was stationary in his parked car. Not one of the reports indicates that they were in pursuit of my client."

"Mr. Gabrelli," said the judge, "I'm inclined to agree that the state has not presented sufficient evidence to convince this court that the police were in hot pursuit, as that term has been interpreted by the courts. However, I would like for you to address the second issue. What about the state's contention that the police were concerned for your client's safety? The state alleges that they were concerned that your client might be in need of medical attention, and that delay may have placed his life in jeopardy."

"I would first remind the court that it is the state's burden to prove a warrant wasn't required. However, the facts of this case do not support the state's argument," Duncan said. "We need look no further than Exhibit T. Officers McLaughlin and Kacy were first on the scene. They describe the defendant as being asleep in his vehicle. Over thirty minutes passed between the time they arrived on the scene and the time backup arrived. If they were concerned for the defendant's safety or well-being, they would have jumped the fence and come to his aid. But they did not. Why? Because they were not concerned for his safety, they did not believe he was in some physical harm; they thought he was asleep."

Duncan could hear the prosecutors squirming in their chairs.

"I would ask the court take a look at Exhibits F, G, and H again, Your Honor, together with Exhibits U, V, and W. As the court can see, U, V and W are reports written by the same officers who wrote reports F, G, and H. The officers admitted in their deposition testimony that U, V, and W are in fact the original reports that they prepared on the day of my client's arrest, and that they subsequently replaced their reports with F, G, and H at a later date.

"As the court can see, there is no statement contained in any of the original reports that would indicate that the officers had any concern for the safety or well-being of my client. However, two weeks after the original reports were prepared, they were replaced with reports that include statements by each officer indicating that they discussed their concerns for my client's safety prior to entering my client's Malibu compound.

"Exhibits U, V, and W were not turned over by the prosecution. In fact, the defense would have never discovered these documents had we not received them from an anonymous source."

"Yes, I am very disturbed that the discovery rules may have been violated here. I don't know how you got your hands on these exhibits, but I am profoundly disturbed by these reports," Judge Polan interjected.

Duncan knew exactly where they came from. Mr. Bartelli had so many police officers on his payroll that even the code of silence that exists between officers could not conceal their lies. "I would remind the court that during the depositions of these same officers, they originally denied the existence of the original reports. It was only after the defense provided the officers with copies that they miraculously regained their recollection of having prepared two separate reports.

"The officers who prepared reports D and E did not change their reports, and those reports make no reference to any discussion about my client's health or well-being."

"Yes, counsel. I can't say it enough; I am very concerned about the circumstances surrounding these reports. I will no doubt be seeking an explanation of those inconsistencies in a separate investigation." Judge Polan cast a disapproving glare toward the prosecution's table. "Please continue, counsel."

"At this time I would like to present defense's exhibit L. Exhibit L is the complete videotape taken by WKTZ News on the day of my client's arrest. The tape has an audio track, which our experts have enhanced. May we turn down the lights?"

Before Commander Thompson had posted officers to crowd control, the tape was running. Thompson was not aware he was being recorded. The tape depicted Thompson speaking to several other officers.

"Should I call an ambulance?" one of the officers asked Thompson.

"What, for that drunken bastard? No, he doesn't need an ambulance, but he may by the time we're done with him."

"You know who he is?"

"I know, and I'm not impressed. Fuck him and his daddy," Thompson replied.

Duncan played and then replayed that portion of the video for effect.

Duncan slowed the tape down when the tape showed Santino being dragged out of the car and slammed face first onto the concrete driveway. With the tape playing in the background, Duncan began to speak.

"This video does not depict officers who are concerned for the health of my client. Rather, it shows a violent assault on a helpless man. Please turn up the lights."

The entire courtroom could hear Webb's butt pucker as he watched Santino's face bounce off the driveway.

"The evidence is overwhelming that the police did not enter the property to protect my client. But even if that were not true, this court would still be bound to grant defendant's motion.

"I've cited the US Supreme Court case, Wagner v. the United States. The Supreme Court held that 'if a governmental agency enters private property to protect the health or welfare of another without first obtaining a warrant, their right to trespass lasts only as long as the emergency exists. Thereafter, they must immediately vacate the private property and obtain a warrant before reentry. Further, during the existence of the emergency, the governmental agency may not take any action or initiate any search that is not directly associated with protecting the health or welfare of another.'

"The ruling in the Wagner case makes inadmissible any evidence obtained from violation of the emergency entry rule.

"The WKTZ video shows that no emergency existed in this case. More important, it proves that all the evidence recovered by the police was obtained after my client was handcuffed and any perceived emergency had been eliminated."

"Mr. Gabrelli, I have a pretty good picture of what happened here. Unless you have an objection, I would like to hear from the prosecution."

"Certainly, Your Honor. I anticipated a much longer presentation. If I may inquire, Your Honor, will I be permitted an opportunity to complete my presentation?"

"Yes, should it become necessary," Judge Polan said, strongly indicating that the prosecution had no chance of prevailing.

Webb walked to the rostrum.

"Good morning, Your Honor, Nathan Webb for the prosecution."

"Yes, counsel, I know who you represent, my concern is *how* you represent your client. Your client is this state, and as a citizen of this state, I am deeply concerned about how the case is being prosecuted."

"I understand, Your Honor. I can assure this court that my office is addressing some of the issues that the court has expressed concerns about."

"So your office is reviewing your office. Is that supposed to ease my mind?"

"With all due respect, Your Honor, I do not believe that there has been any misconduct by my office. I understand that there have been some questionable actions on the part of a small number of officers. But that should not reflect on the DA's office."

"Counsel, I don't know who's responsible, but I can assure you that there will be an investigation in this case."

"My office welcomes that review, Your Honor."

Judge Polan did not look the least bit impressed.

"May I address the motions before the court?"

"Yes, but first tell me this: Are you going to present any evidence that is not contained in the pleading filed by your office with this court?"

Webb was already off script and starting to squirm. "Well, Your Honor, there may be a few things that were not included, but primarily, I would like to address the issues discussed by defendant's counsel," Webb replied, trying to keep his composure.

"I gave your office two continuances to file supplemental briefs. Pray tell me, what is not in your pleadings?"

Webb began to fumble through his notes. "One moment, please."

A long two minutes passed before Webb addressed the court. "My apologies to the court. I misspoke. I believe my briefs contain all my arguments."

"Good, because I read your briefs. I am confident that I fully understand your arguments, so unless you have something more to add, I'm prepared to rule in this case."

"Your Honor, you allowed defense counsel to present his case. I would respectfully ask that you afford the prosecution the same opportunity," Webb said defiantly.

"Let me correct you, counsel. I allowed defense counsel to argue part of its pleadings. And I must admit that I was hoping that defense counsel would shoot himself in the foot, so that I would not have to rule as I must in this case. Unfortunately, he read these pleadings, too. So unless you have something more to add, I'm prepared to rule in this case."

"I would just like to make my objection for the record, Your Honor. I would prefer to state my case on the record before the court rules."

Polan was visibly displeased. "Okay, Mr. Webb, you want to waste this court's time, go right ahead. Make your case."

The district attorney, who had been sitting in as an observer, approached the rostrum and whispered into Webb's ear then returned to his seat.

"Your Honor, the state submits based on the record before the court."

"Before I rule, let me say that I have made many difficult decisions during my twenty-five years on the bench. I must tell you that I struggled hardest with this one. It is clear that the prosecution's case will be substantially more difficult to prove if I grant these motions.

"I am also mindful that a young girl was murdered. While I make no findings of guilt or innocence, the evidence subject to these motions is compelling and chilling. However, there is a maxim in the law, 'tough cases make bad law.' In my heart, I want to deny these motions, but as a judge I am compelled to grant them.

"The evidence is overwhelmingly in favor of granting the motions based on the current state of the law. Therefore, the ruling of this court is that the search and seizure violated the defendant's rights, under the constitutions of both California and of the United States. As a result of those violations, I am compelled to rule that all the evidence delineated in the motions to exclude may not be used by the prosecution in this case."

CHAPTER 21

THE PROSECUTION KNEW from the beginning of the case that Duncan would bring motions to exclude the evidence. However, they never thought—not even for a minute—that the court would grant them. They had provided the court with an escape route by arguing that the police had legal cause to justify entry and to search Santino and the Malibu property. Due to the heinous nature of the crime and the high-profile defendant, the prosecution was convinced that the judge would not exclude the evidence.

Granting the motions to exclude evidence broke the back of the state's case.

It quickly became clear what the district attorney had whispered in Webb's ear. "You're off the case."

Duncan received notice that Sheila Cross would be taking over the prosecution's case the morning after the hearings on the motions to exclude evidence were granted.

What a bitch. Duncan thought as he read the notice.

The prosecution scrambled to reconstruct its case from the evidence found at the scene of the crime.

"Those incompetent necrophiliacs." Cross could not believe what she was reading.

"Get me the coroner's office on the telephone."

The fire had badly mutilated the young girl's body and destroyed much of the physical evidence. However, the ineptitude of the Los Angeles County coroner further added to the prosecution's problems.

"I don't care if you're overworked and understaffed," Cross screamed into the receiver. "That's not my problem. However, your incompetence is my problem. How can you fuck up an autopsy? Isn't that what you guys do for a living?"

"You no talk me like that. I read newspaper. Your office inconfident," Dr. Kong lashed back in his best broken English.

Evidence related to the murder had been misplaced and mislabeled by the coroner. The written report of the autopsy contained inaccuracies and inconsistencies, including incorrectly identifying the location of several of the victim's injuries, indicating the existence of fractures that did not exist. In short, the report was riddled with mistakes. At least one of the audiotapes recorded by the coroner during the autopsy was unaccounted for.

Cross attempted to sound civil. "I can read, too. Did you see the governor's comments in the *Times* this morning? Look, Dr. Kong, for better or worse, we're in this together. We had better put some lipstick on this pig, or we'll both be looking for jobs."

"Leepsteek on pig?"

"It's a figure of speech. I'm just saying we need to work together."

They agreed to meet the following day to discuss the evidence.

The heat on the coroner and the district attorney's office to salvage the Santino case was growing more and more intense with every passing day. The governor—together with other prominent politicians—began to distance themselves from the case. These were the same politicians who, only months earlier, were falling all over themselves to get photo ops with anyone connected to the prosecution.

As the trial drew nearer, Duncan continued to fortify his defense. He was becoming increasingly confident that his experts could convince the jury that the coroner was inept and that the jury would find the coroner's testimony unreliable.

The coroner's testimony was supposed to be the icing on the cake for the prosecution. It was clear that the prosecution had built its entire case around the evidence found at Santino's Malibu home. Without that evidence, there was very little to support the sexual assault and sodomy charges.

CHAPTER 22

WITH THE PROSECUTION'S case in disarray, the defense team was preparing to launch the second phase of its attack.

Duncan and Cohen were putting the final touches on a variety of pretrial motions seeking dismissal of all the charges alleged in the complaint, with the exception of the murder and arson charges.

"I don't mean to question your judgment, but I wouldn't file these motions if I were lead counsel."

"That's why you're not lead counsel, Mr. Cohen."

"You're the boss," Cohen replied, still convinced that he was right.

"Let me guess. You think that because there is virtually no evidence to support the rape and sodomy charges, the jury will see how weak the prosecution's case is, causing them to doubt the validity of the remaining charges?"

"Something like that."

"That's what I thought. You're an idiot," Duncan said, sounding exasperated.

Cohen was more amused than insulted by Duncan's almost childlike rebuke.

"There are two firm rules in the law. Don't fight battles you don't absolutely have to fight. And never be stupid enough to believe that you know what a jury is going to do. You would have us violate both rules. And I thought you were the smart one. If you don't understand what we are doing, then what must those other neophytes be thinking? Stella, get Stanley, Dixon, Thaler, and Hurey in here." Duncan deplored stupidity.

"Gentlemen, if you're going to work this hard, you should at least be learning something. It has come to my attention that you don't have a clue about our trial strategy."

All four attorneys simultaneously looked at Cohen with suspicious eyes.

"Hey, don't look at me, I'm the idiot. At least you're only neophytes. So there is still hope for you guys."

Duncan cast a disapproving glare Cohen's way, but he could not completely hide his appreciation of the comic relief that showed on his face.

"It was important to narrow the issues presented to the jury. I didn't want them to hear anything regarding the rape charges. There will almost certainly be women on the jury. We must keep any evidence of rape out. Women in particular have a natural bias against anyone charged with rape. Don't ever forget that. Now get back to work."

—⁄⁄⁄—

Cross was leaning back in her chair reading the defense's pretrial motions when the district attorney burst into her office.

"Have you read Gabrelli's motions?"

"Looking at them right now. It's good work, wish I had the staff to put these kind of pleadings together," Cross said almost casually.

"I don't care what kind of staff he has, we can't lose this one. I want every person in this office working on this."

Cross smiled. "You can't be serious. We're going to get our ass kicked if we oppose these motions."

"What?"

"That Gabrelli, he's a smart one. He knows we can't win. He wants us to commit our already thin resources into opposing this motion. There is a time to fight and a time to capitulate. Guess which time this is, boss."

"Are we going to just let these motions go unopposed?"

"No. We will steal his thunder. We'll dismiss the charges before the hearing."

The DA reached over and closed the office door. "Good idea. At the same time, we might want to let stories slip to the press that the conduct of the police and coroner has forced us to focus on the murder. It's time to start covering our butts, just in case this whole thing goes south."

"I'll leave the stories to you. I have enough to do just getting ready for trial."

"Tell me the truth. Can we win this one, Sheila?"

"We can win. But I wouldn't bet on it."

"It's too late, Sheila, we already have."

—m—

"They've dismissed all the indictments, except murder and arson. It looks like they're throwing in the towel," Stanley said handing the dismissal notice across the table to Duncan.

"She's good. If she were a lot younger and much prettier, I could fall for that gal."

"It's good news, right?" Hurey said hesitantly.

"I was trying to suck her into a battle she can't win. I tried to deplete her resources, and she didn't take the bait. Damn, she's good. I want my Webb back," Duncan said with a smile.

"How does it help them to roll over? Even a weak opposition would have been better than no opposition at all."

"Dixon, you should stick to research and writing. Strategy is not your strong suit. If she files weak papers and loses, she gets blamed for doing a bad job. If she does great paperwork and loses, she has wasted her valuable time, and the press crucifies her anyway. This way she gets to spin the story. Keep your eyes on the news, boys. Someone's about to get dumped on big-time."

Despite his pretrial successes, Duncan was still concerned that the prosecution might be able to present enough forensic and circumstantial evidence to convict Santino.

"Okay, guys let's get back to work. Remember, without a witness to the murder, this case has become a battle of circumstantial evidence and experts. Let's make sure our experts are ready."

CHAPTER 23

DUNCAN ASSUMED PERSONAL responsibility for preparing Santino for trial. In the months that led up to the trial, he secretly employed a speech therapist to soften the mafioso harshness of his client's voice, acting coaches to relax his physical appearance and angry facial expressions, and a psychologist to help Santino control his legendary temper.

Beauticians, makeup artists, and manicurists were kept on staff to make sure that every time Santino went out in public, he was perfectly groomed. Using the lessons learned from the Nixon/Kennedy presidential debates, Duncan made sure that Santino shaved twice a day.

Santino greeted Duncan with a handshake. "Yous bain doowin good?"

"'Yous' 'doowin'? You've been taking voice lessons for two months!" Duncan exclaimed in disbelief.

"I'm just fuckin wit ya."

"It's your ass, Santino. You want to end up in prison, keep jerking around."

"I'm here, ain't I? Ya, I meant to tell you, I'd rather meet these guys at their offices. It's a drag driving to your office every day."

"I explained this to you ten times. The terms of your bail are clear, you must stay at your Malibu home or your father's home, and you can only drive to your attorney's office and doctors' offices. Break those rules even once and have no doubt that you will spend the next year in jail awaiting trial. Besides, I don't want the press to know we're working on your image. That's why you have been staying at your father's house and why you come here. If word gets out of your makeover, it will be all over the news. You need to just tough it out for a few more months."

While Duncan was babysitting Santino, the rest of the defense team was making sure that the pieces of the defense puzzle fit together snugly.

Private investigators were digging into the backgrounds of all the witnesses scheduled to testify for the prosecution.

Duncan had personally interviewed all of the state's witnesses, many on more than one occasion. Employing his folksy hometown Southern drawl, he was able to elicit considerable personal information.

After securing their trust, he launched tenacious attacks on the credibility of each witness. Leaks to the press regarding their personal lives were beginning to pay off.

It came as no surprise to Duncan that virtually every witness had skeletons in their closets. They were homosexuals, adulterers, criminals, and at least one pedophile. Their dirty little secrets (some real and some invented by the defense team) became front-page news.

Like sharks, the press ripped and tore at the witnesses' moral veneer. The witnesses were no longer the sideshow, they were the story. Paparazzi followed them relentlessly. Out of fear and intimidation, they began to get convenient lapses of memory. They had lost their appetite for justice and simply wanted this trial out of their lives.

Mr. Bartelli was also doing his part for the cause. Witnesses began to have trouble remembering what they had seen. One of the witnesses from the motel apparently decided to return to his home in Mexico. Permanently. Rumors of witness intimidation and coercion were rampant but were never proved.

The defense had dug up so much dirt on everyone—from the investigating police officers to the coroner's office—that it became a full-time job for Hurey and Thaler to leak the information to the press.

After a year of the press toeing the prosecution's line, the daily articles and press reports began to reverse direction. They started to make it look like Duncan had a chance of winning an acquittal. The thought of trouncing the prosecution in such a high-profile case pleased him to no end. In truth, Duncan preferred being seen as the underdog.

CHAPTER 24

THE DISCOVERY MOTIONS and the general pretrial wrangling between the prosecution and defense caused the case to drag on for almost a year before it was ready to go to trial.

In the weeks preceding the trial, it became obvious that the prosecution's case had almost completely imploded. The media reports were gradually leaning toward acquittal, and it was clearly making the prosecutor nervous. It didn't go unnoticed by Duncan that this was the same press that had ridiculed him for taking the case in the first place.

There was more at stake than just the prosecutor's win/loss record. It was common knowledge that District Attorney Edward Duffy was up for reelection. A year ago, he was practically guaranteed to win reelection. Losing this case could snatch defeat from the jaws of a victorious reelection campaign.

"I thought I said no calls."

"I think you're going to want to take this one, Mr. Gabrelli." Duncan's ears perked up when Stella said, "Edward Duffy on line one."

"Put him on hold. Get Cohen and the other boys in here. I want them to hear this."

Duncan pushed the speaker button on the phone. "Ed, how's the reelection campaign going?" Duncan said fully aware that it was not going well.

"Just fine, Duncan, just fine."

"Good, good, glad to hear it. I don't mean to be short, but things are a little hectic around here. How can I be of service to you?"

"Duncan I have something to say for your ears only. Is this a private line?"

With Hurey, Thaler, Dixon, Cohen, and Stanley sitting directly in front of him, Duncan said, "Yes. Just the two of us."

"Duncan, I think we should meet."

"Love to, Ed, maybe we can get together for dinner after the trial." Duncan knew full well that Ed meant that he wanted to meet before the trial; he was just messing with Ed's mind a bit in a show for his troops, who were hanging on every word.

The DA was not amused. "Don't fuck with me. You know damn well why I'm calling. We're going to settle this case, just me and you. I will be at your home tomorrow night at nine o'clock."

"I'll be there," Duncan replied.

One second after Duncan hung up the telephone, Hurey, Thaler, Dixon, and Stanley jumped up, screaming a victory cry. Cohen and Dixon were dancing around, pounding the table.

It was not until they noticed the lack of emotion on Duncan's face that they stopped.

"Break a smile for a change, they're going to settle. The DA would not have called himself unless the deal was too good to pass up."

"Sit down and keep quiet. I didn't call you in here to hear my call with the DA; I called you in here to listen to your client."

"Stella. Get me Mr. Bartelli on the telephone, please."

"Good morning, Mr. Bartelli."

"Good morning."

"There has been a development we should discuss. I just got off the phone with Edward Duffy. They want to make a deal."

"Duffy called you?"

"I just hung up the phone two minutes ago."

"What's the deal?"

"I don't know, but he must be scared shitless. He's not taking any chances that the settlement might be prematurely leaked to the press. He insisted that just the two of us meet in person to discuss the offer. We agreed to meet tomorrow night at my place."

"Listen to me, Duncan. No jail time. Do you hear me? No jail time!"

Duncan knew that the prosecution couldn't offer *any* deal that did not include jail time. However, he saw no reason to argue about the terms of a deal that hadn't even been offered. "I hear you, sir. Let's just listen to what he has to say."

"Listen to Duffy until your ears fall off, as long as you can still hear me. There will be no jail time for Santino."

"I understand. I will call you tomorrow night after the meeting."

The jubilation in the office had disappeared.

"The DA isn't going to offer no jail time," Cohen said, as the wind rushed from his lungs.

"You're probably right. But it doesn't cost anything to listen. However, the bigger lesson that you need to learn today is don't assume that your client is going to do the smart thing. Back to work, gentlemen."

The next evening at 9:00 p.m. sharp, Duffy arrived at Duncan's home. After quickly exchanging obligatory pleasantries, the two men got to the task at hand.

"Let me get right to the point. If your client is convicted, he's going to go to jail for a long time. I sure wouldn't want to be in your shoes if you lose the case that sends Vincenzo Bartelli's son to jail for the rest of his life. To be fair, I'm sure you know that the last thing I need during an election year is to lose this case. So I think we can help each other out here. I'm prepared to reduce the charges to involuntary manslaughter and guarantee that Santino spends no more than three years in jail."

There was no question in Duncan's mind that the prosecution was making the best offer it could make and still save face. It was either accept or go to trial. They had nothing more to give. "Let me be completely candid. My client will not accept a deal that includes jail time."

"Are you fucking kidding me? My office could never offer that kind of deal! We're already going to get a lot of heat if Santino gets only three years. Hell, he will be out in fifteen months with good behavior. I'm only prepared to make this offer because, with a little help from my friends in the press, I think I can spin the plea bargain into looking like a win. Look, Duncan," Duffy said irritably as he stood to leave, "This is it. I don't have anything left to offer."

"I understand. Let me take this to my client. I'll call you tomorrow with my client's response."

With that the two men shook hands, and Duncan showed Duffy to the door.

Duncan's experience told him that the deal was never going to get any sweeter. It was tantamount to surrender in chess. Had he been representing anyone else in the country, the case would be over. But he was representing the son of Vincenzo Bartelli. He picked up the phone and called Mr. Bartelli just minutes after Duffy left.

"Good evening, Mr. Bartelli."

"Get to it. What was the offer?" Mr. Bartelli was not in the mood for small talk.

"The offer includes three years jail time, out in fifteen months with good behavior."

"No deal. I thought I made that clear."

Duncan didn't want to say what he was about to say, but he had no choice. "Mr. Bartelli, I'm ethically required to communicate the offer to my client."

"You just did."

The line went dead.

Duncan stood there, receiver in hand, shaking his head more in frustration than in disbelief.

CHAPTER 25

DUNCAN WAS DETERMINED to at least make sure that Santino understood the potential ramifications of declining the deal. Of course, he knew that meant making Bartelli understand first.

During the year that preceded the trial, Mr. Bartelli had become a fixture in Duncan's life. He used his son's trial as an excuse to look in on Duncan from time to time. Often, he would show up at Duncan's office unannounced to discuss the case. Meetings turned into lunches, lunches turned into dinners. As their relationship grew stronger, he began to invite Duncan to swank social affairs.

Their mutual respect had blossomed into genuine affection for each other. In under a year, their relationship had gone through a metamorphosis. It was as if Duncan was becoming part of the Bartelli family. The growing depth of their relationship did not go unnoticed by Santino.

What Duncan did not know was that long before he had been asked (or more accurately, ordered) to represent Santino, Bartelli had been following his progress with the firm.

Unbeknown to Duncan, he'd represented several of Mr. Bartelli's associates prior to taking Santino's case. He was unaware of the fact that the vast majority of Mr. Bartelli's associates appeared (to the rest of the world) to be legitimate businessmen, bankers and white-collar professionals mostly, who on occasion would extend favors to Mr. Bartelli.

It would not be until later in their relationship that Duncan would learn just how *many* important people were in Mr. Bartelli's pocket.

Sandler Helms, the firm's most senior partner, had been a trusted counselor and adviser to Mr. Bartelli for decades. However, he was nearly sixty-five and had twice survived heart attacks. He was getting too old to handle the excitement of Mr. Bartelli's world and wanted to retire. For years Mr. Bartelli had been promising to find an attorney to take his place. Helms finally knew his retirement was not far off when he saw the interest Mr. Bartelli had taken in Duncan.

Duncan, who had never known the closeness of a father-son relationship, began to look forward to his meetings and conversations with Mr. Bartelli. Now he hoped that he could use their newly formed bond to convince him to allow Santino to accept the plea offer.

Duncan knew that Santino should take the deal. Even before he disclosed the deal to his client, he also knew that Mr. Bartelli would not let his son agree to it.

On at least three occasions he strongly advised both Santino and Mr. Bartelli to authorize him to make the deal.

This is insane. Why can't he see that his son should accept the deal? he thought as he reluctantly picked up the telephone to call the district attorney's office to reject the deal. Duncan was right. When it came to Santino's trial, he was not dealing with a sane man.

At least that's what Duncan thought at the time.

CHAPTER 26

ONE WEEK LATER the trial went forward as scheduled. It was not uncommon for the district attorney's office to leak small amounts of evidence to the press in an effort to contaminate the jury pool. The leaks relating to Santino's case could have sunk the Titanic.

Duncan always considered picking the jury to be the most important part of a criminal trial. The stakes were higher than ever before, so he paid particular attention to jury selection in Santino's case.

Due to the firestorm of publicity that surrounded the case, the court ordered that the jury be sequestered during the trial. Even so, Duncan was keenly aware that information the jury pool had already learned about the case could influence their judgment when it came time to render a verdict.

Two companies were retained by the defense to analyze the jury selection. Wealth, age, sex, race, and religion were just a few of the many factors considered in making their predictions. They employed a variety of methods and techniques, including psychological profiling and handwriting analysis to help determine which potential jurors would most favor the defense.

Having always relied on his own experience and instinct to select his juries, Duncan was uncomfortable with the idea of using "experts." However, Duncan forced himself to consider their findings, and in the end combined his own instincts with their expertise to make the final determination of whom to keep on the jury and whom to keep off. By the time *voir dire* was completed, Duncan was more than ready to do battle.

Notwithstanding the multitude of problems with its case, the prosecution did its best to set forth a compelling argument for conviction. It called twenty-seven lay witnesses and nine expert witnesses in support of its case. Despite its valiant efforts, with every point the prosecution scored, Duncan scored two on cross-examination.

The prosecution rested forty-two days after making its opening argument. It was now the defense's turn. Had Duncan not put on a defense, there was a very good chance that Santino would have been found not guilty.

But he wasn't going to take any chances. Scientists and professors from the most prestigious institutions of learning in the country, including Princeton, Harvard, Berkeley, and Duke were put on the stand to attack the forensic evidence presented by the prosecution.

Defense experts testified that they were sure beyond any doubt that—considering the amount of drugs and alcohol that would have been in Santino's blood at the time of the murder—he would have never been capable of driving the forty-five miles from the crime scene to his home in Malibu.

Blood samples hadn't been taken from Santino until the morning following the murder. However, the experts used large color charts and graphs to explain in simple terms how they were able to calculate the amounts of alcohol and drugs in his system almost seven hours earlier based on Santino's weight, age, sex, and the alcohol and drug levels in his blood at the time of his arrest. They presented a compelling argument that it would have been impossible for anyone to operate a vehicle. It was a testament to how unreliable experts can be, inasmuch as Santino *had* driven home that night.

The defense called thirteen expert witnesses during the trial, each challenging separate aspects of the prosecution's case. Duncan laid the groundwork to support his theory that Santino was being framed by the government. He presented evidence that various governmental agencies doctored or falsified reports. He produced a retired FBI officer who testified that he had been present during a meeting at FBI headquarters where framing both Vincenzo and Santino was discussed. God only knows what Mr. Bartelli had to pay to secure *that* testimony. But Duncan was sure of one thing: the agent was off the FBI's Christmas card list.

The coroner's clumsiness added credence to the conspiracy theory. Missing reports, missing tapes, lost evidence. It all supported the defense's case.

To add to the prosecution's woes, Santino's speech lessons, professional groomers, and behavioral conditioning were working to perfection. The jurors' faces revealed that they were connecting with Santino in a positive way. Santino looked like a frightened choirboy sitting at the defense table. By the end of the trial, the jury would have awarded monetary damages against the government for damaging Santino's reputation if they could have.

All of his pretrial work had paid off. Duncan controlled the direction of the trial like a maestro controls his orchestra.

He played the jury as only he could do.

When the jury foreman read the not guilty verdict, a hush fell over the courtroom. There were no cheers and no jeers, just the soft shuffle of feet exiting the courtroom. The court thanked the jurors for their service, and the judge retired to his chambers.

Duncan individually thanked the jurors before they left the court. They were about to become twelve of the most hated people in the country. He should have felt sorry for the jurors, but he was too busy feeling good about himself.

The press had provided the country with all the evidence, including the evidence that had been excluded by the court. To their credit, based on the evidence that the jury *did* hear and see, it would have been difficult for them to find Santino guilty beyond a reasonable doubt.

They would wish, however, they had found him guilty anyway. They were lampooned by the press, and the public considered them nothing short of stupid.

Two months after the verdict was read, the judge voluntarily retired. He knew that Santino was guilty. Being loyal to his oath to follow the law caused him to set a murderer free. Watching Santino walk out a free man was the last straw—he could not sit on the bench and let even one more criminal go free.

CHAPTER 27

THE COURTROOM WAS almost empty when Duncan placed the last of his files in his briefcase. The hard silence that had fallen over the courtroom was suddenly breached by a solitary sound. It was Jessica's mother crying. She was not screaming or yelling. She sounded more like a small child sobbing. The soft and painful sound of her heart breaking rose gently into the air.

Duncan did not want to confront Mrs. Lopez, but he could not help but look over his shoulder at the small frail-looking Latin woman. When their eyes met, he was shocked by his reaction, or more accurately, his lack of reaction.

He didn't feel even the slightest twinge of remorse for stealing her vengeance. The sight of her tears left him hollow. He didn't feel sorry for her. He didn't even feel sad for her. He didn't feel anything for her. At that moment, he didn't feel anything for any of the players in this grotesque play.

It was that day—that very moment—when Duncan Gabrelli was revealed to himself. Looking into his soul, he was able to see who he was at his core.

He had been living a dualistic life for many years. The forces of good and evil were constantly at war for dominion of his soul. His work fostered his most base instincts. He was cold and calculating, ruthless and cruel. In his mind, the ends always justified the means.

But there was another Duncan Gabrelli, generous and kind. The one his mother raised him to be, the one he once wanted to be. But his mother's murder had shaken the roots of his faith in the church, humanity and himself.

Looking into Mrs. Lopez's eyes, he was forced to admit that the darker side of his personality now ruled. That realization would change the course of his life forever.

As Duncan exited the courtroom he heard Mrs. Lopez call out, "Hell has made a place for you."

"I know Mrs. Lopez. I know."

The press half expected Duncan to do victory laps around the courthouse.

"Mr. Gabrelli, does your client believe he's been vindicated by today's verdict?"

"Mr. Gabrelli, what's your reaction to the verdict?"

"Mr. Gabrelli?"

"Mr. Gabrelli!"

To their surprise, Duncan made no statements as he left the courthouse.

There was nothing he could say. Everyone in the country (except twelve jurors) knew his client was guilty. To suggest otherwise would have made him look like a fool.

Santino, the fool, couldn't resist the draw of the cameras. He was standing in front of a dozen microphones when Duncan caught up with him.

After months of the best instruction available, Santino ripped off the mask of refinement to reveal the beast that dwelled within. "Fucking cops tried to frame me. They tried to frame me."

Duncan grabbed his client's arm, "We have no comment." He dragged Santino down the courthouse steps, through the throng of reporters and spectators, to the black-on-black limousine parked at the curb.

"Why don't you stop and take a bow. You kicked the DA's ass. You're my attorney from now on. You're beautiful, fucking beautiful."

I'd kill myself before I'd represent your dumb ass again, Duncan thought. "Just get in, Santino. Just get in the car."

Vincenzo was in the limo when they arrived.

"Good work, Duncan. Damn good work."

"Thank you, sir."

Santino didn't stop talking the entire way back to Duncan's office.

Seeing that Duncan looked distracted, Vincenzo broke in. "You look deep in thought. What's on your mind?"

"Nothing, sir. I missed lunch. I was just thinking how good a thick slice of prime rib from Ruth's Chris would taste about now."

CHAPTER 28

MR. BARTELLI'S UNWAVERING confidence in Duncan's abilities caused him to reject the plea bargain. That conviction was also evidenced by the fact that—in advance of the verdict—he had planned a lavish party to celebrate his son's acquittal. The party had been in the planning stages for months. However, he had hedged his bet by not sending the invitations until the day the verdict was read.

Duncan was not particularly interested in attending the party. He had just saved his job, his firm, and probably his life. He was emotionally spent. Attending a black-tie affair was the last thing on his to-do list. Even so, Mr. Bartelli was not the kind of man who looked favorably on the rejection of a personal invitation. He would have considered declining the invitation anyway if he hadn't been aware that the party was—at least in part—being thrown to congratulate him.

Feeling an obligation to attend, he thought that he should take a date to the affair. It would give him an excuse to leave early should he get too bored. A date would also act as a defense against the flock of socialite groupies who attended most of the high-society galas.

It was not conceit; Duncan had done quite well for himself with women over the years. Relying on his wit and natural charm, he had had more than his share of casual sexual relationships.

As his reputation and financial fortunes grew, so too did his desirability quotient. Without trying, he had become one of the most eligible bachelors on the social scene. He was a big hit at all the upscale social gatherings and never more than a phone call away from waking up with a beautiful successful-attorney's-wife wannabe.

He hadn't abused his good fortune with women. Not because he was a caring or considerate man, but because he was working so hard. There were simply not enough hours in the day to think about women, not even beautiful women. In truth, even if he had more time, he was a solitary person. He was so entertained by his work and his criminal obsession that he was one of the few men on the planet whose mind was not perpetually preoccupied with sex.

Scrolling through the names in his Rolodex he stopped at Victoria McPherson's name. He hadn't seen her in many months. As he stared at the card, he remembered that he hadn't returned at least two messages from Victoria before she gave up and stopped calling. Even so, he was confident that Victoria would welcome the invitation.

Someone answered the phone on the second ring. "Victoria? So, have you missed me?"

She apparently had no problem recognizing his voice. "Ever so much. I'm so glad you called. Where have you been keeping yourself?"

"I wish I had a more interesting answer. But tragically, I live in my office these days."

"I've been reading about you in the paper. You're quite the celebrity."

Duncan chuckled. "More infamous than famous, I'm afraid. However, that's why I'm calling."

"I'm not sure I get the connection, but if it takes a murder to get you to call, that works just fine for me."

He laughed again. "I've been invited to a party to celebrate the acquittal."

"Yes, everyone I know has been trying to get invited. Rumor is it's going to be quite the affair."

"Would you do me the honor of being my date?"

She made no pretense of playing hard to get. "I would love to."

"Excellent. I'll pick you up at seven o'clock," he said, and hung up the phone without so much as a single additional pleasantry.

Victoria was from a wealthy Georgian family and spent most of her time at social and charity events. She received a degree from some Ivy League college back East, a degree she never had any intention of putting to practical use. She was twenty-five years old and in the market for a husband and a family for her nannies and servants to care for.

Tall and thin with blond hair that fell to her waist, she was a glamorous-looking young woman. She would make some unlucky man a great show wife.

However, she was barking up the wrong tree. Duncan was not the slightest bit interested in marrying Victoria, or any other person. Strangely enough, that appearance of aloofness made Victoria that much more determined to pursue Duncan.

She'd been invited for two reasons. She had the social skills to mingle in any crowd and wouldn't be overtly offended by the likes of Mr. Bartelli and his "family," and, of equal importance, she was great in bed. It had been a long time, and he was in the mood to participate in some serious carnal activity.

CHAPTER 29

VICTORIA AND DUNCAN arrived at the palatial Beverly Hills estate on prestigious Hillcrest Drive in a black limousine. The estate was encircled by fourteen-foot-high hedges. Two men in dark suits stood at the entrance. With their stoic facial expressions and stiff postures they could have easily passed for FBI agents. They were instead the elite of Mr. Bartelli's security force.

One of the men asked to see their invitation. After a brief examination, the man raised his hand to signal the guard in the security booth. The ornate brass-and-steel gates swung open, and the limousine drove through the gates and proceeded slowly up the long horseshoe-shaped driveway.

It was no accident that once inside the gates, Mr. Bartelli's guests were completely shielded from the prying eyes of outsiders.

The exterior of the mansion was beyond impressive. Twenty solid marble pillars lined the front of the main residence, with Greek and Roman statues standing sentry between them. Sculptures of angels and other religious icons were carved into the face of the building, while others sat on the spires at the roofs edge.

Duncan estimated the main building to be at least twenty thousand square feet. There were also two guesthouses on the property, each approximately five thousand square feet.

The limousine stopped in front of the massive hardwood entry doors, and a gentleman in a servant-style tuxedo opened the limousine door. Duncan was the first to exit the limousine and (ever so gallantly) presented his hand to Victoria as she stepped out onto the red carpet.

While the exterior of the mansion was impressive, it paled in comparison to the splendor of the interior of the residence. It was decorated with ornate rugs and tapestries. An enormous Lalique crystal chandelier hung in the foyer. Smaller, but equally beautiful, chandeliers hung in almost every room.

The furniture was from the finest American craftsmen, including pieces from Baker and Kyndal's Winterthur collection. Many of the rooms were decorated with priceless antiques. It was clear that Mr. Bartelli knew how to spend money, and that he enjoyed the finer things in life.

It suddenly struck Duncan as a little strange that, notwithstanding the fact that he and Mr. Bartelli had become very close over the past year, he had never been invited to Mr. Bartelli's home before that night.

Duncan and Victoria were escorted through the residence and out the back where the party had been staged. The mansion sat on a massive plot of land by Beverly Hills standards. Large white canopies had been erected behind the main house.

Strands of colored lights adorned the trees and plants. Tall, thin, cast-iron columns with spires of fire shooting skyward from their tops flickered in the night sky, providing both decoration and lighting for the event. The flickering flames cast elegant shadows across the tables that dotted the grounds. The tables formed a large horseshoe shape around a hardwood dance floor.

At the head of the dance floor, a thirty-piece orchestra was playing classical music, and people were already gliding across the dance floor in their tuxedos and designer gowns. Both Duncan and Victoria had been to many very fancy social affairs but neither had seen anything quite so grand.

Mr. Bartelli, who had been talking to a group of a dozen or so guests, cut his conversation off in midsentence when he saw Duncan enter the grounds. He immediately excused himself and made his way over to where Duncan and Victoria were standing. Duncan extended his hand as he approached, but to his surprise, Mr. Bartelli threw his arms around him in a bear hug.

Duncan was a little uncomfortable with the display of affection shown by a man who had, only a year earlier, all but threatened to kill him. However, he returned the embrace so as not to embarrass or offend Mr. Bartelli.

The embrace lasted longer than Duncan thought it should. He was glad to feel Mr. Bartelli release his arms and start to step back away from him. As he stepped back, he grabbed Duncan's hand firmly and shook it long and hard.

Leaning forward, Mr. Bartelli whispered in his ear, "You saved my son. I am *forever* in your debt."

When a man like Mr. Bartelli says that he is forever in your debt, he means that he is forever in your debt, and Duncan knew it.

"Come, let me introduce you to some of my guests," Mr. Bartelli shouted above the din of the party.

It was a regular who's who of the social elite. Politicians, business moguls, Hollywood luminaries, all the rich and beautiful were there. Even some of the politicians who had originally voiced strong opinions regarding Santino's guilt were there.

With all of the negative press, Duncan would have thought that many of these guests would have declined the invitation. He smiled as he thought that Mr. Bartelli's invitations must be even harder to turn down than even he originally contemplated.

Servers dressed in matching costumes scurried about the grounds serving hors d'oeuvres for well over an hour before a rather large black fellow with an impressively deep voice announced to the crowd, "Dinner is served."

As guests started making their way back to their tables, an army of smartly dressed waiters and waitresses appeared out of nowhere, carrying trays bearing the first course of the meal. Course after course of some of the most wonderfully flavorful foods followed, each one expertly prepared. Mr. Bartelli had employed the services of some of the finest chefs in all of California to prepare the evening's meal.

The flavors of each successive course complemented the course before. It was like dining at ten of the finest Los Angeles restaurants at once. An endless river of fine wines and champagne flowed throughout the meal and late into the night.

Mr. Bartelli had arranged for Duncan and his guest to be seated at his table, a considerable honor in light of the prestigious guest list.

Dinner conversation consisted mostly of boring social banter. There was no discussion of the trial or the acquittal during the meal. As dessert was being served, Mr. Bartelli stood up from the table to say a few words to his guests. It took only a moment for his guests to quiet down. The massive grounds fell silent.

"A toast!" he barked as if he was giving the entire august assemblage an order.

Grabbing his glass, he reached down and placed his hand on Santino's shoulder. "My only son is here with me today as a result of the efforts of one man. His tireless efforts and unparalleled brilliance has brought my son back home to me."

With those words, his eyes shifted to Duncan. "Duncan Gabrelli, you have my undying gratitude. *Salud!*"

The sound of fine St. Louis crystal stemware clinking together rang out, and the sound rose up into the air, drifting in the breeze like a gentle mist.

He spoke for several more minutes, bestowing even more praise on Duncan before he offered up a final toast and sat down.

A chorus of "Speech! Speech! Speech!" rose up from the guests. Duncan was not prepared for either the accolades or the insistent call for him to speak. He really didn't want to give a speech, for the same reason he didn't address the press after the verdict: everyone at the event knew Santino was guilty. They had simply chosen to ignore that fact for the sake of having a good time. It was as if they were hiding behind the jury's verdict to ease their conscience. If Duncan stood up and professed Santino's innocence, it would only remind the crowd that they were here to celebrate a murderer's escape from justice.

However, the calls for him to speak had grown even louder, and there was little chance of a silent escape. When his host chimed in, he knew there was no way out.

As he stood to his feet, a roar of applause rose with him. His mind was racing. *Perhaps a little humor to break the ice.*

"Unaccustomed as I am to public speaking..." The guests immediately broke out into a chorus of laughter.

After allowing a brief moment for the guests to quiet down, but without letting the laughter completely die out—an old comedian's trick taught to him by a friend who performed stand-up—he continued, "I'm going to do you all a big favor tonight and keep this short." Again a chorus of laughter rose.

It was time to say something substantive. "It is with great pride that I accept the praise and accolades bestowed upon me by our host. We all know him to be a man of few words. When he spares some of those words to give praise or thanks, you know that they are heartfelt.

"When Mr. Bartelli's name is mentioned, many images come to mind. Having gotten to know him over the course of the last year, I can tell you that he is, above all else, a father. I watched him support his son through the worst of times, in a way that only a father who truly loves his son can do. Please raise your glasses with me in a toast to a man I am proud to call my friend. Vincenzo Bartelli. *Salud!*"

Applause and the ringing of crystal glasses again filled the air, this time louder and longer than before.

Some in the crowd may have felt that he had taken considerable liberties in calling Mr. Bartelli his friend. After all, the guests saw him as a (very) well-paid employee who had only known him for a relatively short time. But the truth was that he and Mr. Bartelli had become friends, maybe even more than just friends. In any event, he was sure that Mr. Bartelli would accept his words as a compliment. It wasn't his best speech; it may have been his shortest, but under the circumstances, it was good enough. He was just glad to be back in his seat again.

CHAPTER 30

AFTER DINNER MR. BARTELLI turned to Victoria. "May I borrow your date for a few minutes?"

She politely consented, adding, "Don't keep him too long. He owes me a few dances."

"I'd have no respect for Duncan if he let me keep him from such a lovely lady for even one second more than necessary."

The two men excused themselves from the table and walked back to the main house. After passing through a maze of doors and hallways, they entered a large study. The room was furnished with several large leather couches and matching oversize chairs. The walls were lined three stories high with row after row of leather-bound books on every imaginable subject. Matching spiral staircases on each side of the room led to a second-story walkway that wrapped around the entire room.

"Please take a seat. I have some things I would like to discuss with you," Mr. Bartelli said in a lower and more friendly tone than Duncan had ever heard from him. They had had numerous meetings during his son's ordeal. He had come to like Mr. Bartelli very much, and he could tell that the feeling was mutual.

Mr. Bartelli started the conversation as soon as Duncan sat down. "I have a gift for you, for saving my son."

"Sir, you really don't need to give me anything. Perhaps you haven't had a chance to review the bills in your son's case. I can assure you that my firm has been more than adequately compensated for our services," Duncan replied, only partly in jest.

"I know, I've seen the bills," he said with a smile. "But this is a personal gift, from me to you. I like you, and I trust you, Duncan. I can't say that about many people."

"That is very generous of you to say. Thank you, sir," he replied, adding that now-famous southern drawl to his voice in an effort to sound extrasincere.

Upon hearing the change in his voice, Mr. Bartelli's brow pinched just a little, as if to let him know that he was aware of what Duncan had just tried to do. In his own way, Mr. Bartelli had just scolded him, in the manner that a father might shoot a disapproving look to his son.

Duncan regretted employing the little trick even before Mr. Bartelli's scolding. His look left Duncan feeling a little embarrassed.

The slightly awkward moment passed quickly, and Mr. Bartelli continued. "What do you want? A new home perhaps?" he suggested as he stood and walked over to a liquor cabinet. With the question still floating through the air, he took out a decanter of Martel Supreme XO cognac.

"A drink?"

"Please," Duncan responded. He needed a drink now more than ever before in his life.

Before he could muster a response, Mr. Bartelli said, "There is a nice little property not far from here. It's yours if you want it. Just say the word." He locked eyes with Duncan's in search of a reaction.

Duncan knew that there were no 'little properties' anywhere near this place, and that even a fixer-upper in this neighborhood would be worth well into the millions of dollars.

"Mr. Bartelli, if you want to write me a big fat bonus check, it would be greatly appreciated, sir, but you have something else I want."

Mr. Bartelli looked intrigued. "So what, pray tell me, is on your mind, young man."

Duncan was filled with excitement and apprehension. "I want to know everything you know about crime, about criminals, motives, and methods. Everything."

Now it was his turn to wait for a reaction. Mr. Bartelli had been standing until that moment. With a look of contemplation on his face, he took a seat and said, "Well, that brings me to the next subject I would like to discuss with you. I want you to work for me."

After another short pause, he continued, "It's not clear to me why you are so fascinated by the things I know, but if you work exclusively for me and my associates, you will have access to all the information your heart desires. But know this: with that information comes a duty and a great responsibility. If you ever breach that duty, if you ever fail to honor that responsibility, there will be no place in the world for you to hide from my vengeance. No safe place on the planet. Do you understand what I am telling you?"

Duncan's brain was racing to process the offer. "I need time to think about your generous invitation. As you know, I have obligations and commitments to my firm. I would, in effect, be stealing one of the firm's largest clients, something I am not prepared to do behind their backs. I need to discuss the matter with the partners of the firm."

Mr. Bartelli was pleased by the response. Any other could have had devastating ramifications for Duncan. "I have already made arrangements with your firm. I have taken care of everything."

Duncan could hardly believe what he was hearing. *Can it be true that he really has already obtained the blessing of the firm?*

"What other concerns do you have?" Mr. Bartelli inquired.

Duncan's mind was still stuck on the idea that Mr. Bartelli had already spoken to his firm, and that his firm had effectively traded him like an athlete to another team. It was like Babe Ruth, in the prime of his career, waking up one day to find that his locker had been cleaned out and that he had been traded back to the Red Sox without notice or consultation.

He did not like being treated like a commodity. By going to his firm before talking to him, he had been left with no real choice in the matter.

On the other hand, the fact that Mr. Bartelli would go through this much trouble to retain his services was a sign of great confidence and trust.

As his mind struggled to formulate a response, he decided to accept as true the fact that his firm had given its blessing. If that was in fact true, then a few issues popped instantly into his head.

"Well, Mr. Bartelli, a solo attorney—without offices, support staff, and legal assistance—would be of little practical value to you. Further, standing out there on my own, apart from a major firm, is going to make me an easy target for every state and federal agency that wants to teach lawyers a lesson about representing individuals with undesirable reputations such as yourself. Albeit undeservedly," Duncan said with a slight tone of comedic sarcasm.

Mr. Bartelli was again pleased to see how quickly Duncan thought on his feet. He also recognized the sarcasm in Duncan's voice, and it brought a smile to his face. *The cocky little bastard reminds me of me when I was that age.*

"You don't need to blow smoke up my ass, young man. My reputation is every bit deserved. However, I'm way ahead of you, as you will soon find to be the case in most matters. When I said I have made arrangements with your firm, I didn't mean that you should *leave* the firm. On the contrary, you will be made a full partner of the firm, as promised. The only difference will be that you will work exclusively for me, protecting my various business concerns. Well, maybe not the only difference. In addition to the compensation you receive as a partner of the firm, I will pay you an additional one million dollars a year, plus bonuses, of course."

Duncan was trying not to look stunned, but he couldn't hide the deer-in-the-headlights look that enveloped his face. Mr. Bartelli, on the other hand, bore the look of a hunter locked in on his prey. The reversal of roles was making Duncan uncomfortable.

Reaching into his pocket, Mr. Bartelli took out a set of keys and slid them across the glass tabletop toward Duncan. "Here's your first bonus."

Duncan assumed they were keys to a new (and no doubt very expensive) automobile until Mr. Bartelli said, "Congratulations on your new home. Your escrow closed today. The address is on the key ring."

Hillcrest Road.

From the address, the property had to be within a few blocks of where he was sitting.

Trying to maintain his composure, he did not hesitate, although he probably should have. "I look forward to working for you."

"Good. Now that we have taken care of our business, let's go back and join my guests. I'm sure that your lovely young girlfriend is ready to get that dance you promised her."

CHAPTER 31

DUNCAN DIDN'T TELL Victoria about his conversation with Mr. Bartelli, nor would he. However, she could sense his excitement. When he returned from his meeting, Duncan whisked Victoria from the table and out to the dance floor.

His feet were barely touching the ground as they danced to song after song. They were both wonderful dancers. Duncan's mother had compelled him to take countless ballroom dancing lessons as a young boy. While his friends spent their Saturday afternoons playing games and riding bikes, he danced.

He did his best to hide that fact from his friends. At first, the stories he would tell his friends were simple, doctors' appointments or dental work, but you can only have so many medical emergencies before ten-year-old boys become suspicious. When his friends began to ask questions, the stories became more and more fantastic. He actually had some of the other boys convinced that his mom was a secret agent for the government, and that his Saturdays were spent traveling the world on secret missions to protect the world from evil. The stories were so compelling, that no one seemed to question how he managed to travel to Russia on Saturday morning and get back home that same night for dinner.

Duncan did not like lying to his friends, because it was morally wrong, and it was getting to be hard work. He might have been able to overcome the religious and moral conflict in his soul, but the extra studying was more than he was prepared to endure.

He had been keeping journals of the stories he had been telling just to keep the lies straight in his head. Duncan had spent countless hours rifling through the encyclopedia and at the public library researching Russia, China, and other faraway lands, to make his stories sound credible. Setting aside the fact that he would have needed a time machine to adequately explain his travels, his facts and details were accurate to the smallest detail, at least according to the folks at *Encyclopedia Britannica.*

He had been taking lessons for over a year when he finally concluded that enough was enough. One Friday afternoon, right after school, he pulled his best friend, Bobby, aside and told him the truth.

"I have a secret, but you can't tell anyone. You promise?"

"Sure, cross my heart and hope to die, I swear."

"You swear?"

"Yes, I swear. So what's up?"

"Okay, you swore. My mom makes me take dance lessons every Saturday at noon."

"Wow!" Bobby immediately exclaimed. "So all those stories you have been telling about your mom being a secret agent and all, they're not true?"

"Sorry, Bobby, I didn't want to lie, but you understand, right?"

"Sure, I wouldn't want anyone to know if my mom made me take dance lessons. But, man those stories were good." It made Duncan smile to hear that, because he'd worked very hard to make them interesting and believable.

"Sounds bad, man," Bobby said with a look on his face like he had just eaten a worm.

"It is not that bad, I guess. I kind of like it, but I don't want anyone else to know. You promised, not one soul. You promise?" Duncan asked again with emphasis.

This time, Bobby made the sign of a cross with his hand over his heart. "Cross my heart and hope to die."

Bobby looked thoughtful for a moment, which was not normal for Bobby. He was not a particularly bright boy, and deep thinking was not his strong suit. "I got to get home. I promised my dad I would help him with...(There was a short pause) the car, yeah, the car, I promised him I would help him fix the car. I'll talk to you later." And off Bobby ran down the street.

Bobby had promised not to tell the other boys, and he kept that promise for as long as it took him and his PF Flyers to run to Ted's house, and then to Barney's house, and then to Stan's house. When Saturday noon came rolling around, no fewer than fifteen of Duncan's schoolmates were camped out on Duncan's doorstep. The story of his dance lessons had been modified and exaggerated with each telling. By that point, most of the boys expected Duncan to step out of his house in a pink tutu.

Looking out the window, Duncan begged his mother not to make him go to dance lessons that day. But at exactly noon, Lucia, with Duncan in tow, made their way down the walkway lined with little boys, and off they went to dance school.

For two weeks Duncan did not say even one word to Bobby, but as kids do, they found a way to put it behind them. Bobby promised never to break his word again. He crossed his heart and hoped to die again, but this time "for realzees," and Duncan got to slug Bobby in the arm twice, as hard as he could, and they were best friends again.

Moms, on the other hand, do not get off that easy. For years to come Duncan would quietly curse (never using any of the really bad words) his mother under his breath every Saturday at noon. Lucia did not care if he was the butt of jokes at school. "Jokes or no jokes, you are going to learn to dance," she would say, and off to the instruction they would go, every Saturday at noon.

But on this night, the night of the grand party thrown in his honor by Mr. Bartelli, he was quietly singing his mother's praises. All those lessons were making him the envy of every eligible young woman at the party, as they watched Victoria with both scorn and jealousy. Some of the older guests stopped dancing and stood quietly admiring the beautiful spectacle of their two bodies gliding in perfect harmony across the hardwood floor. Even Mr. Bartelli seemed to find some degree of pleasure in watching his new barrister put on such a display of poise and grace.

Despite his air of sophistication, Duncan was wired. He had a look of wild abandon in his eyes that Victoria had never seen in any man's eyes. It scared her almost as much as it excited her.

It was almost midnight by the time that they had said their goodbyes and were back in the limousine. He instructed the chauffeur to drive down the coast. "Take the Pacific Coast Highway home and drive slowly," were his only words to his driver before he closed the blackout glass between the driver's compartment and the back of the limousine. He wasn't particularly interested in an ocean view, but he knew that the coast route would make for a long slow drive to Malibu.

He pulled Victoria close to him and began to kiss her passionately. He wanted her and was in no mood to wait.

In an effort to remove her gown, he began tugging at the zipper. He hadn't noticed that the gown was molded to her body with a formidable defense system of zippers, hooks, and buttons. After a few minutes it became clear that he was going to need some assistance.

Victoria, also caught up in his infectious excitement, became impatient with his lack of progress and came to his aid. The relatively small confines did not hamper her efforts to extricate herself from the dress. Within seconds she was gently tossing the last of her undergarments to the far end of the limousine.

While she was removing her clothes, Duncan had been making considerable headway at removing his own. The soft lights in the rear of the limousine cast shadows in the curvature of Victoria's form. Her features were magnificent, and he hungered to have her.

They made heated, passionate love to each other during the drive down the coast. She allowed him to explore her body in ways she'd never allowed anyone before. The intensity of their lovemaking drenched them in each other's lusty sweat.

When they were on the verge of exhaustion, they collapsed together as one onto the limousine floor. It had been too long between such moments for both of them. The experience reminded Duncan how much of life he had been missing.

Victoria cracked open the sunroof just far enough to let the cool, moist, ocean air wash over their bodies. With Victoria's warm and supple body lying on top of him, he marveled at the magnificence of the stars through the opening in the sunroof. Her hair fell gently all around him, and he was swept away by the serenity of the moment. He lost all track of time and drifted off to sleep.

He awoke to the feeling of Victoria's gentle fingers running through his hair. She was already dressed and had placed his tuxedo jacket over his naked body.

Lying there with his eyes closed, he heard her gentle voice whispering in his ear. The limousine was about to pull into her driveway. It was one thirty in the morning when they arrived at Victoria's home. He was just fastening the last buttons on his shirt when the limousine came to a complete stop.

She invited him to stay the night, but he was spent both physically and emotionally, so he graciously declined the invitation. Duncan slipped on his trousers and jacket. They walked to her door and again kissed each other passionately. They embraced for almost fifteen minutes before she opened the door and disappeared inside the stately home.

Before she let him go, she made him promise to return her calls and to get back together soon. He promised.

It was a promise he would not keep.

CHAPTER 32

DUNCAN MOVED INTO his new home two weeks after the party. He had been right—it was less than a mile from Mr. Bartelli's palatial estate. It was not as opulent as Mr. Bartelli's, but it was still much larger and more elegant than he needed (or even wanted). The residence had more than nine thousand square feet of living space. Both the interior and exterior of the home featured magnificent architecture and design.

Moving from a three-thousand-square-foot home to a nine-thousand-square-foot estate was quite a change. He had only enough furniture for a third of the rooms in the home. His furniture, though not inexpensive, appeared cheap and out of place in his new home.

He would have loved to spend the time required to properly decorate his lovely new residence, but there simply were not enough hours in the day to handle both the legal demands of his new client and home decoration. Even with half a dozen junior associates and an army of legal assistants and secretaries, he had very little time to call his own.

However, he found solace in the fact that his newfound wealth made it possible for him to employ the services of Jean Maurice, one of the best decorators in Beverly Hills. Jean was in great demand, and Duncan had to pull a few strings to convince him to take the job. Jean was a wispy sort of fellow who made no pretense about being gay. While Jean's sexual preference made no difference to Duncan, he thought it best not to introduce Jean to Mr. Bartelli. Duncan's experience with Mr. Bartelli had shown him that he was at least a little homophobic.

The first thing Jean did was to call Goodwill to take away all the furniture Duncan had brought from his old home. He did this without as much as a Post-it note to Duncan. Upon learning this, Duncan became so enraged that he almost fired Jean on the spot. When he calmed down, he remembered that he had agreed to leave the decorating decisions completely in Jean's hands. Deep down inside, he also knew that Jean was right—his old furniture simply did not fit his new lifestyle, but it still pissed him off.

His decision to keep Jean turned out to be monumentally correct. By the time he had finished working his magic, Duncan was in awe of Jean's talent. He had only seen such splendor in magazines. Each room seemed more impressive than the last. Jean had spared no expense—a fact painfully known to Duncan—in making the place a dream home.

The large kitchen sported commercial-quality Wolf ranges, two Sub-Zero refrigeration units, and a half dozen matching appliances. The walls were lined with teak cabinets, matching the teak floor. A large center island made the kitchen as functional as it was beautiful. Marble counter tops, deep sinks, and the finest fixtures completed the kitchen's look. Duncan enjoyed cooking, and he was ecstatic about the look and feel of his new kitchen.

Of all the rooms in the house, he thought that the study was the most spectacular. It was not quite as large as the study in Mr. Bartelli's home. Even so, it was massive by most standards.

Jean had so brilliantly used the space in the study that the room felt much larger room than it was. Three of the four walls were lined from floor to ceiling with maple bookcases with leaded glass fronts. Ornate edging and wainscoting accented the bookcases and walls. The oversize executive's cherrywood desk and matching conference table filled the room with an aura of class and sophistication. Much like in Mr. Bartelli's study, two spiral staircases provided access to a second-story walkway that circled the room.

When Duncan found time to spend at home, he spent almost all of it in his study. He so loved the feel of the room that he dedicated it to his analysis of criminal behavior. He had a locksmith install locks in the study door to which he had the only key. Using one of Mr. Bartelli's famed contractors, he had a security system installed—independent from the security system that protected the remainder of the home—to protect his private sanctuary.

Two computer systems were installed in the study. Four televisions and videotape recorders were mounted high on the wall in front of his desk. An audio-visual projector could be raised and lowered from the center of the large conference table, and a viewing screen was concealed under the second-story walkway when not in use.

The study became the center of his universe. He could examine case files into the wee hours of the morning without interruption.

CHAPTER 33

NOTWITHSTANDING THE LONG hours spent working and traveling, his new employment pleased him immensely. Mr. Bartelli had been right—their association provided Duncan with a wealth of information about criminal activity. His associates were involved in every type of criminal enterprise. Duncan was able to delve into the inner workings of the criminal mind as never before.

Now he was dividing his time between only three things: working, analyzing criminal cases, and sleeping. All work and no play made Duncan a very dull boy.

His compulsion to analyze the criminal mind was no longer a hobby; it was an obsession. Charts and graphs were strewn all over the study. He didn't allow anyone to enter the room—not even the maid unless he was there—so it frequently looked in shambles. Despite its unkempt appearance, he had the room organized just the way he wanted it. He spent many long nights sorting through the stacks of case files.

His mission was to design the perfect crime. But no matter how he searched, he just could not discover all the elements of the perfect crime. There were just too many contingencies that appeared to be outside the control of the criminal; if there was an answer to the problem of how to control all the contingencies and variables, that answer eluded him.

Of particular fascination to him were crimes involving murder. He knew from personal experience that both state and federal agencies spend a disproportionate amount of their time, energy, and resources attempting to solve murder cases. Therefore, it was more difficult to get away with murder than virtually any other type of crime.

His obsession with murder was moving him ever closer to the darker side of his nature. He found himself dreaming about murders. The dreams came on slowly at first, maybe once a month, then once a week. After a time, they came every night. Increasingly violent and disturbing, the violence escalated with each dream. At first, they seemed like bad dreams, nightmares that struck fear into Duncan's heart. He began to dread the thought of sleep for fear of the depth of his depraved thoughts. The details of the murderous dreams were taken directly from the files that he had studied and analyzed for years. Everything, every detail, every aspect of the murders was crisp and clear, except for the face of the murderer.

His entire existence was wrapped tightly around crime and criminals. His fascination with murder and murderers in particular was growing exponentially.

One night he had a particularly horrific dream. Duncan woke in a cold sweat, but not in fear. He had had an epiphany. In the deepest, blackest, most secret parts of his soul, he saw himself. That dream had unmasked the killer that had been haunting his dreams, a person whom he did not recognize at first. But that night he could clearly see the killer's face. Duncan turned on the light beside his bed and stared at the mirror on the wall. There he was again, the murderer. Right there in the mirror.

He wanted—no; he needed—to kill someone, anyone, just to prove that he could do it without getting caught. He was driven to succeed where his clients had always failed. That was his epiphany. He was a murderer; or at least that's what he wanted to be.

The more he tried to suppress this deviant desire, the more he was compelled to succumb to it. He was far too intelligent to deny that his obsession had become unhealthy, but he just simply didn't care. That night would prove to be the turning point that drove him down a murderous path.

CHAPTER 34

DUNCAN MARVELED at Mr. Bartelli's operation, known by those very few powerful men in control as the "syndicate."

He was the head of a criminal organization that reached the four corners of the globe. At the heart of the operation were hundreds of legitimate businesses—at least in appearance. The syndicate used its control of these businesses and their shareholders to launder money.

The businesses were different in many ways, but they were all primarily used to scrub income from illegal operations until the money was as clean as light.

It was Mr. Helms, the partner who had originally introduced Duncan to Mr. Bartelli, who had been the mastermind behind much of the corporate structure of the syndicate. Mr. Helms had been far more brilliant than Duncan had known. There was no paper trail to link the businesses to the syndicate.

Always the businesses were incorporated. There were businesses incorporated in every state in the United States. The stocks in the corporations were frequently owned by other corporations, which were in turn owned by other corporations, which were themselves owned by offshore corporations.

In every case, there were no common owners of any of the stock in the separate corporations.

When Duncan took over his firm's representation of Mr. Bartelli's legal matters, the design of the syndicate's operational structure had been in place for many years. It was designed to prevent some pencil pusher or bean counter, who might stumble upon one business operation, from taking down the entire syndicate. If one operation was discovered, the remaining operations were insulated.

There were only a handful of people in the organization who knew the inner workings of the syndicate. Duncan had become one of them. Even still, he was sure that there were things about the syndicate's business activities that *he* knew nothing about.

Mr. Bartelli's primary—and most profitable—business was the drug trade. His organization shipped product from every well-known drug-producing country in the world (and some not so well known). If you sold drugs anywhere in North America, the odds were very good that Mr. Bartelli had financially benefited from the transaction.

The level of sophistication of the syndicate was far more complex than anyone could have imagined. It was mind boggling, to say the least. The syndicate was effectively running the most profitable business operation in the United States (perhaps the world) and was doing it without the government's knowledge or control.

Mr. Bartelli frequently complained to Duncan, mostly in jest, that the syndicate paid millions in taxes to the US government as its money was being laundered. "That same government is spending those same millions to put me out of business."

It did seem a little ironic to Duncan that the drug dealers were funding the war on drugs. He found a considerable amount of humor in the symbiotic relationship that existed between the syndicate and the federal agencies that sought to shut it down.

CHAPTER 35

ONLY A HANDFUL of people in the syndicate knew who was really running the show.

In *The Godfather*, the layers of people who stood between the lowly drug pusher on the street and the bosses of the crime families were called buffers. The modern criminal syndicate was nothing *but* buffers.

Players were transacting multimillion-dollar deals having never even met one another. To avoid detection, there were no contracts, invoices, or written documents of any kind. The drug trade is a cash-and-carry type of business on the street level. But on the high end, where multimillion-dollar agreements are made, the players depended on each other's reputations to guarantee payment. Millions of dollars' worth of drugs were shipped every day on the promise of payment. If a company employed such practices in the legitimate business world, it would not be in business very long.

Despite the large sums of cash involved, very few people ever tried to rip off the syndicate. The rules were simple: you cheat the syndicate, and you die. And on the high end, it was not just your life on the line; your wife, your children, your in-laws, and your dog were all fair game.

While the police might spend a disproportionate amount of money attempting to solve murder cases, the syndicate had an endless budget to commit murder. The syndicate played by its own set of rules, and woe be upon the fool who broke them.

CHAPTER 36

YEARS EARLIER DUNCAN had been wrong, when he had described Mr. Bartelli as a killer. He was not a killer. In fact, but for very rare exceptions, he never even *ordered* anyone to be killed. In almost every situation, the enforcement of the fuck-with-the-syndicate-and-die rule was farmed out to independent contractors who had no connection to the syndicate. These independent contractors were murderers for hire and provided the service known as "wet work."

Whenever possible—and it was almost always possible—the independent contractors didn't even know who had contracted the hit. The process was simple. Money and a name were provided, and the contractor took care of the rest.

To the untrained mind, one might think that the syndicate had found the way to commit the perfect murder. With no connection to the murderer, there was no way to track the murder back to the syndicate. But in real terms, the syndicate was no closer to committing the perfect murder than was Duncan. Based on his knowledge of how murders were contracted, he saw little need to spend much time or energy examining how the murders were actually committed.

He knew that once a hit was contracted out, the person accepting the contract was nothing more than a clearinghouse for that murder contract. The contract was frequently jobbed out to another level of subcontractors, with the original contractor retaining a piece of the action when the job was done. It was not uncommon for a contract to change hands several times before it landed in the hands of the person who would actually perform the hit.

Once employed, the prospective murderer was given a small amount of cash up front, the name of the victim, and a "cold piece" (an unregistered gun with the serial numbers removed). After that, the murderer was on his own.

The subcontractors' recruiting methods were simple. They would hang out where people have lost hope—where poverty, drugs, and alcohol motivated people to commit unconscionable acts. Ex-cons or gang members were their dregs of choice. Among these societal castaways there were always those willing to risk the little they had in the hopes of making enough money to change their lives—or maybe just buy their next high.

By the time the murder was committed, the murderer had no connection with either the syndicate or even the original contractor. Therefore, even if they were caught—and they almost always were—the murderers had no idea who hired them or why. Frequently, gang allegiances prevented them from implicating anyone else.

In the final analysis, Duncan decided neither the syndicate nor those who contracted its wet work were even *trying* to commit the perfect murder. Quite the opposite, in fact: they didn't care if the murderer got caught.

To Duncan's mind, the murders lacked the purity of pulling the trigger or embedding the knife. It was the one-on-one nature of the crime that made it *your* crime.

Hell, it's like hiring Jack Nicklaus to play in a golf tournament for you, he thought. *Sure, you were likely to win. But where's the sport in that?*

CHAPTER 37

DUNCAN HAD BEEN responsible for handling the legal arm of the syndicate for over two years when, one fiery summer day in June, he was returning from Texas after handling an arraignment hearing. The weather had been extremely hot, and he was just starting to cool down as he reclined in his first-class seat. He was hoping to catch a few hours of sleep, but his head instantly filled with charts, graphs, and case files, all the information and statistics he had been compiling over the years.

It was getting harder and harder for him to keep the thousands of cases from flooding, uninvited, into his head.

Just as he had about pushed the last of it from his mind, he felt a tap on his shoulder, arresting him from the brink of sleep. Startled, his entire body stiffened slightly, and his eyes popped open.

"I'm sorry to disturb you," said the sixtyish-looking woman in the seat behind him, "but I know you."

His face had been on the front page of every paper in the country at one time or another, so it was no surprise to him that she might have seen him before. He didn't recognize her, at least not at first.

"I'm Barbara Page. You represented my son almost five years ago."

It came back to Duncan almost immediately. Her son, David, had been a troubled young man. He had gotten into more than his share of trouble with the law. He was one of those rich-and-famous children who lived to punish their parents for giving them too much, for being too generous.

David had graduated to real crime as an adult. After being arrested for armed robbery he ended up in Duncan's office. In one of his earlier strokes of genius, Duncan had been able to get David assigned to a halfway house for six months and three years' probation.

The seat beside Duncan was empty. Mrs. Page, as if she'd been invited by his recognition of her, moved forward to sit beside him. He really did not mind. He was awake now, and there were still several hours to kill before they touched down in Los Angeles.

"So how is David?" Duncan asked.

She'd been looking directly at Duncan, but her eyes turned to the floor, and she began to shake her head slowly. "I'm afraid he is no longer with us."

He assumed that she meant he was dead, but she could have just as easily meant that he moved away or was in jail. Just to make sure, he said, "Excuse me?"

"Yes, he was murdered."

In an almost transparent attempt to appear emotionally moved, he replied, "I'm sorry to hear that. He was a good son." In fact, Duncan could not have cared less, and he knew that David had been a horrible son.

Not detecting his lack of sincerity, she looked up and gave Duncan a sorrowful smile. "Thank you for your kind words, but we both know he was bad. But he tried. God knows he tried to change."

Mrs. Page proceeded to tell him the story of her son's passing. He had been shot to death outside a bowling alley. Listening intently, he took pleasure in the fact that she'd chosen to talk about his favorite topic: murder. He seldom had the opportunity to discuss a murder from the perspective of the victim's family.

When she'd finished telling her story, she took out a tissue and wiped away the solitary tear that had formed in the corner of her eye. It had been years since his death, and she was running out of tears to cry over her son. By the end of her story, it appeared to Duncan that a burden had actually been lifted by her son's passing. But she could not bring herself to express that emotion.

From his perspective, she'd left the most important part of the story out. *Was the killer apprehended?*

Seeing that she'd emotionally drained herself in the telling of the story, he hesitated for a moment to allow her the opportunity to regain her composure, all the time hoping that she would fill in the blank without being asked. It was clear that she hadn't spoken in such detail about her son's passing for some time. She was awash with emotion and appeared too distraught to continue—at least not without a little prodding.

His curiosity finally overcame his consideration for her feelings. Besides, she'd awakened him from a much-needed nap.

He turned to her and asked in his sweetest southern tone, "Did they catch your son's murderer?"

The question came out much more direct and curt than he had intended. He had become so anxious to hear the answer, he really did not consider how he might pose the question.

Mrs. Page forced a cooperative smile to her face. "No."

For a moment he thought that he was going to have to be even more direct in his questioning, but after a moment of contemplation she continued. "That was the strange thing about David's death. With all the trouble he had caused during his lifetime, and with all the pain he had caused, it finally looked like he was getting his life back on the right track. He had been drug-free and alcohol-free for six months. He had stopped hanging around with the people he considered bad influences. On the day he was killed he had gone to the bowling alley to relax and have a little fun. As David was leaving, a car drove by, and he was shot in the face. The police think that he was mistaken for someone else, maybe a gang member. He was just in the wrong place at the wrong time. I guess that's the way it is with random acts of violence. No one knows why they happen, not even the police."

In that moment, a light went on over Duncan's head. *Random acts, of course. That's the answer, that's the key.*

He was so excited that he leaned sideways toward Mrs. Page and almost kissed her. Instead, at the last moment he slid his head beside hers and gave her a brief hug. Such emotional displays were uncommon for him, and he quickly released his awkward hold on her and sat up straight in his chair.

Random victims, random places. It makes perfect sense. That is the key to the perfect murder.

CHAPTER 38

DUNCAN'S EXCITEMENT WAS palpable. He impatiently counted the minutes until his plane landed. Duncan's chauffeur, Benton, was waiting at the gate when his plane arrived at Los Angeles International Airport.

Benton was an English gentleman in his late forties. His résumé included the distinction of having had been previously employed by a distant relation of the royal family of England. He had been recommended to Duncan by one of the partners at his firm. While Benton had an impressive pedigree and the recommendation of a respected colleague, in truth, Duncan hired him because he liked to hear him speak in his highbrow British accent. Benton reminded him of Mr. Fender, his former guardian. Mr. Fender had left his employ shortly after Duncan graduated Cambridge. Mr. Fender decided to remain in England rather than return to the States. It was only then that Duncan realized how much he'd enjoyed Mr. Fender's companionship.

If he was being honest—although he would have never admitted it, not even to himself—what he really liked the most was that Benton looked like the chauffeur of someone of importance and prominence.

The airplane had taxied to the gate about ten minutes behind schedule. Benton watched as he made his way down the exit ramp and entered the airport terminal. Duncan was so distracted that he didn't even acknowledge Benton.

It was part of Benton's job to recognize Duncan's moods and facial expressions. It was clear that something was weighing heavy on Duncan's mind. To avoid interrupting his train of thought, and without so much as a "Good day, sir," he took the carry-on bag and briefcase out of Duncan's hands, and the two men moved through the airport terminal.

As was frequently the case, Duncan had traveled light. Bypassing baggage claim, they proceeded directly to the parking structure. He was so anxious to get back to his home and private sanctum that he found himself jogging through the airport lobby. It was all Benton could do just to keep up with him as they sped through the airport lobby and out to the parking lot. It must have been a comical sight, Duncan in the lead, now almost at a full run, with Benton, who didn't even know how to *talk* fast, much less run, hot on his heels, struggling to look dignified while the bags he held swung wildly from side to side.

He was sitting in the limousine before he even acknowledged Benton's presence. The sweat pouring down Benton's forehead and his labored breathing went unnoticed. "Home please, and close the screen."

Those were the only words he said to Benton until they reached his Beverly Hills home almost an hour later.

Not having taken any notes while he was talking to Mrs. Page during the flight, once in the limo he took a notepad out of his briefcase and began to furiously write down his thoughts and questions.

The reason he could not find the answers he had been seeking for so long began to expose itself. The mistakes he had made were in his logic, not his analysis. He had fallen into the trap of addressing the problem in conventional ways.

This riddle required unconventional thinking, and he began to feel very average for not having considered such an alternative analysis earlier. He hated feeling average. He was smarter than most people, and he knew it. The thought of being or acting average was as distasteful as any feeling he could imagine.

His failure to think "outside the box" reminded him of a story that a client had told him years earlier. The client owned and operated a string of movie theaters located in small towns in Michigan, Vermont, New Hampshire, and Maine. The client would go into small towns that either didn't have a movie theater or had only a one- or two-screen facility. If the population density supported it, he would build a six-screen or larger theater and run the smaller operations out of business.

The client had been considering an abandoned supermarket for conversion into a movie theater in a small town in Michigan. However, the architect he employed to design the project concluded that the ceiling in the market was too low to accommodate the large movie screens and elevated seating. The cost of removing the roof and increasing the height of the building would have exceeded the project's budget.

Because the project showed great profit potential, the client flew to Michigan to meet with his architect. After walking through the project site for less than ten minutes, he turned to his architect and promptly fired him.

A new architect was employed, and the theater opened for business six months later. As it turned, out the question wasn't how much it would cost to raise the roof. Rather, it was how much it would cost to lower the floor.

The moral of the story was simple. Some problems just require you to think outside the box. It was time for Duncan to do just that.

CHAPTER 39

I T WAS ALMOST eight thirty that evening when Duncan closed the door of his study behind him and began to rummage through the towering piles of charts and files. With each chart and file he reviewed, the common theme became clearer.

In each case, the criminal had an intended victim or was in the process of committing a specific crime at a specific location. In almost every case the criminal had a relationship or connection with either the victim or the location where the murder took place. In case after case, the ties between the crime and the criminal would ensnare the criminal like a fly stuck in the silky strands of a spider web.

Continuing to read and analyze files into the early hours of the morning, Duncan began to see so clearly what only the day before had been invisible to him. The one element that was missing in every case was the element of randomness.

While it may have appeared that serial killers were killing at random, the case files made it clear that there were always clues that tied the killings together and eventually back to the perpetrator. Even the most elusive serial killers targeted a specific type of victim, be they prostitutes, homosexuals, elderly, or children.

Duncan began to reorganize the cases and review them in groups. The group of cases that involved criminals who select a specific victim proved to be the easiest for the authorities to solve. He discovered that, as an almost universal rule, when the killer selected a specific victim, the killer was connected in obvious ways, such as family, friendship, or romantic involvement.

For reasons that strained logic or reason, people seemed to believe they could get away with murdering someone they were close to. But only rarely did this type of killer evade justice for very long.

Similarly, he found that the groups of cases involving the murder of one's enemies were also expeditiously resolved. In most cases, the bad blood between the killer and victim was known to third parties who provided information to the police, resulting in the killer's arrest.

Most interesting to Duncan were the smaller number of cases involving serial killers. They were without doubt the most difficult cases for authorities to crack.

For the most part, serial killers fell into one of two categories. The first group included those who murdered random victims but used a specific method of committing the murder, such as only using guns, knives, or strangulation. The second group included those who killed victims of a particular race, sex, age, or other identifiable characteristic.

It was as if they were leaving a calling card behind. As if they wanted to get caught. And just like in all the other types of cases, the clues they left behind would eventually come back to haunt them.

While it was considerably more complicated to solve cases involving serial killers—particularly when only the type of victim is selected—the files revealed that they too were virtually always brought to justice.

Adding to the likelihood of apprehension was the fact that the federal government frequently provided local authorities with support in serial murder cases. Unlike the state agencies, the federal agencies had nearly limitless resources to track down serial killers. Their substantial assets and considerable expertise made evasion almost impossible.

If the cases told him anything, they told him that the last thing a killer wanted was the federal government pursuing him.

There was another group of cases where the murders occurred during the commission of an unrelated crime, such as murders committed spontaneously during a burglary, robbery, or rape. While this type of killing frequently involved a random victim, the criminal's connection to the unrelated crime resulted in his apprehension and eventually to his conviction.

Duncan thought it strange how often the murderer helped the authorities solve the case. *Murderers as a group are not the sharpest tools in the shed.*

As if the clues they accidentally left behind weren't enough to get them convicted, murderers frequently took trophies from their victims. Sometimes the trophies were nothing more than a personal item, like a ring or a photograph. The more aggressive trophy hunters were known to take body parts.

He could not help but dwell on how often the killer played the biggest role in his or her own apprehension (he thought *him or her*, but he knew that the vast majority of murders involved male killers). The case files unmasked another truth—that while one aspect of the crime might be random, without eliminating *all* connections to the crime, the killers were destined to be caught.

Duncan had pored over these same files countless times, hours and hours of review and analysis, but never before had they been so revealing.

Random act! It must be a random act, random in every way. This thought played over and over in his head.

This epiphany disclosed one last truth—he no longer needed any of the files. They had provided him all the information they would ever divulge. All the mistakes, misjudgments, and lapses of judgment contained in the documents were already etched in his memory.

It may not have been in the forefront of his mind at the time, but somewhere in the shadowy recesses of his subconscious, he knew it was time to get rid of documents that might someday be used as evidence against him.

The sun was almost ready to crest the horizon when he closed and locked his study and headed up the circular staircase to his bedroom. Friday had turned into Saturday, and he was looking forward to sleeping the day away. The last thing he remembered before falling fast asleep was looking at the alarm clock: 4:28 a.m.

PART IV

THE MURDER OF
SANTINO BARTELLI

CHAPTER 40

AT 6:46 A.M. on Saturday, Duncan woke on the seventh ring of the telephone. He thought about not answering it until he saw the light flashing on his private line. Only Stella and Mr. Bartelli had the unlisted number.

Duncan was in the middle of a huge yawn as he picked up the phone. It was Mr. Bartelli, and something was definitely wrong. It sounded like he was crying, and there was the unmistakable sound of crisis in his voice. Duncan was still half-asleep. The idea that Mr. Bartelli would be crying made him question if he was dreaming the whole thing up.

"They killed my son; the bastards have killed my boy."

The news instantly woke Duncan up and sent him into attorney mode. "Don't say another word! I'll be there in five minutes. Until I get there, don't call anyone, don't talk to anyone. Do you understand what I'm telling you, sir?" Duncan did not want Mr. Bartelli to say anything in a state of anger over the telephone.

"I understand."

Duncan did not even take time to shower; he threw on yesterday's clothes and ran out the door at breakneck speed. Less than five minutes had passed since he hung up the telephone, and his black Cadillac Seville was already pulling up to the front gate of Mr. Bartelli's estate.

Duncan's mind was racing. *Who killed Santino? Why? Was Mr. Bartelli in personal danger?* There was increased security at the front gate, but he was immediately recognized, and the massive gate began to swing open.

The Cadillac sped up the driveway. Slamming the gearshift into park, Duncan swung open the door and was climbing out of the vehicle even before the vehicle had slid to a complete stop.

He raced toward the entry door and entered without knocking. He found Mr. Bartelli sitting in one of the large overstuffed chairs in his study. As Duncan entered the room, Mr. Bartelli rose from his seat, and the two men embraced. While there was much to say, the two men held the embrace in silence for several minutes.

What little Duncan knew of his father came from stories his mother would tell him as a boy. His father had been killed in an automobile accident when he was only three years old. His mother had never remarried.

Not having a father figure had made him generally uncomfortable expressing any emotions around other men. In fact, Duncan had never exchanged such an emotional moment with anyone.

For the first time in his life, he was experiencing a heartfelt connection with another person's grief and sorrow. No one had comforted Duncan when his mother was murdered. But during this unfamiliar embrace, in a strange but touching way, he was deriving as much solace as Mr. Bartelli.

He was so caught up in the moment that he felt a tear begin to swell in the corner of his eye. It was more emotion than he could handle. Patting Mr. Bartelli on the back, he pulled away.

"Please, let's sit down."

Nodding his head in agreement, Mr. Bartelli returned to the leather chair. Duncan pulled the ottoman close to where Mr. Bartelli was sitting and sat down. The men began to talk very quietly.

Whatever Duncan may have been feeling inside, he was first and foremost Mr. Bartelli's attorney. "I'm not comfortable talking here," Duncan said. "Perhaps we should go for a drive."

"My son is dead, and you want to play attorney? I have better electronic surveillance equipment than the goddamn FBI. I have the place swept for bugs every day. We're alone, completely alone."

"Sorry, sir. I only want to protect you. What happened?"

"I know. I know." Looking down at the floor, Mr. Bartelli began to tell of Santino's unspeakable demise.

Santino's body had been found aboard his forty-seven-foot yacht, the *Player*, earlier that morning at the Royal Marina and Private Yacht Club in San Diego, California.

Mr. Bartelli's associates controlled most of the unions that worked the waterfront in San Diego. Even in his badly beaten state, Santino was immediately recognized by a union worker, who then did what any good union employee would do. He called his union boss before calling the authorities.

The union boss called the local mob boss, Stan Gusman, who called Mr. Bartelli. Gusman made sure that no one called the police until he examined the crime scene and reported the bad news to Mr. Bartelli.

Santino had been beaten to death. Several of his fingers were missing, and all of his teeth had been knocked out. From the look of the body, Gusman deduced that Santino had been tortured for a long time before he was killed.

When the local police arrived on the scene, they too immediately recognized Santino. The decision was made to cordon off the crime-scene until the chief of police, Captain Bernard Shipman, arrived. No one was allowed within two hundred yards of Santino's body, and no statements were made to the press regarding the identity of the murder victim.

While in transit to the crime scene, Captain Shipman called several government officials and the FBI, seeking their input on how to handle the firestorm of media coverage that was sure to follow the release of the victim's identity.

The San Diego Police Department—as was true with most police departments in the country—had informants that leaked information to the press when big stories were about to break.

By the time Captain Shipman arrived at the crime scene, the front gates of the marina were already blocked by swarms of reporters. Much to his chagrin, the press seemed to know more about the case than he did.

The media had uncovered the fact that Santino was the murder victim, and that he had been badly beaten. As the patrol car carrying Captain Shipman rolled by the hordes of reporters, they pelted him with questions.

The police refused to release much detail about the murder to Mr. Bartelli. They wanted to be careful not to provide any information to him, or anyone else, that might compromise the investigation.

Despite the fact that there was no love lost between the police and Mr. Bartelli, the police were forced to extend him certain courtesies. To avoid an escalation of the media circus already at the marina, the police arranged to have Mr. Bartelli identify his son's body at the morgue. The police agreed to make the body available for identification at five o'clock that Saturday afternoon.

"Do you think this is syndicate business?" Duncan asked.

"It's too soon to tell. But anything's possible."

"I'm very concerned about your safety until we find out more about Santino's death. Have you arranged security for this afternoon?"

"I've already taken care of that. But I was hoping that you'd come with me to identify Santino."

Duncan considered it an honor that Mr. Bartelli would request his company during such a solemn and personal moment. "Certainly, anything I can do—just name it."

"That means more to me than I can tell ya."

Duncan nodded, acknowledging Mr. Bartelli's appreciation.

"Does anyone on the council know about this yet?" Duncan asked, referring to the governing board of the syndicate.

"Probably. The crews on the docks will have put out the word by now."

"I don't know how to say this without seeming insensitive, but perhaps you should contact some of the members yourself. Let them hear it from you."

"You're right, I don't want these sharks thinking there's blood in the water. I'll call everyone this afternoon."

That's an odd metaphor under the circumstances, Duncan thought.

"If I find out that any of them had a hand in this, I'm going to carve their hearts out with a dull fucking spoon."

Reaching over, Duncan placed his hand on Mr. Bartelli's shoulder. The grateful smile let Duncan know that he appreciated the gesture.

"When the time comes, I'll hold them down for you. But for now, we need to make sure that everyone on the council understands that you're on top of this. It's the wrong time to appear weak."

The two men sat and talked for hours. Mr. Bartelli's mood swung like a pendulum between sorrow and anger. Duncan let him vent his anger without interruption. After a long and rambling oration, he finally stopped talking and rested his forehead in his hands. Tears began to splatter on the tops of his black patent-leather shoes.

Sensing the time was right; Duncan put his lawyer's hat back on.

"I know it's hard, but Santino's death is going to bring with it a massive amount of publicity. It's important that you keep a low profile until things calm down."

Though Mr. Bartelli was listening intently, periodically his desire for vengeance would reach a new boiling point.

"I'm going to dedicate everything I have to finding and killing the sons of bitches who murdered my boy."

While Mr. Bartelli held Duncan in high esteem for his legal acumen, Mr. Bartelli had no idea that he was also talking to one of the country's foremost authorities on criminal behavior—the very man he would need to locate his son's killer.

CHAPTER 41

THE EYES OF every government agency that ever wanted Mr. Bartelli locked away would be focused on him now more than ever. They would expect him to seek revenge, and they would be looking to catch him in the act.

The syndicate would be watching him as well. The last thing they wanted was to have the FBI breathing down the neck of their leader. If he acted emotionally or irrationally, he could become a liability. And no one—not even Mr. Bartelli himself—wanted to become a liability to the syndicate.

It was a time for patience and reason, and Duncan was the only one in the room embodying either quality.

At ten thirty that Saturday morning the two men were still talking.

If Duncan had learned anything in the past four hours, it was that Mr. Bartelli was prepared to do anything to get his revenge. Duncan was sure that the minute they were done talking, Mr. Bartelli would use his influence and power to cast a wide and indiscriminate net to locate the murderer of his son.

He feared, and rightfully so, that Mr. Bartelli was going to allow anger to cloud his judgment. The hammer he intended to bring down on the murderer's head could easily fall on his own.

If I don't take control, things are going to get dangerously out of control, Duncan thought. "I can find your son's killer. I need for you to leave this matter in my hands. I promise you this: if I don't find the killer in thirty days, I'll support any action you choose to take. Just give me thirty days to take care of this matter for you."

The conviction behind his promise brought more tears to Mr. Bartelli's eyes. The room fell silent.

Two facts would have been known to a man in Mr. Bartelli's position of power. One, Duncan would have to exert a substantial amount of power and influence to obtain the information necessary to unmask the killer. And two, Duncan would have to violate the law, and the code of ethics governing attorney conduct.

Above all, Duncan was offering to place *everything* on the line for him. Even Mr. Bartelli must have been surprised by how casually Duncan had volunteered everything he owned, including his livelihood, to protect a grieving father from himself.

With all the emotional strength he had remaining, Mr. Bartelli forced a smile to his face, "Look, my boy. I appreciate what you're trying to do. But you're swimming with sharks now. The people we're looking for won't be wearing five-thousand-dollar suits or playing golf at the Riviera. Someone's going to have to get their hands very dirty chumming the water. No! This is not something you can do for me. This is something I've got to take care of myself."

"With all due respect, sir, this isn't about what I do, or even what *you* do. It's about what I *know*. Someday we can discuss *how* I know. But for now, let it be enough that *I know* how to catch the killer. You need to trust me on this. I'm already one step ahead of these assholes, and they don't even know it yet." Duncan replied with great self-assurance in his tone.

"I'm impressed by your confidence. But you can't possibly understand how precarious my situation is right now. If my son's death is related to my business, then I need to act quickly and decisively, or I'm a dead man. Even *you* wouldn't be safe."

He paused, giving Duncan the opportunity to reconsider his offer.

Duncan was just that much more emphatic. "Thirty days. Just give me thirty days."

Mr. Bartelli began stroking his chin with his right hand as he leaned back in his chair. "Maybe you're right. I'll put out some feelers, but I'll lay low for a while, a short while! You have one week from today, if you don't bring the murderer's balls to me on a silver platter by then...Well, then we do things my way, *capisce*?"

"Seven days!" Duncan exclaimed.

"Don't look at it as seven days. Think of it as the amount of time God took to create the heavens and the earth. Seven days. No more."

Duncan wanted to argue, but he was a good enough negotiator to know that Mr. Bartelli had given all he was prepared to give.

Duncan stood up as if to leave.

"Stay," Mr. Bartelli offered. "Have lunch with me. It'll take at least two hours to drive to San Diego, so we don't need to leave for the coroner's office until three."

"I need to pick up some documents from home, take a shower, and make a few phone calls before we leave, if I'm going to stay on God's pace," Duncan said, fighting back a smile. "I don't want any of the calls to be traced back to your house. I'll be back in a few hours."

The two men embraced again, and Duncan left. He drove home and began the daunting task of identifying Santino's killer. With only seven days, he couldn't waste time.

CHAPTER 42

MOST INFLUENTIAL PEOPLE don't truly realize just how powerful they truly are. Under normal circumstances, Duncan didn't have that problem. He was powerful, and he knew it. But today, even Duncan was surprised by the breadth of his influence.

It was early afternoon Saturday, and most state and city employees were off through the weekend. But Duncan and his firm were well connected. He called several well-placed city employees at home to seek their help.

Before returning to pick up Mr. Bartelli, Duncan called Bart Perkins, a midlevel paper pusher in police headquarters.

"Bart. How you doing?"

"I know why you're calling. Looks like your boy ain't getting away with murder after all."

In order to befriend people like Bart, Duncan was compelled to sink to their level. "Yeah, another pillar of the community bites the dust."

"You need crime scene reports? Right?"

"Exactly. And I need them faxed to me right away."

"Are you kidding? I can get them, but it's going to take a few days. This place is crawling with brass."

"No good. I need them now."

After a moment, Duncan said, "Are you there?"

"Yeah, I'm here. I'll get them, but it's going to cost ya."

"How does double sound?"

"Not as good as triple!"

"Triple it is, then. But that includes everything. Any new stuff comes in, I expect to see it immediately."

"You got it. It will take a few hours."

"Thanks, Bart. Say hi to your gorgeous wife and kids."

In truth, Duncan found Bart's wife to be brutally unattractive, but it was all part of the game.

Several other calls yielded a promise to fax a copy of the evidence logs (which described in detail the evidence that was found at the crime scene). This information would be logged as soon as the officers returned to the station later that afternoon. Duncan's contacts assured him that he would receive copies as soon as the officer reports were filed.

His last call before leaving was to David Schwartz, the San Diego County coroner.

"David, it's been a while. How's the family?"

"Hey, it's good to hear your voice, too. Although I must confess that I expected this call several hours ago."

"To be honest, it took me a while to find your home number," Duncan replied.

"Well you're the only one in the state who is having trouble finding me, because my phone has been ringing off the hook."

"I'll bet."

"Just between us, do they know who killed him?"

"Not yet, unless the cops are holding that information back."

"Well if they were, I'm sure your client, with his connections, would know about it before I would," David said with a chuckle in his voice.

"You're probably right."

"Okay, enough of the small talk. I know you called me for a favor, so go ahead and ask, but I got to tell you, there isn't much I can do for you on this one."

"If it's okay with you, I'd rather talk in person."

"Now I know for sure I can't help you. But it will be nice to spend some time with an old friend. When and where?"

David hadn't planned to be at the morgue for the identification. However, he agreed to be there that afternoon.

Both Duncan and Mr. Bartelli were lucky that the body hadn't been found in Los Angeles. They would have received no cooperation from the LA coroner's office after the thrashing Duncan put on them during Santino's murder trial. The time that had passed since Santino's acquittal—over two years—hadn't diminished the coroner's seething hatred for Duncan.

Fortunately, the body was found in San Diego, and Schwartz was, as luck would have it, a personal friend of Duncan's.

They'd been introduced to each other years earlier at some swank social gathering. They quickly discovered that they shared a mutual compulsion for excellence that which made them instant best friends. While they did not socialize often, they had kept in touch and held each other in high regard.

Duncan considered him a friend, and he hoped that Schwartz felt the same, because now he needed to exploit that friendship.

As a rule, Duncan rarely—to the point that saying never would not be grossly inaccurate—called in favors from his many powerful acquaintances. He didn't mind paying off the working poor, but rich people wanted more than money, they wanted you to be in their debt. Learning to survive on his superior intellect and talent, he seldom saw the need to place himself in a position where he would be in anyone's debt.

He was about to make a whole series of exceptions to that rule.

David Schwartz, though a friend, was not just going to let him waltz into the coroner's office and examine whatever evidence he wanted. At least not for free. Schwartz was no fool, and he would know the value of the information. He would also know that Mr. Bartelli could afford to pay for it. *Yes, it's going to cost a pretty penny to get David's cooperation*, Duncan thought.

Even as Duncan was talking on the telephone, he was reviewing some of his files and charts. These particular files were murder cases involving torture or unusual levels of brutality. Over the years he had carefully dissected these files, preparing psychological profiles of the murderers. These profiles would help him begin his search.

After completing his calls, he grabbed the files, a camera, and several rolls of film, and raced out the door. Benton drove Duncan back to Mr. Bartelli's residence in the limo, allowing him a few extra minutes to read. With the information contained in his files, together with the limited information he derived from Mr. Bartelli, Duncan began formulating a profile of the killer.

Key in his mind was the constant theme in such murders—hatred. In almost every case involving torture, the murderer hated the victim.

Mr. Bartelli agreed to let Benton drive them to the morgue. One of Mr. Bartelli's bodyguards sat in the front seat with Benton. There were two escort vehicles (each containing two bodyguards), one leading the way and the second protecting their rear. The three vehicles caravanned their way down the 405 freeway toward San Diego.

"Benton, close the screen. We need some privacy."

"Did you call the members of the board?"

"Most of them," Mr. Bartelli replied.

"How did they react to the news?"

"Some already knew. The others sounded shocked. All of them seemed a little afraid of what I might do."

"Did you get the sense that they might be involved?"

"No. But I put some feelers out. I will know more in a couple of days."

"We need to talk about Santino. Do you mind answering a few questions?"

"I'm not a fucking daisy. Just ask," Mr. Bartelli snapped at hearing the coddling tone of Duncan's voice.

"I don't know how involved you were in Santino's personal life. But is there anyone who stands out in your mind, someone who hated him?"

Mr. Bartelli smiled a sad smile. "We lived in different worlds. I loved Santino. But he was a world-class prick. Most everyone was afraid of him or hated him or both."

"This is more than hate or fear. There was passion here. Whoever did this enjoyed it."

"I'm afraid I won't be of much help to you. I just don't know."

"Was he a big drinker, maybe do lots of drugs?"

"Some of both I'm sure, but nothing too crazy. He was hooked on girls. He loved the girls. He always had lots of girls, ever since he was in junior high."

Duncan noticed Mr. Bartelli suddenly looked uncomfortable with the question.

"I know it's hard to talk about, but what happened to the Lopez girl—could there have been others?"

"Hard to talk about? You keep treating me like a little girl, and I'll throw your ass out of this car, right here in the middle of the fucking freeway. No. Not like that. But he'd been in trouble before."

"What kind of trouble?" Duncan asked, but he was thinking. *How can he be just telling me this? What if this had come up during Santino's trial?"*

"Just some things with girls."

"I'm sorry, but if you don't want to be treated like a little girl, then answer like a man. What kind of things?"

If Duncan was trying to be funny, Mr. Bartelli was not amused. "You got brass balls, kid, but talk to me like that again, and I will cut them off. You hear what I am telling you?"

Mr. Bartelli did not wait for a response from Duncan before continuing, "Like S and M. He went too far a couple of times. I had to get him out of trouble."

"What did he do to the girls?"

Finally, Mr. Bartelli surrendered. "It was pretty sick shit, what he did to those girls. He would hurt them; hurt them bad. I don't understand it. It was just the way he was."

Mr. Bartelli was now visibly uncomfortable discussing the issue, and it showed on his face. Duncan couldn't tell if the discomfort was because of the personal nature of the information, or because of his disgust at his son's vile behavior.

"Did you meet any of these girls?"

"Maybe, I don't remember. But they weren't the kind of girls you bring home to meet your dad. He knew better than that."

The details Mr. Bartelli disclosed of his son's strange sexual desires painted a portrait of a deeply troubled young man. One needed to look no further than the murder of Jessica Lopez to see just how troubled Santino was. Mr. Bartelli had used his power and influence—and a good deal of money—to extricate his son from troubles related to his deviant excesses.

"Duncan. Enough for right now. You're starting to piss me off. Let's talk about this another time."

"Sure. I understand."

"You couldn't possibly understand." Mr. Bartelli was right. No one could understand, not Duncan, not anyone, the depth of his sorrow, and the height of his disappointment in Santino.

During the rest of the drive, he brought Mr. Bartelli up to speed on some of his preliminary investigation efforts.

"The coroner's name is David Schwartz. We're pretty good friends."

Mr. Bartelli was still a little irritated. "Good. If I ever need an autopsy, you can get me a deal."

"Well, sir, you need one right now."

"What the fuck does that mean?"

"I mean that I believe that David can help us find Santino's murderer."

"What can David tell us that we're not going to see for ourselves in about an hour?"

"A great deal, sir. The autopsy will tell us a lot about the killer."

"Like what?"

"God, where to start? Is the killer right-handed, was there more than one murderer, what type of weapons were used? From the depth of the wounds, we can even get an idea of the physical characteristics of the killer. There could be blood and fluid evidence. It's a long list, sir."

"Stop saying 'sir.' You do that when you think I'm mad at you. I'm not mad. I just have a lot on my plate right now," Mr. Bartelli said as he stared out the window.

"I know, sir," Duncan said, emphasizing the word out of respect, rather than sarcasm, and Mr. Bartelli instinctively knew it.

It could have gone without saying that Duncan had an unlimited budget to acquire any information he needed, but Mr. Bartelli said it anyway. "I'm sold. Don't tell me what it costs; just get this guy on our team."

"I also talked to some of my friends downtown. I hope to have the police reports and evidence logs by the time we get back to LA."

"I'm impressed, and I don't impress easily."

Duncan smiled. "Yeah, tell me about it."

For any average attorney, obtaining access to such evidence—especially in a high-profile case—would have been impossible. But he was no average attorney.

Their limousine pulled up in front of the coroner's office fifteen minutes before the scheduled 5:00 p.m. meeting, stopping in the "No Parking Anytime" zone directly in front of the main entrance.

While the press *had* gotten wind of Santino's murder, they had focused on the crime scene. Only a handful of reporters had the foresight to stake out the coroner's office.

Duncan called ahead from the car to make sure that David knew they would be arriving a few minutes early. Surrounded by bodyguards, Duncan and Mr. Bartelli were escorted into the building. Two of Mr. Bartelli's bodyguards waited just inside the large glass doors of the office. The remaining three bodyguards waited in a small lobby near the door of the viewing room.

Santino's body was lying on a gurney draped with an aqua-blue sheet. Both Duncan and Mr. Bartelli were surprised when David Schwartz entered the room with a police lieutenant in tow. Duncan was a little disappointed in himself that he hadn't prepared Mr. Bartelli for the near certainty that the police would be present during the viewing.

Schwartz shook hands with both Duncan and Mr. Bartelli. He mumbled a few words of condolence before getting down to business. "Be prepared. The body is disfigured, bruised, and swollen." David immediately pulled back the sheet.

It had been many years since Mr. Bartelli had seen a body beaten this badly. His informant's description didn't even begin to describe the injuries inflicted.

The police officer asked, "Is this your son, Mr. Bartelli?"

Mr. Bartelli did not respond.

"Yes, this is Santino Bartelli," Duncan replied.

"As you can see, there is quite a bit of swelling over the entire body. Virtually every bone is broken. Quite extraordinary, actually. We rarely see these kind of injuries outside of a plane crash or some other horrific accident."

David was not known for his bedside manner. However, his insensitivity made even Duncan cringe. Duncan reached out and put his hand on David's shoulder. "That will do."

Santino's skull had been cracked open like a ripe summer watermelon. His face was so swollen that it was barely recognizable—even by his own father. The little finger on his left hand was missing, as was part of his right thumb and right ear.

From the battered remains, it was clear that the murderer had gone to great lengths to inflict pain. He wanted him to suffer.

Mr. Bartelli showed no emotion at the sight of his son's battered body. After a moment he spoke. "That's my son, God rest his soul." Mr. Bartelli immediately turned to exit the viewing room. Duncan was in awe of his strength.

As Mr. Bartelli was leaving the viewing room, the police officer approached him. "Mr. Bartelli. I am Lieutenant Green of the San Diego PD. Duncan always found it odd that police officers never volunteered their first names. "May I ask you a few questions?"

Duncan was miffed that the lieutenant hadn't directed his inquiry to him, so he politely but firmly interjected, "No. My client will not be answering any questions today."

"If he doesn't want to talk here, perhaps we should discuss this further at the station."

Duncan, neither intimidated nor amused, went completely out of character. "Sure. He can tell you to eat shit here *or* at the station, if you prefer. Give me just a minute to contact the press so that he's quoted accurately."

Lieutenant Green instantly realized that he was out of his depth. "Perhaps another time, then? My deepest condolences, Mr. Bartelli. Please excuse me; I should get back to the station."

With his boss safely in the hands of the three bodyguards, Duncan followed David back to his private office. He was confident David was a good enough friend that—even if he wasn't prepared to cooperate—he wouldn't betray him just for asking, so he jumped right in the deep end of the pool.

"I'm asking for your help on this one."

"I told you on the telephone. I'm not sure there is much I can do, but I'll do what I can," David replied.

"Good. What I need is access to all the evidence and autopsy reports."

Both men knew full well that if anyone ever discovered David had allowed Duncan such early access, it would mean David's job, and possibly criminal charges.

"You've been drinking, right? No, you stopped and had a lobotomy on the way over here. Are you nuts?"

"Calm down my friend. I'm n—"

"You fucking calm down! It's not your ass on the line. Besides, where the hell do you get off asking me to break the law?"

"Look, David, we're just talking here. We are going to see all this stuff eventually anyway, we just want it first. So please let me finish."

David, though visibly irritated, listened to what his friend was selling.

"David, I'm not asking you to take this risk for free. There's money. Lots and lots of money."

Suddenly, David's concern for the sanctity of the law began to evaporate. "How much money?"

"What's it going to take?"

"Don't fucking play attorney with me, this is your game. How much?"

"How much money did you make last year?"

"Sixty-eight, give or take."

"Let's round it up to seventy. Cash?"

That was much more than he thought Duncan was going to offer, but he tried not to look excited. "Is that your opening bid?"

"Now who's being a dick? Take the money before I change my mind."

Duncan would have paid much more. Had David taken two minutes, before jumping at the offer, to think about why Duncan wanted the information so quickly, he would have realized just how valuable the information was. Duncan was right; he was going to see all this information eventually anyway. Therefore, there was only one reason to want to see it first; he wanted to find the killer before the police did.

Before their meeting ended, Duncan got a private viewing of the body, together with the promise of complete access to all the evidence and autopsy reports.

Friendship may have opened the door, but money closed the deal. It turned out to be a purely financial arrangement. In truth, Duncan preferred it that way.

David planned on starting the autopsy on Sunday in hopes of avoiding the publicity that would surely arrive with the new work week. Starting on Sunday had the additional advantage of making it easier to get Duncan into the autopsy undetected.

The two men devised a plan to slip Duncan into the office through a back door accessible only through an underground parking garage. The entrance was occasionally used by celebrities and other high-profile individuals to bypass the press—a surprising number of celebrities have run-ins with death in California. Though they planned on meeting the very next day, Duncan insisted on taking a few photos of Santino's body before he left.

When Duncan, Mr. Bartelli, and their entourage exited the coroner's office at approximately 5:40 p.m., the steps were crowded with reporters from every major network. Trucks and vans bearing the logos of both local and national media stations lined the street.

As the bodyguards wedged out a passage through the wall of reporters, Duncan kept repeating "No comment" until the limo door closed behind him. Some of the news vans followed the caravan, only giving up the pursuit when it was clear that the vehicles were heading back to Los Angeles.

Once inside the limo, the effect of seeing his disfigured son finally melted Mr. Bartelli's stoic mask. He broke into tears of sorrow, anger, and frustration.

Through the tears, he said in a maniacal voice, "I am going to make them pay. My hand to God, I am going to make them pay."

As the limo drove on, he began to regain his composure. "What did he say?"

"David's in. I will meet him back here tomorrow."

The news seemed to lift his spirits. "Good, what did it cost me?"

"I thought you told me not to tell you."

"Where's my fucking gun?" Duncan laughed a nervous laughter, not completely sure Mr. Bartelli was kidding. "Seventy."

"Seventy thousand?! Damn, you may be a great litigator, but you suck as a negotiator."

"No. No. No. That seventy is on you."

"How's that?"

"Seven days? Hell, you're lucky it didn't cost three times that much."

CHAPTER 43

AFTER DROPPING OFF Mr. Bartelli, Duncan had Benton drive him home. The faxes he had been promised were lying in a large pile on the floor, still connected to the fax machine, like the tail of a kite. He hadn't expected such a large fax, but he was glad he remembered to replace the roll of fax paper before he left. Locking the door to the study behind him, he got down to the daunting task of identifying Santino's killer.

He had taken literally thousands of photographs of crime scenes over the years. By necessity, more than desire, he had formed a strong interest in photography. Because there were frequently pictures that he didn't want viewed by anyone but himself, he had a room off the library converted into his own private darkroom.

Under the glow of a single red light, he developed the photographs he had taken at the coroner's office. Hanging the photos one by one on little clips that dangled down from long lines that stretched the length of the darkroom he waited, not so patiently, for them to dry. Having exhausted what little patience he possessed, he pulled down the still damp photos, careful not to let them stick to each other, and slipped back into the library where he nestled down into his leather chair.

He sat at his desk and examined each photograph for clues. Minutes turned into hours as he hunched over his desk, studying the pictures and reviewing the police reports until just after one o'clock in the morning.

Still tired from his lack of sleep the night before, with his six thirty meeting in San Diego drawing ever closer, he reluctantly retired to his bedroom. Less than three hours later, he was showered, shaved, and ready to leave.

Grabbing his knapsack full of cameras and film, he took one last sip of coffee and was out the door at five o'clock.

The hordes of reporters had long since gone, and a lone media van stood sentry in front of the morgue. At six thirty he slipped unnoticed into the building through the parking garage. Ten minutes later he was inside the examination room.

"Duncan. I'm going to be recording much of this, so you can't make a sound during the autopsy. Don't talk, cough, sneeze, don't even fart."

"They can identify the 'farter' from the sound?" Duncan mused out loud.

By the look on David's face, Duncan could see that he was not amused and more than a little nervous.

"Got it."

The autopsy was a slow and laborious procedure, but Duncan was nevertheless completely fascinated by the process.

David began the autopsy of Santino's body. Before making a cut, David made a thorough examination of the entire body, starting at the tips of the toes working his way up to the hair on Santino's head.

He pulled down the microphone, which was suspended from a cable above the table. First lifting Santino's right foot and then his left, he said, "There is visible bruising and swelling beginning at the tips of the distal and middle phalanges extending the entire length of both feet."

Squeezing the skin, as he worked his way along the feet and up the legs, he continued, "There appear to be multiple fractures of each of the proximal phalanges and metatarsal bones in both the right and left foot, the toenails are missing on all but the large toe on the right foot. The calcaneus is shattered on the left foot...3 cm stab wound...fractured tibia...4 cm stab wound...multiple fractures along fibulas...slashing wound...5 cm severing patellar ligament...crushed patella...femur multiple fractures...7 cm stab wound...dislocated head of femur...broken pubis and ilium...fractured humerus...fractured clavicle...fractured...fractured...fractured..."

Three hours passed, and David hadn't made a single incision. He meticulously measured the length and depths of each cut, describing its precise location on the corpse.

"Stab wound, 6 cm deep, appears to have been made with a jagged-edged instrument, approximately four inches wide, wound not fatal...stab wound, 2 cm deep, appears to have been made with a dull instrument, approximately one inch wide, wound not fatal..."

All told, David described seventy-three knife wounds, caused by as many as fifteen different instruments.

David was very good at his job. His descriptions of the wounds, and his commentary on what types of weapons might have caused the injuries were extraordinarily helpful in assisting Duncan to understand precisely how Santino was murdered. The impressions David had regarding why certain wounds might have been inflicted also provided considerable insight into the motivations of the murderer or murderers.

Based on the varying depths of the wounds, David suspected that they might have been inflicted by individuals of different heights and strengths.

He concluded that some of the wounds were so shallow that they were probably inflicted by weaker blows—perhaps even by a female.

Duncan was also recording the autopsy. He wasn't sure if David would have consented, so he concealed his recorder in his jacket pocket. Several times during the autopsy he thought David heard the recorder click off when the tape was full. But David was so engrossed in his work that he never even noticed Duncan leave the room to insert new tapes.

Examination of Santino's clothes also proved extraordinarily valuable. Santino's clothes were covered with blood. As a result of the degree of violence involved in the murder, his clothes were ripped in many different places. David removed small portions of blood-soaked cloth to send out for analysis and typing. At the same time, he cut samples for Duncan to take with him for independent analysis. Duncan hoped that the samples would contain DNA from the murderer and would perhaps provide clues as to his identity.

He worked for hours, taking only small breaks to get a cup of coffee or to relieve himself. Lunch was a doughnut and more coffee. At four fifteen, David was ready to call it a day.

"There is a lot more to do, but I'm too tired to focus. I will come back tomorrow and finish up."

"I understand. It's a long process. I'll call you tomorrow."

"Sounds good."

"Anything I need to know before I get out of here?"

"There's one thing. You probably already knew this, but they kept this guy alive a long time. The blow that split his head open killed him. I'm pretty sure that many of his injuries came hours, maybe even days before he died. I'll know more when I get some of the labs back."

"Thanks, David. You do good work."

"That's why I get the big bucks."

"Oh no, I'm the reason you get them."

Both men laughed.

At four thirty, Duncan left with a doggy-bag of evidence, including hair samples, swatches of clothing, blood samples, and tissue samples retrieved from under Santino's fingernails.

Duncan had taken more than a hundred photographs of Santino's wounds. He also carried with him David's promise to provide any additional evidence discovered later, including the laboratory reports as they became available.

Duncan had no intention of waiting to get the evidence analyzed. However, it was Sunday, and every laboratory in the state was closed. He would have to pull some more strings to have a laboratory begin analyzing the evidence today.

In anticipation of the problem, he had called his secretary at home during a break in the autopsy. He had her drive to his office to locate Stephen Braumowitz's home number. Braumowitz owned one of the most respected private laboratories in the country.

Duncan, as well as other lawyers in his firm, had used the laboratory to analyze blood and tissue samples in many criminal cases over the years. Braumowitz did good work. But more important, he knew how to keep his mouth shut.

Duncan was not about to let a little thing like the laboratory being closed deter him. It was almost seven o'clock when he reached Braumowitz by telephone.

"Steve, I have a project I need your help with."

"Sure thing. I will be in my office first thing in the morning."

"No. I need to get started on this right away."

"It's Sunday, and it's seven o'clock."

"I own a watch and a calendar. Steve, I need you to get started tonight."

"Duncan, there's not much I can do without my staff."

"I understand. How long will it take you to get them in the lab?"

"You want me to get my employees out of bed and start tonight?" Braumowitz asked in disbelief.

"That is exactly what I want you to do," Duncan replied. "I'm sorry. I forgot to say the magic words. Money is no object."

Duncan now had Braumowitz's attention. "It's not that I don't trust you. But what does that mean?"

"Whatever your normal fee is, I want you to triple it. No, quadruple it. But I don't want your doors to close for even one second until I have every ounce of information that you can squeeze out of this evidence."

"I will head into the lab immediately. My staff will be ready when the samples get there." Stephen's cadence was almost military.

"One more thing—not a word of your work gets leaked to the street. Not a word! No one on your staff is to know where the samples came from, what case you are working on, or who you're working for."

"I take it that *I* don't want to know where these samples came from."

No answer was forthcoming. "See you in thirty." Stephen hung up the phone and headed for his lab.

Duncan also drove directly to the laboratory.

"Nice puppies," Duncan said as he laughed.

Stephen was still wearing slippers with stuffed puppy toys with long floppy ears attached to the front.

"Don't laugh. My little girl got these for me. It's a fashion statement. What you got for me?"

"Blood, hair, tissue, and cloth."

"What are you looking for?"

"Anything. Everything. Run every test you can think of."

"God bless you. My wife thanks you, my children thank you, my bank account thanks you."

"Very funny. Seriously. I want you to call me with every piece of evidence you extract from this stuff. I don't care how small. I want to know immediately."

"You'll be hearing from me a lot, then."

"Good."

After leaving the laboratory Duncan drove to a one-hour photo in Hollywood that he knew stayed open late. He was going to have to make good time to get in the door before it closed at nine.

The hundreds of photographs he had taken during the autopsy were far more than he was in the mood to develop in his small darkroom. Besides, time was of the essence; it would take far too long for him to develop them one at a time.

He had taken photographs to this particular photo shop before, and the pimply faced kid behind the counter recognized him immediately.

It was ten minutes until nine, and bold red lettering on a large sign put customers on notice that no film would be accepted for development within an hour of closing time.

"I'm sorry, Mr. Gabrelli, but we're closing in ten minutes. If you leave your film, I will get it done in the morning."

Duncan reached in his pocket and pulled out a hundred-dollar bill. The closing time magically changed to ten o'clock.

"Thanks Mr. Gabrelli, must be important."

Duncan did not respond.

"What's on these rolls anyway?"

Duncan looked at the name tag pinned to the kid's shirt. "It's Timmy, right?"

"Yes, sir."

"Timmy, you're right. It is very important. I can't let you see what's on this film."

Pointing at the machine behind the counter, he said, "Here's what we're going to do, Timmy. You put the film in there, and I will take it when it comes out there."

Forty-five minutes later, Duncan and his bag of photos were headed home.

CHAPTER 44

BACK IN HIS study, Duncan began to examine the tall stack of photographs.

The pictures depicted the savagery of the beating. *The murderer knew Santino, enough to hate him with a passion.* Duncan theorized that the police would assume the murder was mob-related. After all, it was the obvious explanation.

It just doesn't make any sense. He was more familiar with the inner workings of the syndicate than the police would ever be. *This is not how it would be done. It's just not how it would be done.* The key was Santino's stature, or lack thereof, in the syndicate.

Santino had the look of a mobster, and the press liked to portray him as an important figure in organized crime. But in reality, Santino had almost *no* part in running the syndicate. He was, as his father had once described him, a world-class prick. Not even his father considered him worthy of the respect due the syndicate's elite.

It was common knowledge that Santino had many enemies. A great many of those enemies would be standing in line to get their piece of him—if his dad's name were not Vincenzo Bartelli.

On a visceral level, that realization is what bothered Duncan. *No one in the syndicate would be stupid enough to go after Santino, precisely because he was the son of Vincenzo Bartelli.*

Equally disturbing was the fact that the murder had almost none of the indicia of a mob hit. *How can the cops be so smart and so stupid at the same time? They all must get their ideas about the mob from the movies.*

Duncan knew that when a player was taken out, the job was done by professionals, quick and neat. If the murderer thought Santino was a real player, the hit would have had an entirely different look; it would have been clean.

If no one in their right mind would have killed Santino, then that left open only one possibility, that some crazy son of a bitch killed him.

Duncan was aware that insanity might account for the severity of the beating, but the photographs taken at the morgue evidenced premeditation. The killer was methodical.

The torture was designed to inflict constant pain. The infliction of pain appeared to be in the forefront of the murderer's mind. Small cuts on Santino's back and chest weren't deep enough to cause any serious injury; they were intended to make him suffer. Deeper, jagged cuts on the buttocks were not, by themselves, life-threatening but were deeper than necessary if pain was the only goal.

Those cuts evidenced a desire for vengeance.

Santino's penis had been filleted and his testicles completely severed, which made Duncan believe that vengeance was sexually motivated.

As much as Duncan wanted to believe that Santino was the victim of some deranged murderer, his experience did not support that conclusion. He had read hundreds of police investigators' interviews of murderers, many of whom were criminally insane. The types of injuries found on Santino's body were simply not consistent with the attack of a crazy person.

There was an absolute method present in Santino's murderer's madness.

The more he let his mind expand beyond the obvious, the more the murder had the feel of a personal vendetta.

I don't know what this is yet, but one thing is sure: it wasn't random.

CHAPTER 45

MR. BARTELLI'S DISCLOSURES about his son's propensity for deviant sexual desires kept playing in Duncan's mind. The mutilation of Santino's genitals and buttocks was consistent with sexually motivated crimes.

Something in the pit of his stomach made him believe Santino's prurient behavior was connected to his murder. Duncan was heading in the right direction; he could feel it.

While thumbing through the photographs, a picture of Santino's left hand caught Duncan's attention. He was suddenly reminded of a conversation he had with Santino at the acquittal party.

It's missing.

At the party, he noticed that Santino was wearing a platinum-and-gold ring on the little finger of his left hand. On the face of the ring, in very small script, were two words. From where Duncan was seated, he couldn't make out the words.

Idle curiosity caused him to ask Santino about the inscription. Apparently the words were intentionally designed to be difficult to read.

Santino explained in a devilish tone, "It says, 'You're fucked.' And if you're close enough to read it, then you are!"

Santino took such a sadistic pleasure in answering, that Duncan realized that he'd answered the question before with the same stupid answer. The double entendre of sexuality and brutality was not lost on Duncan.

He remembered smiling so as not to offend Santino, but he immediately regretted asking the question and giving Santino the opportunity to say that idiotic line for the hundred-and-first time.

The murderer had taken more than just Santino's finger; he had also taken the ring.

The murderer took a trophy.

The clock on the mantel chimed midnight. His lack of sleep over the past three days had left his body exhausted and his mind muddled.

I need to get some sleep. I'll revisit this in the morning.

CHAPTER 46

I T WAS NOT until almost ten o'clock Monday morning that Duncan finally opened his eyes. He just lay still in bed for a few minutes, enjoying the comfort of his king-size bed and silk sheets, until his eyes caught the message light flashing on his answering machine. He'd never heard the telephone ring.

The message was from Braumowitz.

"Duncan, it's Stephen. We need to talk. Check your fax, I sent you over some of the preliminary test results. Give me a call at the lab."

Duncan went directly to the study, still in his robe and slippers, and began reading through the reports.

The tests revealed four different blood types on Santino's clothes. Even more interesting were the tests done on the strands of hair. The hair belonged to Santino and two others, one being a female.

Fucking unbelievable! He was killed by a woman. A woman did this to him? Duncan thought as he read the report.

While it seemed incomprehensible that Santino had been killed by a female, it was the first bit of evidence that made any sense.

"Good morning, Mr. Bartelli."

"Hey, Duncan. Good to hear your voice."

"I need to see you this morning."

"Sure. You can come now if you want."

"I need to put some notes together first. How does noon sound?"

"Good. Good. I'll have the chef make something special."

"See you soon."

He arrived at 11:58 and was escorted by one of Mr. Bartelli's housekeepers to a small balcony in the back of the mansion. Duncan had enjoyed meals with Mr. Bartelli on that same balcony many times over the last year.

Mr. Bartelli was sitting at an ornate wrought-iron, glass-topped table. It was set for lunch with bone china and Waterford crystal glasses and goblets. The solid-silver utensils sat atop frilly little, white napkins. In the center of the table sat a modest white vase supporting two orchids: one purple and one white. The color of the orchids perfectly matched the china pattern.

Someone had taken such great care in displaying the items on the table that Duncan was a little uncomfortable touching anything.

"You made it." He was so pleased to see Duncan step out onto the balcony that he jumped up and gave him a hug.

I'm going to have to get used to this. Duncan thought. But for now, such embraces still made Duncan feel uneasy.

"Sit down, sit down. I missed you these last two days. So, let me know. What have you been up to? What have you dug up?" Mr. Bartelli inquired with a tone that lacked expectation.

"Well, quite a bit, sir."

He began to lay out his theories.

"It's beginning to look like Santino's—" Duncan paused to find a polite way to say what he had to say. "Santino's unusual sexual appetite may have been a factor in his murder."

Duncan walked Mr. Bartelli through the test results and the photographic evidence. Mr. Bartelli could hardly believe how much Duncan had accomplished in the past forty-eight hours.

"I'm going to need to talk to some of Santino's sexual partners."

"Santino knew a lot of girls," Mr. Bartelli responded proudly.

"I don't mean to suggest anything, but if he was having sex with men, I'll need to know that, too."

Duncan knew that Mr. Bartelli was homophobic; however, he had no idea just how homophobic. But he was about to find out, "Sex with males!" blasted Mr. Bartelli. With anger painted on his face, Mr. Bartelli exploded straight up from his seat. As he rose, his legs caught under the ledge of the table lifting it a foot off the floor.

The expensive china and crystal went sailing over the second-floor railing, shattering into thousands of little pieces on the concrete patio below. Only the sheer weight of the table kept it from flying over the railing as well.

The table slammed back down on the floor of the balcony with such force that it shook Duncan's feet like a small California tremor. Duncan's orange juice spilled down the front of his shirt and the crystal glass smashed against his chair, directly between his legs. As if to emphasize his anger, Mr. Bartelli took his left arm and swept the remaining plates and dishes over the railing.

The veins on his neck were so engorged that Duncan thought that they might burst. He was enraged to the point of being unable to form coherent words.

Finally, he thrust his left index finger toward Duncan's face, stopping just inches from his nose. He wanted to say something, but only a blood-curdling yelp came out. Without uttering one intelligible word, he withdrew his finger and stomped into the house.

Sitting there with a lap full of broken crystal, Duncan was stunned. For the first time in his life, he was truly speechless.

What the hell just happened? Does he want me to leave? Should I wait?

For just a second he considered the possibility that Mr. Bartelli might return any minute to blow his head off. But the thought was fleeting. *He wouldn't hurt me,* he convinced himself.

For the life of him, he couldn't make sense of Mr. Bartelli's rage at the insinuation that Santino may have experimented with homosexual behavior. It seemed strange that Mr. Bartelli was not offended by the gross and sadistic sexual practices his son inflicted on women but would lose his mind over the thought that his son had sex with a man.

There was nothing in Duncan's background that could have prepared him for Mr. Bartelli's reaction. He had been reared in a home where his mother emphasized tolerance and understanding. Despite being a devout Catholic, her extremely liberal views were etched in Duncan's way of thinking. She may have been convinced that all homosexuals were going to hell, but that did not mean that you should hate them. Better that you should feel sad for their eternal souls was her way of thinking. Duncan was a heterosexual, but he had no particular problem with the homosexual lifestyle.

Mr. Bartelli, on the other hand, had a very definite opinion on the subject. He thought homosexuality an anathema. He wasn't prepared to deal with even the *suggestion* that Santino might have been gay.

The longest five minutes of Duncan's life passed before Mr. Bartelli came back out onto the balcony. Before he could say a word, Mr. Bartelli began apologizing profusely for his outburst.

"Look, my memories of Santino are all I have left. It's hard enough dealing with his murder."

"Sir. You don't need to apologize."

"I hate fags, plain and simple. They disgust me."

"I didn't mean to suggest that Santino was gay. I just can't afford to ignore any possibility."

"Homosexuality is an abomination unto God. As a Catholic, you must know how the Church feels about homos," Mr. Bartelli preached.

While Mr. Bartelli led the life of a criminal, he strangely saw himself as a practicing Catholic. The irony was difficult for Duncan to reconcile, but he was not about to say anything that might further offend him.

"I can assure you of one goddamn thing; I would never let a fucking faggot work for me. And another thing, Italians hate fags."

Duncan was so relieved that Mr. Bartelli had calmed down that he could barely concentrate on the long-winded apology/explanation.

Mr. Bartelli continued with his diatribe for several more minutes before Duncan had a chance to respond.

"I was completely out of line. I treated you like a client, and not like my dear friend. Please forgive my insensitivity."

"Let's just drop it," Mr. Bartelli said, as he rang a small brass bell he had concealed in his hand.

Moments later, three young, frightened maids slipped out from behind the curtains. They quickly and quietly cleaned up the mess.

Duncan picked up a napkin from the floor and gently wiped away the small shards of crystal stuck to his pants. A fourth maid appeared with a clean shirt. Duncan excused himself to wash up and change before they resumed their conversation.

In less than five minutes the table was cleared and new china, crystal, and silver adorned the table. By the time Duncan returned, even the mess on the concrete below had been cleaned. Looking neat and clean and no worse for the argument, Duncan took his seat at the freshly set table.

In a fashion that only men can do, Duncan and Mr. Bartelli resumed their discussion as if nothing had happened.

CHAPTER 47

"YOU'LL NEED TO talk to Santino's best friend, Anthony Visco. They were inseparable. Best friends since they were three years old. No one knows more about Santino than he does. He will be able to give you a full record of Santino's *girl*friends." Duncan wasn't about to take the bait, refusing to acknowledge Mr. Bartelli's emphasis on the word "girl."

Even before Duncan could ask how to reach Visco, Mr. Bartelli began dialing the phone sitting on a small stand one of the maids had placed next to his chair.

"Tony, I need to see you right away. How quickly can you get here? Great. I'll see you in ten."

A maid brought a rolling tray with breakfast fare. "Eat. Eat. We'll meet with him downstairs when we're done."

For the first time in three days, Duncan let himself think about something other than identifying Santino's murderer.

For the next ten minutes, they talked about the weather, baseball (a passion of Mr. Bartelli's), local restaurants, and other such meaningless things. While their conversation was brief, it felt great to discuss something unimportant.

"Sir, Mr. Visco has arrived," a butler announced.

"Tell him we'll be down in ten. Have him wait in the study."

Duncan had formulated an image of what Santino's best friend might look like. Anthony fit the bill perfectly. He had dark tanned skin, deep green eyes, and chiseled facial features. He was short and thick. His squat, muscular physique made him look a little like a fireplug.

Anthony left the first three buttons of his shirt unbuttoned exposing his matted chest hair, thick gold chains, and heavy gold medallions.

I bet you're a real hit with the girls, Duncan thought.

Anthony threw his arms around Mr. Bartelli.

"I'm so sorry, Mr. B. I miss Santino so much."

"I know. We all miss Santino. Thank you for coming."

"Anything for you, Mr. B. You know that."

"You're a good kid. This is Mr. Gabrelli. He needs to ask you some questions."

"Hello, sir. No problem. Anything I can do to help."

"Hello. Do you mind if I call you Tony?"

"Sure. All my friends do."

Duncan got right to the business at hand. "I need to know everything you know about Santino's sex life."

Not expecting that type of questioning, Tony cast a questioning look at Mr. Bartelli.

"It's important. Just tell Duncan what you know," Mr. Bartelli said reassuringly.

Santino was a sexually prolific young man. Taking copious notes, Duncan made a list of all the names of Santino's girlfriends; it was impressively long. It would have been much longer, but for the fact that Santino had sex with so many girls, that Tony couldn't remember many of the girls' names. In many cases, he admitted that they never even *knew* the girls' names.

"*Wow. It's a strange new world.* The conversation was making Duncan feel old.

The stories of Santino's sexual exploits went a long way toward healing some of the wounds inflicted on the balcony earlier in the day. Duncan could see a look of relief on Mr. Bartelli's face. However, the stories were so graphic and violent that any sense of pride he might have had in his son began to vanish with each new disturbing story.

Tony admitted to joining Santino in beating young girls on a regular basis. From his account, most of the girls participated willingly. Some even craved the abuse. At least that was the story Tony was selling.

"Tell me about the girls who did not willingly participate. Girls, let's say, that might have it in for Santino?"

"There weren't many, only three, maybe four. You know, only the cockteasers. You know the type. Sometimes we had to teach them a lesson."

"No, Tony, I don't know the type. Tell me more."

Tony discussed problems Santino had with several girls; however, nothing sounded particularly interesting.

It was clear, however, that he and Santino were best friends, because he knew all the details—things that only a best friend would know. He was providing useful information, but Duncan had a sneaking suspicion that Tony was not being completely forthcoming.

It's hard to imagine what could be more vulgar than what you're telling me. But you're holding something back. Maybe you're not comfortable discussing this in front of Mr. Bartelli, Duncan thought.

As tactfully as humanly possible (and with the expressed desire not to offend Mr. Bartelli for the second time that day), Duncan politely asked if he could speak to Tony in private.

Mr. Bartelli welcomed the excuse to leave. Hearing about his son's conduct was making him physically ill.

Before leaving, he looked Tony directly in the eyes. "Answer all of Duncan's questions."

Anthony had never seen anyone ask Mr. Bartelli to leave a room. Staring at each other, Duncan saw a look of awe in his half-glazed green eyes.

Duncan wasted no time. "Okay. He's gone. Tell me what you didn't want Mr. Bartelli to hear." He'd been right. Tony was uncomfortable discussing many details in front of Santino's father.

The gory details began to spew from his mouth like vomit. In the several years prior to Santino's murder, they had participated in some very unconventional sexual practices, including torture and mutilation. Santino had taken particular pleasure in inflicting pain on his partners.

Santino was the most deviant individual Duncan had ever heard of, and that was saying something, in light of the type of clients he represented.

Santino employed every imaginable method of torture on his sexual partners. Beatings were just the beginning. A medical appliance, belts, knives, steel wool, were just a few of the instruments of torture used to inflict pain. He burned girls with cigarettes, even branding some of them like cattle. He would jam live animals—snakes, mice, gerbils—into young girls' vaginas and anuses.

So many evil things were done to so many girls on the list that Duncan began to believe that they *all* could have killed Santino.

As unbelievable as it sounded, Tony stuck firmly to his story. "I'm telling you the truth. These girls liked this stuff. They almost always came back for more."

Instinctively, Duncan was inclined to believe that Tony had to blame the girls in order to live with what he and Santino had done to them, but there was sincerity in Tony's voice.

Duncan had read a number of cases where girls were accidently killed during sex acts involving torture. He recalled that the physiological profiles in those cases made it clear that death was rarely the goal. When a death occurred, it was accidental.

"We were just having some fun. But sometimes Santino let it get a little out of control."

"Out of control in what way?"

"Look, most of the girls wanted drugs and sex. The sex was great, and the drugs just made it crazier."

"I'm sure it did. But what did you mean when you said Santino let it get out of control?"

"Well, it started becoming a contest between me and Santino. We would pick out a girl and bet who could get her first."

"Get her?"

"Yeah, you know, fuck her."

"I get the picture."

"Well there were some girls at the parties that were pretty stuck-up. You know, they would come to the party dressed like they wanted it then not give it up. Everyone knew they wanted it, they were just playing hard to get," Tony paused, looking like a man trying to find a way to justify rape. "They all gave it up eventually—most of them when they were stoned, but they wanted it. All girls want sex when they're stoned, you know."

Wanting to get the whole story, Duncan said, "I'm sure that's true," all the while thinking, *You evil little fuck.*

"Well, a friend of ours turned us onto this great drug called roofies. Man, it took *all* of a girl's inhibitions away."

"Doesn't that drug knock the girls out?"

"Well, sometimes. That's what I meant by Santino letting it get a little out of control. He didn't care if a girl was out cold. He got a kick out of beating and fucking 'em. He would joke around, saying that the sex was better, because the bitches would finally shut the fuck up. Santino would slip the drug into the girls' drinks when they weren't lookin'."

Tony went on to describe in great detail the vile and disgusting sexual acts Santino performed on his unsuspecting victims.

"He once told me that he wanted to fuck dead people, but I don't think he ever did. He'd have told me."

"Were you ever present when Santino used roofies on a girl?"

"Hey, I was at all the parties. Yeah, I saw him put it in their drinks."

For the first time during the questioning, Tony seemed to understand just how grotesque their actions were, hanging his head.

Duncan could no longer disguise his contempt. Santino and Tony were cut from the same cloth. Only Tony had been a puppet, dancing like a marionette controlled by his now-deceased best friend. He sprang up from his chair and stared down at Anthony. "How many girls did Santino secretly give roofies to?"

It wasn't until that moment that Tony recognized Duncan as the attorney who had won Santino's acquittal years earlier.

Even as he waited for Tony's response, the name Jessica Lopez kept running through Duncan's mind. Santino's sexually predatory nature resulted in Jessica's death. It had been some time since that name had come to his mind.

"Three. Maybe four. No, three. It's possible that there were others, but it's not likely. If there were, I would have heard 'bout 'em. Santino loved to brag."

"What can you tell me about the three girls?"

"Not too much. I think one of them was a runaway. She was pretty young, thirteen, maybe fourteen years old. She said she was from a broken home or something back East. It could have been Virginia or maybe Maryland, I'm not sure. I remember hearing some of her friends saying that social services had picked her up."

"Do you know when that happened?"

"It would have been over a year ago. They said she'd been placed in a foster home up north somewhere. But I have no idea where."

"How about the other two?"

"I think one was named Carol, or maybe Kathy. She was one of those runaways who hung out at the clubs, dreaming of being picked up by some handsome prince who would take care of her. She wasn't from here. And I know for a fact that she left the state over a year ago. The whole scene out here messed with her head."

"Did she have any family out here?"

"No, I don't think so."

While Duncan listened patiently about the first two girls, he was biting his tongue, waiting to hear about Jessica. "What about the third young girl?"

"That was...you know, that was the girl that Santino...I mean, that was the girl that died. You know, the one that Santino got into all that trouble over. You know the murder trial thing and all that stuff."

"Jessica Lopez."

"Yeah, that's the one, Jessica. That was a bad scene, a really bad scene."

"What do you know about Jessica?"

"Just that I met her that night at the party."

"Did she hang out at the clubs and parties?"

"No. I would have noticed her. She was fine. Long black hair, very pretty. I wanted her, but Santino made a move on her first."

"Anything else you can tell me about Jessica?"

"No. Not really. Well, there was some talk that she had a badass brother who was going to get even with Santino, some Mexican gang dude. But that was years ago. I'm not even sure if she had a brother."

Furiously, Duncan searched his memory for details about Jessica and her family. Her mother had sat in the first row, directly behind the prosecutor's table, every day of the trial. He didn't recall any other family members present. Even so, he recalled reading his investigators' reports and the police interviews of Jessica's mother. There was a brother, he recalled.

The family was originally from a small town in Mexico, not too far from Guadalajara. *What was the name of that town? Pegueros? That's it, Pegueros.*

The difference between the first two girls Santino had savaged and Jessica was that she was a local girl. She had family that lived in the area.

Also, Jessica was—as the prosecution made painfully clear during the trial—a good girl, an innocent girl. In that moment, the sobs of Jessica's mother once again echoed in his head.

His mind was so preoccupied that he had all but forgotten that Tony was still in the room.

"Is that all?"

"Yes. Yes. Thank you for your help. Can I call you if I have any more questions?"

"Yes. Anytime," Tony said, but he was hoping he would never meet Duncan again.

"I don't want you discussing these matters with anyone."

"Sure. I promise."

To drive home the point, Duncan reminded Tony how "disappointed" Mr. Bartelli would be if he discovered that Tony violated that promise.

Duncan was in a state of anxious excitement. Tony had innocently provided the key to the murderer's identity. If he was right, Santino's murder was connected to Jessica's death. Now it was up to him to expose that connection.

CHAPTER 48

DUNCAN CHOSE NOT to discuss his suspicions with Mr. Bartelli.

He didn't want to disclose too much information before he had more proof. First, he didn't want to get Mr. Bartelli's hopes up without more evidence to back up his theory. Second, he was concerned that Mr. Bartelli might overreact, doing something that everyone would regret.

"So, what did we learn from Tony? Not that much, I imagine; nice kid, but not too smart," Mr. Bartelli asked, almost rhetorically.

"You may be right. I'm not sure he told me anything I didn't already know. But I want to check out some of his story," Duncan said, heading for the front door.

"You're always on the run; stay awhile."

"I'd love to, but I need to get a few files from the office before Stella leaves. I'll call you when I get back to the house."

At approximately three thirty, Duncan pulled out of the gates of Mr. Bartelli's estate and headed back to his office in Century City.

While on the road, he called Stella. Her name always reminded him of Brando in *On the Waterfront*. More frequently than she liked, Duncan would mimic Marlon Brando's gravelly voice when he called the office. *Stella... Stella...*

He was too preoccupied to entertain Stella with impressions today.

"Good afternoon, sir."

"Stella. I need you to box up all the discovery files in the Santino case. I don't want any pleading or exhibits, just discovery documents; all the depositions, interviews, interrogatories, all of it."

"Yes, I am familiar with what documents are included in discovery files," Stella replied, a little irritated that Duncan felt the need to describe in such detail what should be included.

"Yes, I know you do, my dear," Duncan replied, indicating his complete and unconditional surrender. "And may I extend to you my heartfelt apologies for doubting your knowledge in this, your area of expertise."

"Okay, okay, I get it. You don't want to fight. Too bad, I think I could have taken you today." Stella chuckled out loud.

"Now, can I stop kissing your butt long enough for you to get this done?" Okay, maybe it was not a complete and unconditional surrender, but it was about as close as Duncan came to giving in. "Have them ready by the time I get there. Get some law clerks to help you get them down to the parking garage. I won't be coming in."

"When will you be here?"

"I'm just leaving Mr. Bartelli's house. Maybe twenty minutes."

"It there anything else?"

"Yes, I need you to look up some telephone numbers. Get me the numbers for..."

Stella quickly jotted down the names as he reeled them off. "I'll have them at valet parking when you arrive."

When he was five minutes from his office, he called Stella again. As he should have expected, the receptionist informed him that Stella was already on her way down to the parking garage.

Stella, two law clerks, and twenty-three boxes of files were waiting for him when he pulled up. The boxes that wouldn't fit in the Cadillac's large trunk were stacked to the ceiling in the back and passenger seats.

"Here's the list of numbers you asked for. I put in their addresses just in case you needed them."

Duncan couldn't help but think what a difficult job it must have been to locate and box all the files in only fifteen minutes.

"Thank you. Good job."

"That's why you love me, sir," Stella's response reeked of sarcasm.

"That's supposed to be our secret," Duncan said, ignoring her insincerity.

"Sir, you have some messages."

"Unless they're critical, put everything off until next week."

"I'll take care of them."

Duncan had Benton set the boxes just inside the door to his study while he ran into the kitchen to make a sandwich to eat while he reviewed the files.

Benton was a little taken aback at the instruction. No one had been allowed to set even one foot into the study unaccompanied.

Back at his desk, door locked, he proceeded to gobble down a cold turkey sandwich while he perused the files and made some phone calls. His first call was to Mr. Bartelli. Even though he had nothing new to report, he had promised to call. Mr. Bartelli seemed to sense that Duncan knew more than he was letting on, but his confidence in Duncan's loyalty and judgment quenched his thirst to know just what it was.

Duncan next called Stephen Braumowitz at the laboratory.

"I thought this was important," Braumowitz said, mostly in jest, but a little irritated.

"It is. It's just on a long list of very important things. What's new?"

"When was the last time you checked your fax and answering machines?"

"This morning, I got the test reports. Hold on. Let me change phones."

Duncan walked across the study, only to find another long roll of faxes lying on the floor. Stephen had been faxing updates every few hours.

Duncan was a little embarrassed that he hadn't checked before calling. *Fuck him. I'm paying for this show.*

Ripping off the fax on his way to his desk, he picked up the telephone.

"So what am I looking at?" Duncan asked, still trying to swallow a bite of his sandwich.

"Well, some of the tests are back from the blood on the clothes samples. They identified several different blood types. Both A negative and O positive were present. They're both pretty common. Santino is A negative, so it's probably his. We're running more tests to make sure."

"Whose blood type is A negative?"

"Come on Duncan, I read the papers. I haven't told anyone. But don't treat me like an idiot."

"Let's just say you're correct for the sake of argument, how would you know Santino's blood type?" Almost before the last word escaped his lips, "That's right; you did the blood work during his trial several years ago. You had that information from my file."

Duncan did not definitively confirm nor deny Stephen's assumption, but they both knew Stephen was correct.

"What else did you find?'

"We identified traces of AB negative, a much rarer blood type, only eight out of a thousand people in the general population have it."

In the course of his practice, Duncan had reviewed hundreds of medical reports. He knew that AB negative was extremely rare.

"How rare is it in the Spanish population?"

"Very. Maybe twenty in every ten thousand."

Even without his photographic memory, Duncan might have remembered that Jessica's blood type was O negative; it too was relatively rare. But, his incredible ability to recall even obscure facts also brought to mind that the medical records presented during Jessica's murder trial revealed that her mother also had O negative blood.

"Tell me, Steve. If my mother had O negative blood, could her children have AB negative?"

Stephen broke the bad news. "No. That would not be possible, no matter what the father's blood type was."

Damn. Duncan thought, *Even if Jessica has a brother, it can't be his blood.*

While the news was disappointing, it didn't necessarily exclude anyone from being involved in the murder. He kept reminding himself to think outside the box. Duncan was still convinced that there was a connection between Jessica's and Santino's murders. *I'm over-looking something that ties these murders together.*

Despondent, Duncan said, "Let me go over these faxes you sent. I'll call you later after I've had a chance to study them. Be sure to call me if you find anything else."

The last call Duncan made was to Winston Security Services. The company provided security for most of the politicians, movie stars, and big shots in LA. Within an hour of the call, two plainclothes security guards were stationed at his front gate.

Duncan believed that he was getting close to identifying the killer. However, if he was wrong, and Santino's murder had been a mob hit, his life could be in danger. It was common knowledge among syndicate members that Duncan was a trusted friend and confidante of Mr. Bartelli. If someone was looking to harm those close to Mr. Bartelli, Duncan would be high on their list.

It was the first time since he learned of Santino's murder that he even considered the fact that his life could be in danger. Mr. Bartelli would have been glad to provide him with security; all he needed to do was ask. But Duncan felt that it would be safer and cleaner to use an outside company, at least for the next few days.

CHAPTER 49

THAT NIGHT DUNCAN pored over the Santino files. While the police never considered Lopez's family as suspects in her murder, they did interview her mother, Maria, on several occasions.

The files revealed that his memory had been correct. Her family was from the small Mexican town of Pegueros, in the state of Jalisco, an hour northeast of Guadalajara.

From his investigator's reports he knew that Jessica's father had died five years prior to her murder. The file didn't provide any information regarding how he had died. However, it did reveal that Jessica had a brother, Juan.

Why didn't Juan come to the trial? I wonder.

He quickly found the answer. Juan couldn't have attended the trial. He was serving a stretch for armed robbery at Folsom Prison in San Francisco. It wasn't clear from the police interviews when he was scheduled to be released.

Duncan checked his watch. It was just after seven o'clock. *Good thing prisons are open all night.* The thought drew a smile to his face.

At least, they were if you knew the right people. Duncan had connections in every prison in California. Reaching across his desk, he spun his rolodex until it stopped on the letter F. "Folsom," he said out loud as he picked up the telephone.

A pleasant voice answered the line, "Folsom Prison, how may I direct your call?"

"Yes, could you please connect me to the night watch commander's desk?"

"Who's calling, please?"

"Attorney Duncan Gabrelli."

"One moment, please."

"Lieutenant Allan," the stern voice sounded like music to Duncan's ears. *It's getting to be a small world,* he thought. As fate would have it, he knew Lieutenant Bill Allan.

Before Duncan had become a high-powered criminal lawyer, he had defended Allan's cousin against charges of breaking and entering. Using just a little razzle-dazzle, he was able to get the charges dropped. Bill Allan had voiced that overused expression: "If there's ever anything I can do to repay you, just let me know." Duncan was about to call in that marker.

"Mr. Gabrelli. It's been a long time. How are you?"

"Very well. Please call me Duncan."

The two men exchanged pleasantries for a few moments before Duncan got to the point of his phone call.

"Bill, I need a little information about an inmate. At least, he was an inmate a year ago."

"That shouldn't be a problem. What do you need to know?"

"Can you help me find out if you still have a Juan Lopez in custody?" Asking for Juan Lopez in Folsom Prison was a little like asking the operator for the telephone number of John Smith in Utah.

Bill was surprisingly eager to help. "Let me put you on hold for a moment." Bill walked over to the Records Room to look for Juan's file. Only a few minutes passed before Bill was back on the line. "I always pay my debts." Apparently Bill hadn't forgotten his promise.

Through a process of elimination, he was able to locate Juan Lopez's file. Juan was still serving the tail end of a six-year stretch. With good behavior, Juan was scheduled for release in ten months.

You can't commit a murder while you're in jail. For the second time that day, he had heard news that didn't support his theory.

"Just out of curiosity, has anyone sharing a cell with Juan Lopez been released in the last several years?" He was grasping at straws, but he was running out of ideas. Only a minute or so passed before Bill's voice came back on the line.

"Yes. Only one. Jaime Sanchez was released almost three weeks ago. Here, let me pull his file for you."

His words instantaneously renewed Duncan's faith in his instincts. *Maybe you can't commit a murder while you're in jail, but you can orchestrate one,* he thought.

The fact that Bill was bending over backward to provide information was far more than he could have hoped for. While he was on a roll, Duncan thought that he might as well continue to press his luck.

"Does the file give an address for Sanchez?"

"Yes, it does. It also gives the name and telephone number for his probation officer, if you need it."

"That would be a big help."

Allan read off the contact information, still appearing eager to help.

"Is there anything else I can do for you?"

"Yes, as a matter of fact, there is. Does Sanchez's file include his blood type?"

Duncan knew that the information was in the file. The only question was whether Bill would disclose medical information.

"It's right here. AB negative."

Duncan almost jumped through the ceiling. "Can I get a photograph of Sanchez?"

"There is a photo in the file, but I can't send that to you. It's against the regs," Bill replied apologetically. It seemed like a strange reply in light of the fact that he had already violated the 'regs' in at least a dozen different ways.

"I understand. Not a problem. You've already been a tremendous help."

The two men spoke for a few more minutes about nothing in particular before he thanked Bill again and hung up the phone.

Obtaining copies of Sanchez's mug shots would be easy.

CHAPTER 50

DUNCAN WAS NOW confident that he had found a reliable connection between Santino's and Jessica's murders. He was feeling more than a little cocky about having done it in half the time Mr. Bartelli had given him. However, there were still a few loose ends to tie up.

There were the strands of hair found on Santino's clothes. The latest reports from Braumowitz identified the hair sample as female and likely from a Hispanic.

From the hair color, coarseness, and texture, Braumowitz surmised that the woman was in her mid-to-late fifties.

There was also the human tissue found under Santino's sole remaining fingernail. It contained trace amounts of type O positive blood. While a common blood type, Jessica's mother was type O positive. The strand of hair and the tissue led Duncan to conclude that Maria Lopez had been present during Santino's torture and murder; a conclusion that seemed almost surreal.

She'd appeared so small and frail at her daughter's trial.

How could that sweet lady be involved in something this violent? I guess hell has made a place for her, too.

His mind drifted back to the day that Santino's verdict was read. He recalled that he had lacked emotion toward Maria Lopez. He was not so sure what he felt now.

She had, after all, lost her daughter at the murderous hands of Santino. It would take a cold and forbidding heart to blame her for seeking revenge.

One thing was for sure. When he told Mr. Bartelli about her involvement in the murder, she was as good as dead.

I hold her life in my hands. This must be what God feels like. He wasn't sure what to do. After considering the matter for a long while, he decided to sleep on it. *I'll decide in the morning.*

CHAPTER 51

WHEN DUNCAN AWOKE the next morning, the first thing on his mind was, *What the hell was I thinking? Of course I'm going to tell Mr. Bartelli. Fuck her. It's not my problem. Fuck them all.*

He wasn't going to lie to one of the most powerful and dangerous men in the world to save her life. He hadn't cared about her during Santino's trial, and he didn't care now. *Fuck her*, he thought again as he shook his head in disbelief. *How could I have even considered keeping quiet about this?*

At seven thirty, he called Mr. Bartelli, who was known to be an early riser. He was already sitting down to breakfast when Duncan called.

"Good morning, my boy." Duncan had noticed that since Santino's death, Mr. Bartelli had been saying "my boy" much more frequently. Even so, he couldn't bring himself to say anything but "sir" in reply.

"Good morning, sir. We need to talk. Can I come over?"

"Of course. Of course you can. You sound excited. What's up?"

"I'll fill you in when I get there."

"Then hurry up and get your ass over here. We'll have some breakfast."

Five minutes later, the two men were sitting down to breakfast on the same balcony and at the same table where Mr. Bartelli had nearly lost his mind the day before.

During breakfast Duncan reminded himself, *I still need to get copies of Sanchez's mug shots.* Looking down at his watch he realized that it was too early to reach anyone. He jotted down a quick cryptic note in a ragged daybook. Despite having an almost perfect memory, he was still anal about making notes to himself. He was equally anal about destroying those notes the minute a task was completed.

"So tell me, my boy, what's got your underwear in a bunch?" Mr. Bartelli asked through a mouthful of scrambled eggs.

Duncan slid a piece of paper across the table, on which he had written the names Juan Lopez, Maria Lopez, and Jaime Sanchez.

"What's this?"

"The names of Santino's murderers."

Mr. Bartelli almost choked on his eggs, and as he coughed, small bits of egg came flying across the table in Duncan's direction. Taking a gulp of water, he sat there, staring down at the paper in stunned silence. When the initial shock subsided, he looked up at Duncan and said, "Are you sure?"

"I'm sure. I'm waiting on the results of a few more tests from the lab, but they're the killers."

Duncan was beginning to lay out the evidence that led him to the murderers when he noticed Mr. Bartelli's hands were shaking. Suddenly he exploded in anger. "I'm going to kill those murderous bastards today! Where are they?"

Duncan grabbed the wrought-iron table firmly with both hands. "You're not going to throw my food over the railing again, are you, sir? Because I am really very hungry," he said, hoping his attempt at humor would defuse the situation.

It *did* force a smile to Mr. Bartelli's face.

"I've got a private dick looking for them right now. I will know where one of them is today, tomorrow at the latest."

Mr. Bartelli started to get up. "I'll find these fucks."

"Please just wait a minute."

Seeing the concern on Duncan's face, Mr. Bartelli sat back down.

"While I've kept my investigation as covert as possible, I did have to shake a few bushes to get the information. An officer at Folsom was instrumental in confirming my theory. You must know that if Sanchez and Lopez suddenly end up dead, he would likely report our conversation to the authorities."

"Fuck that. They're dead."

"I know that. But you need to stop and think about this. Even if he didn't make the connection, it would take the police all of ten minutes to figure out you had some connection to the murders."

"The cops have been investigating me for years. You think that bothers me?"

"No. But it should. I'm only sure of one thing. If bodies just start showing up at the morgue—particularly if they're bodies of people that both of us have direct connections with—the police are going to start asking questions. They're not *all* complete fools."

Mr. Bartelli may have taken issue with him on the existence of intelligence in the police department, but it was true that he'd be the primary suspect.

Duncan had anticipated Mr. Bartelli's instinctive reaction. "I've already begun developing a plan to deal with your son's murderers. But developing that plan will take time and a considerable amount of patience on your part."

"I'm listening. But it had better be good. Otherwise, I'm killing these fucks today."

"Look, the police want to believe that Santino's death was a syndicate-related crime. We know that's not true, but they don't. So let them believe it and close the case."

"Great, so the police will suspect me of a murder, so what's new? Tell me, is there a plan coming? Because watching the police fuck up the investigation isn't a plan."

"Perhaps you missed the *patience* aspect of the plan. Just hear me out."

"I'm not in the mood for your wit, boy. The plan, get to the point," Mr. Bartelli responded gruffly.

"It's essential that all three murderers be dealt with at the same time. If Sanchez is killed first, Juan and Mrs. Lopez might panic and go to the police, even if it means being prosecuted for Santino's murder."

Among the slew of ugly scenarios Duncan had considered, he could visualize a jury having sympathy for the mother of a murdered daughter and acquitting her of the crime.

"I can have them killed today. One word from me, and they'll be dead."

"Yes, and if you only wanted them killed and to make their bodies disappear, then you wouldn't need my input. However, I've known you long enough to know that you're going to want your pound of flesh."

"You don't know dick about me."

"Let me guess—you're going to want to be present? Perhaps even participate?"

Mr. Bartelli was simultaneously proud and irritated to see that Duncan knew him that well. "The plan, get to the fucking plan."

"What plan? We just found out who the killers are. We are *developing* a plan. After we analyze all our options, we'll formulate something definite. Patience!"

"You say patience one more time, and I'll throw *you* over the balcony," Mr. Bartelli said only half joking.

"Look, I want these guys dead, too. But I'm not going to let you go off half-cocked."

"Listen to me carefully, Duncan. These three pieces of shit are about to die the worst death they could ever imagine," he barked. "There is no room for argument on this point. Have I made myself clear?"

Duncan nodded. "I'm not suggesting that you *not* kill them. I'm only asking that you consider the ramifications of acting in anger and haste. We need to handle these matters with care and caution."

Duncan needed to establish a little credibility. It was one thing to possess the intellect to find the killers; it was another thing altogether to suggest he had the skills to plan their murders. It was time to explain how he had come to know so much about the criminal mind.

"Mr. Bartelli, there is a lot that you don't know about me."

"Less than you might think, young man," Mr. Bartelli responded brashly.

Duncan wasn't sure what he meant, but he refused to be distracted. "I have dedicated my life to analyzing and decoding criminal files."

With confidence he continued, "I know more about why and how crimes are committed and solved than any man on the planet." His bold words were beginning to get Mr. Bartelli's attention.

"I have access to inside information that is unobtainable, except to a handful of people in the country," Duncan continued.

"'I have access to inside information.' You sound like a fucking stockbroker. You're a fucking attorney, for God's sake, which in my book is somewhere below a stockbroker. What the fuck could you know about this subject that I couldn't write a book about?"

"With all due respect, your business is drugs, not murder. Murder is at best incidental to your business."

Mr. Bartelli was officially offended at that point. "You don't have any idea what my business is. You only know what I want you to know. That's it."

"Mr. Bartelli! I'm not trying to one-up you. I'm trying to help you."

"Then try telling me what you know, and stop telling me what I know."

"If knowing what it takes to commit a successful murder was art, I'd be Rembrandt, Van Gogh, or fucking Matisse."

"Now you sound like a fucking used car salesman."

"Okay. What I know is that the advances in forensics have made it almost impossible to get away with murder. What are left at a crime scene—blood, hair, tissue, the corpse itself—are road maps, directing the cops to the killer, and 96.8 percent of all murderers are identified as a direct result of examination of the evidence left at the crime scene. Not informants, not witnesses, not interrogations, not psychics, or prayers asking God to intervene."

Duncan continued to reel off statistic after statistic. It was beginning to sound like an advanced-level college lecture on criminology.

"Murderers who kill someone they have personal connections with are caught and convicted more than ninety-three percent of the time. That percentage goes down only slightly when the murder is planned."

He was not excited about allowing Mr. Bartelli to buck such horrible odds. His relationship with Mr. Bartelli had become even more powerful in the short time since Santino's death. Duncan was forging a bond with Mr. Bartelli, solidified in Santino's blood.

"Sir, the bottom line is that the murderers provide most of the evidence that is needed to catch them."

Mr. Bartelli was still finding it somewhat ironic that Duncan was giving *him* advice on how to kill someone, but he was listening.

"Sir. There are people in the government who would love nothing more than to put you through a murder trial. They wouldn't even care if there was sufficient evidence to prosecute you. They would throw as much mud at the wall as they could, in the hopes that something would stick in a jury's mind. Please, at least listen to me."

"So what do you want me to do? Assuming that I believe that you know what the hell you're talking about. What do you want me to do with this scum?"

Duncan thought that calling Mrs. Lopez scum was just a little hypocritical, but he ignored the temptation to point it out.

"First, I don't care what you do to these fucks." Fuck was a word that he never used prior to meeting Mr. Bartelli. However it was increasingly finding its way into his vocabulary, at least in his conversations with Mr. Bartelli. "However, when you're done collecting your payback, the bodies must disappear. I mean from the face of the earth. Dust to dust."

Spending a day observing Santino's autopsy had confirmed what Duncan already knew. The evidence the corpse provides almost always unmasks the murderer's identity.

It was almost ten when Duncan, exhausted from the intensity of the conversation, asked Mr. Bartelli to excuse him for a few minutes while he made some calls. In truth, Duncan was equally interested in getting a moment to regroup and relax his mind.

"I need to get a few photos of our friend Sanchez. May I use the phone in your study for a few minutes?"

"Good idea. I would hate to cut the balls off the wrong guy."

Only ten minutes later Duncan returned to continue his discussion. "You get 'em?"

"They'll be delivered this afternoon."

"The photographs or his balls?"

"One will get you the other," Duncan said with a grin.

The two men continued to analyze their options throughout the morning. At 11:10 a.m., Stella tracked Duncan down. He stepped into a small parlor to take the call. "Stella, my love, what can I help you with?"

She hadn't identified herself to Mr. Bartelli's butler. Even so, she was not impressed that Duncan knew it was her. *You're a genius. Who else but me would know you might be at Mr. Bartelli's? Duh!"* is what she thought, but, "How did you know it was me?" is what she said. She saw stroking his enormous ego as part of her job and was a master at it.

"The private investigator called several times."

"Did he leave a message?"

"Only a number. He didn't say it was important, but there was something about his tone. I thought you might want to know he called."

Her intuitive nature was one of the qualities Duncan admired most about her. Taking out a small notebook, he wrote down the investigator's telephone number.

"Anything else?"

"Nothing I can't handle."

"I'll call later, goodbye."

A smile came to Duncan's face. He knew that his abrupt goodbye would have left Stella muttering to herself, the same little rant he had overheard her say at least a thousand times. *Thank you, Stella. Good job, Stella. What would I do without you, Stella? You are so lucky to have me and someday, you're going to tell me.*

Mr. Bartelli joined him in the parlor about the same time he said goodbye to Stella.

"Sorry, sir, one more call."

"Take your time."

The phone rang, and a young woman's voice came on the line. "Milton's Investigative Services."

"Hello. This is Duncan Gabrelli returning Milton's call."

Duncan had used Milton's services for years and considered him to be a personal friend. More important, Milton was one of the most discreet people he had ever met.

"Good morning, Mr. Gabrelli. He's been waiting for your call. I'll connect you."

The first thing Duncan heard from Milton was a sigh, apparently believing he had bad news.

"Hi, Duncan. She was easy to find, but it looks like she's on the move soon," Milton said, dispensing with the customary pleasantries and cutting directly to the chase. "I was able to get a few pictures of her."

"Where's she living now?"

"She's in Sylmar. It looks like she lives there with a Latin male. I got some pictures of him, too; thought you might want to see them."

"Boyfriend or friend-friend?"

"Too young, he's a friend-friend."

"What else did you come up with?"

"Talked to some of the neighbors. She moved to the mostly Latino community after her daughter was killed. But it looks like she's planning on returning to Mexico. Couldn't find out exactly where in Mexico, but it's a small town not far from Guadalajara."

The name of Lopez's hometown was already etched in Duncan's memory. *She's heading for Pegueros.*

"Do me a favor, Milton."

"Sure thing."

Insulating Mr. Bartelli was still in the forefront of Duncan's mind. *Better have them sent to my place.* "Have the photographs and your report messengered to my home."

"You got it. I'll have them delivered within the hour."

"One more thing. I want you to find someone else for me."

Duncan gave Milton all the information he had on Sanchez.

"Call his PO. That should get you started."

"How much time do I have?"

"None. I need to know yesterday."

"Got it. I'll get right on it."

"One last thing, Milton. Don't keep any copies of the photos. Put the negatives in with the photos you send over. Are we completely clear on that point?"

"Absolutely. No copies."

Having some time to burn, he began to scan the rows and rows of bookshelves that lined the walls of Mr. Bartelli's massive study. Somewhere in the thousands of books, he hoped there would be at least one that contained information about Pegueros.

"Sir, any books on Mexico?"

"Don't you think it's about time you started calling me Vinnie?" Mr. Bartelli quipped.

"As you wish, sir," he said with a smirk. "Now how about those books?"

"Mexico? Mexico? Let me check."

Pulling a list from his desk, he began to scan the book titles. After a moment, he stopped and pointed at a row of books near the top of the thirty-foot-tall bookshelf.

"Help yourself," he said plopping himself down into an over-stuffed leather chair.

"Yeah right! Call you Vinnie until there are ladders to climb, then it's back to 'boss,'" Duncan mumbled, loud enough for Mr. Bartelli to hear. "Wait until you get my bill this month. I get paid triple time for hazardous duties."

He climbed a long ladder that led to the second-story walkway. Sliding another ladder directly under the books Mr. Bartelli identified, he gingerly resumed his ascent.

"What are you looking for in Mexico?"

"Santino's murderer."

"They're in Mexico?"

"Not yet."

"Don't make me climb that ladder and kick your ass."

Duncan looked down from the long, steep ladder. "Right! You're climbing this ladder."

Mr. Bartelli stood up.

"Okay. I believe you. If I'm right, Mrs. Lopez will be there soon. Very soon."

"Where in Mexico?"

"Hold on a minute, and I'll show you."

Studying the spines of the books, he took three very thick and deceptively heavy books off the shelves and climbed down.

"You know I'm not putting these back," he said with a defiant smile as he reached the floor.

The books contained a great deal of general information about the people, topography, and agriculture of Mexico. However, only one book made specific reference to Pegueros.

Duncan pointed at the book. "Right here."

There was only a short blurb, which Duncan read aloud. "Pegueros...a small town with approximately five thousand residents. Its inhabitants scratch out a living from the red clay fields that stretch across the valley floor between Tepatitlan and El Valle de Guadalupe."

A map in the book revealed that Pegueros was located deep in the heart of Mexico, approximately seventy-five miles outside of Guadalajara. *Far from the borders and protections of the United States.*

As he stared at the pages of the book, Duncan couldn't help but think, *Mrs. Lopez is killing herself. She may feel safer in her hometown, but she'll be in the heart of Mr. Bartelli's vengeance. Once she leaves the United States, she's as good as dead.*

CHAPTER 52

M R. BARTELLI AND Duncan stayed in the study, continuing their discussions through lunch and into the early afternoon. Duncan continued to urge forbearance (being careful not to use the word patience, just in case), while Mr. Bartelli insisted on swift and violent retribution.

"Juan's in jail; we know where Lopez is; I'll know where Sanchez is by tomorrow. When all the pieces are in place, we'll design a plan."

Mr. Bartelli let Duncan's words sink in for a moment before responding. "You've accomplished more than I thought possible. I owe you, so I'll tell you what. I won't take any action without first consulting you. Fair enough?"

"It's all I'm going to get, so I'll take it."

"You're a smart kid."

"Let me get out of here. I've got me a killer to find. I'll call you tonight, if I find out anything new."

At approximately two thirty, Duncan pulled out of Mr. Bartelli's driveway. When he arrived home he went directly to his study. Just outside the door, sitting on a small table perched against the wall, were the two medium-size envelopes he had been expecting. One contained the pictures that Milton had taken, the other the mug shots of Jaime Sanchez.

Locking the door behind him, he sat at his desk and reached for a letter opener. Looking first at the Sanchez photos, he found four separate series of mug shots and a rap sheet.

Sanchez had been a prolific criminal, albeit not particularly lucky or smart. Arrested on thirteen different occasions for everything from shoplifting to armed robbery, he had served two stretches at Folsom and one in Attica in upstate New York, as well as many shorter incarcerations in local jails. *He's the classic habitual criminal.*

Sanchez bore the marks of both a gang member and prison thug. The tattoos on his neck and forearms were crudely done. Over the years Duncan had familiarized himself with the symbols and marking of the gangs that made the criminal justice system their home away from home.

So you're a Latin King. His shaved head and goatee completed the badass look. They gave his face a menacing appearance. *If nothing else, you'll be easy to identify.*

After examining Sanchez's photographs, he grabbed the envelope containing Milton's photos. Having seen Mrs. Lopez every day during the course of Santino's trial, he was not particularly interested in the photos. The only reason for opening the envelope was to see if there was anything informative in Milton's report.

As he was pulling the report out of the envelope, almost half of the twenty pictures came tumbling out. Some landed on his desk, and others fluttered to the floor. Ignoring the photos for the moment, he glanced at the report. He wasn't sure what he hoped to find, but whatever it was, it wasn't there.

The mild irritation he was feeling was magnified by the mess he had made. Removing the remaining pictures from the envelope, he casually glanced at them, not giving them much consideration.

As he leaned over from his chair to pick up the pictures from the floor, he stopped suddenly, staring hard at one picture in particular.

"It's Sanchez, that stupid son of a bitch," he said aloud. Milton had said he'd taken pictures of another person living with Mrs. Lopez, but in Duncan's wildest imagination he never expected that person to be Sanchez.

Picking up the picture, he couldn't keep from saying his thoughts aloud again, as if he were questioning someone in the room. "How stupid can this guy be?"

He could hardly believe his eyes. If history had taught him anything, it was that criminals were dumb. But Sanchez was making the rest of his ilk look like brain surgeons by comparison.

How could a guy who killed the son of the world's most notorious crime boss not be looking for a rock to crawl under? Why would he go anywhere near Mrs. Lopez? How could he not think that she would—at the very least—be suspected of involvement in the murder?

At least a hundred similar (and equally unanswerable) questions flew through his mind as he stared at the photograph.

After taking a moment to catch his breath, he examined the remainder of the photos, finding Sanchez in a second and then a third.

Duncan was so engrossed in his discovery, that the sound of the telephone ringing made him flinch.

"Mr. Gabrelli. I found Sanchez!" Milton exclaimed, without so much as a hello.

"Me, too. You must be a mind reader; I was just about to call you."

"Then you know he's living with Lopez."

"Yes, he's in the photos you sent to the house."

"Do you want me to keep an eye on this guy?"

"Yes. Don't let Lopez or Sanchez out of your sight until I tell you otherwise."

"Yes, sir. Sorry I didn't know this earlier, but none of the neighbors knew who this guy was when I asked earlier today."

"No problem. Just don't lose them."

"I'm on it."

It didn't take Duncan long to understand the significance of Sanchez's presence in the photographs. Mrs. Lopez was a woman of modest means—she wouldn't have the financial resources to ship her belongings back to Mexico. *No, she'd be driving back to Mexico.*

It started him thinking. *A trip by automobile between Los Angeles and Pegueros would be difficult. She'd have to navigate her way through parts of Mexico where banditos roam the desolate highways like vultures. The police are only slightly less dangerous than the banditos. It's very unlikely she'd attempt the journey on her own. Damn. He's going with her to Mexico,* Duncan shook his head in disbelief.

Well, maybe it's not completely stupid. What are his choices? Not many came to mind.

He's no longer safe in the United States. He's fresh out of prison. He probably has no friends, here or in Mexico, at least not any that want an ex-con living with them.

Sanchez clearly wasn't smart enough to realize that there was no place to hide from Mr. Bartelli's wrath.

Sanchez must have owed Juan Lopez a big favor. To commit Santino's murder and then take Juan's mother to Mexico, he must have owed Juan a monstrous favor.

For all Duncan knew, it could have been a gang-related debt, or a prison thing. But whatever his reasons were for participating in Santino's murder, he had made the most costly mistake of his life.

"Sir, Mr. Gabrelli is on your private line," the butler announced.

"I'll take it in my office." Mr. Bartelli broke into a jog as he headed toward his office.

"Don't tell me. You miss me already?" Mr. Bartelli said, catching his breath as he picked up the receiver.

"I found him. Are you okay? You sound out of breath."

"Don't worry about me; I'm the picture of health," Mr. Bartelli replied, just as a deep, loud cough forced Duncan to pull the receiver from his ear.

"Yeah, 'the picture of health'? You might want to use that treadmill that is gathering dust over there."

"Okay, doctor. You mind getting to the point, you broke into my workout." He could hear Duncan laughing on the other end of the line, "Fuck you, I could have been working out."

"Right," Duncan said in total disbelief. "As I was saying, I found him."

"Jesus, you've only been gone for twenty minutes. You already know where he is?"

"I'd rather talk in person. But I have someone keeping an eye on him."

"So you're coming over?"

"I can't, sir. I was thinking lunch tomorrow. I'll be there at eleven thirty, if that's okay with you."

"Why so long? Come now."

"Sorry sir, but I need to take care of a few matters first. Lunch would be best."

"You keep amazing me, son, and I'm seldom amazed by anyone."

Son. It sounded good in Duncan's ear. "Thank you, sir. I will see you tomorrow."

CHAPTER 53

WITH SANCHEZ AND Mrs. Lopez fleeing to Mexico, Duncan knew that there would be little he could do to stop Bartelli from killing them both as soon as they crossed the border. And not just kill them—it was sure to be gruesome and brutal.

While murder was hard to get away with in the United States, such was not the case in Mexico.

Poverty had forced many Mexicans to leave their homeland in search of work. Entire families would sneak across the border, melting into the large Spanish speaking populations residing in California and other border states. Keeping track of its citizenry was further hampered by corruption at every level of the government and the lack of resources. The whereabouts of two Mexicans would be too deep in the minutiae for anyone to care about.

Mr. Bartelli had many powerful political connections in the United States, but they paled in comparison to his influence in Mexico. Even if a US agency attempted to investigate the disappearances of Sanchez and Lopez, they would find little assistance from the Mexican authorities.

Looks like Mr. Bartelli is going to Mexico. I'd better find a way to get him there undetected.

With the US government keeping tabs on Mr. Bartelli, it wasn't going to be as easy as it sounded.

Whatever the plan, Duncan needed to prepare himself for the possibility that *he* might be investigated for the murders.

While US authorities wouldn't get much help from across the border, Duncan's activities over the past week would surely direct the police straight to his front door.

It's time to purge myself of all the evidence related to my Santino investigation.

As quickly as that thought came to mind, it dawned on him that it was time to destroy *all* his personal files. *I've already learned all I can from them; they could only get me into trouble now.*

He had purchased a commercial shredder years earlier in anticipation of this day. It had sat unused under a gray cover in a small room just off the study. Like a vulture, it stood watch over the mounds of research that it was destined to consume. Its patience was about to be rewarded.

He wouldn't be saying goodbye to his obsession. Rather, he was taking it to the next level. To move on, he had no choice but to rid himself of all remnants of the research. There could be no trace left to later connect him to the murders he planned to commit.

He had dreamed about what it would feel like to murder another human being for so long, that it seemed more like a fantasy than reality. But the truth was that he had been ready for a long time. Santino's murder was just the shove he needed.

Staring around the room, he wondered, *If Santino hadn't been murdered, would I have ever let my obsession leave the confines of this study?*

Duncan could have gone on with his research for many years, never choosing to become a murderer. *Have I been using my professed desire to study as an excuse to avoid taking the next step?* It was a question he had asked himself many times.

Now he had to consider the possibility that the answer was yes.

It pained him deeply to watch his years of labor disappear into the shredder's teeth. The pages looked like they were being attacked by a swarm of piranhas, as they were ripped into tiny pieces. Page after page disappeared into its jaws.

The chimes from the clock on the wall counted out the hours. He hadn't realized just how much paperwork had been generated or how many files compiled. The pure volume of shredded paper was impressive. Using large black plastic garbage bags he filled bag after bag, until the last of the twenty bags he'd found in the gardener's shed were full.

It was one o'clock, but only about a third of his files had been destroyed. Exhausted both physically and mentally, he decided to start again in the morning.

As he lay in bed, he thought, *No one will ever benefit from my years of hard work and study.* Drifting into a deep sleep, his last thought was, *I could have used the information for good.*

CHAPTER 54

A T 7:35 A.M., Duncan was awake but resisted opening his eyes. It was his habit to keep his room at a slightly cooler temperature than was comfortable for most people. Waking to a cold room, wrapped snugly in his silk sheets and a down comforter, was one of life's little pleasures.

This morning he had additional motivation for not wanting to get out of bed. Having spent most of the night dismantling his life's work, he wasn't in any hurry to get back to the project.

He promised to meet Mr. Bartelli at eleven-thirty. Lying there, he contemplated rescheduling their meeting for later in the day. Considering the mood he was in, he could have easily convinced himself to stay in bed all day. But Mr. Bartelli was already champing at the bit. If he did not show up for lunch, there was no telling what Mr. Bartelli might do.

The last piece of the puzzle was the connection between Mrs. Lopez and Sanchez and their impending departure to Mexico. Mr. Bartelli needed (and more important, expected) to be informed of such important information without further delay.

Reaching a compromise with himself, Duncan decided to treat himself to breakfast in bed, rather than resuming the shredding operation.

He rarely took breakfast in bed and *never* stayed in bed past eight. The house staff assumed that he was ill when he called down at eight thirty to have his breakfast brought to his room.

At ten forty-five he finally forced himself to leave the sublimely comfortable confines of his bed just in time to shower, shave, and get out his front door at twenty-five minutes after eleven.

Duncan's driver, also concerned that he might be ill, offered to drive him the short distance to Mr. Bartelli's home. The sympathetic tone of Benton's voice brought a confused look to Duncan's face. "No, thank you, I can drive myself."

Mr. Bartelli met Duncan as he pulled to the end of the driveway. "Come walk with me a moment. Let's stretch our legs a bit," he suggested. The two men began to walk around the perimeter of the massive estate.

"So tell me. What was so important that I had to wait all night and half the day to find out where the murderer of Santino is hiding?"

"I'm sorry. But it was important."

"Okay. We'll let that be your secret for now. So, where is Sanchez?"

"It appears that Lopez and Sanchez are planning to head for Mexico together."

"They're going to Mexico together?"

"Yes. Sanchez has been staying at Lopez's home. It looks like he is going to drive her back to her hometown."

Mr. Bartelli began to act almost giddy with excitement. Duncan couldn't help but think that *giddy* was an inappropriate response to the news. These people had killed his son, and nothing was going to bring him back. He would have thought that Mr. Bartelli would have expressed conviction or anger. His appearance of almost childlike happiness was a little disconcerting.

"Why didn't you tell me this last night?"

"You know I don't trust the telephone, and there's a lot of planning to do."

"That brings us back to why you didn't come by last night."

"I'm very sorry, but I just couldn't make it last night. I felt it was important that we discuss these matters after we had the benefit of a good night's sleep."

What he really meant was, he didn't want Mr. Bartelli to jump the gun and make a mess of the murders. But discretion was clearly the better part of valor, so he sugarcoated his response—just a little. "I have someone watching them, but perhaps you should have men you trust keeping an eye on them," Duncan suggested. "We'll need to know when they leave town."

"You disappoint me, my boy. You didn't really think I was just going to sit back and make you do *all* the work? I've had around-the-clock surveillance on her since you told me about her involvement," Mr. Bartelli confessed, with a look of one-upmanship painted on his face.

Duncan's surprise quickly turned into disappointment in himself. *How could I think that he would simply sit back and do nothing?*

The two men cut their walk short and headed back to the comfort of the study to begin developing a plan of action.

When they reached the house, Mr. Bartelli excused himself, explaining that he needed to make just a few calls before they got down to business.

"Should I be concerned about whom you're calling?" Duncan said sheepishly.

Mr. Bartelli did not respond. When he returned, Duncan began to discuss some thoughts that he had on Lopez's and Sanchez's deaths.

"Because these murders are going to be brutal and laden with revenge, making sure that the bodies are never found is of the utmost importance," he said for the hundredth time. He was beginning to sound like a man with Alzheimer's, the way he continually reminded Mr. Bartelli how critically important it was that the bodies disappear.

"Do you realize how many times you have told me that?"

Duncan ignored the question. "It will also be vital to any plan that Mrs. Lopez and Sanchez establish their presence in Mexico before the murders occur. There must be no question in anyone's mind that the two vanished while they were in Mexico."

Through his research, Duncan had discovered that both Lopez and Sanchez had originally entered the United States illegally, and neither had become a naturalized citizen. Therefore, when they went missing in Mexico, there would be no legitimate reason for any US government agency to investigate the matter.

Mr. Bartelli's political connections (both in Mexico and the United States) could find cover behind the argument that the disappearances would be a domestic issue for the Mexican government.

For the first time since Santino's death, they were in complete agreement about something. The murders would take place in Mexico after the two arrived in Pegueros.

Lunch was served in the study to allow the two men the opportunity to continue discussing the details. As they were eating, Mr. Bartelli received a call.

"Yes, I understand. Get a full description of the vehicle, including license plate. Yes, good work. Keep me informed."

Duncan could only hear one side of the conversation, but it was enough.

"Our prey is already on the move," Mr. Bartelli said in a calm voice. "They're loading up their belongings. It appears that they intend to leave today."

They spent the remainder of the afternoon planning. Despite his admonitions, Mr. Bartelli insisted on being present for, and participating in, the murders. Pleading with Mr. Bartelli to allow him to go in his place came to no avail. While he was clearly moved by Duncan's offer, there wasn't a chance in hell that he would accept.

Duncan was considering Mr. Bartelli's well-being when he offered to go to Mexico on his behalf. But he also had ulterior motives. Moving ever closer to his psychotic desire to commit the perfect murder, there were still lingering doubts that plagued him. Until now, his thoughts of murder had all been completely theoretical. While he had seen countless pictures of murder victims and hundreds of bodies at the morgue, he had never witnessed anyone being killed.

Actually experiencing murder was a different animal altogether. It was not clear in his mind how he would react. This would be his opportunity to find out if he had the *cojones* to kill. *I need to see if I have the stomach and the nerve. This is my chance.*

These murders were going to be extraordinarily violent. If he could handle these, he could handle anything.

Mr. Bartelli, while grateful for the offer, not only refused to let Duncan go in his place, but he also made it clear that Duncan could not accompany him to Mexico.

Duncan sensed that Mr. Bartelli had interpreted his offer as a gesture of affection and admiration. Playing on the emotion of the moment, he hoped that he could talk Mr. Bartelli into changing his mind. He did everything he could to play on their bond. But no matter how he tried, Mr. Bartelli flatly refused to allow Duncan to have any part in the actual murders.

Dejected, he eventually surrendered, accepting the idea that he was going to miss this golden opportunity to test his mettle under the most extreme of circumstances.

CHAPTER 55

THE FINAL PLAN was set. Mr. Bartelli would take an unchartered flight in a private plane. To avoid any record of him being in Mexico, his name would not appear on the flight manifest.

Duncan would take Mr. Bartelli and two of his most trusted bodyguards to a small airfield in San Diego. From there, the small airplane would take the three men hopscotching across Mexico to Guadalajara.

Associates of Mr. Bartelli would arrange for Lopez and Sanchez to be delivered to a large pig farm just outside of Guadalajara.

One of the major concessions made by Mr. Bartelli was that he would not be present for the murder of Juan Lopez. The plan originally called for killing all three at the same time and place.

He only consented because it was clear that Juan Lopez didn't physically participate in the murder of Santino, and waiting for Juan's release from Folsom would set the plan back by over a year.

Now that Mrs. Lopez and Sanchez were heading for Mexico, delay was impossible. Mr. Bartelli wasn't about to let either of them disappear into one of the thousands of Mexico's small towns.

While it would likely take weeks for the news of their disappearance to reach Juan, Mr. Bartelli had no intention of letting him live that long. They agreed that Juan should be taken care of as soon as possible after Mrs. Lopez and Sanchez were dealt with.

The drive from Los Angeles to Guadalajara was approximately forty hours, if they drove straight through. Considering the harshness of the drive through the desert, Duncan calculated that the trip would actually take at least three days.

The real concern in the back of both of their minds was, *What if they aren't going to Pegueros?* It would be impossible to follow them all the way to Pegueros. The long, desolate roads in Mexico would make it too easy to detect someone tailing them.

Therefore, the plan called for Mr. Bartelli's men to follow the car just beyond the Mexican border. From that point on, Mr. Bartelli would use his people on the other side of the border to make sure spotters were stationed along the route.

If they were truly going to Pegueros, there was only one major highway that they could take. There were contingency plans, but both men were banking on them taking that highway.

Duncan had also expressed concern that Sanchez might be just driving Lopez to Pegueros and not staying, or maybe not even driving her all the way. The spotters along the route would need to alert Mr. Bartelli immediately if Sanchez separated from Lopez before reaching Pegueros.

Last, they were concerned that if they didn't act quickly enough, Sanchez could leave Pegueros before they arranged for his abduction. If they allowed that to happen, he could easily vanish forever into the vastness of Mexico.

Because Pegueros was such a small town, neither Mr. Bartelli nor any of his associates knew anyone who actually lived in the town, whom they could trust to provide surveillance. However, his contacts in Mexico assured him that they would remedy that problem before Lopez and Sanchez arrived.

The plan had been conceived quickly, and there were many things that could go wrong. However, Lopez and Sanchez were already on the move, and there was no time to second-guess themselves or the plan.

There were far more people involved in the conspiracy than Duncan would have liked. In an effort to cull the number, he made sure that only essential information was provided to anyone involved.

Mr. Bartelli had chosen his most trusted bodyguard, Robert Percer, whom everyone called Stretch, to track Lopez and Sanchez just beyond the Mexican border. Duncan was not sure how Stretch got his nickname, but he had heard a rumor that it had something to do with an abnormally long appendage. Trusted or not, Mr. Bartelli always played his cards close to the vest; Stretch was told nothing about whom he was following or why.

Initially, no one in Mexico was told the identities of the two people they were instructed to track, or *why*. The spotters were provided with only a description of the car and a general description of its occupants.

It was becoming clear that Duncan had been absolutely correct. Lopez and Sanchez were reportedly on the main highway headed toward Pegueros. Updated reports came in on the hour and revealed that they were proceeding on schedule.

However, they were getting closer and closer to Pegueros and Mr. Bartelli still hadn't heard a word from his contacts regarding the recruitment of a local informant to provide surveillance inside the small Mexican town.

As it turned out, the people of Pegueros were so virtuous and hardworking, that Mr. Bartelli's associates were having trouble finding anyone even related to a resident of the very religious local community who had any connection whatsoever with organized crime. It took three full days to locate Carlos Martinez. He worked for one of the Mexican drug cartels and was the nephew of one of the residents of Pegueros. Carlos was immediately sent to Pegueros to keep an eye out for the arrival of Mr. Bartelli's prey.

Pegueros is a devoutly religious town with deep roots in the Catholic faith. As is true with most small Mexican towns, there are no secrets; everyone knows everyone else's personal business. To his family's chagrin, it was common knowledge that Carlos was connected to the drug cartel. That connection was a smudge on his family name and honor, leaving the family to wear his badge of disgrace. Even so, their culture never turns family away, so while his arrival was an unwelcome surprise, he was greeted with open arms by his family.

Carlos arrived for the unexpected and not particularly welcome family visit only three hours before Lopez's 1974 Chevy station wagon made its way down the narrow dusty main street pulling a small storage trailer.

CHAPTER 56

THE BOOK IN Mr. Bartelli's library had said almost everything there was to say about this town that was smaller than even a speck on the map. The old cliché, "If you were driving by the town and blinked, you could miss it altogether" fit this dust hole perfectly. With the exception of the huge Catholic church, the town was devoid of significance.

The church was a different story. The beautifully ornate structure stood tall in the very center of the town. Carvings and sculptures adorned its exterior. Its gold dome and spires stood sentry over the sleepy residents.

The interior of the church was even grander than the exterior. Large antique tapestries hung from the ceiling. Artists had drawn breathtaking murals of the ten Stations of the Cross around the interior walls of the main chapel. Hand-carved pews escorted the red carpet down the center of the church to the altar. Behind the altar hung a massive hand-carved depiction of Jesus nailed to the cross. Its opulence appeared out of place in such an impoverished town. As beautiful as the church was, there was something offensive about its grandeur in the midst of such poverty.

In front of the church was a large cobblestone town square. Behind the church was an even larger brick courtyard. The locals used both areas to congregate before and after church services.

Once a year—in honor of the town's patron saint, Sagrado Corazon de Jesus—the town threw a massive fiesta that lasted nine days and nights.

During the fiesta, the church was surrounded by tents, tables, and chairs. Mariachi bands and vendors were staggered throughout the square and courtyard.

Neither Mr. Bartelli nor Duncan realized that their prey's arrival would coincide with the beginning of the fiesta. It would later dawn on Duncan that it was probably no coincidence that Lopez chose this particular time to return home.

It was not until Carlos relayed the information of their arrival that they learned the fiesta was scheduled to begin in just two days.

Carlos had many fond memories of the fiestas he attended during his youth. His insight would prove invaluable.

He made it known that during the fiesta the entire town partied with nonstop drinking, dancing, and general hell-raising. It was quite common for people to stay out all night during the fiestas and even stay at the homes of neighbors or friends for days at a time. He suggested that it was possible that neither Lopez nor Sanchez would be missed for several days if they disappeared during the fiesta.

Both Duncan and Mr. Bartelli concluded that it would be the perfect time to spirit the two out of town.

There was an added advantage to kidnaping them during the fiesta: family and friends of those who resided in Pegueros would return home, like swallows to San Juan Capistrano, to join in the annual festivities. With plenty of unfamiliar faces in town for the celebrations, a professional crew could slip into town unnoticed among the many new faces.

CHAPTER 57

ON THE SECOND night of the fiesta at about eleven, six of Mr. Bartelli's associates were on the outskirts of Pegueros.

Three of the men were in a 1973 dark-green Chevy panel van with blacked-out rear windows. The other three men followed close behind in a late-model Lincoln Continental. They had arranged to pick up Carlos on the outskirts of town. When the driver of the van saw a solitary figure standing by the side of the road, he pulled over, and Carlos jumped in.

While Carlos was not the senior man, due to his familiarity with the town, he had been instructed to take logistical control of the abductions.

"Carlos, *estos son Miguel y Jose. Yo soy Esteban.*"

"*Buenas noches.*"

"Buenas noches."

"*Hablan Ingles?*"

"Si."

Carlos confirmed that everyone spoke English. "Good, most of the people in town don't, so we should."

"Sure. Where are they?" Esteban asked firmly and without emotion.

"They're staying with Lopez's older sister, Claudia."

"Let's go take a look."

Claudia, like her younger sister, was a widow. She lived alone in a small house approximately a mile from the center of town. Her children had long since left the quiet streets of Pegueros far behind. They had all left for the United States, seeking a more prosperous life.

With Carlos navigating, the van and the Lincoln drove slowly by Claudia's home. The house couldn't have been better situated. Unlike the houses in the center of town, each sharing a common wall with its neighbor, her house stood alone on a small plot of land.

There were no lights on inside or outside the house. On most nights that would have meant that the occupants were asleep, but this was the second night of the fiesta—it was much more likely that everyone was still celebrating in the square.

Lopez's station wagon was parked in the front of the house. The small storage trailer had been disconnected and parked on the east side of the house.

Confident that the house was empty, the crew turned their vehicles around and pulled to a stop directly in front of Claudia's home. Esteban got out to talk to his *compadres* in the Lincoln. He ordered them to make sure no one was home.

As was typical of small towns in Mexico, the front door was unlocked, allowing the men to quietly enter the house.

The other men waited in the van for almost five minutes before there was a knock at the passenger-side window. They had gotten lucky—the house was not empty. Mrs. Lopez, still exhausted from the journey and slightly inebriated from the consumption of tequila earlier in the evening, had walked back to the house alone. She was sound asleep when the three men entered. They had taken her completely by surprise.

Before she had a chance to even open her eyes, a hand pressed hard against her face, covering her mouth. One of the men plopped down hard on her chest, forcing most of the air from her lungs. She tried to scream, but the firm hand covering her mouth muted her pained voice.

They bound her wrists and ankles, stuffing a gag deep in her mouth. They were under strict instructions not to harm either her or Sanchez, so while they were firm, they took special precaution not to inflict any injury.

She refused to disclose Sanchez's whereabouts, but her defiance was of little concern to them. They already knew where to find a man like Sanchez. Free alcohol—he would be drinking and partying.

After a brief conversation with the men in the house, Esteban, Carlos, and the men in the van drove away toward the center of town. The other men stayed behind to make sure Claudia's home was left undisturbed. They even made the bed where Lopez had been sleeping. When they were done, they carried Lopez out of the house, placing her in the rear seat of the Lincoln.

Two men jumped in the Lincoln, one in the driver's seat, the other in the back with Lopez. The third man connected the travel trailer to Lopez's station wagon, and the two vehicles headed out of town toward Guadalajara.

It would be left up to the men in the van to abduct Sanchez.

CHAPTER 58

THE FIESTA WAS in full swing. A half dozen mariachi bands were playing simultaneously in different locations in front of and behind the church. The cascade of sounds blended into a noise that barely resembled music.

The town of five thousand residents had swollen to almost fifteen thousand, the majority of whom were in the courtyards singing, dancing, and drinking heavily. Tequila and beer were flowing like a river through the dry and dissolute town.

It was impossible to find a place to park anywhere close to the center of town. Old dusty cars and trucks lined every street. It was difficult to drive down the narrow streets without hitting the cars that had been left jutting out from the sidewalks. Esteban decided to have Miguel drive around until the van was needed. Carlos would contact the driver by walkie-talkie as soon as they grabbed Sanchez.

Carlos and the two men jumped out and began their search for Sanchez. It was eleven thirty, and the crowds in the front courtyard were waiting for the fireworks display that was set to begin at midnight.

A large metal structure had been haphazardly erected in the center of the courtyard. It had several large wheels attached to its sides and one giant wheel at its top. Dangerously large amounts of pyrotechnics had been strapped to the massive structure.

For each night of the fiesta, one of the prominent members of the town sponsored the fireworks display. The larger the display, the more affluent the town member was thought to be. On that night, one of the former residents of the town, who had become quite wealthy in the United States, was about to impress the townspeople with the largest fireworks display the small town had ever seen. It would be the perfect distraction if they could locate Sanchez before the show started.

However, the mass of humanity that was milling around the courtyard made their job a difficult one. The three men split up and walked through the throngs of people that filled the square. They met up again at the front steps of the church. Sanchez was nowhere to be found.

Esteban took Jose and headed around the east side of the church while Carlos walked around the west.

The east side of the church was a brightly lit wide road filled with vendors and concession stands. The two men walked slowly scrutinizing each face, careful not to let Sanchez slip by unnoticed.

The west side was a dark narrow alley. The only people Carlos encountered were a young couple attempting to hide their lusty intentions from their parents and neighbors.

The courtyard behind the church had only a scattered crowd, mostly old men who had no particular interest in seeing, or hearing for that matter, the fireworks.

As Carlos emerged from the alley, he immediately spotted Sanchez sitting with a group of old men at a table near the back of the church. Empty beer bottles littered the table in front of him. His droopy eyes and hunched shoulders announced that many of the bottles had belonged to him.

Carlos continued walking around the back of the church until he met up with the other two men. Occupying an empty table close to where Sanchez was sitting, they began to discuss how best to accomplish the abduction.

From the slurred voices, it was clear that the men sitting with Sanchez were also drunk.

They needed to get Sanchez away from the table, out of sight of the other men.

While contemplating their strategy, they heard Sanchez exclaim in a loud, grotesque voice, *"Tengo que miar,"* which roughly translated means "I have to take a piss."

One of the old men at the table laughed and pointed toward the alley on the west side of the church. *"El baño."* The toilet.

It was not uncommon for the older men, who were too lazy or just too drunk to make their way home, to use the alley beside the church as a restroom.

It was five minutes before midnight when Sanchez managed to muster enough energy to escape the force of gravity that had seemingly cemented his ass to the chair. On wobbly legs, he slowly staggered toward the alley.

They gave Sanchez a brief head start before following. He had already unzipped his pants and was using the wall of the church to hold himself up while he tried—without much success—to avoid pissing down his pants.

The crackling noise of the walkie-talkie was drowned out by the sound of fireworks exploding high above their heads. It filled the night sky with light and a deafening noise. Carlos told the driver to pick them up in the alley.

As Sanchez shook the last few drops of urine onto his pants, Esteban removed a blackjack from his pocket and struck Sanchez hard just above his left temple. Sanchez crumbled in a heap onto the urine-soaked ground. The blow to Sanchez's head was not as hard as it appeared. However, he was so drunk that he fell to the ground with the look of a dead man.

Carlos was first enraged and then scared. "We were not supposed to hurt this guy, asshole!" he said in Spanish.

While Carlos may have been in logistical control of the operation, he was in no position to talk down to a made soldier in the Mexican mafia. "He's not dead, but *you* will be if you ever talk to me like that again, *cabrón,*" the short, stocky Esteban snapped back in a blend of Spanish and English.

Carlos bent down to check on Sanchez, all the while praying the blow hadn't killed him. He was out cold, but he was breathing. Carlos let out an audible sigh of relief upon seeing the drunken man's chest moving up and down.

Only moments later the van turned down the narrow alley. Carlos's eyes were scanning the alley in all directions. The young lovers were staring up at the fireworks. They hadn't even noticed the van drive by them.

The limp body was quickly thrown in the van. All the men except Carlos jumped in. Miguel threw the van in reverse and backed out of the alley. The men headed out of town to meet up with the others in Guadalajara.

Carlos had been instructed to stay behind—if the situation permitted—and assess the town's reaction to the disappearances. In truth, he had no desire to spend two hours in a van with a Mexican Mafia thug he had just insulted. Staying in Pegueros would be much safer, at least for now.

He checked once more to make sure no one had witnessed the event. Seeing no one, he walked the length of the alley, entering unnoticed into the courtyard to watch the fireworks.

CHAPTER 59

AT 11:00 P.M. Los Angeles time (1:00 a.m. Guadalajara time) Mr. Bartelli received a call informing him that both Lopez and Sanchez were en route to Guadalajara. It was time to avenge his son's murder. He immediately called Duncan, waking him from a deep sleep.

Duncan had gone to bed early for the first time in years. Only the day before, he had completed the project of destroying all of his files. He had worked through the night until the job was finally completed at three o'clock.

Just when he thought there would be no more sleepless nights, the phone shattered the silence of the room at 3:47 a.m.

He was so tired that he sounded incoherent over the telephone. For a moment Mr. Bartelli thought he had dialed the wrong number. He'd called Duncan at all hours of the day or night and had never caught him sleeping.

Upon recognizing the voice on the other end of the line, Duncan instantly knew that it was time for Mr. Bartelli to catch his flight to Mexico.

"When do you want to leave?" Duncan asked in a groggy voice, sounding more drunk than tired.

"First thing in the morning."

Duncan's eyes refused to focus. "What time is it?"

"Go back to sleep. Pick me up at six o'clock sharp."

Without thinking, Duncan hung up the phone not waiting to hear if Mr. Bartelli was finished talking. After setting the alarm for 5:25 a.m., Duncan quickly fell back to sleep.

Mr. Bartelli was a little miffed with Duncan for the abrupt ending to the call. He thought about calling him back, but his excitement tempered his anger. He finally had his son's murderers.

Duncan pulled into Mr. Bartelli's driveway at exactly six. There were two blacked-out Chevy Impalas parked in the drive. Each one had three men inside. He assumed that the vehicles were their escorts to San Diego. Mr. Bartelli rarely left his estate without at least a half dozen armed guards. He would be traveling a little light this time.

Duncan was not pleased that their plan required Mr. Bartelli to leave the country with only two bodyguards. His associates in Mexico agreed to provide security for him and his entourage once they arrived in Guadalajara. But getting Mr. Bartelli safely from San Diego to Guadalajara concerned him.

As he pulled his Cadillac to a stop, Mr. Bartelli emerged from his front door flanked by two bodyguards. Duncan didn't even have time to get out of the car before the three men and several light bags were in the trunk of his car.

"Let's go, we have a plane to catch," Mr. Bartelli said as he closed the door firmly behind him. "There has been a slight change in plans. We will be leaving from the Van Nuys Airport," he told Duncan without explanation. The Van Nuys Airport was a very small airfield located in the San Fernando Valley about twenty miles outside of downtown Los Angeles.

Duncan was taken aback by two things his boss had said. He didn't like changing the plan. They had spent a considerable amount of time developing it, and changes at the last minute could jeopardize the entire plan.

Secondly, Mr. Bartelli had said "we" will be leaving. While he could have meant him and his bodyguards, it sounded more like Duncan was going.

"What do you mean by 'we will be going'? Am I going with you?" He had all but begged to go during the planning stages, but his request had been flatly refused.

While he waited for an answer, he couldn't help but think, *Why the change of plan and heart?*

"You were always coming. It was better that you didn't know until now."

Mr. Bartelli was a very cautious man and saw no good reason to let Duncan know the truth until the last minute.

"I'm scheduled to fly to Texas to meet with one of your associates tomorrow morning," Duncan said.

"Already taken care of. I made that appointment to make sure your calendar would be open for the next few days."

It was a short drive to the Van Nuys Airport. When the caravan drove out to the airplane hangars, a twin-engine Cessna was already fired up and ready to take off.

"The plane seats six very uncomfortably," Mr. Bartelli said with a chuckle.

The four men got into the airplane, which immediately taxied out onto the runway. Once the plane was in the air, Mr. Bartelli explained that they would fly to San Diego, top off the fuel tanks, and then continue on.

"Has the Juan Lopez matter been taken care of?" Duncan asked.

"I made the call last night. He's probably already dead," Mr. Bartelli said matter-of-factly.

Juan was dead. He had been found lying in a pool of blood on the shower-room floor that very morning. Someone had stabbed him seventy-three times in the chest, back, and face. It was no coincidence that Juan received the exact number of stab wounds that had been inflicted on Santino. While there were three guards on duty and at least fifty inmates in the general area of the showers, no one saw a thing.

It was just another gang-related jailhouse killing in a California prison.

CHAPTER 60

I T WASN'T IN Mr. Bartelli's nature to explain the reasons behind decisions he made. He never fully explained *why* he'd waited until the last minute to tell Duncan he was coming to Mexico. Undoubtedly, it had much to do with his emotional connection to Duncan.

Since Santino's death, Mr. Bartelli had increasing demonstrated in both word and deed that Duncan's affection meant more to him than almost anything in the world. Perhaps even more than his love for his murdered son Santino.

The relationship between the two had been a strange one from its very inception. Even before they were formally introduced, Duncan had formed impressions about Mr. Bartelli that were founded in misconception and rumor. Mr. Bartelli, on the other hand, knew almost everything there was to know about Duncan—at least, he *thought* that he did.

While Duncan would eventually learn a great deal about Mr. Bartelli's business affairs, he knew very little about Mr. Bartelli's personal life.

From the time her son was just five years old, Mr. Bartelli had made sure that Lucia Cabella received financial support to raise her only son. Growing up, it never occurred to Duncan to *ask* where the money came from to pay their bills or to send him to private schools. It never crossed his mind to ask how they were able to take vacations and travel.

After his mother's murder, the boarding schools and colleges were all paid by an anonymous benefactor. Duncan blindly accepted the story that it was part of his inheritance.

For a man who prided himself on details, it was strange that he never even thought to ask where the money came from; the money was just always there. Perhaps somewhere deep inside he didn't want to know.

Many years would pass before he would learn that everything he had accomplished had been financed by Mr. Bartelli. It was Mr. Bartelli who had paid his tuition from the time he entered elementary school on through law school.

Even his promise to attend law school, made to his mother when he was still too little to understand its import, was part of Mr. Bartelli's master plan. It had been he who made sure that Lucia exacted that promise. It was Mr. Bartelli who wanted Duncan to become an attorney. And, as usual, he would get his way even if it took a mother's guilt to make it happen.

It had been Mr. Bartelli who made sure that Weiss, Barron & Helms vigorously recruited him out of law school. And it was no accident that WB&H had made him such a spectacular employment offer.

Without ever having a clue, his entire life—his destiny—had been orchestrated by Mr. Bartelli.

And why not? Mr. Bartelli's blood was running through his veins.

CHAPTER 61

DUNCAN'S MOTHER, LUCIA, met the young Vincenzo Bartelli when she was only eighteen years old. Lucia was the most beautiful creature he had ever seen. He was almost ten years Lucia's senior, which in that era was considered an acceptable difference in ages. Working in his favor was the fact that both he and Lucia came from Catholic families.

However, there was one insurmountable obstacle standing between them and obtaining her parents' consent: Vincenzo's father was part of the crime family that controlled the west side of Chicago, a fact well known to all the members of the large but tight-knit Italian community.

Most Italian families would have seen him as a great catch for their daughter; such was not the case with Lucia's parents. They saw the mob as a blight on the Italian community and the reputation of all Italians.

While the Catholic Church turned a blind eye to the Italian mob, her parents would not. They saw it as their religious obligation to prevent their daughter from consorting with such a man. Vincenzo was guilty by association, or in this case by birth, and Lucia's family refused to give their consent.

Her parents made it crystal clear that she was strictly forbidden from associating with Vincenzo. Being a good Catholic girl, she tried hard to obey them, but she was as enamored with Vincenzo as he was with her.

The two met clandestinely for several months, spending every available moment together. The big ears and wide eyes of the Italian community forced the two lovers to spend their time in secret, out from under the watchful eyes of their community.

To her, he appeared wise and mysterious. Her innocence prevented her from seeing the trouble she was pursuing until it was too late.

Vincenzo was a worldly young man with substantial experience with women, but he had fallen deeply in love with Lucia. He wanted to marry her, but her parents stood fast to their convictions.

There was still an outside chance they could convince her parents to give their blessing, had the two been more patient.

But patience is a virtue frequently lacking in the hearts of those young and in love. After only a few months, it was clear that Lucia was with child. She could no longer quietly seek absolution for her sins at confession; this would soon be known to the world.

Her parents took the news as badly as she'd expected. Not only had she shamed herself, but if word got out that she defiled herself, then her entire family would bear her disgrace. Such were the morals and traditions of the day, particularly in her culture. There was only one thing that Lucia and her family could do.

A week after telling her parents, they sent her away. She was spirited out of town, literally under the cover of darkness, never to return. Lucia wanted to say goodbye to her Vinnie, but there was no way to reach him, locked away in her bedroom. She was sent to a Catholic convent to give birth to her son far from the prying eyes of her community.

Vincenzo's heart was broken. He begged her parents, but they would not disclose her whereabouts.

After giving birth, Lucia and her newborn son were moved south to Georgia. Her parents were able to provide some limited financial support. However, after a year, she stopped hearing from them altogether. Perhaps they were motivated by their religious beliefs, pride, or guilt, but the result was the same: she was on her own.

Lucia's letters to her parents began to be returned unopened. After a while, she stopped trying. Deep down, she accepted the fact that her parents had let her go.

She'd named her son Duncan, after Vincenzo's grandfather. She struggled to make a living, finding steady work in a local market. They lived modestly, but she and Duncan were building a happy and loving home in their small one-bedroom apartment.

CHAPTER 62

ON DUNCAN'S FIFTH birthday, his life changed forever. Lucia had planned a small party for his birthday.

On that beautiful sunny day a black limousine rolled to a stop in front of her building. The expensive vehicle (and the extraordinarily large gentleman who exited it carrying several ornately wrapped packages) looked conspicuously out of place.

However, inside the apartment, the spectacle went unnoticed. The large man knocked loudly on Lucia's front door. When she answered, even the brightly wrapped packages couldn't subdue her feeling of unease at seeing the sheer girth of the man in the black suit filling her doorway. For a moment she couldn't catch her breath, which forced her to release a soft sigh of surprise before she could speak.

The menacing-looking man (who was probably used to such reactions) looked down at her "Are you Lucia Cabella?" His voice was delicate, more suited to a man half his size.

She replied, "Yes, I am. May I help you?"

"I've been instructed to deliver these packages to you."

And without another word, the mammoth man stepped past Lucia, careful not to step on any of the half dozen small children playing on the floor beneath his size-fifteen feet. With surprising grace and agility he navigated the fifteen feet to the couch in the front room, where he deposited the gifts. He began to scan the room, as if he were looking for someone he knew.

Lucia was still standing frozen at the front door. The eyes of every adult in the room were focused on the man in black.

Duncan was standing in front of the small kitchen table, doing his best to control the temptation to poke his finger in the chocolate-covered birthday cake Lucia had baked. The man's eyes fixed on Duncan. He walked over to him and bent down on one knee beside little Duncan. Even on one knee, the man's sheer girth blocked Lucia's view of her son.

A panicked feeling came over her that snapped Lucia from her near trance. She came up quickly behind the big man.

Just as she was about to say something (she wasn't sure what), she heard him say, "Happy birthday, little man." He reached out to shake Duncan's hand. The little boy's fingers disappeared into his enormous palm.

With that, the man stood to his feet, turning back toward the front door. He hadn't expected Lucia to be standing so close behind him. It was all he could do to stop quickly enough to avoid running her over.

Looking her directly in the eyes, he reached into his vest pocket. As he did, half the parents in the room audibly gasped. He pulled out two large envelopes, which he handed to Lucia.

"This is for you, madam," he said, looking back down at Duncan. The man smiled, tipped his hat to Lucia, and then turned to leave.

"Excuse me, sir. Do I know you?"

The man did not respond.

"Who are you?" she asked firmly, but in a polite tone.

The man looked over his shoulder at her. "The answers to all your questions are in those envelopes." With that he was gone.

Everyone in the room stood in silence, waiting for an explanation from Lucia. "Who was that man? What's in the packages? What's in the envelopes?" they asked.

Lucia was asking herself the very same questions. After all, before that day, she'd never met the man. And yet he seemed to know her and Duncan.

While everyone stood stunned, the birthday boy had made his way to the couch. The sound of tearing wrapping paper drew the room's attention to little Duncan.

Lucia was about to stop him, until she noticed his name neatly printed on each one. They contained a new baseball glove, roller skates, a bag of assorted candies, and a toy truck.

Lucia had never been able to afford such extravagant presents. Seeing the excitement explode onto her son's face brought tears to her eyes.

When the last of the packages was unwrapped, there were still no clues as to who had sent them. All eyes immediately turned back to the envelopes that Lucia still clutched with both hands tightly against her bosom. Opening one of the envelopes, she saw a thick bundle of cash in large bills. The sight of such a large sum of money snatched the air out of her chest. Her legs became weak and she was forced to take a seat on the couch to keep from collapsing to the floor.

Just as she was beginning to regain her composure, she looked back down at the money and felt faint again. Catching her breath, she opened the second envelope. It contained what looked like a legal document. It was a deed to a home.

Tears began streaming down her cheeks. If her guests weren't already mystified by the events of the last few minutes, her tears surely brought a whole new series of questions to their minds.

There was another surprise in the envelope. It was a savings account passbook from a local bank. It was in her name. The balance: $10,000.

Her eyes rolled back in her head, and she toppled face first onto the floor, just missing a baby crawling in front of her.

Several minutes later, when she came to, she was still clutching the envelope. Her friends helped her back up onto the couch, where she sat without moving a muscle for several minutes. She was almost too afraid to look back into the envelopes; for fear that her heart couldn't stand any more excitement.

There was one last item inside, a single piece of paper. Her bene-factor had written, "I will always love you. Take care of our boy." The note was not signed, but it didn't need to be. It could only be one person, her beloved Vincenzo. There was no question about it—she'd loved only one man.

The deed was to a modest home located in a town Lucia had never even heard of in California. *Where is Tarzana?* She thought.

It wouldn't be until several days later that she would learn that she was the owner of a small three-bedroom home located in the hills that separated the beaches of Santa Monica from the San Fernando Valley.

At first, she wasn't quite sure what to do with the money or the deed to a home so far way. She didn't want his money; she wanted the man she loved.

Even after five years, she was—and would always be—in love with him. In her heart she knew that if he could, he would be with her. After considerable contemplation, she concluded that the gift meant that he wanted her to raise their son in California. That was all she needed to know.

Giving two weeks' notice to her employer, she and little Duncan moved to their new home.

CHAPTER 63

VINCENZO HAD STARTED looking for Lucia the day after her parents forced her to leave Chicago. As months turned to years, he had all but given up hope of locating his lost love. Even after he met the woman whom he would eventually marry (almost two years after Lucia vanished), he continued to hold out hope that he would find his beloved Lucia and the child he had never met.

Her parents had been only partially correct about his father. He wasn't *part* of a crime family. He was what every crime family wished it could be.

Vincenzo Bartelli Sr. was one of the masterminds who transformed the mob into a much more organized and civilized operation. His crime family would eventually become what is known today as the syndicate.

Way ahead of his time, Mr. Bartelli Sr. could see that the real money was in the trafficking of illegal narcotics. Recognizing that the profitability of other criminal activity—loan sharking, gambling, theft—paled in comparison to drugs allowed him to eventually gain control over almost all of the drug trafficking in the world.

His real genius lay in his understanding that the syndicate needed to employ more brain and less brawn. The days of gunfights in the street were over. He knew that the syndicate didn't need more thugs; it needed more attorneys and accountants. Employing some of the most expensive legal minds in the country, he was able to use the law to construct and protect the syndicate.

The attorneys created layer after layer of shell corporations to launder money. The accountants found loopholes in the tax laws to avoid paying taxes on much of the money the corporations washed.

The federal government ferreted out smaller, less organized drug traffickers, while the syndicate's influence grew. Its control would spread across the country and eventually throughout the world.

The syndicate was run much in the same way corporations are. There was a board of directors that through the years maintained varying levels of control over the general direction of the syndicate. But it was Bartelli Sr. that controlled its day-to-day operations.

When his father retired, all the day-to-day operations of the syndicate were turned over to Vincenzo Bartelli.

It was through his father's business connections that Vincenzo was able to locate Lucia and his son in Georgia. However, by the time he found her, he had already been married for three years and was expecting a child. As much as he loved Lucia, he had already begun a new life. His responsibilities to his marriage, to his Catholic faith, and to the syndicate made it impossible to be with Lucia.

He did, however, do his best to provide support for Lucia and little Duncan. Continuing to provide that support for the rest of their lives, he maintained a close watch over his second family.

As the years passed, Lucia and Vincenzo would talk by telephone. He would frequently ask to see her, but she always declined. He was married, and she would do nothing to break that bond.

A hopeless romantic to the end, she never remarried. She chose instead to dedicate her life to raising her only child.

CHAPTER 64

THE FLIGHT FROM San Diego to Guadalajara was grueling. One of Duncan's big concerns was that the airplane would be mistaken by DEA monitors as a drug smuggler. Therefore the pilot was instructed to fly low over the US border to avoid detection. Turbulence rocked the airplane violently as it flew at frighteningly low altitudes.

As if the turbulence were not enough, the small airplane had to make several stops to take on fuel. The takeoffs and landings were taking their toll on everyone, especially Duncan.

"You're looking a little peaked. Are you okay?" Vincenzo asked, more to poke fun at Duncan than out of concern.

"No. And you're not funny."

"Don't get sick in my plane, or I'll have David throw your ass out," Vincenzo said, nodding to his bodyguard. Playing along, David cast an "I'll do it" glare at Duncan.

"Yeah, you guys are a riot."

After a long and uncomfortable trip, the twin-engine Cessna set down on a small private airfield just outside of Guadalajara. As they rolled down the dirt runway, four Lincoln Continentals and a black stretch Cadillac limousine followed their dusty trail.

When the airplane and vehicle escort came to a complete stop, a herd of men brandishing automatic weapons poured out of the Lincolns. As he looked out the window, Duncan thought, *If this is an ambush, we're dead men.*

It was, however, just a very impressive showing of security by their hosts. The armed men created a human shield for a small Latin gentleman named Roberto Rodriguez.

Rodriguez was a very important man; at least he was on *this* airfield. He stood at the base of the steps with an awestruck look of anticipation on his face. Rodriguez was, in fact, an important man, but from the look on his face, he could've just as easily been waiting for the pope to step off the plane.

A bodyguard exited the airplane first, followed by Mr. Bartelli, Duncan, and then the last bodyguard. Stepping past the bodyguard, Rodriguez bowed his head as he reached out for Mr. Bartelli's hand. Accepting the extended hand palm down, Rodriguez kissed the back of his hand repeatedly.

"Don Roberto, what a pleasure to see you again, my good friend," Mr. Bartelli spoke in perfect Spanish. Duncan's three years of Spanish classes were finally coming to use.

"It's an honor to have you visit my home, Don Bartelli," Rodriguez responded in English, his thick Latin accent slurring most of his words into a single guttural phrase.

It would have been easier to understand if he had spoken in Spanish, Duncan thought.

"I have taken care of everything, just as you have requested. I'm at your service. My men have pledged their lives to protect you and your men during your stay."

Mr. Bartelli again replied in Spanish, "Thank you, my dear friend. I have the utmost confidence in you."

The conversation was so formal that it appeared staged. *Sounds more like lines in a play than a conversation between friends,* Duncan thought.

"It must have been a long flight. Would you like to freshen up before we visit your friends, Don Bartelli?"

"No. Take me to the farm. Let me see my son's murderers."

Ordering three of his men to stay behind to guard the plane, Rodriguez waved his hand, and the limo pulled forward. Rodriguez, Duncan, Mr. Bartelli, and his two bodyguards climbed in.

Rodriguez instructed the men to take the pilot directly to his ranch. The rest of the men piled into the three remaining vehicles and escorted the limo to the farm.

CHAPTER 65

THE PIG FARM was a twenty-minute drive from the airport. When Mr. Bartelli decided to use the farm, Duncan had conjured up some pretty unsavory images of what the place would look like.

Duncan stared out the window of the limo as the vehicles made their way down a long dirt road.

"When will we get to the farm, Mr. Rodriguez?" Duncan inquired.

"We've been on it for the last five minutes," Rodriguez's bodyguard responded.

Rodriguez glared at the guard. "Please forgive him, Mr. Gabrelli. My English is not so good. He is used to translating for me. He meant no disrespect."

"No. No. It's fine. You haven't seen Mr. Bartelli for a long time. Here, you two talk, I'll talk to...I'm sorry, I don't know your name."

The guard looked to his boss, who nodded his head, giving the man permission to speak to Duncan.

"My name is Jesus."

"So, Jesus, it must be a large piece of land."

"Yes, it is very large. The farm encompasses over six hundred acres of land. However, only a small portion of the land is used to raise pigs. Most of the land is used to grow the food used to feed the pigs and farmhands."

"You speak English very well. Did you learn it here?"

"No, in the United States."

"It's a beautiful place. Greener than I expected."

"Yes. It's a very nice place, as long as you don't stand downwind of the holding pens."

Duncan laughed. "Tell me a little bit about the operation."

Jesus was glad to oblige. "The farm is divided into two sections. The north side is used to house the pigs. Their pens are elevated over a concrete ravine. The floors are made of two-inch-wide wood slats spaced about six inches apart. That allows the pigs' feces to drop down onto the ravine. It's washed down into large holding ponds. It's used as fertilizer to grow food to feed the pigs, and the whole process begins again."

"You must have given this tour before," Duncan said with a smile.

"Not really. Not many visitors come to the farm; and even fewer leave." The sinister smile on Jesus's face left no need for explanation.

Duncan could see large buildings on the horizon as they got closer. "What are they used for?"

"The large ones are the slaughterhouses where the pigs are made ready for market. The smaller ones are bunkhouses and living quarters."

"It sure looks different than I imagined." *It's a fitting place for them to die.* Duncan kept that thought to himself.

While Jesus entertained Duncan, Rodriguez and Bartelli held a conversation in Spanish.

"We're holding them in one of the slaughterhouses."

"Was there any problem getting them here?"

"No. It went exactly as planned."

"Good. Good. They're in good health then?"

"Sanchez has a nice bump on the head, but they didn't put up much of a fight."

When the vehicles reached the entrance of the farm, they turned south and stopped in front of the largest of the slaughterhouses. One of Rodriguez's men slid open the huge hangar-type door, and the limo and one of the Lincolns drove inside. The men from the remaining two vehicles took up defensive positions outside.

Once the building was secured, the men exited the limo. Rodriguez, Mr. Bartelli, and Duncan walked down a long hallway lined with doors on either side.

Halfway down the hall, Rodriguez opened a door. Maria Lopez was sitting on a concrete bench with her hands and feet chained together. The long chains ran through big metal rings embedded in the concrete walls. Except for a blindfold and a gag, she'd been stripped naked.

"Sanchez is just down the hall," said Mr. Rodriguez.

Lopez's body began to quiver when she heard the men talking. She looked fragile and scared. Mr. Bartelli watched without emotion as a trickle of urine ran down her leg. He wasn't in the least bit moved by the obvious intensity of her fear. A torrent of rage filled his chest. He wanted to kill her that very instant.

A strong stench of human excrement filled his nostrils as he entered the room. She hadn't been allowed to use the bathroom facilities. The chains restricted her movement, but she relieved herself as far away from where she was sitting as possible.

Walking slowly over to where she was sitting, Mr. Bartelli removed a handkerchief from his pocket, wiped off a section of the cement bench directly beside her, and sat down.

Suppressing his rage, and in a gentle and controlled tone, he softly whispered into her ear so that only she could hear. "I understand why you murdered my son. I respect you for having the courage. You did what you had to do, and now I will do what I must do. May God have mercy on both of our souls."

Until that moment, she hadn't been told why she'd been abducted or by whom. While she certainly had a strong suspicion, it was not until she heard Mr. Bartelli make reference to his son that she knew for sure. Strangely, she seemed to find comfort in that knowledge, notwithstanding the fact that she must have realized it meant she would die.

Standing up, Mr. Bartelli asked to be taken to see Sanchez.

Sanchez was sitting in a room almost identical to Lopez's. He too was chained, but he was neither blindfolded nor gagged. Even stripped naked, he was a hard-looking man. The markings of his thug lifestyle added to his gritty look.

Mr. Bartelli could see from the expression on his face that he was not intensely afraid. Duncan felt a twinge of intimidation facing this man. *Damn, he's about to die, and he still has the balls to give us a fuck-you stare.*

Mr. Bartelli, on the other hand, was not impressed. He'd wiped that same stupid look off the faces of men much tougher than Sanchez would prove to be. "You're going to answer a few questions for me before I kill you."

In what would be one of his last showings of bravado, Sanchez responded in a mixture of broken English and Spanish. He spewed profanities for several minutes (the *Reader's Digest* version of his response was the same as his glaring look: fuck you).

There would be no kind or understanding words for him. Whatever his reason for participating in Santino's murder, Mr. Bartelli would show no mercy. Sanchez was less than human in his eyes and deserving of death. A fate that would not be far in the offing.

CHAPTER 66

LOCATED IN THE center of the slaughterhouse was a thirty-foot-wide circular pen with four-foot-high walls. Around three-quarters of the enclosure was bleacher-style seating, nine seats deep. It served a variety of functions. Sometimes it was used to show and auction off prized hogs. Other times cockfights or dogfights were held there. That day, it was to be used for the torture of Sanchez.

On Mr. Bartelli's order, Sanchez was dragged naked into the arena. His arms and hands were secured to the wide, flat armrests of a heavy metal chair in the center of the pen. His legs were spread apart and tied to the legs of the chair.

The chair was fitted with metal rings that were staked into the dirt floor. Beside the chair sat an old, sturdy wooden table.

Mr. Bartelli had Lopez brought out and seated on one of the benches closest to the pen, to witness Sanchez's torture up close.

Lopez and Sanchez were left alone, while Rodriguez, Mr. Bartelli, and Duncan secretly watched and listened from a narrow walkway that ran below the bleacher seats.

The sounds of Mrs. Lopez's sobs echoed throughout the empty building.

"I'm so sorry, Señor Sanchez."

Sanchez was not very talkative. Tugging on his restraints, he was more interested in attempting to free himself. His struggling only managed to tighten the ropes that bound him to the chair.

After about twenty minutes, Mr. Bartelli walked back into the arena and sat down next to Lopez. Duncan took a seat directly across from them, strategically choosing his seat in hopes of getting a good view of both the torture and the reactions of Mr. Bartelli and Lopez.

Roberto Rodriguez entered the arena last. He walked directly down the path to the center of the pen. In his right hand he carried a large black leather bag, just a little larger than the kind doctors carry. It appeared to Duncan that the bag must be quite heavy based on the strained look on Rodriguez's face. In his left hand he was carrying a small wooden stool.

Being asked to conduct the interrogation of Sanchez was considered a personal honor, and Rodriguez accepted it with great pride.

No one else was allowed in the arena. None of the security personnel were permitted to witness any of the violence that was to be perpetrated.

When he reached the center of the pen, Rodriguez set the stool on the floor directly in front of Sanchez. Yanking at the handle of the black bag, he leaned his body hard to his left to help lift the bag higher into the air. Just clearing the lip of the wooden table, the bag landed heavily on its top with a loud clank.

Pulling a pair of skintight leather gloves from his pocket, he squeezed his thick callused hands into them. As if he were preparing for surgery, he began removing the contents of the bag, placing each of the items neatly on the table. Now Duncan understood why the bag looked so heavy. It contained four different size hammers (the largest was a five-pound baby sledgehammer). The bag held a dozen different knives, small saws, ice picks, and an array of other tools, some of which Duncan didn't even recognize.

Looks of horror were painted on the faces of both Sanchez and Lopez. Mr. Bartelli had seen this show before. He carefully watched the faces of his son's murderers, entertained by their fear.

Duncan was enthralled by the pure terror that electrified the arena. Nothing had even *happened*, and yet he was so stimulated by what he was watching that he felt himself getting an erection. Disgusted by his reaction, he mentally fought the sensation until the erection was gone.

Mr. Bartelli was softly talking to Lopez, but Duncan couldn't hear what was being said. It was, however, clear that she was terrified. She was shivering wildly, as if she were having a seizure.

Unexpectedly, a voice boomed from the center of the arena. "Did you kill Santino Bartelli?" Rodriguez bellowed.

Sanchez (first in Spanish and then in English) denied having anything to do with Santino's death. Before his denials finished leaving his lips, a small ball-peen hammer came crashing down on the little toe of his left foot. It flattened like dough under a rolling pin, causing blood to splatter in a small circle around his foot.

A chorus of profanities rose up from arena. Alternating between English and Spanish, he cursed his torturer.

"*Chingate cabrón! Tu madre es una* fucking cunt! You cock-sucking *pinche puto!*" FUCK!

"Wrong answer," and the hammer fell again, this time on the small toe of the right foot.

Clenching his teeth, Sanchez groaned loud and long.

"Did you kill Santino Bartelli?"

When no answer was forthcoming, the hammer crashed down for a third time.

Grimacing, Sanchez screamed in pain. "Fuck you, *cabrón!* Fuck you!"

"Wrong answer again," Rodriguez whispered as the hammer crushed the thumb of his right hand.

Sanchez tugged wildly against his restraints. Not so much to free himself, as it was a reaction to the intense pain that was racking his body.

"*No mas, no mas.* Yes, I killed him, you motherfucker," he confessed, still finding the *cojones* to talk tough.

"Good, now we're getting somewhere. Who helped you?"

The silence was broken by the cracking of bones in his right index finger. After allowing a moment for him to stop flailing, Rodriguez raised the hammer again.

"No, please, no one helped me, man. No one. Please. *No mas.*" Tragically, Sanchez was not aware that everyone in the room already knew that Maria Lopez was present during Santino's murder.

Sanchez would find out the hard way. The strike left the middle finger of his left hand throbbing.

The blows continued to fall, alternating from limb to limb so as not to allow a blockage of pain to form in any one part of the body. Rodriguez left little doubt that he knew how to inflict pain.

Sanchez was on the verge of passing out. "Mercy, *por favor*, mercy!" Lopez began screaming uncontrollably. "Just tell the truth, tell them everything!"

Hearing her brave call, Sanchez mustered one last burst of courage, and in a slurred voice said, "Fuck you," just before he passed out.

Passing out was not going to save him. A bucket of cold water brought him back just in time to hear Rodriguez say the words he didn't ever want to hear again.

"Wrong answer."

There was a sharp pain in his right thigh. The hit wasn't designed to break anything—it was just a wake-up call. "That must have hurt like hell," Rodriguez said, mocking his suffering.

"Who helped you?"

The pain had grown too great to resist further. In a whimpering voice he sobbed, "Victor Perez and Maria Lopez."

Who the hell is Victor Perez? Mr. Bartelli and Duncan thought simultaneously. How could they have overlooked this possibility? Neither man expected to hear any name other than Lopez.

Mr. Bartelli motioned for Rodriguez to come to the edge of the arena. Duncan quickly made his way over as well, and the three men discussed the revelation in a whisper. When they were done talking, Rodriguez returned to Sanchez and began questioning him about Victor Perez.

Having finally surrendered to his pain, he freely disclosed the information without need for additional torture. He explained that he, Perez, and Juan Lopez belonged to the same street gang. Perez had only helped in the abduction of Santino but didn't participate in the murder. He hadn't spoken to Perez since the murder and hadn't told him that he was leaving the country. As far as he knew, Perez didn't even know the name of the person they had abducted. Perez was just helping out a fellow gangbanger. It was even possible that Perez didn't know Sanchez had killed the man he helped abduct.

Sanchez continued to pour out information, providing Perez's address, phone number, and physical description. After extracting the information about Perez, Mr. Bartelli suggested that they take a break to resolve "the Perez problem." Lopez was led back to her cell, and Sanchez was left tied to his chair.

It was a twenty-minute drive to Rodriguez's ranch. To call it a *residence* grossly understated the magnificence of the estate. From the outside, it resembled a military compound. Massive electrified fences surrounded the sprawling grounds. Armed guards were literally everywhere Duncan looked.

Even with cheap labor, this place must have cost a fortune to build, Duncan thought.

Huge Greek statues and fountains adorned the grounds. While there were a considerable number of smaller buildings inside the compound, the main home was a massive two-story *hacienda* with all the trappings of the most expensive homes in Beverly Hills.

Entering the home through the large hand-carved oak doors, Duncan marveled at the eclectic mixture of furnishings from around the world. Mr. Bartelli, who had obviously visited his friend's home before, excused himself, entering a small antechamber to make some calls.

It took less than an hour for Mr. Bartelli to make the necessary arrangements to deal with the Perez problem. Because Perez hadn't actually participated in Santino's murder, Mr. Bartelli felt no need to participate in his disposal. More importantly, they needed to resolve this Perez problem with dispatch. Making sure he was dead—and soon—was the most important thing.

Rodriguez had phoned ahead to have dinner prepared. The three men dined on tender carnitas, jumbo shrimp, and lobster.

Dinner was followed by a little friendly conversation, cognac, and Cuban cigars. When they had let their meal settle sufficiently, it was time to go back to the farm and let the torture begin again, this time in earnest.

With Lopez back in her seat of honor, Rodriguez continued to torture Sanchez late into the night. He began by driving an icepick deep into Sanchez's left thigh. Having Sanchez's complete attention, he methodically engaged in the infliction of pain. Using dull, rusty saws and clippers, Rodriguez slowly and methodically, inflicted pain, cutting away several fingers and one ear. Sanchez began to pass out more frequently as his nervous system reached overload.

It was important to Mr. Bartelli that Sanchez not die too quickly. Seeing he might be on the brink of death, it was decided to resume the torture in the morning.

Tourniquets were applied. Rodriguez took special care to make sure all the bleeding had stopped; it wasn't time for Sanchez to die—at least, not yet.

Sanchez, unable to walk under his own power, was dragged back to his holding cell, where he was covered with a thick poncho to protect him from the cool night air. God forbid that he should catch a cold and not be well enough to be tortured properly. Lopez was likewise returned to her room.

"Perhaps we should post someone to keep an eye on Sanchez. It would be a shame to have him die too soon."

"Certainly, Don Bartelli."

Rodriguez motioned to his bodyguard. "Carlos, I want Sanchez kept alive. Make sure that he does not die tonight."

"Si, Don Rodriguez. He will not die."

The security force escorted the three men back to the house to get some much-needed sleep.

CHAPTER 67

AFTER A FULL night's sleep, a large breakfast was served. As one might expect, there were piles of sausages and bacon, and enough eggs and tortillas to feed a small army.

Duncan was careful not to consume too much food for fear that his stomach might become unsettled by the next round of torture. Once breakfast was over, the men returned to the slaughterhouse and to the task at hand.

Duncan was surprised when Mr. Bartelli personally took over the torture. Unlike Rodriguez, he wasn't looking for information; he was only looking to inflict pain.

There was one question. "Where is my son's ring? You took my son's ring. Where is it?"

Mr. Bartelli knew that Lopez would have no use for a ring that was inscribed, "You're fucked."

Sanchez was in such pain that he could not even remember taking the ring. His poor memory would cost him. Mr. Bartelli took out a large pair of tinsnips and promptly snipped off Sanchez's ring finger.

Not surprisingly, it came back to Sanchez what ring Mr. Bartelli was talking about. "It is in my bag, in my bag, the one in the trailer. It's in my bag."

It was not clear to Duncan why Mr. Bartelli cared about the ring. After all, what was Vincenzo Bartelli going to do with a ring inscribed, "You're fucked." Maybe he thought the ring could give the police a clue, or maybe he just wanted to have it back because it belonged to Santino, or maybe he just wanted a reason to cut off Sanchez's finger. Duncan would never know. He never asked, and Bartelli never said why. But Duncan never saw the ring again.

Mr. Bartelli picked up a thin piece of wire off the table and wrapped it tightly around the nub of Sanchez's ring finger, "I would not want you to bleed to death," he said sarcastically.

The torture went on for three more days. Sanchez would pass out from the pain only to be revived and forced to endure even more extreme torture. Large hogs were periodically brought into the arena. They would bite and rip at the flesh on his arms, legs, and thighs.

His fingers, toes, and eventually his penis were cut off. He was forced to watch as the hogs were fed his amputated body parts.

Lopez was also compelled to observe every hideous moment of the torture. When it became too grotesque, she would faint. The torture would be stopped until she could be revived since Mr. Bartelli didn't want her to miss even one second of Sanchez's agony.

On several occasions as she watched the horrifyingly brutal acts, she soiled herself. Showing not the slightest bit of compassion, Mr. Bartelli made her sit in her excrement until the day's torture was done.

Toward the end, Sanchez became delusional. For all practical purposes he went completely insane. On the fourth day, when it appeared that Sanchez was beyond feeling the pain, Mr. Bartelli called a stop to the torture.

Mr. Bartelli sat on the stool, watching Sanchez's body twitch and jerk uncontrollably. Though the movements were clearly involuntary, he still derived a degree of pleasure from watching the body respond to that day's assault.

Mr. Bartelli stood up suddenly. The look on his face appeared almost devilish. It was as if he had devised a way to inflict even more pain. But it was not Sanchez's pain on his mind.

Having Lopez's restraints removed, he had Rodriguez escort her into the arena. She stood there naked and crying in front of Sanchez's battered and twitching body.

Rodriguez lurched back as Mr. Bartelli handed her one of the knives from the now blood-soaked table. Surprised by the events, and in an effort to protect Mr. Bartelli, Rodriguez drew a small-caliber pistol from his belt.

"I will make you a deal, Señora. Kill him, and I will let your sister live." Mr. Bartelli looked down at his watch. "You have two minutes to make up your mind, not one second more."

The first minute passed quickly. Lopez stood there staring at the bloody knife in her quivering hand.

At the one minute mark, Mr. Bartelli began to count down the seconds. "Sixty...fifty-five...fifty..."

She began to beg and plead with Mr. Bartelli. "Please, please don't hurt my sister!"

"...thirty...twenty-five...twenty..."

"No! Please. For God's sake, don't make me do this."

"...ten...nine...eight...seven..."

There was no time to think; no time to rationalize. She might have been better off attempting to kill Mr. Bartelli. But just as the countdown reached one, she cried out, "God forgive me," and plunged the knife deep into Sanchez's chest.

With the knife protruding from his chest, he slumped over dead. Lopez fell to the blood-drenched dirt floor, weeping hysterically. She cried for several minutes before looking up at Mr. Bartelli. He bent until their noses were nearly touching. Staring into her eyes, he whispered emotionlessly, "It's your turn."

CHAPTER 68

THE RESTRAINTS WERE removed, and two men were called in to carry Sanchez's lifeless body out of the building, dumping it into one of the pens containing large male hogs. The hogs squealed and snorted as they fought over his carcass.

Lopez tried to resist being bound to the chair, but she was far too small and weak to put up much of a fight. Bartelli watched as she squirmed and fought against the ropes. Duncan, who had been watching Mr. Bartelli intently, noticed the expression on his face transform from that of a killer to that of a redeemer. In that moment Mr. Bartelli had undergone a metamorphosis.

But into what?

She sat there in silence as Mr. Bartelli pulled the small stool close and began to speak to her in Spanish. His voice had a gentle, almost apologetic, tone.

"As you are by now painfully aware, I'm not a man to be trifled with. I know, as do you, that my son was responsible for the tragic death of your daughter. If I had it in my power to change that, I would. I wish you had your daughter back. I wish I had my son back. But they are gone, and there is nothing that either of us can do to change that reality. I apologize to you for the pain my son has caused you, may God rest his soul. But I do not forgive you for the pain you have caused me."

Duncan had never heard Mr. Bartelli apologize to *anyone*. The sound of the words echoed in his ears.

Etched in the reflection from Lopez's aging eyes was the unmistakable look of someone that was preparing to die that day. However, Mr. Bartelli's gentle words were helping her accept that fate.

As if they were two old friends saying their goodbyes, she interrupted him and said, "I will burn in hell for the sins I have committed on this earth. Even God can't save my soul from Satan's eternal fires. I accept that you must take your vengeance on me. But please, I beg you; do not hurt my sister or my only son."

Until that very moment, Mr. Bartelli had every intention of subjecting her to the same unimaginable tortures Sanchez had received. But as he listened to her, the image of Santino raping and killing her fourteen-year-old daughter flashed vividly in his mind.

He'd intended to tell her that her son was already dead, and even intended to tell her that he had killed her sister, although he had no intention of doing so. But for the first time in his life, he felt true remorse. Not for what he'd done, but for what he was about to do.

He no longer wanted to kill this fragile woman. She'd already endured more pain than she deserved. She hadn't put this play into motion—Santino had.

"This ends here! Worry not, little mother, for your sister and son, they are safe. It ends right here."

With those words, he took a .45-caliber revolver from his vest pocket. At point-blank range, he shot Maria Lopez twice in the heart. She died instantly. It was the closest thing to mercy he'd ever shown to someone he considered an enemy.

Neither Rodriguez nor Duncan expected his impromptu use of a gun. Apparently, neither did any of the bodyguards protecting these important men. Disobeying express orders not to enter the arena, the sound of gunshots brought both of Mr. Bartelli's bodyguards and two of Rodriguez's men racing into the arena with guns drawn.

In the confusion of the moment, a gun battle almost broke out between the two groups of men. Fortunately, the men quickly recognized that their respective bosses were in no danger. While they would later laugh about the incident, all three men could have been killed in the commotion.

After order was restored, Lopez's body was disposed of in the same manner as Sanchez's.

Returning to Rodriguez's home, the men sat around smoking cigars and drinking for hours. The next morning the men visited the hog pen where they had deposited the bodies. Duncan appeared to be the only one amazed by the fact that there was nothing remaining of the two human beings but a faded blood-stain in the dirt.

The hogs had devoured everything, bones and all.

CHAPTER 69

AFTER EXCHANGING LONG-WINDED expressions of gratitude with his host, Mr. Bartelli and his entourage were on their
way back to the United States. The flight home was more arduous
than Duncan had recalled. The small plane felt more cramped and the
takeoffs and landings were rougher. The plane appeared to be flying
slower, and he began to feel a little claustrophobic.

As they closed in on the US border, Duncan was happy he had
arranged slightly different transportation for the trip home.

They landed just on the outskirts of Tijuana, where a limousine
and a blacked-out four-door Cadillac were waiting to take the plane-
load of men across the border.

It was common knowledge that the DEA paid very little attention
to small airplanes flying to Mexico, but paid meticulous attention to
small airplanes flying in *from* Mexico. While there was nothing illegal
on the plane, Duncan didn't want to subject Mr. Bartelli to any random inspection. He thought that there would be far less chance of
being detained driving across the border.

Besides, Mr. Bartelli's name didn't appear on any flight manifest,
and the last thing Duncan wanted was to have to explain why they
were in Mexico. As it stood, only a very few individuals knew of their
whereabouts, and Duncan intended to keep it that way.

Out of an abundance of caution, Mr. Bartelli had his men leave all
their firearms with the pilot, just in case the vehicles were searched at
the border. There would be weapons waiting on the other side of the
border for the drive home.

One of the security guards sat up front with the driver, and the
others followed behind in the Cadillac. The two vehicles crossed

the border without incident. Within minutes of entering the United States, two Lincoln sedans pulled up alongside the limo.

Duncan, startled to see the vehicles with their menacing-looking occupants, immediately snatched up the telephone receiver to alert the driver.

Mr. Bartelli grabbed his hand, forcing the telephone back down into its cradle. "They're with us. I left the travel plans to you, not security."

A look of relief swept over Duncan's face.

The two men spent the drive home talking, but not a word was said about the events in Mexico. The bond between the two men had been made even stronger by the events in Mexico, but only Mr. Bartelli knew how strong. They were, after all, father and son, even if Duncan didn't know it.

Once back in Los Angeles, life returned to normal—or at least, normal for Duncan. He was back to representing Mr. Bartelli's associates and business interests around the world.

However, the relationship between the two men had completed its own transformation. He no longer treated Mr. Bartelli like a client or a boss. There was a new closeness between them. It was more than a little ironic that he *felt* Mr. Bartelli was treating him like a son.

There were a variety of reasons why Mr. Bartelli chose not to tell Duncan the truth about being his father. Being his son brought with it a level of risk and responsibility that could endanger Duncan's life. He had only one son now; he had no intention of placing him at risk.

For Duncan, the trip to Mexico provided the input into his own personality that he had been looking for. In fact, it had revealed a side of him that perhaps even *he* wasn't prepared to admit existed.

More important, the trip had answered the question he had so often asked himself. *Yes.* He *could* face murder in the eye and not flinch.

He'd not just planned a murder, he had witnessed every gory second of it. Remembering how he'd become sexually aroused by its brutality still left a feeling of shame and disgust. However, it made him realize just how much he craved the excitement.

Everything he'd experienced during the trip made him more determined to take the next step. It was time to use his knowledge, his expertise, and his cunning. There would be no cause, no revenge, no fear, and no hatred, only the sheer rush from the act itself.

How, when, where, and whom shall I murder? Duncan thought as he drifted off to sleep his first night back. These thoughts filled his dreams that night and every night that would follow. Each night he dreamed of new victims and new methods of murder.

PART V

THE BIRTH OF A MURDERER

CHAPTER 70

THE SUM OF his research had led him to the conclusion that it was the *randomness* of the act that reduced the risk of being caught. Even so, he thought it was a bit of an oxymoron to plan a *random* act. But it was all about manipulating and eliminating variables, and that took planning.

Everything must be committed to memory. The creation of documents of any kind might later incriminate me.

That was precisely why he had destroyed all of his research. There must never be anything in his possession that might connect him to his crimes.

For a normal person, it would have been nearly impossible to commit every detail to memory, but Duncan was not a normal person. Using his photographic memory, he was able to store an endless amount of information in his brain. While there are many people who have incredible capacities to memorize data, Duncan was one of the chosen few who possessed the talent and ability to analyze and put that information to practical use.

His substantial trial experience had trained him to outline and organize large volumes of information in his head. Criminal trials had honed his talent to modify and change his plans on the fly. Like a seasoned politician, he was able to adapt his arguments and strategies, disguising the weaknesses of his case and taking full advantage of its strengths.

Confident in his intellectual abilities, there was now the matter of how to cloak his physical identity. After all, he had experienced more than his share of public exposure. His face had been on the front page of almost every major newspaper in America at one time or another.

While he was by no means a celebrity, he was well known and had to face the possibility that someone might recognize him.

Years of interviewing witnesses had taught him that the vast majority of people have poor memories. He had read any number of studies that confirmed that fact, including one in the Harvard Medical Journal, in which it was reported that, on average, people begin forgetting details of things they had said, seen, or done within minutes. Unless there was some preexisting relationship or an otherwise unusual feature, one's ability to recall faces and body characteristics was almost nonexistent after twenty minutes.

The reports notwithstanding, he would have to become a human chameleon, able to disappear into any environment.

Where to commit the murders was a variable he *could* control. As a starting point, he decided that his crimes should be committed in parts of the country where he was less recognizable—places where the reputation of a big-city attorney was of little consequence and of even less use. Anyplace where the legal communities were large was ruled out. He was much more likely to be recognized by members of his peer group.

But no matter how small the legal community, there was always the possibility that some criminal attorney wannabe might recognize him. So he would need to be able to disguise his physical appearance in other ways.

He smiled as he recalled one of the funny (yet common) mistakes criminals made: the use of disguises. Getting caught wearing (or even possessing) a disguise was an open invitation for police to suspect you of a crime. Time and time again he had read case files where individuals were apprehended not because the police knew that a crime had been committed, but because their suspicion was raised by poorly conceived disguises. What those cases taught him was that the best disguise is no disguise at all.

A criminal who dresses in all black to hide in the darkness is destined to get caught the minute someone turns on a light. The best disguise is one that makes you look like everyone around you. Blend into your environment, melt into the community. Even a naked man would blend into a nudist colony.

However, it was only common sense that the more the body was covered in clothes, the harder it would be for someone to describe his features.

The East Coast, maybe the Midwest, someplace cold would be most suitable for committing such crimes. Hats, scarves, and gloves would be commonplace.

He had traveled extensively in his defense of the syndicate. They had made him acutely aware of how different the fashions are, not just from state to state but from town to town. Unlike most people who don't consider (at least not on a conscious level) the signals that are sent out by the clothes people wear, Duncan was fascinated by what he could discern from people's attire.

Some of the signals were obvious, like preachers, policemen, firemen, and hookers. But there are many more subtle messages, such as aggression, anger, rebellion, conservatism, wealth, grief, loss, and stupidity. The list was endless. Obtaining a better understanding of those signals was critical to his ability to disappear in a crowd.

Using the design of the syndicate as his model, he set up layers of corporations, each eventually owned by offshore corporations, to obtain information about the dress and customs of cities and towns across the country. In the Internet age, his scheme might appear excessively elaborate, but before information could be obtained with a single click of a mouse, newspapers ruled the information universe. He subscribed to every local newspaper and church newsletter in little towns across the country.

The corporations were a buffer between him and the towns, through which news of local events and trends would eventually end up in Duncan's library. The extravagance of the ruse was a testament to the extremes to which he was prepared to go in his effort to protect his identity and to disconnect himself from the community.

He was starting to get his arms around the question of where, but there were many other variables to consider, including time of day, lighting, population density, economics of the community. He would be taking a long list of considerations into account before he took action.

At first, the task of manipulating the variables was daunting. But that was also the beauty of the process. Each crime would have a unique and random nature, because by their very nature, the variables would mutate depending on the community in which the crime was committed.

Duncan would spend all of his free time over the next several months perfecting his outline, laying the foundation for the perfect crime.

CHAPTER 71

AFTER YEARS OF contemplation, Duncan was ready. More than that, he was eager. But he'd been avoiding one problem that had plagued him since even before the trip to Mexico.

The popularity and notoriety he'd garnered in the general public was nothing compared to how well known he must be to the FBI. There was little doubt in his mind that his photograph hung prominently on the walls of those agencies next to the many crime figures he had defended over the years.

His relationship with Mr. Bartelli, now as much personal as it was business, made him an even larger target for surveillance. Cringing a little, he thought, *My God, they must have a thousand photographs of me entering and leaving Mr. Bartelli's home.*

For the first time in years, he allowed doubt to creep into his mind. He wondered why he'd risk all he had and all he'd become to commit these meaningless crimes. *Why kill anyone? To what end?* It should have appeared completely illogical to such a brilliant mind. But such is the fine line between the brilliant and the insane.

For that brief moment, he entertained the idea of denying his inner demons. But as quickly as it appeared, the doubt was gone.

What to do about my relationships with the syndicate and Mr. Bartelli? The answer was as simple as it was obvious. At the very least, he had to stop being the front man for the syndicate's legal problems.

That would prove to be easier said than done. *You just don't quit the mob,* he thought.

The relationship he shared with Mr. Bartelli was becoming obvious to others in the syndicate. He'd become much more than just its attorney. Associates he met had begun to show him respect that was normally reserved for the board members, or even Mr. Bartelli himself.

Those in the highest levels of the organization were suggesting that Duncan might be the syndicate's heir apparent. Whether that was true or not wouldn't alter the fact that he was no longer just its attorney.

There was an unspoken, yet universally accepted rule, that once you're in, you're in the syndicate for life. Inasmuch as Duncan had no particular desire to die, he'd have to find an exception to that rule.

The final word on all things relating to the syndicate was pretty much up to Mr. Bartelli. If he couldn't help, no one could. And it was just as likely that he would *not* help.

What was best for the syndicate had always been the basis for all Mr. Bartelli's actions. If he believed it to be in the best interest of the syndicate, he would require Duncan to stay. But one thing was absolutely sure. If Duncan was allowed to disconnect himself from the syndicate, he could only do so with Mr. Bartelli's blessing.

CHAPTER 72

I N THE MONTHS that passed after returning from Mexico, the two men spent considerably more time in each other's company. Even as he spent most nights in contemplation of murder, he made sure to make room for Mr. Bartelli in his life. When he'd return from business trips, his first stop was always Mr. Bartelli's home.

When Duncan was returning from five days of meetings in New York, he called Mr. Bartelli from the airport.

"I'm at baggage pickup. Just calling to let you know I'm on my way over."

Waiting impatiently near the front of the house, listening for Duncan's car to arrive, Mr. Bartelli felt like a child awaiting the arrival of his best friend. It had been nearly a week since he had last seen his son, and he was looking forward to spending the day together.

Mr. Bartelli came running out of the front door as Duncan's shiny new Cadillac rolled to a stop in the driveway. He wrapped both arms around Duncan's waist and lifted him off the ground. It was one of those hugs that would have caused Duncan excruciating discomfort had it been by anyone other than Mr. Bartelli.

"I've missed you, son. Where have you been keeping yourself?" he said as he released his grip from Duncan's waist. Grabbing Duncan's arm, he began dragging him toward the front door.

"Just doing God's work," Duncan replied with a chuckle as he struggled to keep pace with Mr. Bartelli.

"You don't need to call me God anymore. Master will do just fine," Mr. Bartelli said, letting out a long deep laugh. Duncan couldn't recall ever hearing him laugh so heartily. Its tone brought a sincere smile to his face.

"Stop pulling on me, old man. You're going to tear my arm off!" Duncan said jokingly, making a halfhearted effort to free himself. This was the first time Duncan had any recollection of calling him anything other than Mr. Bartelli or sir.

If their exchanges didn't seem strange to each other, it did to the half dozen bodyguards and gardeners who had never heard anyone speak to Mr. Bartelli in that manner. Nor had they ever seen Mr. Bartelli show such affection to anyone, not even Santino.

They looked like frat brothers, poking and jabbing and pulling at each other. The trip to Mexico had expanded—or more accurately, broken down—the boundaries between them.

In any event, neither man seemed to notice the change in attitude. Duncan did, however, take notice of one word. For the second time since they met, Mr. Bartelli had referred to him as *son*. In the context in which it was said, it could've meant absolutely nothing, just a word, just another form of greeting. But Mr. Bartelli had always been meticulous in his choice of words. Certainly he'd never used that word in reference to anyone other than Santino. It made Duncan feel very special.

The two men made their way out onto the balcony to eat breakfast. Although Duncan had shared meals on that same balcony on many occasions since Santino's murder, every time he did, he was reminded of the time that Mr. Bartelli had gotten so mad that he'd nearly thrown him over the railing. It didn't seem funny at the time, but the memory brought a broad smile to his face.

He had spent the last several months contemplating how to broach the subject. Now that he was in the moment, he was having trouble finding the words to tell Mr. Bartelli he wanted to extricate himself from the syndicate and its business.

I'd better butter him up a bit first. "Sir, I can't tell you how much I have enjoyed joining you for breakfast over the years."

"Me, too, my boy. Me, too. I thought I told you to call me 'Vinnie.'"

He'd asked him to call him Vinnie on dozens of occasions. As much as he wanted to, Duncan had never been able to bring himself to address him by his full first name, let alone Vinnie.

"Just a few minutes ago it was Master instead of God. It's quite a jump from Master to Vinnie, so I think I'll stick with Mr. Bartelli or sir for now," Duncan said, trying to keep a straight face.

There would be so much he couldn't explain, so much he couldn't disclose about his reasons for needing separation. His major concern was that Mr. Bartelli might misinterpret his meaning altogether and take it personally. After all, for all intents and purposes, Mr. Bartelli *was* the syndicate.

The conversation over breakfast was so personal and comfortable that he chose to wait until later in the day to talk about such unpleasantness. It was the first time in months he wasn't going into the office on a Saturday. His plan was to spend the entire day with Mr. Bartelli. There would be ample time to discuss representation of the syndicate later.

After completing their morning meal they retired to a private screening room. Mr. Bartelli's home theater had a full-scale projector and large screen that retracted into the ceiling when not in use. There was also a massive overhead projection television that could be viewed on a hundred-inch screen, also concealed in the ceiling. As was true with everything he owned, the projection equipment and sound systems were the highest quality available.

The large overstuffed chairs and billowing ottomans were comfortable beyond belief. The chairs made watching their favorite shows an extraordinarily pleasant experience.

Duncan had only one complaint about the room. He felt so relaxed in it that he frequently had trouble staying awake. On several occasions over the past months, he would wake up to find that both he and Mr. Bartelli had fallen asleep in the middle of some old movie.

Summers and Saturdays meant only one thing to Mr. Bartelli: baseball.

He loved baseball. He owned first-row seats behind home plate, first-row seats down the first-base line, and a private box at both Dodger Stadium *and* Wrigley Field. Being from Chicago, he was a die-hard Cubs fan, but there was room in his sporting heart for his hometown Dodgers.

On this particular Saturday morning, the Dodgers were on the road playing San Francisco, and the Yankees were playing an afternoon doubleheader.

"What a great way to waste a day," they said in unison.

The coincidence would have been uncanny had they not uttered that identical phrase on at least fifty prior occasions.

Servants had already brought in trays of snacks and drinks. Sinking deep into their chairs, they began the hard work of wasting the day away. For the past week, Mr. Bartelli had been looking forward to a complete day of vegging out with his son and best friend.

For Duncan, however, neither the soft chair nor the sublime surroundings could relieve the anxiety that he was feeling in his chest. He just couldn't wait any longer.

"Vinnie, I need to discuss some matters with you," he said, trying to keep his voice from cracking.

"Vinnie? What the hell? Vinnie? Holy crap, this must be important," Mr. Bartelli said with a touch of both pride and comedic relief in his voice. That had been the first time Duncan had ever called him Vinnie.

Important or not, this was Baseball Day. "Can't it wait? You sound so serious, and this is Baseball Saturday, for God's sake!"

"No, sir, I don't think that it can wait. I've been meaning to talk to you for months, and it's time that I discussed this matter with you."

Grabbing the remote control, Mr. Bartelli muted the television. He could tell from Duncan's voice that the matter must be important, but he wasn't yet convinced that he needed to turn the game off altogether.

Mr. Bartelli sat forward in his chair and said, "Speak to me, my son. What's on your mind?"

He did it again, he called me son again. It seemed strange to him, and a little frustrating, how a simple word like *son* could take a cold and calculating person such as himself and turn him into a bowl of Jell-O. In light of what he was about to ask, the word weighed particularly heavy on his mind.

Duncan had concocted a variety of different reasons and explanations as to why he needed to surrender his high-profile position in the syndicate. However, after much deliberation, he'd narrowed his arguments to only one.

He was never going to be able to cut all ties with the syndicate. He simply knew too much. The only option was to move *up* the ladder. But not too far up. He needed to obtain the authority to delegate more of his work to other attorneys.

"I need your help."

"Anything, just name it." He responded as any father might, though he would later regret giving such a carte blanche response.

"I have been counsel for your business affairs for almost a decade." In fact, he'd represented the syndicate for closer to eight years. Even if he included the time spent in his representation of Santino, he had only known Mr. Bartelli for just shy of nine years.

Mr. Bartelli cut him off again. "Yes, and a damned fine job you have done. I don't know what I'd have done without you."

While flattering, the praise only made what he was about to say harder. "Thank you, but please let me finish."

His words caused Mr. Bartelli to sit up straight. He switched off the television and stared at Duncan intently.

"I am going to be forty years old in three months. I know that's young by most standards, but I have things I want to do, places I want to see. I have worked seven days a week my entire adult life. What do I have to show for my hard work? Lots of money to be sure, but I forfeited my life in exchange.

"I want a family. A family, that's a joke, I don't even have time to go on dates. Hell, I haven't even been properly laid in years. The long and short of it is that I want to slow down. What I need to do is turn over the responsibilities of representing the syndicate to another attorney."

In truth, Duncan had no desire to have a family, but he felt it made his cause more compelling and defensible. His words sounded more rambling than he intended. He didn't like admitting it to himself, but he was not handling the pressure very well. "What I would like to do, with your permission of course, is to take on more of a supervisory role in the legal affairs of the syndicate. Work behind the scenes. Allow other attorneys to handle the day-to-day legal affairs."

Mr. Bartelli's face became stern. "Do you know how long Sandler Helms handled the legal affairs for the syndicate before you took over?"

The question was meant to be rhetorical, but Duncan seized what he saw as an opportunity and answered it anyway. "Yes, I do. Twenty years too many. Four heart attacks later, the man is dead. He lived a full nine months after he left the firm. That is precisely my point. I don't want to end up like Helms. He had no life, no family, and not even the people he served so faithfully, for those many years, mourn his passing."

Helm's passing had regrettably slipped Mr. Bartelli's mind. He immediately wished it hadn't. Not just because it supported Duncan's argument, but because he really did miss his old friend.

To use one of Mr. Bartelli's favorite analogies, he'd served up a slow pitch over the plate, and Duncan hit it out of the park.

Mr. Bartelli let what Duncan said sink in for a moment before responding. "Look, you can't imagine how difficult it would be to grant your request. While I'm a very powerful man, even *I* must answer to others in the organization. This is no small thing that you are asking."

Mr. Bartelli was being completely honest. The head of the legal team was the one truly weak link in the syndicate's armor. The level of trust must be complete. If that person ever turned on the syndicate, the entire operation would be placed at risk.

"Vinnie, I'm not asking to be relieved as counsel for the syndicate. Far from it. I just need to have the authority to delegate more of the mundane duties. I will still be the only person with any information regarding the inner workings of your businesses."

Calling him Vinnie a second time was not as calculated as it must have sounded; it just slipped out. It took both men by complete surprise, but for different reasons, Duncan for having said it again, and Mr. Bartelli, because it did not seem as genuine as the first time.

Taking a second to regroup, Duncan was prepared to proffer an even more compelling reason to grant his request. In the weeks preceding this meeting, he'd concluded that it was actually in the syndicate's best interest to use more than one firm to handle its staggeringly large volume of legal problems.

It had begun to concern Duncan that all the work that had gone into creating layers upon layers of corporate entities could be unmasked by simply reviewing his firm's client list. The firm had offices in almost every major city in the United States. With his firm representing the vast majority of the syndicate's criminal matters, it would have been relatively easy for anyone paying even a *modest* amount of attention to make the connection.

Duncan explained in great detail the risks involved in not diversifying the legal representation of the syndicate. "How some snotnosed desk jockey at the FBI hasn't figured that out by now is amazing," Duncan declared.

Still feeling a little uncomfortable with having been called Vinnie a second time and feeling a bit like he was being played, Mr. Bartelli grudgingly began to consider the ramifications of Duncan's request. The more he thought about it, the more the idea actually made sense. There were countless firms that would love to take over some of the less important cases. On the surface it would appear that the new firms would be representing legitimate businesses and businessmen accused of illegal acts.

The syndicate was so well organized that there was no legitimate connection between the firm's clients and the syndicate. In fact, only a handful of individuals in the entire world had access to the information that connected those businesses.

The two men continued to discuss the effects that the reshuffling might have on all concerned. By the end of their discussion, they agreed that the syndicate should implement an even more aggressive diversification of its legal affairs than even Duncan had originally contemplated.

They finally agreed that his firm should be farming out many of the less significant legal matters—and even some higher-profile cases—to take the spotlight off both Duncan and his firm.

Both men were humbled and privately embarrassed for not considering this problem sooner, but neither could bring himself to admit it out loud.

They spent the rest of the morning outlining an outsourcing framework. The new order of things would relieve Duncan of all but the most critical duties. Mr. Bartelli ordered him to immediately implement the diversification plan.

"Well, immediately after the baseball games. After all, it *is* Baseball Saturday," Mr. Bartelli said with a smile. "*Now* can we watch a little baseball?"

Mr. Bartelli picked up the controller and turned the television back on. The first of the two Yankee games was just about to start.

Two things Duncan had said were still echoing in his mind. They hadn't said a word to each other for over an hour when he could no longer hold back.

"'Haven't been properly laid in years'? Son, we got to get you a girlfriend, or laid at the *very* least. Now why don't you ever come to me with simple problems like that? That's a problem I *can* fix. And who the fuck said you could call me Vinnie, anyways?"

Both men laughed hysterically.

CHAPTER 73

I T TOOK DUNCAN the better part of three months of preparation to implement the reorganization of the syndicate's legal arm. While he would still take the lead in evaluating its legal needs, he was given broad power to delegate the work to other firms as he deemed appropriate.

There were still two weeks left before his fortieth birthday and the job was nearly complete. However, he was going to have to wait until after his birthday to finish the job.

Duncan's goal in the reorganization of the firm was to lower his profile and notoriety with the press. Much to his chagrin, Mr. Bartelli was not helping him to reach that goal. He had planned a grandiose affair to celebrate Duncan's fortieth. All of Hollywood would be there. Every politician, businessman, everyone who was anyone would be there.

It was his worst nightmare come true. Duncan tried to convince Mr. Bartelli to tone down what was escalating into the social event of the year, but he was unstoppable. The gala event was going to make the party thrown for Santino's acquittal look like a backyard barbecue.

On a Thursday afternoon two days prior to the birthday celebration, Mr. Bartelli called Duncan at his office.

"I'm picking you up in ten minutes."

Duncan was very busy, but he could tell from the tone of the call that he wasn't being given a choice in the matter.

"Do you mind telling me what is so important?"

His inquiry was answered by a dial tone.

Nine minutes later a black limousine pulled up in front of Duncan's building. He slid inside beside Mr. Bartelli.

Even before he could open his mouth, Mr. Bartelli cut him off. "Don't even bother to ask any questions, you will find out soon enough. We'll be there in fifteen minutes. So just relax and have a drink."

Be where? He was, however, put somewhat at ease by Mr. Bartelli's demeanor. There were no signs that he was irritated or concerned. In fact, he looked almost smug, like a cat that had just eaten the pet mouse.

Exactly fifteen minutes later, they pulled up behind a blacked-out Suburban parked at the gate of a large estate in Bel Air. Looking over his shoulder, Duncan saw a second Suburban pull up behind them. *One thing was sure when traveling with Mr. Bartelli—you always felt safe,* Duncan thought.

The security cameras placed on both sides of the entrance turned toward the limo. A moment later, the massive gates swung open, and the vehicles drove up a long driveway that horseshoed around a beautiful marble statue and pond.

Bodyguards opened the doors on both sides of the limo. The two men stepped out and were escorted to the front door of a magnificent Mediterranean-style mansion. Two servants dressed in French-cut tuxedos swung open the ornate double doors. Mr. Bartelli and Duncan entered what looked more like a palace than a home.

A particularly striking and elegant-looking woman (she was probably fifty, but she looked much younger) entered the large foyer. She walked directly to Mr. Bartelli and began to speak in French.

Much to Duncan's surprise, he responded in French! You could have knocked Duncan over with a feather. *Since when does he speak French?* Every time he thought he had this man figured out, Mr. Bartelli revealed another side of himself.

After a brief conversation, he turned to Duncan. He could tell from the look on Duncan's face that he was impressed.

"There are many things that you don't know about me, boy. Don't ever forget that. Now, let me introduce you to a dear friend of mine. Francesca Devereux."

Francesca politely bowed her head in greeting. Mr. Bartelli reached into his vest pocket, pulling out a sealed envelope, and handed it to Duncan.

"Now, it is very important that this matter be handled with the utmost delicacy and discretion. It is critical that you follow these instructions to the letter," Mr. Bartelli said, almost whispering.

Duncan started to open the envelope, but Mr. Bartelli stopped him. "Not until I've gone. Don't fuck this up; it's important to me that this be handled well." With that, he turned to leave.

"Handle what?" Duncan called. But his question was ignored.

The large entry doors swung open again. He watched Mr. Bartelli climb in the limousine and drive away. He continued to watch anxiously as the three vehicles passed through the front gate.

Staring at the letter, he felt very uncomfortable. The whole cloak-and-dagger game was very out of character for Mr. Bartelli. Duncan knew most of the syndicate's secrets. His discretion had never been questioned before, nor had his ability to handle its business. His relationship with Mr. Bartelli made this sort of secrecy very disconcerting.

And then, as he read the letter, a smile swept over his face.

Haven't been properly laid in years? Well we can't have that! I will send a car for you tomorrow afternoon at 4:00. Francesca has been given strict instructions that you are not to leave this house until you have been properly laid by every one of the young ladies I have chosen for you. Do not disappoint me.

Happy Birthday,
Vinnie

Beads of sweat began popping up on his forehead as Francesca slipped her arm under his. She led him down a flight of stairs toward a door at the end of a long hallway. He didn't want to be rude, but

Francesca was not his type. She was a lovely woman, but he had no desire to sleep with a woman ten years his senior.

Francesca opened the door, placed her hand on the small of his back, and gently nudged him inside. The room was massive, the largest he had ever seen. There was a custom-made circular bed in its center, the size of three king-size mattresses.

Three of the most beautiful women on earth stood in a row beside a massage table, completely naked.

While he stood there stunned, Francesca spoke over his shoulder in a thick, sensual accent. "Barbara, Susan, and Bernice will be your masseuses."

She clapped her hands, and two more young ladies, equally lovely, stepped into the room. "Greta and Bertha will bathe you." She clapped again, and four additional beauties entered the room. "Carla, Debbie, Shin Lee, and Sophie will make sure that you remember your visit with us for the rest of your life." Francesca closed the door behind him.

The girls looked like they had fallen out of the pages of *Vogue*, *Cosmopolitan*, and *Playboy*. As it turned out, two of them actually had.

In addition to selecting women of unsurpassed beauty, it was clear that someone had taken special care to make sure a diverse assortment of nationalities were represented. These goddesses were several steps above even the most expensive call girls.

Few people on the planet could afford the services provided by Francesca and her extraordinary girls. Duncan would be the only client that the girls would entertain that night, which only added to the mystique of this high-class brothel.

He spent the rest of that day and all of the night being massaged until he was as loose as Play-Doh, bathed until his skin was rubbed pink, and fucked until he was, well, "properly laid." When he was too spent to join in, he lounged on the bed and watched the girls pleasure each other.

What he lacked in stamina, he made up in repetition. After hours and hours of feeding his sexual appetite, he eventually fell into a deep sleep, the kind of sleep that only total exhaustion can bring on.

The next morning, thanks to the efforts of two girls he hadn't even met the night before, he awoke midclimax. Apparently there had been a changing of the guard that morning.

It was a feeling he'd never experienced. Then again, during the past twelve hours he'd already checked off an impressive number of life experiences he hoped to have before he died. Unable to move, he lay there with his eyes wide open.

He'd fallen asleep among all nine of the girls from the night before; now only three of them remained. The two new girls who had awakened him in such a spectacular fashion were joined by three other new girls.

The morning and early afternoon were spent eating, bathing, and fornicating—not necessarily in that order. By day's end, Duncan realized that he'd been spending far too much time working and far too little time chasing women. In the past twenty-four hours, he was given a major-league lesson on just what he'd been missing.

The limo arrived at exactly four o'clock. He felt a little like Cinderella. His fairy godfather had told him that the party would end at exactly four that afternoon, and it did.

CHAPTER 74

THE CHANGE IN his responsibilities as counsel for the syndicate was dramatic. It was like starting life all over again.

For as long as he could remember, he'd had no free time. Now there was time. Time to let his mind run wild, and it did. It was awash with murderous scenarios. He spent hours and hours in preparing himself to commit murder.

The choice had been made. The first victim would be killed in Rhode Island. Having traveled there on several occasions for business, he always considered it to be the armpit of America, particularly in the winter, when the entire state was transformed into a large slushy mud puddle. It inspired the wonderfully gloomy atmosphere that the state was so rightly known for.

The residents seemed to take on the mood of their state, never looking anyone in the eyes, always focused on their shoes. Duncan was never sure if Rhode Islanders were looking down to avoid the omnipresent puddles, or if the aura of depression was just so overwhelming that they couldn't bear engaging one another.

One of the syndicate's smaller operations needed counsel in Providence. Duncan was scheduled to make several trips there over the next few months to evaluate which firm should provide their legal representation. His trip would give him perfect cover.

Extensive research led him to choose the small town of North Kingstown. Learning as much as he could about the local community became his solitary focus. He'd been reading the *Standard Times* for several months. The newspaper provided a wealth of information about the city's people, fashions, and overall customs.

What he found particularly inviting about the town was that it played host to a military base. As such, it had a large transient population. The town, while small, was constantly being repopulated with new faces, so much so that the local citizenry went out of their way to ignore military personnel and their families. Duncan thought it ironic that while the city derived substantial economic advantages from the military's presence, the local citizenry still treated the soldiers like second-class citizens.

Using his maze of corporate shells, he purchased attire that would allow him to blend in. The cold weather provided him with the ability to mask his identity with clothes that could cover almost every inch of his body.

It was just over twenty miles between Providence and North Kingstown, and there was plenty of public transportation available between the two cities.

He thought long and hard about his choice of murder weapons. Each type of weapon had its own pros and cons. He would eventually discover that the choice of weapon was one of the most important considerations in his planning.

In addition to the experience derived from his association with criminals, Duncan read everything he could find on the use of weapons of all types.

Knives, if used properly, provided a stealthy way of committing murder. But they also had the potential to make a messy kill. Blood-splatter analysis was a powerful tool used to link killers to victims. There was also the problem of subduing the victim. Victims were frequently not dispatched with the first penetration. Wounded victims tend to struggle and scream, which increased the risk of apprehension. For that reason, cutting instruments were inherently unreliable.

Poisons, while effective, tended to be slow to take effect. They were also usually difficult to administer.

Duncan was at least initially partial to the idea of using a firearm for his first murder. However, guns had their own special set of problems. They were loud and could be awkward to conceal and maneuver. The rule of thumb was, the larger the caliber, the bigger and louder the gun.

He eventually settled on a .22-caliber revolver with a silencer attachment. Twenty-twos are small and relatively quiet, usually sounding more like a popgun or firecracker.

There were some drawbacks to revolvers. They only accommodated five rounds of ammunition and were more difficult to reload than automatics. On the plus side, revolvers were far less likely to jam—the slide that ejected spent cartridges in automatic weapons could malfunction in close quarters. Duncan had read several cases where the automatic pistols snagged on the victim's clothing, preventing them from discharging.

Because his plans called for killing at close range, reducing the risk of malfunction outweighed his concern about reloading. Besides, if he needed more than five rounds, his ability to reload was likely going to be the least of his problems.

Many people were under the misconception that a .22 pistol lacked the firepower to stop a house cat, much less a full-grown person. Such naiveté made Duncan laugh. He knew that the stopping power of a weapon had less to do with the caliber and more to do with the ammunition. Having seen photographs of victims shot with .22-caliber Magnum hollow-point bullets, he was acutely aware of what such a gun could do to the human body. Magnum cartridges were longer than normal .22 shells. Once the bullet hit its target, it expanded. Having lost its aerodynamic shape, the hollow-point tended to change directions, sometimes fracturing into several pieces. The fragments bounced around inside the victim, tearing through vital organs.

The .22-caliber pistol would provide more than enough killing power, of that he was sure.

CHAPTER 75

*D*AMN. *IT'S COLD as hell*, Duncan thought as he stepped off the city bus in the center of North Kingstown on a blustery Thursday evening. Although it couldn't be seen through the forbiddingly overcast skies, the sun had just crept beneath the horizon.

His research had served him well, he blended in perfectly. His hat dipped down low across his forehead. A scarf was pulled up high, just below his lower lip. The glasses he was wearing were not prescription; they just provided one more way to hide his facial features. When he looked toward the ground, his entire face was obscured.

It had been raining most of the day. The temperature had dropped below freezing earlier that morning, and there were still some of the remnants of melting snow on the ground. Misjudging the length of his stride, he inadvertently stepped into a shallow mud puddle. *Yes, just as I remembered, the armpit of the country,* Duncan thought to himself, forcing a nervous smile.

He wasn't a superstitious man, but he couldn't help but think how unlucky he was to be in town for only five minutes before stepping in a puddle. Water seeped into his right shoe, and his foot began to feel the early evening chill immediately. A little water in his shoe wasn't going to deter him, but it *did* piss him off.

Walking down the street, he began to have a strange series of physical sensations. He couldn't tell if it was nervousness or anxiety, but he was experiencing tightness in his chest. His clothes felt heavy, and he began to perspire under the weight of the layers that draped every inch of his body.

After a moment, he noticed he was walking faster than the pedestrians around him. He felt his heart racing uncontrollably. A drop of sweat rolled down his forehead, washing into his eye. The salty drop caused his eye to burn, and he began to blink rapidly from the irritation.

Realizing his abnormal behavior could bring unwanted attention, he slowed his pace and tried to regain his composure. He was a man unfamiliar with feeling even the slightest bit out of control. However, even this sudden and unexpected surge of emotion didn't arouse any thoughts of abandoning the project.

Duncan made a conscious effort to muster his legendary poise. It took only a moment for him to regain his sense of purpose and confidence.

When all the physical sensations disappeared, his mind began to flood with years of research and theory. *What exactly am I looking for? Random! Who is random? What is random?*

He'd examined these same questions on hundreds of occasions, but in the moment they seemed even more abstract.

Before he knew it, he'd walked nearly a mile. As he neared the end of the main road, he noticed a bar. Shelley's. He recognized the name from the local newspapers.

As if an alarm had gone off inside his head, he was once again focused on the task at hand. Questions stopped clogging his mind as he considered the possibility that this would be the place where he'd commit his first murder.

Shelley's was one of those truly local bars. A small, loyal neighborhood clientele barely provided enough profit to keep the establishment's doors open for business. The large picture windows in the front of the bar were adorned with flashing neon beer signs and one OPEN sign with the light for the E burned out.

It was just after seven in the evening when Duncan first strolled by the bar. The sky was heavily overcast, blotting out the moon. The neon lights cut only a small swath in the darkness.

There was enough room between the neon signs for Duncan to see several patrons sitting at the bar, and a middle-aged couple playing pool in the back.

There was only a small amount of street parking available in the front of the bar, but there was a large unpaved and poorly lit parking lot behind the establishment. Shelley's was attached to a strip mall on the north side, but all the shops had closed hours earlier.

On the south side of the building was a fenced-in vacant lot overgrown with weeds and wild shrubs. A driveway separated the bar from the lot, providing access to the parking lot behind the bar.

Walking past the bar, he disappeared into the darkness in front of the vacant lot. He leaned against a chain-link fence and observed the bar. He was completely shrouded in darkness. The combination of the overcast sky and his dark clothes made him virtually invisible.

He watched as an older-model Chevy truck pulled down the driveway and behind the bar.

There were no windows or lights on the south side of the bar. The only light behind the bar came from a single naked bulb hanging above the rear door.

Straining to get a better look at the individual getting out of the truck, he was unable to tell if the figure was male or female. However, that question was quickly answered when the individual began to take a piss against the rear wheel of the truck. When he finished with an impressively long excretion of bodily fluids, the man walked back down the driveway and entered the bar through the front door.

It occurred to Duncan that if the man was a local—and from his conduct, he most likely was—then he would have entered through the back door if that option was available. *For God's sake, he was too lazy to wait the twenty seconds it would've taken to go inside and piss. He certainly would've used the back door if he could've,* Duncan thought.

The only person to enter the bar over the next half hour was the man in the old truck. Deciding that the area behind the bar might provide the right location to commit his crime, Duncan walked around back to take a better look.

He was correct. The back door was covered by a large cast-iron cage with a large padlock. There would be no way for patrons or employees to enter the lot from the back of the building.

They are almost assuredly breaking a building code by having that door locked, Duncan thought idly. It brought a perverse smile to his face. He was there to kill someone, yet he couldn't help but think the bar was violating some zoning law.

Shelley's faced north, and the rear lot separated the bar from a long line of small businesses facing to the south. Walking across the lot, he found that the small-appliance store, the shoe-repair shop, and all the other businesses were closed for the day.

Heading back toward the bar, he muttered aloud, "How perf—"

But before he could even complete the sentence, he spotted a vehicle coming down the driveway, its headlights twinkling off the chain-link fence. Squatting down in the weeds, he watched as the light-blue Rambler rolled slowly around the side of the building. The bulb above the bar's door backlit the driver just enough to reveal her long hair and feminine outline.

There were only four vehicles parked behind the bar. Even so, the driver slowly maneuvered her car through the lot like she was trying to find the last remaining spot in a crowded lot. She pulled past the old truck, finally turning the vehicle toward the bar and backing to a stop deep in the south corner of the lot.

The care that she was taking in parking this old Rambler (which had more dents than flat panels) struck him as oddly interesting. *She could just as easily have been parking a new Mercedes.*

There was no time to do anything, not even change his mind. *This is random* crackled like thunder in his head as he stood up and made his way toward the Rambler. He approached from the rear as quietly as he could. When it was clear she hadn't noticed his approach, he knelt down behind the rear of the car and waited for her to open the door.

Paula Morton was rummaging through her purse in the darkness. For reasons that didn't at first make any sense, she didn't turn on the car's interior light.

In her youth, Paula had been a better-than-average-looking girl. She'd foregone her education, choosing instead to believe the lies that young men tell to punch holes in young girls' panties.

By the time she discovered the evil men do, she'd already squandered what little opportunity was available to a young women in that shit hole of a town. While she still bore the outline of a fine-looking woman, up close Paula displayed the hard look of someone who had lived a tough life. It was etched on her face, and even deeper in her soul.

She'd spent the better part of the last six years frequenting Shelley's. There was a time when she still believed that Prince Charming would rescue her from a lifetime of bad choices. But reality had long since chased that fantasy away. Now she spent most of her nights teasing the local men at the bar—both married and not—with her provocative attire and sexual innuendo.

Paula rarely gave her fellow bar-mates anything more than a good lie to spin for their friends. However, every now and again she would drink just enough to surrender to her loneliness. Such indiscretions had gained her an undeserved loose reputation.

It was not Prince Charming coming for her this night. It was the Grim Reaper.

Duncan was overcome by a strange and stimulating sense of calm. As he removed his fur-lined gloves, steam rose from his warm hands as they met the cold night air. He pulled a pair of thin rubber gloves over his tingling hands.

His original plan was just to shoot her in the head and immediately make his getaway. But at the last second he changed his mind. *There's something I want to say to you. No. I shouldn't. I need to at least see her face. If she screams, I'll just kill her.*

Thinking that he should try to open the door to the car himself, he decided not to run the risk that it might be locked. Then it dawned on him that he hadn't considered the fact that the interior light would come on when she opened the door. Before he had a chance to contemplate the blunder, the driver's-side door swung open. To his surprise no light came on. *It must have been broken, that's why she didn't turn it on earlier. What luck!*

The fact that he'd gotten lucky didn't stop him from mentally thrashing himself. It wasn't like him to overlook such obvious details.

Before the woman's foot touched the ground, Duncan darted out from behind the car. He stood in the door opening to prevent her from closing the door and blocking any means of escape. When she looked up, she was staring into the barrel of his pistol.

She let out a startled gasp, which almost got her shot immediately. But the sound was just soft enough to keep him from pulling back on the trigger.

He put his finger to his lips as a signal for her to keep quiet, which she acknowledged with a nod of her head.

"Take what you want. Just don't hurt me. Take anything," she said in a soft but frantic whisper. With emphasis on "anything," she tried to make it clear that she meant anything Duncan wanted.

By not killing her immediately, he'd already increased the odds that he would get caught. But in those seconds of delay, he'd found the excitement that was the very essence of his desire to kill.

The look of horror and fear on her face sent a shiver down his spine. Absolute power, unchallengeable and merciless, was his to dispense at his whim. He was his victim's master, her god. *There is no greater feeling on earth!* he thought.

As he whispered instructions, he simultaneously motioned for Paula to lie back on the front seat of the car. Without making a sound, she complied. Accepting without struggle what she thought to be her fate. Without being asked, she unbuttoned her blouse, exposing her bra. Reaching down she grabbed the hem of her long loose skirt. The long slits up both sides exposed the full length of her long slender legs.

Pulling the skirt up to her thighs, she revealed her pantyless form. She arched her back, lifting her butt just enough to slide the skirt under, leaving it resting on her flat stomach.

From the economy of motion used in preparing herself to be taken, Duncan concluded that this wouldn't be the first time she'd had sex in the front seat of an automobile.

Paula was not happy about being forced to have sex at gunpoint, but believing that rape was the worst thing that was about to happen, she was overcome with a feeling of relief. She'd been the victim of date rape on two occasions. She was strong enough to deal with the emotional aftermath.

For reasons she didn't totally understand, Paula had fantasized about being raped by a total stranger. On some strange level, she was starting to find the experience a little erotic and stimulating.

Duncan lifted the flap of her skirt off her stomach and tossed it over her face. With her legs spread apart (as far as possible in the cramped space) she lay there motionless, expecting him to penetrate her any second. Blinded by her own skirt, she never saw him point the pistol at her head.

He held it less than twelve inches from her face and fired two rounds into her head. Her head bounced up off the seat with each shot. The first bullet entered her skull directly between her eyes, killing her instantly. The skirt acted as a shield from the blood that gushed from the wounds.

The pistol let out muffled noise, more like a popgun than an instrument of death. There was a small echo inside the vehicle, but it quickly evaporated into the darkness. Seconds later, the lot behind the bar was once again deathly silent.

Duncan grabbed the woman's legs, swung them inside the car, and closed the door. He took only a few seconds to look around, making sure no one had seen him. Then he left.

To avoid having to walk by the bar again, he exited onto the next street over. It was a decision he would later regret.

Duncan had been wearing a reversible overcoat and had switched the coat around before he reached the bus stop. The coat played two roles. First, it made him look different from the man who had walked in front of Shelley's bar less than an hour ago. Second, it would hide any blood that might have found its way onto the outside of his coat.

Feeling powerful and fulfilled, he had no remorse or guilt. It was everything he'd thought it would be and more. Before reaching the bus, he wanted to kill again.

CHAPTER 76

I T WAS NOT until the Saturday that followed the murder of Paula Morton that Duncan was able to get his hands on the late Friday edition of the North Kingstown *Standard Times*. His first murder was front-page news.

I got the front page. It made him feel important, even if it was only the local newspaper.

The local police and the district attorney's office each attempted to secure their fifteen minutes of fame. They held repeated press conferences vowing to arrest and convict the perpetrator of this "dastardly and cowardly act."

"We are going to avenge the death of a beloved member of our community," they announced in the local papers. "The victim was an upstanding member of the community, born and raised in North Kingstown."

There was not much information in the initial reports. Mostly, the papers described the crime scene and provided a background report on the victim—a thirty-eight-year-old mother of one adult son.

The initial stories made Paula out to be a woman of virtue as well as a pillar of the community. However, subsequent articles began to paint a far less flattering picture of her life. The local authorities originally theorized that it was a "rape gone bad." In the days that followed her murder, the police questioned many of the patrons who frequented Shelley's. Several of the married patrons of the bar found themselves having to confess to having relations with Paula. Reportedly, at least one of them was now heading for divorce court.

As days turned into weeks, and weeks to months, the police were under considerable pressure to make an arrest. Not surprisingly, the newspaper's description of Paula had turned a full 180 degrees, falling only slightly short of calling her a hooker who got what was coming to her.

Duncan had seen the press do this to victims in the past. The local authorities had gotten the fame they wanted, but they hadn't delivered the killer. It was going to be much easier to justify letting this one go unsolved if the victim was not as sympathetic.

Duncan knew that the release of information contained in the investigative reports was generally prohibited, unless it would aid in the apprehension of the criminal. Notwithstanding such policies, he also knew that it was a standard practice to release unflattering information about a victim if it would deflect the negative press directed at the police and district attorney's office.

The press was taking the bait; information was leaked about Paula almost every day. By the time they got done slandering her reputation, nobody seemed to care that she'd been killed. What's one less hooker? was the general opinion in the community.

Almost as tragic as her physical murder was the murder of her memory. While Paula may not have been a pillar of the community, she wasn't a harlot either. Duncan found a considerable amount of humor in the fact that an innocent victim's reputation had been murdered along with her.

Most of all, it pleased him that he was the cause of it all.

CHAPTER 77

BACK HOME IN Beverly Hills, Duncan locked himself away in the study and began to dissect the Paula Morton murder. There had been so many errors in judgment that he quickly became angry with himself, cursing under his breath. His feeling of exultation was clouded by the knowledge that he could have accounted for many more variables.

In his mind, he replayed over and over the events that took place in North Kingstown until every second was accounted for. Of particular concern were his initial emotional and physical reactions. Even his stepping into the puddle was a sign that he'd lost his focus. He would need to work on maintaining his composure in the future.

More disturbing was his failure to recognize variables that were *clearly* within his control. Not accounting for the interior light of the car was just the tip of the iceberg.

He had also failed to thoroughly examine his escape route. While he surveyed the lot behind Shelley's Bar, he hadn't noticed that the street behind the lot was a cul-de-sac. By the time he realized his error, he was forced to walk almost a half mile through residential neighborhoods to get back to the bus stop. The mistake caused him to miss an earlier bus back to Providence. The next bus came a full thirty minutes later.

He compounded this mistake by failing to bring reading materials that would make him look too occupied to socialize. Fortunately, he wasn't confronted by any lonely pain-in-the-ass riders looking to make a new friend.

He was equally disturbed by his last-minute decision to delay killing his victim. *If she'd screamed...my God, what was I thinking?*

As Duncan sipped from a large snifter of brandy, he shook his head in disgust at his ineptitude. There was little doubt in his mind that, had the victim's body been discovered immediately, he'd certainly be behind bars.

As critical as he was on others, he was even harder on himself. *I fucked up. That's got to change. I just got lucky this time.*

He was generally displeased that he hadn't looked into his victim's eyes as he pulled the trigger. *After all, my little Paula didn't even know she was about to die. She thought she was getting laid, for God's sake. She could have been smiling, for all I know.*

Despite his self-condemnation for his feeble first attempt at committing the perfect crime, he was done beating himself up, and ready to plan his next murder.

There was the feeling that he'd been cheated by fate. He wanted his first victim to be a man. The idea that he might someday be considered a woman-killer was disturbing. Had he arrived at the bar only twenty minutes earlier, the old man in the Chevy truck would have been his first victim.

The very nature of random acts prevented him from having complete control over the victim, but he hoped his next one would be a man.

CHAPTER 78

DUNCAN DIDN'T TARRY in seeking out his next victim. Paula had been dead for less than a week, and he was already investigating small towns in Colorado. He liked the idea of committing the murder farther west, not just because it was closer to Los Angeles, but also because it created a large geographic expanse between the murders.

Colorado's seasonably cold weather again allowed him the opportunity to disguise his appearance. As was true in North Kingstown, there was always an influx of new faces in ski resorts. He had business in Denver in just two weeks. That would give him ample time to select a smaller resort town.

He chose the ski resort at Copper Mountain. Although he'd never been to the resort, he had overheard several members of his firm discussing how much they enjoyed their vacations in the sleepy little town.

What proved to be unique about ski resorts was the fact that there was always an abundance of information available about the towns. Full-color brochures laid out the location, services, and hours of every business in town. Information that might take weeks to amass was instantly at Duncan's fingertips.

However, there were also substantial downsides in choosing such towns. There was usually little to no public transportation. Some hotels provided shuttle services, but the services were only available to their guests. Duncan had no intention of registering in a hotel, so he'd have to obtain alternate transportation.

It was imperative that he enter and exit the town with stealth, spending as little time as possible and leaving as he entered—unnoticed.

He'd have to rent a car in Denver and drive the seventy-five miles to Copper Mountain. The thought of arriving in a rented vehicle that could easily be traced caused Duncan more than a little concern. But it was one of those variables that he couldn't change if he was going to choose a tourist town.

Through his research he discovered that, statistically, the most popular and most frequently rented car was a silver, four-door, mid-size Ford sedan. From his connections on the police force, he had learned that these were also the least ticketed vehicle on the road (red convertibles being the most frequently ticketed).

Accurate weather reports would be vital. An unexpected snow-storm could close the roads, as could even a minor auto accident. Copper Mountain, like most mountain resorts, had only one road leading in and out. He was keenly aware that a single road closure could prevent his escape. If heavy storms were predicted for the area, he'd have to abort the plan.

Weather was one of those variables that were outside of his control. He did, however, purchase a set of snow chains, just in case.

It would become his habit to make all purchases with cash, keeping no receipts and making sure to dispose of every item he purchased. Most items could simply be thrown in a lake, but clothing presented a different problem. His favorite method of disposal was in Goodwill depositories. It wasn't that he wanted to help out those down on their luck—on the contrary—but the new and expensive items he donated almost certainly never reached a Goodwill store. There is a little thief in everyone, and Duncan was sure the workers stole most of the really nice items.

CHAPTER 79

HIS MEETING IN Denver was scheduled for a Tuesday afternoon. His plan called for him to drive to Copper Mountain after the meeting. Among his clients, he was known as a no-nonsense guy. Not being one to socialize, he almost always declined invitations to join them for dinner or drinks after meetings. Therefore, no one would consider it unusual or impolite of him to decline such an offer.

He had Stella arrange accommodations for that Tuesday evening at one of the finest hotels in Denver. However, he'd make his own arrangements for transportation. It wasn't particularly out of the ordinary for him to make his own arrangements. He was never really sure if or when he'd need a car, so he was accustomed to having the hotel provide him with limousine service if needed.

Duncan hated standing in long rental-car lines, so he prearranged to have Hertz deliver a gray four-door Ford sedan to his hotel.

The hotel sent a limo to pick Duncan up at the airport. During the ride, he scanned the local newspaper for weather reports. Nothing had changed since he last checked. Storms had passed through the Copper Mountain area the week before his arrival, dropping almost two feet of fresh powder on the slopes. The forecast for the next few days was mostly cloudy skies, but only intermittent snowfall. He couldn't have hoped for more favorable conditions. The new snow would bring in lots of new faces and the cloudy skies would reduce visibility.

Duncan was standing at the hotel entrance when his client's driver pulled up in a white Rolls-Royce limousine to take him to his one-thirty meeting. He left the rented Ford in the hotel parking lot. After all, he had a reputation to maintain.

He was on his way to meet Benjamin Carter, a longtime business associate of the syndicate and a man whom Mr. Bartelli had, on more than just a few occasions, mentioned in favorable terms.

Carter's name stuck out in his mind, because Mr. Bartelli seldom commented on his relationship with his business associates. If he did say something about them, it generally was in the form of a criticism. Mr. Bartelli had made it clear over the years that Carter was more than just an associate, he was his friend. As such, he was deserving of the utmost respect.

Though in his early sixties, Carter still bore the ruggedly chiseled handsome features of a much-younger man. For his part, Carter was fully aware of Duncan's position with the syndicate and, maybe more important, his personal relationship with Mr. Bartelli. Even very powerful men like Carter were humbled in Mr. Bartelli's presence. Friend or no friend, Mr. Bartelli was treated like a god by everyone connected to the syndicate.

Carter had come up through the ranks of the mob in the days when Mr. Bartelli Sr. ran the operation. He was now the president and chairman of the board of Oasis Enterprises. Oasis was an international conglomerate with holdings all around the world. In addition to its legitimate holdings, it was also a conduit through which smaller subsidiaries laundered large sums of the syndicate's drug money.

Oasis's offices occupied the top five floors of the tallest building in downtown Denver. Duncan rode the private marble-lined elevator (complete with its own operator and overstuffed chairs) up to the reception area just outside of Carter's penthouse office. As he stepped out of the elevator, he was taken aback by the opulence of the room. It struck him that, if the appointments of the reception area were any indication, Carter's office was going to be insanely spectacular.

Before he reached the receptionist's desk, he noticed one of the most strikingly beautiful women he'd ever seen sitting in the corner of the room. Over the years he'd had the privilege of being introduced to countless beautiful women, but with just a glance he could see that there was something quite special about this one.

She was Christina Carter, the only daughter of the man he'd come to see. She was sitting in a rather uncomfortable-looking straight-back chair, hands resting neatly on her lap, her slender legs crossed at an angle. The hem of her lacy white dress settled just below her knee. The chair may have been uncomfortable, but she looked completely content. Her perfect posture seemed to conform to the lines of the chair.

Christina hadn't taken her eyes off Duncan from the moment he'd stepped out of the elevator. The look in her eyes cast the impression that she'd been waiting for him to arrive. He was so distracted by her beauty that he almost walked directly into the receptionist's desk, stopping just in time to avoid what would have been a rather embarrassing collision.

Never making eye contact with the girl behind the large cherrywood desk, he said, "Duncan Gabrelli to see Mr. Carter." Without another word, he changed directions and headed toward the beauty in the straight-back chair. He didn't even hear the girl behind the desk say, "Yes, Mr. Carter is expecting you," as he walked away.

"Do I know you?" he said, now standing directly in front of Ms. Carter.

Before she could respond, the booming voice of Mr. Carter came from just over Duncan's left shoulder, filling the room. "Let me introduce you to my daughter, Christina."

A cool, forbidding sense of unease filled his chest. *That voice. That voice. I know that voice.* Even the sweet distraction of his daughter could not cloud Duncan's memory.

Mr. Carter was standing directly behind him. Duncan turned and nervously shook his hand. "Good afternoon, sir."

Looking at the silver-haired man, he thought to himself. *It's not possible. This couldn't be the man I heard so many years ago.* Fighting back the emotions he'd suppressed for so many years, he looked hard into Carter's weathered face. *It just can't be.*

"When she heard you were coming into town, she asked to meet you. I hope that is okay with you, Mr. Gabrelli."

Without revealing even the slightest emotion, he turned back toward Christina, "It is my privilege. And please call me Duncan."

He incorporated just a hint of the southern drawl that had served him so well with women over the years.

Hoping that Christina would find his soothing southern sensibilities appealing, he reached for her hand, giving it a gentle kiss. At least for the moment it appeared to be working, as her eyes fluttered ever so femininely.

Duncan was amazed (and a little surprised) to find that his reputation had preceded him this far east. In Los Angeles he was recognized in the circles of the social elite as one of the most eligible bachelors. However, that didn't explain why the daughter of one of the wealthiest men in Denver would want to meet him. Then again, he'd always been better at analyzing the complicated questions than he was at recognizing the obvious answers.

Christina was twenty-eight years old, and the only daughter of a very powerful man. She admired powerful men. The fact that her daddy held Duncan in high regard impressed her. His obvious influence with powerful people like her dad, combined with his national notoriety, made him an obvious target for her affection. It is a universal truth that deep down inside, every daughter wants a husband just like "dear old Dad."

"We have work to do, young lady," Carter said in a firm but kind voice. "Perhaps Mr. Gabrelli would do us the honor of joining us for dinner later this evening?"

With each word, Duncan became more certain. It was the voice of the man who'd killed his mother.

The ball was now in Duncan's court. He couldn't accept the invitation if he was going to make the 150-mile round trip between Denver and Copper Mountain. "I am so sorry, but I have already made plans for this evening."

Christina looked hurt and disappointed. Even Carter looked offended. It was as if Duncan had rejected his daughter.

Seeing their reaction, he immediately added, "I was planning to stay in Denver another day. Is it possible to extend that invitation until tomorrow night?"

Carter's offended look relaxed slightly. "I'm sorry, Duncan; I'm leaving on business tomorrow."

Her dad might not be available, but Christina was. She was not about to let pass the opportunity to spend a private evening with Duncan. "Well, I would love to join you for dinner tomorrow night."

Carter looked taken aback by his daughter's forwardness, but then again, she was twenty-eight years old.

Careful not to reveal the seething hatred he was feeling, Duncan turned to Carter. "With your permission, of course."

Despite the fact that he'd had very little control over the actions of his daughter since she was about fourteen, Carter appreciated the courtesy. "Of course, you're all she's been talking about for a week. I would just be a third wheel, anyway. Go have fun." He declared, hoping that he'd embarrassed his daughter (as fathers often do).

"Now if you will excuse us, my dear?"

Christina feigned a look of embarrassment at hearing her father's comments.

"It has been a pleasure meeting you, Christina. I will call you in the morning to make dinner plans."

"I'm available all day tomorrow. Daddy has my number, please feel free to call anytime." She clearly did not feel the least bit ashamed at being so forward, which she deemed to be a rich girl's prerogative.

"I will call you in the morning."

As he entered Carter's office, he couldn't help but think how surreal the last five minutes had been. He'd found the man responsible for his mother's murder and fallen in love—or at least in lust—with that man's daughter. The gods seemed to be smiling down on him. Or maybe not.

The office was just as magnificent as he'd anticipated. The panoramic view of the Denver skyline was extraordinarily beautiful. Only the furnishings in Mr. Bartelli's home rivaled the decor of the office, but it all went unnoticed by Duncan; he had more important things on his mind.

The legal issues presented by Carter were not particularly complicated or serious. There had been several minor investigations by two governmental agencies into Oasis's connection with an offshore bank; they were nothing to get excited about. He could easily hand this matter off to a local firm.

However, before making any final decisions, he thought he'd see how his date with Christina went, while he contemplated how to kill her father. *Maybe some work in Denver won't be so bad.*

CHAPTER 80

DUNCAN WAS IN the mood to murder. Meeting Carter only intensified that desire to kill someone, anyone.

The meeting with Carter lasted less than two hours. By four o'clock he was back at his hotel. He picked up the keys to the rental car at the front desk and checked for messages.

"Good afternoon, Mr. Gabrelli. Here are the keys to your car. It's in valet parking. Just take the elevator to parking level one and show them this ticket." The desk clerk handed Duncan a sealed envelope. "Here are your messages, is there anything else I can help you with tonight?"

"Yes, please have a turkey sandwich and a large glass of milk sent to my room right away."

"No problem, sir. I will take care of it."

Duncan stuck the envelope unopened in his vest pocket and went straight to his room. While he waited for room service, he changed his clothes and checked his bag of supplies for the tenth time. He was growing impatient for his food and anxious to get on the road. Finally, at 4:25 p.m., there was a knock at the door.

"Just leave it next to the sofa. There's a ten for you on the table," Duncan called from the bedroom.

"Thank you, sir."

Duncan left two minutes after the server did; there was no time to eat.

By getting out of Denver under the five o'clock rush, he calculated that the drive would take about two hours. Since it was midweek, he didn't anticipate running into much traffic going up the mountain.

Arriving at Copper Mountain just after sunset fit very nicely into his plan. He'd had only a light lunch, and he could hear his stomach voicing its displeasure with his decision to leave the turkey sandwich behind. But there was no time to stop for a sit-down dinner. He stopped at McDonald's before leaving Denver. It had been many years since he had last eaten fast food. He was surprised at how good the hamburger tasted.

The drive felt long, perhaps because he was the only person on the road obeying the speed limit. He wasn't about to get a ticket.

The long drive gave him an opportunity to contemplate what to do about Mr. Carter. *Was Carter toying with me? Does he realize that Duncan Cabella and Duncan Gabrelli are the same person?*

In final analysis Duncan concluded that it was highly unlikely that Carter knew who he really was. Duncan had been Mr. Bartelli's friend and confidant for far too long for Carter to risk letting Duncan live, if there was any chance that Duncan could identify him. *No, he must not know.*

When he was just outside the resort town, he closed his mind to the Carter issue to focus on the task at hand. *I will deal with you later, Carter!* was his final thought on the matter before preparing to kill.

The streetlights shone bright as he drove down the main street of the resort town just after sunset. Even on a Tuesday, the streets were crowded with snow bunnies. *Doesn't anyone have a job?*

Most of the men were wearing black or gray ski pants, with dark ski jackets, turtleneck sweaters and ski caps. A chill had filled the night air, and everyone was bundled up from head to toe. Prior to entering the town, he had pulled over to change into his black ski pants and jacket. *I'm going to blend right in.*

Based on his review of brochures and local newspapers, he had a fairly good idea where he wanted to start looking for his next victim.

There was a section of town that was known mostly by the locals. It was part of the original town, before the developers created a new main street lined with fancy stores and boutiques.

He parked the car in a crowded parking lot at the end of the main drag, deciding that the car would be less conspicuous among so many others. He headed out on foot to the area he intended to search. On his way, he heard voices coming from an alley between two buildings.

Having just reached the outer edge of town, he stopped to investigate. There was a couple arguing at the other end of the alley. It was hard to tell for sure, with the darkened skies and their cold-weather clothing, but from the sound of their voices and the male's animated body motions, Duncan gauged them to be relatively young.

The massive figure of the man towered over the much smaller female. She was crying as the man flailed about, all the while berating her.

There didn't appear to be anyone else around, but there were too many windows and exposed positions to be sure. For his part, Duncan crouched down in the shadows beside a building and continued to observe the verbal attack for almost five minutes. The young woman's arms dangled loosely by her sides as she absorbed the vulgarity being heaped on her.

When it was clear that he'd completely broken her spirit, with the palms of both hands he shoved her hard just above her breasts. The wisp of a woman went flying backward, slamming against a building then slumping face first into the snow. "You cunt!" were his parting words as he turned and exited behind one of the buildings.

The young woman sat up, resting her head in her hands as she continued to cry in soft, whimpering tones.

Duncan cut back in front of the building and looked down the next alley. He got there just in time to see the man walk past. Jogging down between the buildings, he just caught sight of the burly man walking off toward the tree line, away from town.

The mostly cloudy skies allowed just enough light for Duncan to track the man's shadow as he made his way down a path toward the forest, eventually disappearing into the trees.

He's probably looking for a place where he can be alone and contemplate his assholic behavior.

Barring some unexpected company, this young man was going to be his next victim. Using a penlight he pulled from his pocket,

Duncan made his way down the path, following at a safe distance to avoid detection.

They took a winding path for quite a distance. The farther into the woods the man walked, the better Duncan liked the situation.

A .22-caliber revolver was again his murder weapon of choice. He fancied its light weight and found it to be both quiet and reliable. He made sure, however, to bring a different gun with a different type of ammunition. The gun used in Rhode Island was disposed of at sea, never to be seen again.

Duncan had been closing the distance between them, and he was just about to make his move. Then he heard a soft voice whisper up ahead, "John, is that you?"

Duncan froze in his tracks.

"Yes, it's me," the man replied, just before he tripped over a sapling hidden beneath the snow, which sent him crashing to the ground.

Cursing the invisible obstruction, he screamed, "You cock-sucking motherfucker!" His words echoed in the still night air.

"Are you okay, John?" The woman was carrying a flashlight, and she used it to guide John in her direction. Duncan watched as the two embraced.

"I thought you might have changed your mind," the female voice whispered.

"You know I had to talk to her first. But I'm here now," John responded irritably, rubbing his leg, which he had injured slightly in the fall.

"I hate that we have to keep our love a secret. Look around you. Why do we have to hide in the woods like animals? It is dark and scary out here."

Abandoning the sweet voice she'd used to beckon her lover only moments ago, the woman angrily asked, "I almost left. Five more minutes, and I would have been gone. Oh yeah! And just what did that bitch have to say when you told her? You did tell her, right? Well, did you?"

"Watch your mouth. She's still my wife."

Duncan found it ironic that he could call her *cunt*, but his girl-friend couldn't call her *bitch*.

"She won't be your wife for long, not if you want to be with me."

"I'm here, aren't I?" John said as he pulled her body close to his. Passionately he began to caress and stroke the young girl's body.

At first she appeared to pull away.

"You told her?"

"Yes! I told her. Now come here and kiss me."

Her resolve would prove to be as weak as her morality, as she began to kiss John hard on the mouth. "No, John. Not here, it's too cold. Let's go back to my room."

Ignoring her halfhearted objections, John slipped her jacket off and then his own, laying both on top of the newly fallen snow. Effortlessly lifting her into the air, he gently laid her down on the jackets.

He remained standing as he pulled his ski pants down around his ankles. The young lady had removed her boots, but was having slightly more difficulty removing her ski pants and thermal underwear. Lying on her back she pushed with both hands to extricate herself from the elasticized monster. Reaching down, John grabbed two handfuls of spandex and instantly peeled away the obstacle between him and his lusty desires.

Their lovemaking made enough noise to drown out Duncan's approach. The two were grinding and grunting as he stepped up beside them.

John was the first to notice Duncan. In an aggressive, almost violent tone he yelled, "What the fuck are you looking at, buddy? Get the fuck out of here before I kick your ass."

"Quite a vocabulary you have there, John," Duncan replied sarcastically.

The woman was lying there frantically trying to cover her naked body with a sweater covered with snowflakes.

Seeing the interloper was not going to leave voluntarily, John reluctantly turned his total attention to Duncan. Apparently not wanting to jump up with his erect penis flopping in the cold air, he rolled over onto the snow and slid on his pants before he attempted to stand up.

Duncan shined his small light at John's face, causing him to squint. "I'm going to kick..."

John finally noticed the gun in Duncan's hand as he climbed to one knee. Stopping in midsentence, a look of complete capitulation swept over his face. With a childlike whimper, he begged, "No man, please."

The cries fell on deaf ears. Without even the slightest hesitation, Duncan raised the gun and fired a single shot into the side of John's face. He fell dead in a heap onto the stunned woman's chest. The weight of his massive torso knocked the air from her lungs. Unable to catch her breath, she couldn't scream. Duncan's second shot caught her in the center of her forehead.

For the rest of his life, the looks on the young couple's faces would be etched in his memory. That look would become his drug. From that moment on, he was addicted. He wanted to instill that much fear in *every* victim.

In an instant, his entire motivation for committing murder had changed. Maybe it would be more accurate to say it had evolved. The desire to commit the perfect crime had merged into a need to experience the thrill of the kill. Only seconds had passed, and already he longed to feel the rush of adrenaline again. He needed, as surely as an addict needs his next fix, to take another person's life, without cause, without reason, and without remorse.

The hollow-point bullets had caused massive head wounds. There was no doubt that they both died instantly. Taking one quick look around, he turned and walked back toward the town. Stopping briefly at the edge of the tree line, he stared back toward the town. There was nothing but dim lights looking back at him. The noise coming from the bustling little resort town had smothered the caplike sounds of the pistol.

No one noticed the two men entering the woods, or that only one came out. On his way back to the car, he once again walked by the alley where he'd seen the young woman sobbing. She was gone. She didn't know it yet, but he'd done her a service. She was going to get a new start, thanks to his murderous obsession.

It's a strange world, he thought as he slid into the Ford. *Sometimes doing bad can have a good result in the lives of others.*

He was pleasantly surprised that, even when he obeyed the speed limit, the return trip took less than two hours.

CHAPTER 81

THERE WAS SOMETIIING about the experience of committing the murders that again awoke a ravenous appetite inside him. Fast food was not going to quench his hunger this time. All he could think of during the return trip was carving up a slice out of a thick prime rib. By the time he reached the hotel, his stomach was rumbling uncontrollably.

The events in Copper Mountain had all happened so quickly, he was back in his hotel suite at nine o'clock. Suddenly his mind switched gears. Even his stomach stopped growling.

Carter. That bastard killed Mom. But why? Sitting on the corner of the bed he tried to find the answer to his question. *Why would one of Vinnie's closest associates kill her? It just didn't make any sense. Could I be wrong? No, that is the voice. I know it.*

All the facts pointed to Duncan being right—the voice, the hair, the build, the connection to the syndicate. *It couldn't be a coincidence. But what can I do? I can't kill one of Mr. Bartelli's friends, at least not without his consent.* Duncan would have no choice; he'd have to take this to Mr. Bartelli himself. *Yeah, Vinnie will know what to do.*

Knowing that he could count on Mr. Bartelli's help and counsel eased his mind, and his thoughts immediately turned to a more pleasurable subject.

Maybe I should ask Christina to join me for a late dinner? Is it too late? How can I explain being available after rejecting her father's dinner invitation?

It didn't offend Duncan's increasingly warped sense of morality to transition from contemplating the murder of Carter to fucking his daughter.

In his excited state he threw caution to the wind.

Christina answered the telephone on the first ring. "Well, what a pleasant surprise to hear from you. I didn't expect your call until tomorrow," she said in a half-flustered, half-teasing tone.

"I hope that you'll not find me too forward, but my business resolved itself earlier than I expected. I was hoping I could convince you to join me for a late dinner, if you don't have other plans."

"Now you're not trying to get out of town early on me, are you?" she asked in a sweet but suspicious tone.

In truth, he *was* thinking that if dinner didn't go well, he might leave early the next day. However, he was pleasantly surprised that she knew men well enough to consider the possibility.

Always quick on his feet, Duncan replied, "And forfeit the opportunity of spending two evenings with such a lovely young woman? What kind of fool do you take me for?"

"And just where are you taking me to dinner?"

"Anywhere you like. If you have no preference, I'd be happy to make reservations based on the recommendations of the concie—"

Christina cut him off. "I'll pick you up in front of your hotel in thirty minutes. Dress nice."

He wasn't exactly sure what "dress nice" meant to a twenty-eight-year-old, but he was confident that a six-thousand-dollar custom-fitted suit should qualify.

Exactly thirty minutes later, Christina came screeching to a stop in front of his hotel in a silver Rolls-Royce Corniche convertible. *The family must have a fleet of Rolls-Royces,* he thought to himself.

"Nice car. Is it a rental?"

With a wicked little smile she responded, "Well, sort of. It's Daddy's pride and joy. He never lets *anyone* drive it. So every now and again, I liberate it from him."

"Great, I'm going on a date in a car stolen from one of my clients. You know that you're causing me to violate at least three laws and my attorney-client privilege," he joked, as he slid in through the passenger door.

"First, this isn't a car. It's a Rolls. Second, don't worry, I know this great criminal lawyer." She pressed hard on the accelerator and the Rolls lurched forward.

She'd made reservations at Giovanni's, an intimate Italian restaurant. Despite the impression made by the Rolls, she turned out to be a spectacularly practical woman. She was bright and charming, with a wonderful sense of humor. They spent the entire time at the restaurant talking about nothing in particular. Neither noticed that they barely touched their meals.

The evening passed quickly. Before they knew it, they were the only patrons left in the restaurant. The waiter was politely, but overtly, attempting to push them out the door, and after a few of his none-too-subtle hints, Duncan double tipped the waiter for his trouble and retrieved Christina's jacket. She let him drive, saying that she'd had a little more wine than she was used to drinking.

As they pulled away from the restaurant a black Cadillac started its engine. The Cadillac followed them back to Duncan's hotel, just as it had followed them to the restaurant. They were too involved in each other to notice.

When they arrived, she looked over at Duncan and said, "Are you coming up to my room for a nightcap?"

Duncan laughed out loud. "You *must* have had too much to drink. This is *my* hotel. I should call you a cab."

She smiled. "How much did I drink tonight?"

The question caught him a little off-guard. It dawned on him that she hadn't consumed more than two glasses of wine all night long.

Fighting hard to keep a straight face and employing his smoothest southern delivery, "Ms. Carter, would you do me the honor of joining me for a nightcap?"

Mocking his southern tone, she replied, "Why, certainly, how kind of you to ask."

Duncan tossed the keys to the doorman.

"Will you be needing your car again this evening, sir?"

Not sure how to answer that question without sounding presumptuous, he turned to Christina.

She replied for him, "No. I don't believe we will."

CHAPTER 82

DUNCAN COUNLDN'T RECALL ever feeling quite so happy or content. Lying there awake for almost an hour, he was careful not to rouse the beautiful flower sleeping by his side. *She looks so wonderfully angelic.*

The moment was spoiled when he suddenly remembered that he hadn't let Stella know he was staying in Denver an extra day. It was completely out of character for him not to call and let her know that he had changed his plans.

Slowly and quietly he rolled out of bed and retreating to a separate sitting room. It was almost two back home, and he woke Stella from a deep sleep.

Stella gasped upon hearing that he'd changed his plans without as much as a telephone call. She noticed that he was speaking in a quieter tone than normal.

"I'll call you in the morning with my new itinerary. I think I should stay—" Before he could finish, Stella interrupted, "Are you okay, sir?"

A smile creased his cheeks. "Yes, Stella, I am just fine," he responded at the same time as he heard a sweet voice coming from behind him.

"Already calling another woman?"

Stella gasped out loud. In a sleep-deprived state of confusion, she said, "Sorry for interrupting, Mr. Gabrelli."

The smile on his face grew broader. "Stella, I called you."

"Of course you did. Sorry, sir, I don't know what's come over me."

They were both fully aware what had come over her, but he was finding a great deal of pleasure at hearing her try to extricate her foot from her mouth. He was, however, in too good a mood to let her suffer for too long, so he broke the silence.

"Please alert the pilot about the change in plans. I want to arrive in Los Angeles early Saturday morning; make sure he has my plane ready. Be sure to reschedule my meetings for today."

"Sir, I left several messages for you at the front desk. Mr. Bartelli has been trying to reach you. What should I tell him?"

Crap. He instantly recalled putting the unread messages in his suit pocket. To add insult to injury, he hadn't checked his messages since leaving for Copper Mountain. "I'll call him right away. Did he leave a message?"

"No, sir, he just said to tell you he called as soon as I reached you. He didn't say, but it sounded important."

He was about to ask Stella another question when he felt the long thin fingers of Christina's velvety hand wrap around his penis and gently squeeze. "I'll call in later today!" he blurted abruptly before hanging up the phone.

He knew he should call Mr. Bartelli right away, but every now and again a man had to abandon reason and follow his heart. *Heart?*

What's an hour more or less? he thought as he carried Christina back into the bedroom.

CHAPTER 83

THEIR PASSION COULDN'T hide the fact that there was something bothering Duncan. As much as Christina was enjoying the romantic moment, it was evident that his mind was somewhere else.

Lifting his head off her bosom, she asked, "Where are you?"

His mind was distracted by two names that were floating around in his head, Mr. Bartelli and her dad's. "I'm so sorry, but I need to make a call."

She guessed one of them. "What, Mr. Bartelli can't wait a few hours for the sun to come up?" Although she'd heard him talking to Stella, he hadn't mentioned any names. He was both impressed and intrigued by her deduction.

"What makes you think that I need to call Mr. Bartelli?"

Mr. Bartelli was a name that she'd heard her father mention on many occasions. She was fully aware that he was, for all practical purposes, both her father's boss and his friend. But she thought she might as well toy with Duncan, just a little.

"Well, I can only think of the names of three men important enough to get you out of this bed. The first is my father. If he were trying to track you down, you would have more to worry about than returning a telephone call. The second is the president, but I'm pretty sure that he doesn't consort with lead counsel for the syndicate. The third is, of course, your boss, Mr. Bartelli. So if you're getting out of this bed to call anyone *other* than Mr. Bartelli, you're an idiot. And I'm quite certain that you're not—an idiot, that is."

She is smart, he thought. *I'm going to have to get used to that.*

"You forgot one name: God."

"You call him God if you must. Just call Mr. Bartelli and get your fanny back in this bed."

Casting a "you're cute but not that funny" look in her direction, he threw on a robe and went back into the sitting room to make the call.

With all that had been going on in his life, he hadn't spent much time with Vincenzo over the past month. The two men had become so close over the years that his neglect of that relationship was blatant.

Even something as trivial as not immediately returning his telephone call had become a source of irritation for Mr. Bartelli.

"Where the hell have you been?" Mr. Bartelli barked into the receiver. "I have been trying to reach you for days."

You've only been trying to reach me for hours, not days, Duncan thought. Even so, he saw no point in aggravating Mr. Bartelli any more than he already was, so he just let it go. "I decided to spend another day in Denver to consider the Oasis problem."

"I thought you told me that you didn't believe the Oasis situation was of any consequence," Mr. Bartelli snapped back.

At best, his stated reason for staying in Denver was a white lie. He could have dug himself a deeper hole by expanding the deception, but he knew that, at least in this case, the truth would set him free.

"Yes, I did, but that was before I found out just how gorgeous Mr. Carter's daughter is." Now that was a response that Mr. Bartelli could appreciate. Having previously made sure that he didn't go without female companionship, this would surely be music to his ears.

"Damn it, son, you scared the hell out of me. It's not like you to disappear. Leave a message, do *something* to let me know you're all right, for God's sake," Mr. Bartelli demanded, now sounding more relieved than angry.

Duncan thought it a bit strange. He'd only been out of communication with his office for just over fourteen hours. Mr. Bartelli was acting as if he'd gone missing for weeks. But, in truth, it made him feel good that Mr. Bartelli was so concerned.

"When will you be back in town?"

"Saturday morning. I'm having Stella reschedule my flight."

"Good. I'll check with Stella and have a car pick you up at the airport. Let's have breakfast when you get in. I have some matters I want to discuss with you."

While Duncan would have preferred that Benton meet him, Mr. Bartelli insisted, and Duncan capitulated.

His insistence should have put Duncan on notice that something bigger was happening. However, Duncan's mind was otherwise occupied.

"Breakfast sounds good. I have something very important to talk to you about," Duncan replied.

"Anything you can talk about now?"

"No. I'll see you Saturday."

"She'd better be something very special for you to cause me such grief. Now get back to that lovely girl."

"She is, sir, she is. See you Saturday."

CHAPTER 84

CHRISTINA AND DUNCAN spent the entire next day together. She convinced him to spend the night at her apartment, promising to take him to the airport early the next morning. It was a promise that neither of them wanted to keep when the alarm went off at 3:30 a.m.

They both were making concerted efforts to cause him to delay the flight, each taking every opportunity to caress the other one last time before leaving the apartment. But he had a breakfast appointment with Mr. Bartelli that they both knew he couldn't miss.

At the airport, the two exchanged long embraces and many soft, moist kisses. Duncan felt awkward saying goodbye. He'd grown accustomed to the "love 'em and leave 'em" type of nonrelationship. But it was already different; he didn't want to leave, maybe for the first time in his life.

Even so, the rational side of him kept saying, *You've only known her for two days! Relax, relax, relax.*

As they walked out onto the tarmac, the engine noise of his private jet began to drown out their final goodbyes.

Realizing he only had a few more moments, Duncan took a leap of faith.

In a voice loud enough to be heard over the din of the engines, he said, "I've decided to personally handle the legal representation for Oasis, so I'm going to be spending a lot more time in Denver."

A smile instantly wreathed her face.

Duncan pulled her close, putting his lips to her ear, "But it's more than that. Look. I don't want to scare you off. I know it's only been two wonderful days, but...Well, I've never felt this way about anyone."

"You're not going to scare me off. I knew you were the one the second you stepped off the elevator at my dad's office. Get back here as soon as you can."

Now Duncan was a little scared. "The one?"

They kissed one last passionate kiss before Duncan turned and climbed the steps into his plane.

On the flight home, he tried to figure out just how he could fit Christina into his strange life. *My commitment to my work, my secret compulsion to kill, and now her father—how was all of that going to fit together?*

CHAPTER 85

TWO OF MR. BARTELLI'S personal bodyguards met Duncan at the gate when the airplane landed in Los Angeles. His head was still far too high in the clouds to consider the significance of the level of protection provided simply to drive him from the airport.

The limo pulled through the front gates of Mr. Bartelli's estate forty-five minutes later. Again, the extra security milling around the grounds failed to grab his attention.

It was not until he entered the mansion that he finally recognized that something was wrong. There were armed men stationed throughout the house. He made his way up the stairs toward the balcony.

Just as he reached the entrance to the balcony, a butler informed him that breakfast was being served in the dining room. *That's odd; it's such a beautiful day. Vinnie always takes his breakfast on the balcony. Why is he eating in the dining room?*

When he entered the dining room, Vincenzo rose to give him one of those big hugs Duncan had now grown completely comfortable with receiving. It had gotten to the point where he actually looked forward to them.

"Sit down, sit down. Tell me a story about a young girl of such unsurpassed beauty that you would risk my wrath to be with her," Mr. Bartelli said with a shit-eating grin on his face.

"Have you met her, sir?"

"Oh, maybe years ago, when she was much too young to think of as a woman."

"Well, sir, she is perhaps the most beautiful woman I've ever met."

Mr. Bartelli was just about to take a bite of his toast when he stopped. "Well now. That *is* saying something. I've *personally* introduced you to many of the most glamorous women in the world. Right here in this house, as a matter of fact."

"Yes, sir, you have. And I must confess to you, not one compares." His complete sincerity didn't escape Mr. Bartelli's attention.

Duncan began to describe in great detail how Christina made him feel. Mr. Bartelli didn't expect for the story to be quite so intimate and heartfelt. Knowing Duncan as he did, he expected nothing intimate at all.

That being true, he wasn't quite sure how to react. "Slow down, my son. This sounds pretty serious for someone you've only known for two days. Or have you been keeping this from me?"

"No, it's only been two days. Two of the best I can remember, but not to worry. I'm far too motivated by other things to get bogged down in a relationship at this point in my life," Duncan proclaimed, trying to convince himself as much as he was trying to assure Mr. Bartelli.

Mr. Bartelli focused on his face and paused a minute before saying anything. "Son, you look pretty bogged down in it *already*, if you ask me—if you don't mind my saying so. Besides, weren't you the one crying to me about wanting a family not that long ago?"

Duncan just smiled. "Hey! What's going on around here anyway— all this extra security? And why aren't we having breakfast on the balcony?"

"That's why I had you brought here. We need to talk. There have been some complicating factors within the syndicate of late."

Duncan wasn't sure exactly what was meant by complicating factors, but he was quite sure it wasn't good news. It'd been many years since there had been any disagreements of consequence regarding the internal operation of the syndicate, but that was all about to change.

"We are in the midst of a power struggle and things could get a little dangerous. You need to keep a very low profile for a while. I'm going to provide you with a little security until this blows over," Mr. Bartelli said between mouthfuls of food, just as casually as if he were cautioning him about the start of the flu season.

That certainly explained the extra security he noticed guarding the house. It also explained why they were not eating outside on the balcony today. Apparently Mr. Bartelli had placed himself under house arrest until the matter was resolved. He did not want to give any assassin a clear shot.

However it didn't explain why *Duncan* might need security. After all, he'd been taking a lower profile ever since the syndicate decentralized its legal representation.

In a tone denoting his deep concern, he inquired, "I don't mean to overstep my bounds, but are you in danger, sir?"

"Son, my life is always in danger. It comes with the territory. Look around you. This is what danger buys you. But that's not why I called you here today. I fear that I may have placed you in danger as well," Mr. Bartelli said apologetically.

With that comment, he got Duncan's complete and undivided attention.

"I'm full. Let's continue this conversation in the study."

Duncan looked at his watch and asked, "I know it's Saturday, but I postponed meetings until today. Should I call and cancel?"

"I've already spoken to Stella. All your meetings have been rescheduled."

Once they had settled in the study, Mr. Bartelli asked, "Before we get started, was there something you wanted to talk to me about?"

"No. It's important, but I would rather find out what's going on here first. It can wait."

"Well son, to make any sense of what is happening, I need to come clean with you. There has been something I've wanted to tell you for years. But for many complicated reasons—and perhaps some not so complicated—I was compelled to keep it from you. I apologize in advance for that. But believe me when I say that I always had your best interests at heart."

Duncan sat there spellbound. *Enough of the torturous preamble. Get to the point,* he thought.

"There is no easy way to say this, so I'm just going to say it. You are my son."

Duncan, who had been leaning forward in his chair in anticipation of hearing this deep, dark secret, sat up straight and stared at Mr. Bartelli, waiting for the punch line. When none was forthcoming, he inched to the edge of his chair. For a moment he thought that the old man was losing his mind. *He certainly didn't need to cancel my morning meetings to tell me he loves me like a son.*

Knowing that it couldn't literally be true, he responded the only way that made sense. "You've been like a father to me, sir. It is a great honor that you consider me to be like a son to you."

Vincenzo smiled tenderly. "No, you're not *like* my son. You *are* my son."

There could be no mistaking his meaning now. For reasons that were still very unclear, he apparently truly believed that he was Duncan's father.

What's he thinking? What does he want me to say? He couldn't be my father, Duncan thought as he leaned back in his chair.

After a short but agonizing silence, Duncan responded in a confused and apologetic voice, "Sir, you know how much I care for you. But I don't know what you want me to say. My father is dead. As much as it would please me to be your son"—he paused a moment—"I just don't know what you want me to say."

"I know that it sounds fantastically unbelievable, but please just listen."

Mr. Bartelli began to explain the unexplainable. He left out nothing. A lifetime of a father's love was poured out as the morning drifted into afternoon, and afternoon into evening.

Duncan's head was spinning. It seemed so unreal. However, as Mr. Bartelli traced the tracks of his life, it became increasingly apparent that it was all true. What he perceived as fate and destiny had, in reality, been his father's power at work, staying in the shadows, guiding him down every path.

Both men periodically broke into tears born of joy, sorrow, and forgiveness. Only a very few people had ever seen these men cry.

He was too emotional to see his father as the manipulative and controlling person he'd been for all those years. All he could think was that he had a real, living, breathing father. As a child, that was the wish he made every time he blew out the candles on his birthday cake. Every night's prayers ended with him asking God for a father.

They had been prayers that he believed had gone unheard. Or at least unanswered.

CHAPTER 86

A S HE LET the reality set in he began to contemplate why his father had waited so long to tell him the truth. *Why not tell me after my mother was murdered? Why not tell me after your wife died?* Duncan knew that Mr. Bartelli's wife had passed away before he graduated law school. *Maybe it had something to do with his relationship with Santino, but he had been dead for years. Why not tell me after his murder?*

As if he was reading Duncan's mind, his father said, "I know that you must be wondering why I chose this moment to reveal the truth."

"Yes, why? Why did you wait so long?"

"There were many times when I wanted to tell you, but promises and circumstances prevented it."

It didn't surprise him to hear that a promise to his mother prevented the disclosure prior to her death. The reasons for not telling him after her passing were much more complicated, but at its core, the reasons centered on his relationship with his now deceased son, Santino.

Santino was living under the delusion that he was the heir apparent to his father's control of the syndicate. But, in reality, that was never in the cards. Santino's reasoning was twice flawed.

First, he believed that because control of the syndicate had been passed down from his grandfather to his father, it would someday naturally, in the order of things, be turned over to him. While it was true that Vincenzo was the undisputed boss running the day-to-day operations of the syndicate, there was still a board of directors that oversaw his actions. His father reached his position because the board of directors approved the transfer of power. Without the board's consent, even Vincenzo wouldn't have been the boss.

With his abrasive personality and legendary temper, Santino had insulted or threatened almost every board member. As a result, most of the board didn't like or trust him. There was no chance they would ever approve such a transfer of power.

Secondly, Vincenzo held a deep and abiding conviction that Santino was not capable of accepting the responsibilities that went along with controlling such a far-reaching and influential business operation. He'd always known that Duncan would eventually become a man infinitely better suited to step into his shoes. Duncan was the older of his boys, and therefore by right deserved to be next in line. However, Mr. Bartelli was convinced that when Santino's delusion was eventually unmasked, his son would look for someone to blame.

A sibling who was superior in almost every way would surely be the target. As much as Mr. Bartelli loved both his boys, he knew that Santino's violent side was uncontrollable and unpredictable. To reveal Duncan's existence would surely pit one son against the other.

But to fully explain his reasoning, he needed to provide Duncan with a clear vision of the power struggles that perpetually exist within the syndicate. Finally he was getting to the heart of why he chose this time to disclose their true relationship.

"You know enough about the operation of the syndicate to understand that there is a delicate balance of power."

"Certainly."

"Where power and control of the syndicate rests at any time is always a complicated equation. For many years, there has been little doubt among the board members that *I* control the majority of power. I make or approve all of its day-to-day operational decisions. My alliances and support have made me the undisputed boss."

Mr. Bartelli wasn't telling him anything he didn't already know, but Duncan sat and listened patiently.

"Santino, God rest his soul, was a drain on my power and control for years. While the syndicate is by no means a monarchy, there are those on the board who feared Santino would attempt to wrest control of the syndicate when I retired."

Both Mr. Bartelli and Duncan knew that Santino had only magnified those fears by telling anyone who would listen that he would inherit his father's position within the syndicate.

"When he was alive, I was able to hold a coalition of board members and associates together with my assurances that I would not back any attempts by Santino to gain control upon my retirement."

Duncan was shocked by his admission that he'd effectively conspired against Santino. *He wasn't kidding when he described the balance of power to be delicate and complicated,* Duncan thought.

"God knows that I loved Santino, but he had neither the strength of character nor the intellect required to manage the many diverse interests of the syndicate. You, on the other hand, my son, not only have the intellect, but you also possess the temperament and wisdom."

Duncan was humbled by the confidence his father was expressing in him.

"However, I knew that Santino would never let you step into the position he believed he deserved. He'd have killed you, I'm sure of it. I just couldn't bring myself to have my two sons become mortal enemies. I just couldn't do that," Mr. Bartelli said, hanging his head low.

For the next hour, Mr. Bartelli gave him the history of how the power inside the syndicate had ebbed and flowed over the years. The bottom line was that he—and his father before him—had always sought to reduce the power struggles. Both men had been fair and decisive leaders. The syndicate profited greatly as a result of their leadership. For as long as Mr. Bartelli could remember, the board had played a mostly symbolic role as it related to the control of the syndicate.

In fact, the board would have *preferred* a patriarchal transition, if Mr. Bartelli had a son capable of the task. And why not? It had prospered far in excess of anyone's expectations under the Bartelli family reign. Having an heir to the throne would have made life easier on everyone. Historically, contested transitions of power in the criminal world were almost always messy and expensive.

Santino's obvious failings as a leader led to several factions positioning themselves to seize power when Mr. Bartelli released his stranglehold.

No one expected Mr. Bartelli to surrender his position anytime soon, at least not voluntarily. However, the jockeying for position had been going on for years, just in case the position did open unexpectedly.

'Open unexpectedly.' Now there's a euphemism for you, Duncan thought. *You mean someone kills you.*

Without a clear heir apparent, the possibility of a coup increased substantially. Since Santino's murder, the competition between the factions had ratcheted up considerably.

Years had been spent creating alliances. Influence was now being exerted to coerce support for one person in particular: Leon Horowitz.

The syndicate had diversified over the years. There was a substantial Jewish influence working within the organization, particularly among the associates in New York and Florida. Leon Horowitz had wide support from the Jewish faction. The dust was still settling, but Horowitz had become the front-runner to take over Mr. Bartelli's title.

Normally, identifying a successor apparent would have had a calming influence. However, a wrench had been thrown into the machine.

"The board now knows you're my son. I'm not sure how they found out, but they know."

Unlike Santino, Duncan was respected by the board and the syndicate's associates alike. He was thought of as a brilliant litigator and negotiator. However, the revelation that he was Bartelli's son immediately made him a threat to Horowitz's plan. There was little doubt that the board would back Duncan if he showed an interest in taking his father's position.

Mr. Bartelli paused. "Do you think Leon's going to just let that happen, my son?"

"It's not Horowitz we have to worry about, it's Carter, sir. He told the board. He knows. That's part of what I need to talk to you about."

"I know that Carter is in Horowitz's pocket, but what makes you think he's the one who told the board?"

"You know he's working for Horowitz? I thought he was your friend."

"He was. Perhaps Horowitz made him a better offer. I intend to find out someday, someday soon."

"I'm afraid I have even worse news. It was Carter who killed my mother."

Duncan's accusation caught Mr. Bartelli by complete surprise.

"No chance. Who told you that lie?"

Duncan thought for a moment. "It was you. You were the voice on the telephone the night Mom was killed?"

"Yes. Yes, son, it was me. But what does that have to do with Carter?"

"Remember what I told you that night. I was hiding under the house. I heard Carter's voice. I'll never forget that voice. It's been preserved inside my head for all these years. I knew the minute I heard it in his office on Thursday. It's him. I'm sure of it."

"How can you be sure? How? It's been so long."

"I saw him that night. Just for a split second, but I saw him, his hair, his build, his profile, his voice. It's him. I'd stake my life on it. It's him."

"You just got done telling me that Carter introduced you to his daughter. He is introducing his daughter to someone he is going to have to kill? Explain that to me."

"Keep your friends close and your enemies closer," Duncan replied.

"He is a cold-blooded motherfucker. I have known him a long time, and he is a cold-blooded motherfucker, for sure. That certainly would explain why Carter would help Horowitz. Well, you had better be right; we may both be staking our lives on it."

CHAPTER 87

I T WAS A day for the dropping of bombshells. Not only had Duncan discovered that he was Mr. Bartelli's son, he also discovered that his very *existence* had caused the worst fight for power within the syndicate in over fifty years. To top it off, there were Carter and Christina to consider.

Duncan was dumbfounded by the news. He couldn't help but see the irony in his situation. The harder he tried to extricate himself from the influence of the syndicate, the more control it had over his future.

After hours of conversation, Duncan was mentally and physically exhausted. "Now what do we do?"

Mr. Bartelli laughed. "You're going to have to leave this one to me."

As if Duncan had a choice. While he may have been of considerable help in finding the murderers of Santino, Bartelli wrote the book on all things syndicate. Duncan would have to rely completely on his father to handle this problem.

"What's your plan?"

Having spent his life playing his cards close to his vest, Mr. Bartelli thought it best to wait a little longer to show his cards. "Someone is about to become a victim of his ambition," Mr. Bartelli said with a devilish smile.

Thinking that it might help for his father to know the truth about his future ambitions, Duncan blurted out, "But I have no desire to run the syndicate, if we could only make that clear to Horowitz."

Mr. Bartelli was extremely disappointed by the comment, but Duncan's desires would have little effect on the events that were about to take place.

"Look, this isn't about whether or not you follow in my footsteps. Horowitz has painted himself into a corner. There is no place for him to retreat. He's made far too many promises to back down now. In order to consolidate his power, he's going to have to kill you. I can assure you of only one thing—that will only happen over my dead body."

Duncan looked at his father and smiled.

"Yes, our fates are sealed. Someone's got to go, and I have no intention of going anywhere," Mr. Bartelli said matter-of-factly.

"I wondered why you got so upset when I didn't check in during my stay in Denver."

"You don't know the half of it, son. I didn't find out about Horowitz's plan until you were already there. So Carter guaranteed your safety during your stay."

Duncan's eyes got as big as saucers.

"I was under Carter's protection? When did you find out that Carter had changed horses?"

"I've known for several months that Carter was being disloyal."

"Then why would you put my life in Carter's hands? You trying to get me killed?"

"Don't be a dumb ass. Carter may not be loyal, but he's not stupid. If something happened to our lead counsel while under his protection, I would have held him personally responsible. It was the safest place for you to be."

"Then why did you make such a big deal about my not returning your call that night?"

"Well, somehow Carter's men lost track of you for almost five hours."

"They were *tailing* me?"

"Not very fucking well, apparently! When I called you at the hotel that afternoon you didn't answer. So I called Carter to track you down. He insisted that you went directly to your room after your meeting. I had one of his men check on you. The next thing I get is a frantic call from Carter. Your room is empty, except for an untouched meal."

"Carter's men were in my room?"

"I was told that you had slipped out of the hotel unseen. I thought you were dead for sure. I knew that Carter would not intentionally let anything happen to you, but it never occurred to me that he might unintentionally get you killed," Mr. Bartelli laughed.

"You think that's funny?"

"Only retrospectively, but if it makes you feel any better, I was pretty pissed off at the time." Mr. Bartelli couldn't conceal his smile.

"Very funny. Very fucking funny."

"Anyway, the next thing I hear is that you have magically reappeared in front of the hotel with Carter's daughter. I wasn't a hundred percent sure that you were still alive until I heard your voice later that night. I wasn't mad at you; I was afraid for you. I tell you, I can't ever remember hearing a man sounding as relieved as Carter sounded when he found you fucking his daughter."

Mr. Bartelli began to laugh out loud again.

"Great. He knew I was making love to Christina. I'm surprised he didn't kill me for that."

"Me. Too." Now he was laughing uncontrollably.

"Aren't you missing a pretty important detail? He killed Mom."

"Yes. Well I didn't know that when I placed you in his care. So maybe I misjudged the situation a bit."

"You're being a little cavalier, don't you think?"

Mr. Bartelli wiped all traces of the smile from his face. "I loved your mother then, I love her now. I will take care of Mr. Carter in due time. I have a few fires to put out, but rest assured he's high on my list."

"I know, Dad. I know."

"And by the way, as for your present and future connections to the syndicate, we can discuss that matter later. One problem at a time, son. One problem at a time."

CHAPTER 88

DUNCAN'S LIFE WAS not his own for the next five days. He was under the constant protection of his father's security forces.

Each morning he would be driven to Mr. Bartelli's. They would talk for hours on end about everything they wished they had done together. They were strangers trying to exchange a lifetime of memories over dinners.

Each night, just after seven, he'd be driven back to his house. There, he dedicated most of the evening hours contemplating his life. He was still finding it hard to think of Mr. Bartelli as his father. However, in a strange and wonderful way, he found comfort in the idea that he had a dad.

In the midst of all the chaos going on around him, Christina was still consuming his thoughts. He'd tried, without much success, to reach her by telephone every day since leaving Denver. It appeared inconceivable that she'd simply ignore his calls.

When the car pulled up to his father's driveway on the fifth day of isolation, he noticed that the extra security was gone. Everything seemed to be back to normal, or at least as normal as things got around his dad's house.

Breakfast was being served on the balcony again. It was during breakfast that his father broke the good news. "It appears that Mr. Horowitz had gone missing. Hope he's all right," Mr. Bartelli said jokingly.

"Is he gone? Or, is he *gone*?" Duncan asked.

"Well, the last time I saw him, he was going for a swim. I told him to leave all that cement on the boat, but he insisted on taking it with him," Mr. Bartelli said, almost choking on his toast.

Duncan was visibly relieved by the news. "Thank God. Have you given any more thought to Carter?"

"Quite a bit of thought, as a matter of fact, but now is not the time to deal with that matter. Later."

"Well, sir."

"Call me Dad."

Duncan felt a little silly, "Well, Dad. There are some things I need to take care of in Denver. I'm going to take the weekend off to go see Christina. I haven't heard from her since my first night back. I don't know what I did to get her mad at me, but I'm going to camp outside her apartment until I can find a way to make her fall in love with me again."

A somber look flashed across Mr. Bartelli's face as he reached across the table. Grabbing both of his son's hands in his own, he said, "No, you're not going to Denver. Son, I'm afraid I have bad news."

Before he said another word, somehow Duncan sensed that Christina was dead. His arms, from his shoulders to his fingertips, began to shake.

Only the night before, Duncan had found the strength necessary to break free of the compulsion to kill. There was no doubt in his mind that he'd found the one person that could change his destiny.

"Christina was killed in a car accident three days ago. Under the circumstances, I thought it best to wait to tell you. I'm so sorry, son. I'm truly sorry."

Duncan had only known her for two fantastic days, but he felt as if a piece of his heart had been carved out. He was numb with sorrow.

"Car accident?"

"Not an accident exactly; she was killed by mistake."

"Mistake? Who killed her by mistake?"

"Assassins sent to kill Carter botched the job. Apparently, they got bad intelligence from Carter's inner circle. They mistakenly believed that only Carter drove a particular Rolls-Royce."

"The silver Rolls-Royce Corniche convertible?"

"I think so. She was in the wrong place at the wrong time."

Duncan's first thought was to accuse his father. "You sent them to kill Carter. It was you, wasn't it?"

"No. Duncan, I swear it wasn't me. It was Horowitz."

"But I thought you killed Horowitz."

"Not before he got to Christina. I had nothing to do with her death. My hand to God, it wasn't me who ordered the hit."

"This just doesn't make any sense. If Carter was working for Horowitz, why would he try to kill Carter?"

"It's bigger than Carter and Horowitz. They are pawns in a much bigger game, a game that has been being played for almost thirty years."

"What game?"

"It's complicated."

"Tell me. Help me understand. I need to make sense of this."

"Until you gave me the missing piece of the puzzle, even I didn't understand the breadth of the deceit and deception involved. You made it possible for me to put an end to the game once and for all."

"Dad, stop being so fucking cryptic and tell me what's going on. What puzzle? What game?"

"Look, Carter had been one of my strongest allies for many years. Because Oasis had contacts all over the world, he had influence over several of the board members and a large number of the associates. With him at my side, we were always able to fend off attacks on my control of the operation. I trusted him with my life.

"Since Santino's death, I've thought hard about asking the board to consider you as my replacement. To make that happen I needed Carter's help."

"But I already told you, I don't—"

"I know what you're going to say. Just hear me out. The board would never pick you to take over unless they knew you were my son. So I had Carter leak the truth to several friendly board members."

"Dad! Why would you do that?"

"I had two reasons. I wanted you to take over. But even if you didn't want control, I knew that Horowitz was not the right man for the job. I needed to flush him out before he got too powerful."

"What? You used me as bait?"

"Don't be so dramatic. You're sitting here talking to me, and he's dead. Have a little faith in your old man."

"Unbelievable. I feel like the biggest dunce in the world."

"If you stop interrupting me, I can get to the point of this story."

"How does any of this answer my question? Why did Horowitz try to kill Carter?"

"I'm getting there. I told you. It's complicated. Anyway, when Horowitz learned you were my son, he was left with very few options. Either he was going to forgo his ambition to be boss or he was going to have to attempt a *coup d'état*. To do that, he needed to take action to weaken my support, which would have the effect of weakening support for you."

"Why not just kill you—or me, for that matter? He'd have to do that anyway. Right?" asked Duncan.

"That's much easier said than done. He knew I'd beef up our security. Getting to us would be almost impossible. No. Carter was the only logical target. If he could knock off Carter, he might fragment my support. A move like that might plant doubt in the minds of board members. He hoped that the board would support him to avoid a bloody war."

"So his plan failed because he missed his chance to kill Carter?" asked Duncan.

"No. You see, he got to Carter without having to kill him."

"How? I thought he was one of the most loyal friends you had."

"He was," Mr. Bartelli paused a moment. "Maybe he still is. You see, Carter's loyalty to me was beyond reproach, and he was far too rich to let money buy his loyalty. Therefore, I wrongly assumed that Horowitz couldn't get to him. But that's where I made my mistake. Horowitz didn't offer Carter money; he offered to keep his secret."

"That means that Horowitz already knew that Carter killed my mom. But how?"

"Pure fucking luck. Not such good luck as it turns out, but pure luck just the same. Thirty years ago, Carter was an up-and-comer. He and my dad were close. My dad trusted him, and my dad didn't trust anyone. Anyway, there was a guy, name of Harold Katz, who was part of Carter's crew. Carter's crew killed Lucia. Years later Katz went to work for Horowitz. Just before he took that swim I was telling you about, Horowitz was nice enough to tell me that it was Katz who told him about Carter. At that point it didn't take a genius to put the pieces together. Carter kills Lucia, but her son, Duncan, gets away."

"So he blackmailed Carter into turning against you?"

"That's what he told me. He didn't tell me right away, I had to convince him to come clean, but I can be a pretty convincing guy sometimes."

Duncan had seen that grin before. "So you killed Horowitz?"

"What are you talking about? He went swimming, just like I said."

Duncan began to run his fingers through his hair. "What a tangled web. How can you live like this?"

"It's the life I chose, son. It's the only life I know."

"You never answered the original question. Why did Horowitz try to kill Carter?"

"You know, I asked him that same question. The idiot thought that Carter had tricked him, and was still secretly working with me. I swear, there is simply no honor among thieves." Mr. Bartelli let out a chuckle.

"Hold on. That doesn't explain why Carter killed Mom. Why would anyone want Mom dead?"

"I'm afraid that's my cross to bear. I loved your mother, Duncan. More than I ever loved anything in my life. But I was married before I found Lucia again. I am a Catholic; divorce was not an option. But when my wife died of cancer, God rest her soul, I knew I could finally be with my only true love. Before I asked your mother to marry me, I told my father that I was going to leave the syndicate to marry Lucia."

"Hold on. Why would you have to leave the syndicate?"

"We are talking about your mom, aren't we? As much as she loved me, she loved you more. I knew that there would be no way she was going to let her precious little boy have any connection to the syndicate."

"What was your dad's reaction to your leaving?

"He wasn't happy, but he could see how much I loved Lucia and reluctantly gave his blessing."

"At least Mom knew that you wanted to marry her before she died."

"No. Sadly, she was killed before I could tell her the news. I blamed myself, and rightfully so."

"But she wasn't killed, she was executed. Why? Why would Carter execute Mom?"

"My father told me that he found the killers and had dealt with them. I had no reason to disbelieve the story. However, it wasn't until you told me of Carter's involvement that it became clear to me. It was my father who ordered Lucia's murder."

"To stop you from marrying her?"

"How you can be so smart and say such dumb shit? Open your eyes, son. It didn't matter to him who I married. He did it to keep me from leaving the syndicate."

"Jesus. Your father lied to you all those years. He killed the woman you loved. How can you be so calm, so matter-of-fact?"

"My dad's dead. Lucia's dead. Even if I wanted to do something, it's a little late." He saw the look of exasperation on Duncan's face. "What? You want to me to curse him? Yes, it hurt me to find out he killed Lucia, but he did what he thought was best for me and the syndicate."

"The syndicate. The syndicate. I guess that makes it okay. As long it's what's best for the syndicate."

"Duncan, don't be a child. Powerful men make decisions that get people killed. My dad was one of those men. I'm one of those men. If you're ever to become one, you're going to have to separate your emotion from your reason."

"Separate my emotion from my reason. Are you kidding me? I did that the day my mother was murdered. I had no choice. But you have a choice. You know who the killer is. Tell me, Dad, if it's all about the syndicate, what's going to happen to Carter?"

"I don't know. I have a lot of thinking to do."

"He killed Mom. What's there to think about?"

"Yes, but under orders from my father. This is not a goddamn democracy; he did what he was ordered to do."

"Right. Did he have to turn on you? Was he ordered to do that? How can you trust him again?" Duncan began to raise his voice.

"Now that's a question based on reason, not emotion, a good question. Raising your voice to me is not so well reasoned, but I will give you a pass under the circumstances. Look, I need to look at it from his perspective. He couldn't tell me he killed Lucia and tried to kill my son. And he paid for his sins with his daughter's life."

"So now he's your pal again?"

"It's not about being my pal. It's about what is best for the syndicate. Now that Horowitz is out of the way, maybe it's best to mend fences."

CHAPTER 89

DUNCAN COULDN'T HAVE foreseen the level of pain he would suffer from Christina's passing. The woman he loved was dead. After hearing the news, he stayed in bed for three days, unwilling to face his father, his work, his life.

On the fourth day, Mr. Bartelli put an end to his self-imposed quarantine.

Benton answered the doorbell at seven thirty. "Good morning, Mr. Bartelli."

After an awkward moment of silence, Mr. Bartelli asked, "May we come in?"

With his lower lip quivering, Benton replied, "I'm sorry, sir. But I'm afraid Mr. Gabrelli is not receiving visitors today."

"Benton. Do you see these three rather large men behind me?"

Benton looked up nervously at the three burly men. "Yes, sir."

"Well, they assured me that Duncan is receiving visitors. Now get out of my way before I break you in half."

"Yes, sir. I'll let him know you're here."

"No. Let's just let it be a surprise. Where is he?"

"In his bedroom, sir, I presume."

Pushing Benton out of the doorway, Mr. Bartelli marched up the staircase and barged into Duncan's room.

"Get your ass out of that bed. We're getting out of here."

Shocked to see his father standing at the foot of his bed, "What are you doing here?"

"Is that a real question? I haven't seen you for three days. You don't call. You haven't gone to your office. Get up, take a shower, and get dressed. We're getting out of here."

"Dad. I know that you're trying to help. I appreciate it. I really do. But I need some time alone. I'll be all right. I promise. Just give me a few days."

Mr. Bartelli looked at the clock on the night stand. "It's seven thirty-eight. You've got until eight fifteen to get downstairs. Don't worry about packing, I've got everything covered."

"Where we going?"

Mr. Bartelli's only reply was, "The clock's ticking."

At precisely 8:15, the two men were on their way to the airport.

"It's time to get to know my son and for you to get to know your dad."

Duncan wanted to spend time with Mr. Bartelli to get to know the father he never knew he had. Mr. Bartelli wanted to spend time with the son he always knew he had but was forced to deny existed for over thirty years.

"I know you're right. It's just been a tough week. So where are we off to?" Duncan asked.

"A very special place where we can spend time together, just the two of us. No phones, no work, just white sand beaches and warm tropical breezes."

They were headed for a private island in the Caribbean. They would literally own the island for three weeks. No distractions and time enough to redefine their relationship.

Both men were anxious to make up for lost time.

"Just the two of us. Sounds good."

"Well, just the two of us, and a few maids, butlers, chefs, servers, masseuse and a dozen or so bodyguards. Yeah, just the two of us."

A private ten-passenger Learjet was waiting for them when they reached the airport. As the plane reached cruising altitude, the pilot announced over the intercom. "Looks like clear skies all the way to Denver."

"Denver? We're going to Denver?" Duncan asked.

"I thought that you might want to visit Christina's grave site. I wanted to be with you when you did."

Duncan leaned back in his seat, not saying a word.

"I thought we should pay our respects. I hope you don't mind."

"No. No. I need to say goodbye. Thanks, Dad."

"Does this mean that you have made up your mind about Carter?"

"For now. He's going to pick us up when we arrive."

"My God! Tell me something. What prevents him from killing us both?"

"What prevents us from killing him? Look around you. These six guys aren't here for show. They're here to protect us. It's Carter who wants me to trust him again, not the other way around. Watch and learn."

When the two men and their entourage arrived at the Denver airport, Carter was waiting on the tarmac to greet them. The jet pulled up alongside a single row of three Lincoln Town Cars and a black limousine. As Duncan peered out the window, he thought, *Does the syndicate have an exclusive contract with Lincoln? Why are there always Lincolns waiting for us?* The thought made him laugh.

His father thought the laughter odd in light of their purpose there. However, he chose to chalk it up to anxiety.

Conspicuous by their absence were the bodyguards that were always at Carter's side. Only the lead car had a driver.

Carter greeted Mr. Bartelli by kissing his hand. In a rare display of public affection, Mr. Bartelli wrapped his arms around Carter. "I'm sorry for your loss. I know how hard it is to lose a child."

"Thank you, Mr. Bartelli."

To Duncan's surprise, after releasing Mr. Bartelli, Carter turned and embraced him.

Mr. Bartelli's security force escorted the three men to the stretch limo, situated between two Lincolns. The escorts piled into the remaining vehicles, and the caravan proceeded to the cemetery where Christina was laid to rest.

During the drive, Mr. Bartelli offered Carter a gift. "My friend, I have something for you. I know that it won't bring your lovely daughter back to us, but it may help ease the pain," he handed Carter a sheet of paper.

It was a list of three names, one of which had been crossed off.

"It's the names of your daughter's killers."

Horowitz's name was the name crossed out.

"I took care of Horowitz. The other two are yours to do with what you will."

They were people much closer to Carter's inner circle than he considered possible.

"They don't know that Horowitz gave them up. I know this is no longer your area of expertise, so if you would like, I will handle this matter for you. But I suggest that it be resolved immediately, before they discover they have been betrayed."

As Carter stared at the piece of paper, a cloud of silence fell over the vehicle. "I wanted to tell you, sir. I was afraid," Carter confessed.

"You should have told me. You should have trusted me."

"I had no idea that she was the mother of your son. I was just following your dad's orders. It wasn't until many years later that I discovered what I'd been ordered to do."

"I know my father ordered you to kill Lucia. But that's not what concerns me. Before he died, Horowitz told me you were conspiring with him to take over control of the syndicate."

Mr. Bartelli had neither accused Carter nor asked a question. But the statement was begging a response.

"For many years your family has placed its trust in me. It has been my greatest honor. If you believe I betrayed that trust, you should kill me now. I came here today with no bodyguards to show you I trust you completely."

Duncan, who'd been listening intently, looked confused. *You lying dog. We know you conspired with Horowitz. What's Dad doing?*

"If I wanted you dead, you would be. What kept you alive is my unwavering faith in you."

"Yes. I had to make Horowitz believe I would betray you. I had to keep that secret until I found a way to kill him. I have been, and will always be, completely loyal to you. That loyalty is not for sale."

"Good. I'm glad we cleared that up." Mr. Bartelli swiped his hands together twice. "What is done is done. Let us never speak of these matters again."

The intensity of the conversation left all three men speechless until they reached the cemetery. But Duncan's mind was spinning. Duncan could not believe what he had just heard. After all the intrigue and suspense, decades of lies and deceit, and the murders of Lucia, Christina, and Horowitz, all was to be forgiven?

Standing at Christina's grave site, Carter looked back down at the list Mr. Bartelli had given him before turning to Duncan. "The day you left, my daughter told me that she'd met the man she was going to marry. Thank you for making her last days on this earth happy ones." Carter was trying to fight back the tears.

Duncan didn't know quite what to say. As much as he hated Carter for killing his mother, he felt compassion over the loss of his daughter. "I fell in love with your daughter the day we met in your office. I will never stop loving her."

There was nothing left to say. The two men simply exchanged looks, acknowledging the other's loss; they left it at that. They spent nearly thirty minutes saying their goodbyes, before heading back to the airport.

During their two-hour stop in Denver, Duncan had gained a great deal of respect for Carter. He understood why his father had placed so much trust in him over the years.

Echoing in his head were the words Mr. Bartelli had spoken to Maria Lopez just before killing her. "I do not forgive you for the pain you have caused me." Duncan was not prepared to forgive Carter for his mother's murder, at least not yet.

CHAPTER 90

DURING THEIR TIME on the island, Duncan saw a side of his father he didn't know existed. The side that was prepared to sacrifice everything he had to be with the woman he loved. Mr. Bartelli unmasked the agony he'd endured, at being separated from his beloved Lucia and their son. But Mr. Bartelli had never abandoned Duncan; he was always there. Feeling the pride that only a father can know, he watched from afar as his son excelled in everything he put his hand to.

Looking back on it now, Duncan remembered seeing his father's face at every important stage of his life—his first communion, graduations, and special events—always lurking in the back of the crowd. For the first time, his life began to make sense. The pieces were beginning to fit together.

Duncan used their time alone to make it clear to his father that he didn't want to take over control of the syndicate. In a strange way, Mr. Bartelli was starting to prefer it that way, hoping that his son could live a more normal life. If only his father had known his son's true nature, he might have been able to change the course of things to come. It was not to be.

Both men needed the break from their hectic lives. But the three weeks passed more like three hours. Before they knew it, they were on a flight home.

With Christina gone, his compulsion returned with a burning fury. He'd begin his murder spree in earnest only days after returning to Los Angeles.

The rest made Duncan feel like a new man, but nothing had changed. He was living in the same house, in the same city, and he still possessed the same desire to kill.

He was still working behind the scenes, organizing the outsourcing of legal matters for the syndicate. His new position required him to travel extensively. It was as if a greater power was working to provide him with the opportunity to pursue his murderous desires. He began using his travels to find new victims.

As a result of his acts alone, the national murder rate registered a detectable, albeit modest, uptick. Bodies were being found across the country. They were different ages, sexes, and ethnic and economic backgrounds.

After using the same type of weapon to commit his first two murders, he began using a wider range of weapons. Even the way the weapons were used was different, to the point where no two wounds were inflicted in the same fashion. With no common thread to connect the murders, case files sat on dozens of different detectives' desks gathering dust.

Much like a drug addict's need for his next fix, Duncan had become hooked on the emotional high that he derived from killing. His motivation for committing the crimes had changed. No longer was there the challenge to devise the perfect crime—he'd cleared that hurdle years ago. Satisfying his demented desire to change people's destinies was now the force that drove him to kill.

A quote he'd read during his college years had resurfaced in his head. "A butterfly flapping its wings in Tokyo could cause tornadoes in California," said Edward Lorenz to explain the butterfly effect. It described the sense of power that had consumed Duncan.

His victims would have no more children, who would in turn have no grandchildren, resulting in no great-grandchildren, and so on, and so on. He was beginning to obsess over his perceived power over the universe. "Only gods can rewrite history. Therefore, I must be a god," was his mantra.

While fate and destiny were his to alter as he saw fit, his God complex was driving him to the brink of complete and total insanity.

CHAPTER 91

EVERYTHING HAD CHANGED, and yet nothing had changed, in Duncan's life. He had simply exchanged one obsession for another. Endless hours of analyzing files had been replaced with his meticulous preparation of his nefarious plans. True to his nature, he dedicated every available moment to them.

There was one noticeable difference in his behavior. He started neglecting his relationship with his father. Breaking dates and canceling appointments with his father had become the norm.

Most people would be irritated by such abuse, but one of the most powerful men in the world was not about to tolerate being ignored by *anyone*, especially his own son.

It had been Duncan's routine to stop by Mr. Bartelli's home the day he returned from his trips. Such was his plan in late November.

He flew to Chicago on Thursday, having chosen a nearby town to find his next victim, that same night. *If I fly home Friday morning, I can spend the whole day with Dad.* Duncan thought as he prepared himself to kill again.

It was the same plan he'd executed many times. But from its inception, something was leaving Duncan a little unsettled. He couldn't put his finger on just what it was, but something felt strange.

He'd abandoned plans in the past when reason and logic told him that he should not proceed; however, the decision to abort had never been based on instinct or superstition. There was no logical reason to abort, just a feeling. Priding himself on being a supremely logical person, he decided to ignore his gut feeling.

Everything was going precisely as scripted. His meeting had taken exactly as long as he thought it would. The public transportation to

Brighton, a run-down suburb just outside Chicago, was on schedule. Even with everything going so right, the hair on the back of his neck was still sounding an alarm.

Stop second guessing yourself. Deep in thought, he took little notice of the other three passengers who got off the bus with him. Walking east down the main road, he already knew where he'd find his next victim. The lower-middle-class residences were predominantly Catholic. The church played too large a part in their meaningless lives.

Could it be that I'm going to kill a Catholic? As he walked, it struck him that maybe the source of his unrest was the fact that he was about to kill someone who was most likely Catholic. While the odds were that he had killed one in the past, he'd never knowingly done so.

He was Catholic, after all.

The thoughts about religion faded away momentarily as he turned down a side street.

This is it. I'll find it here. There it was, right in front of him. He instantly knew he was in the right place. However, his thoughts of religion quickly resurfaced. In front of him was a Catholic church.

It was a massive structure. At each corner of the building there were tall spires jutting upward, disappearing into the night sky. The building was painted a dungeon gray, no doubt to keep the devils at bay. The stained-glass windows allowed only a small amount of light to escape into the night from the dimly lit church. The obstructed light made the church appear to glow in the dark.

He wasn't a superstitious man, but the sight of the ominous-looking structure made him think twice about whether the look of the church was a sign from God to abort his plan.

In some towns, the doors of the church never close. This was just that kind of town.

There was one car parked in the lot behind the church. It belonged to his next victim. The lot had no lights, and the cloud-filled sky prevented any illumination from above.

Duncan considered entering the church. Not to commit the crime, but to look at what would certainly be a beautifully ornate religious shrine.

From his religious upbringing, he knew that there were seldom priests in the church after hours. At night, the church became a place to pray and meditate, rather than one to seek religious counsel. Even so, for reasons that were not altogether clear in his mind, he just couldn't walk through the doors.

Needing to know how many people were inside, he cracked the door just enough to peek in. He saw a solitary young man kneeling at the altar, his hands clasped tightly together, deep in prayer.

Stan Kirkland was alone. He had a private cross to bear; seeking forgiveness for something he wasn't prepared to disclose to any mortal. It was for God's ears only.

"Make it good, because it will be your last," Duncan whispered under his breath as he closed the door.

Walking back to the parking lot, he waited in the dark. Every few seconds Duncan did his best to scan the lot. He couldn't shake the feeling that someone was watching him. *How can anyone see me? I can barely see my shoes, it's so dark.* Again, he suppressed his intuitive feelings of danger.

Looking up toward the sky, he thought, *Damn, there's not enough light. How am I supposed to see this kid's death face? Fuck it. Just kill him and get out of here.*

Nodding his head as if he was in agreement with himself, he peered into the dark and waited for a dead man.

As ten minutes turned to fifteen, and fifteen to twenty, the cold night air started nipping at Duncan's nose and ears.

"You must need a lot of forgiveness. Come on, let's get this over with," softly escaped his lips.

When thirty-five minutes passed, Duncan had a stomach-wrenching thought. *Crap! Maybe this isn't his car.*

Just then, Stan entered the lot. As the boy reached for the handle of his car door, Duncan stepped out of the darkness directly behind him. The boy turned quickly, only to find himself face-to-face with his murderer.

The large buck knife had already penetrated Stan's chest and was rapidly approaching his heart. "God sent me. You're not forgiven." The words sounded pretty cold-blooded, even to Duncan.

He hadn't planned to say anything. It just came out. Upon reflection, it was clear the words were really meant for God's ears, not the boy's. He was letting God know that there was a new sheriff in town.

With a gentle shove, the boy's body fell backward against the car and slid to the ground.

Duncan's timing was perfect. He attacked just in time to prevent Stan from opening the car door and illuminating the lot.

He was wearing a thick plastic bag over the hand that held the knife to prevent blood from splattering onto his sleeve. Sliding the bag over the bloodstained knife, he tied the bag and put it back into his pocket.

Pulling the keys from the boy's lifeless hand, he dragged the body behind the vehicle. He knew that there was going to be a light inside the trunk, but it would be small. The risk that the light posed was not nearly as great as leaving the body exposed. By concealing the body in the trunk, it wouldn't be discovered until the next morning—or even later, if he was lucky.

As he lifted the body into the trunk, he squinted into the darkness. Out of the corner of his eye he detected movement near the side wall of the church. The limited light shining through the stain-glass window provided just enough backlighting to reveal the contours of a human form. As quickly as it was there, it was gone.

For years he'd contemplated this eventuality. All his planning hadn't prepared him for the reality of the moment. Fear raced through his body.

The substantial distance between him and the shadowy figure combined with the darkness limited his options. There was no choice but to flee as quickly as possible. *It was too dark. He couldn't have seen anything. Maybe I'm imagining things.*

It was wishful thinking on Duncan's part. Someone had witnessed the murder.

His heart raced as he made his way back to the bus stop. The five-minute wait for the next bus felt like an eternity. Expecting to hear the sirens of patrol cars scouring the neighborhood for the killer, he was never more relieved to see the headlights of a bus rounding the corner.

As he boarded, he slipped his hands into the pocket of his jacket. To his horror, he felt the plastic bag containing the buck knife. He'd always been careful to use weapons that were untraceable. His connections with the syndicate provided him with unlimited access to clean guns and knives. Even so, disposal of the weapon was critical to every plan.

Because lakes and rivers were his preferred depositories, he always made sure there was a body of water somewhere along his exit route. In his haste to distance himself from the shadowy figure, he'd neglected to dispose of the knife.

During the entire forty-minute ride back to Chicago, he expected the bus to be stopped and the passengers questioned. If that happened, he was as good as caught. But it proved to be a rather uneventful ride home.

He spent a good portion of the ride silently berating himself for ignoring his sense of impending danger. He would never do that again.

CHAPTER 92

I T WAS NOT until his plane landed at LAX that he finally released a sigh of relief. Soon he would be back in his beautiful home, in his comfortable bed, with no worries. His confidence was coming back. *The mysterious figure robbed me of a good night's sleep—nothing more.*

Tired and still emotionally exhausted, he was not up for spending the day with his father, as he'd promised. He would have to come up with a very good story if he wanted to cancel. But as hard as he tried, he just couldn't find the energy to go through the exercise of inventing another story. *Screw it. I'll go home, get a little rest, and worry about explanations later.*

His driver picked him up at the airport and drove him directly home. When they arrived, he noticed that the large steel gates were swung wide open, and three Lincoln Town Cars were parked in the drive.

It was an unexpected visit. Apparently his father had anticipated him breaking his appointment. In all the years he had known Mr. Bartelli, he'd never come to his home unannounced.

Whatever the reason, deep in the pit of his stomach Duncan was sure that this wasn't a social visit.

Two of his father's men were guarding the front of his house, and one stood sentry just inside. As Duncan made his way down the hallway, he noticed the door to his study was open a crack.

Well, Dad, just how did you get in there? As he walked closer, he could see the door had been forced open. Mr. Bartelli was sitting at his desk, with a look on his face Duncan had never seen before.

"Close the door and sit down. I need to talk to you," the words were in the form of a command. Duncan complied without hesitation.

Without so much as a hello or how are you, he began to question his son. In fact, it was more like an interrogation.

"Where were you yesterday?" he barked.

"In Chicago," Duncan responded. Easy questions call for easy answers, but the questions were going to get tougher to answer in a hurry. His mind flooded with questions. *Does he know? How does he know? How much does he know?* His tired mind was having difficulty processing what was happening.

Forcing his mind to focus, he attempted to change the subject. "I thought we were going to have breakfast at your house?"

"Where were you last night between eight thirty and midnight?"

At the very least, his father knew about the murder. Duncan was sure of it. He wasn't sure how to play this hand. But he should have known to proceed with extreme caution. Instead he chose to throw caution to the wind. "You know I was outside a church in Brighton. I am equally sure that you know what I did. So what's your next question?"

Mr. Bartelli came flying across the top of the large desk with the speed and agility of an eighteen-year-old. With his fist clenched tight like a hammer, it smashed against the side of Duncan's face.

Caught completely by surprise, Duncan, and the chair he was sitting on, tumbled over. So much force was behind the punch that Mr. Bartelli flipped completely over the desk, landing on the toppled chair. The sound of bodies crashing to the floor brought two bodyguards running, guns drawn.

Duncan hadn't moved since he hit the floor. The left side of his face had already swollen up with a baseball-size knot.

"Just leave us alone. We'll be all right." Mr. Bartelli panted.

"Are you sure, sir? Should I check on Mr. Gabrelli?"

"NO! I will tend to him. Just get out. I need to have a few more words with my son. Close the door behind you."

As the door closed, Duncan was finally starting to move. He'd been briefly knocked unconscious by the punch and was just beginning to regain his bearings.

Reaching down, Mr. Bartelli grabbed his son's hand, helping him back into one of the chairs that was still upright in front of the desk. Not the least bit apologetic, he returned to the chair behind the desk. After a short pause, he shook his head and began to speak.

"What the fuck were you doing killing someone?" he asked rhetorically. "Can a man of your intelligence really be this stupid?" His father chewed him out for the next hour, calling him every nasty name in the book.

"How did you find out?" Duncan asked timidly.

"If you don't mind, answer a few of my questions first, you fucking idiot."

"No, sir," Duncan responded sheepishly.

"When you were in Chicago, I had you followed, if you must know."

I'll have to figure out the hows and whys later, but I'd better come up with a good reason for killing that boy.

"Why did *you* do it?"

It took a second for Duncan to realize that his father wasn't asking what the boy had done to deserve to die, he was asking why *he* did it. The difference between those two questions was subtle, but important. His only concern was having his boy locked away for life.

"You punched me in the face because I didn't let you protect me. Am I the only one that finds that ironic?"

"I don't find that the least bit funny. What the fuck's going on inside your head? Are you retarded or what?"

Rather than try to create a detailed and elaborate ruse, Duncan chose to admit to poor judgment in not seeking assistance from his father.

"Look if you've got a beef with someone, come to me. I don't know why you killed this kid, and I don't care, just don't do anything that stupid ever again. You listening to me, son?" With that Mr. Bartelli walked around the table and gave Duncan a hug.

"I'm sorry, Dad. It'll never happen again. I should have come to you."

Mr. Bartelli lifted the fallen chair back to its feet and sat next to Duncan. "Jesus. I couldn't believe what I was hearing when my man got back."

"Why did you have me followed, anyway?"

"You've been acting very strange lately. I never see you. You cancel appointments. Your erratic behavior made me think that you had gotten yourself involved with drugs or something."

"So why didn't you just ask me?"

"I'm no fool. If you were hooked on drugs, you weren't going to tell me."

"Well, I'm not involved in drugs."

"No. You were just committing a murder," his dad said sarcastically. "Just tell me one thing. Is it done? I don't know why you did it and I don't care, just answer me this. Is it done?"

Duncan looked away quickly. "Yes, Dad, it's done."

"Look me in the eyes when I'm talking to you. Whatever problem you got into with this dead guy, it's done. Right?"

"Yes, I promise you. It's done."

"Good," Mr. Bartelli said, sounding relieved. "Now can we spend a little time together for a fucking change?"

After a long, hard stare, Mr. Bartelli placed his massive hands on either side of Duncan's head and pulled him forward. He lightly kissed Duncan's forehead. "I've been worried about you."

"I know, Dad, but there's no need to worry. I'm okay. Really, I'm okay."

The two men spent the better part of that day together, and had dinner together later that night. It was truly a testament to the depravity that possessed both their souls that Mr. Bartelli was not even interested in knowing why Duncan had committed murder, and that Duncan did not feel the need to even attempt to explain his horrific act.

If he hadn't been so blinded by love, he might have realized that his son had in fact fallen victim to a different type of addiction. Murder.

As it turned out, Duncan had killed a second person that dark night outside of Chicago. Several days after his conversation with Mr. Bartelli, he read that the body of a man with suspected mob connections had been found floating in New York Harbor.

It was the bodyguard who'd witnessed the murder of Stan Kirkland. He'd been the only one, other than his father, who knew the murderer's name. Duncan should have known Mr. Bartelli would not let him live. He was going to protect his son at all costs, even if that meant killing one of his most trusted bodyguards.

PART VI

THE REMAINS OF DUNCAN GABRELLI

CHAPTER 93

STILL REELING FROM the near miss in Chicago, Duncan decided to take a hiatus from his killing spree. But after suffering through withdrawal for almost a month, he could no longer fight his inner demons. Slowly he fell back into his routine, and the murders began again. He would, however, make it a point never to let his nefarious activities cause him to miss—or even be late for—another meeting with his father.

Almost two years passed since the Chicago debacle. The time he'd been spending with his father continued to strengthen their relationship. The altercation in Duncan's library had faded to a distant memory. Life was running smoothly again. So much so that he began to get an intuitive feeling that he was overdue for something bad to happen.

While in Denver handling some minor business matters for Oasis, he received an emergency message from Stella. As fate would have it, he was standing in Carter's office when the call came in. It was the bad news that he had been expecting.

Stella was frantic. "Sir, you need to get back here immediately. Mr. Bartelli has had some kind of stroke." Stella continued talking but he was no longer listening. The word *stroke* kept spinning in his head. His father hadn't been sick for even a day in all the years he'd known him.

"Stop!" he yelled into the telephone. "Where is he now?"

"They've taken him to Cedars-Sinai by helicopter." She paused, waiting for his next question. When none was forthcoming, she continued. "A helicopter is on its way to pick you up on the top of the Oasis building. A private jet is standing by at the airport. I've arranged for a priority takeoff—it will be ready to leave the minute you arrive.

I have a helicopter waiting at the airport in Burbank. It has clearance to land at the hospital."

How she was able to make all the arrangements and obtain the special clearances that quickly was nothing short of miraculous. But Duncan was too consumed by the moment to recognize her efforts.

Anticipating his next question, she said, "Sir, I have tried my best to find out what happened, but there is very little information. He apparently collapsed at his home."

Through the large windows of Carter's office, he could see a helicopter in the distance heading toward the Oasis building. "I'll call you from the jet," he said, dropping the telephone without hanging it up.

Carter only heard one side of the conversation but understood that Mr. Bartelli was obviously in grave condition. "With your permission, I would like to join you," Carter offered.

"I'll fill you in on the way." Duncan was already running toward the elevator.

Seeing the two men go flying by, one of Carter's security personnel followed them to the roof.

"Duncan, what about security? Should I bring some security?"

"There's no room. I'll take care of security once we reach LA."

Duncan didn't find out until his flight landed in Burbank that, even before he'd received the call from Stella, his father had died of a brain hemorrhage.

Stella and four of Mr. Bartelli's security force were waiting for them when they arrived at the helipad in Burbank. She updated him on the additional information she'd been able to obtain. Apparently, during his routine morning workout, while jogging on the treadmill, he'd suffered a brain hemorrhage and collapsed. He died almost instantly.

How could the best doctors in the world not have diagnosed his illness? kept running through Duncan's naturally suspicious mind as he looked for someone to blame.

The doctors at Cedars-Sinai tried in vain to revive him, but the damage to the brain was too severe. There was nothing they could do.

"Mr. Carter. There is nothing you can do for my dad right now. I need you to wait for me at my father's home."

Carter started to protest.

"There's going to be a lot of press. The last thing the syndicate needs is to have you caught up in this. Just wait for me. I won't be long."

Carter realized that Duncan was right. "Certainly."

Duncan arranged for security to take Carter to his father's home in a blacked-out limousine. He gave strict instructions that Carter was to be protected with the highest level of security. "No one is to enter Mr. Bartelli's estate without my personal authorization."

The security personnel looked at each other nervously, confused about how Duncan had the authority to order them to do *anything*.

"That is an order!" he screamed.

"Yes, sir," they replied in unison.

While it appeared that his father had died of natural causes, Duncan knew from experience that things were not always as they appeared. There was the possibility that a coup was already in the works. The last thing he needed was for something to happen to his father's most staunch ally. If Carter was killed, there would certainly be a bloody battle for control of the syndicate.

"Mr. Gabrelli, you should have security with you at all times. Two of us should stay with you," one of the guards said, sounding more like a soldier on a battlefield than a bodyguard.

"Of course. Choose another man and come with me. What's your name?"

"Victor Barlow, sir."

"Very good," he said, committing that name to memory.

After shaking hands, he and Carter parted company.

The helicopter landed on the roof of the hospital within a matter of minutes. As Duncan stepped off, he was immediately flanked by an entourage of bodyguards who were already stationed at the hospital and six members of the hospital staff. They escorted him to a private room where his father's body lay.

He'd called ahead to make sure his father's body was kept in the private and guarded room to prevent anyone from taking unauthorized photographs of him.

When they reached the room, he asked for everyone to wait outside. "I need a moment alone with Mr. Bartelli." He intentionally didn't refer to him as his father. For the time being, only Carter and the board of directors of the syndicate knew that he was Mr. Bartelli's natural-born son, and he wanted to keep it that way, at least for now. The syndicate had kept their relationship a secret. He wasn't yet prepared to have that information disseminated to the world.

To the surprise of the throng of people waiting in the hall, he spent less than fifteen minutes in the room before reemerging. As he exited, he stopped briefly and began barking out orders. Pointing at two of the bodyguards standing in the hallway, "I don't want anyone in this room. No one. Not even hospital personnel. Nobody goes in or out without my permission. Do you understand?"

"Yes, sir," the two men responded. They immediately assumed a military posture on either side of the door.

Pointing his finger at a third guard, whom he recognized as being one of his father's most trusted, he said, "I want you in the room with Mr. Bartelli. Do not leave his side."

"Yes, sir."

"Now, Victor, get me to Mr. Bartelli's house," he ordered as he headed for the exit. It didn't go unnoticed that he'd remembered Victor's name.

The hospital staff stood with jaws open, watching Duncan command his troops. He'd presented such an air of authority that none of the staff questioned his order to prevent access to Mr. Bartelli's room.

Two of the four remaining members of his security force ran ahead to make sure two town cars would be ready to leave the second Duncan reached the exit.

He wanted to keep the news of his father's death under wraps until the syndicate's full board could be contacted. It was important for the stability of the organization that a successor be appointed as quickly as possible to avoid internal power struggles flaring up again.

However, news of Mr. Bartelli's death hit the news wires within hours of his being pronounced dead. Media sources within the medical community had ferreted out the news almost immediately.

CHAPTER 94

MR. BARTELLI'S DEATH was unexpected. Even so, he and Duncan had laid the groundwork to ensure an orderly succession of power, should anything ever happen to him. Duncan would still have to work fast if he was going to implement his father's plans.

Benjamin Carter was the key to its success. Since the murder of his daughter, he'd worked closely with Mr. Bartelli and Duncan to consolidate the power that would be needed to ensure a successful transition. Even as Duncan was heading back to his father's home, Carter was working the phones, making the necessary arrangements for all the members of the board to meet in Mexico. Because members of the board would be flying in from all over the world, the meeting could not be held for three days. While the board was waiting for the meeting to take place, a voice vote unanimously approved Duncan's interim appointment as head of the syndicate.

Carter lent his full support to the interim appointment. With that support, it was a *fait accompli* that the board would make the appointment permanent at its meeting three days hence.

There were still factions that were eager to seize control of the syndicate. However, the memory of Leon Horowitz's failed attempt— and his subsequent disappearance—was a clear reminder that opposing Duncan's appointment could be very dangerous. That was particularly true in light of the support he already had from the board members and associates like Mr. Carter.

The delay in holding the meeting in Mexico allowed Duncan to lay his father's remains to rest. Mr. Bartelli had requested that his funeral be a small, low-key affair. Even in death he wanted to protect the organization that he loved and watched over. The FBI would be keeping a close eye on anyone who attended.

The entire event was a bit surreal. He had his father's remains flown to a small town outside of Chicago where his father had been born and the grandparents he'd never met had been laid to rest.

To Duncan's surprise and horror, it was Brighton, the same town where he'd murdered Stan Kirkland. In fact, it was the same church where his father's spy had observed him committing the murder. The coincidence was too unreal to believe. He recalled the strange feeling of apprehension he'd felt the night of the murder. *No fucking wonder*, he thought.

In the light of day, the church looked completely different. It was a modest gray building, not nearly as ominous as he recalled thinking. It had once been in the center of town. However, "white flight" had taken its toll on the economy. The residents were now primarily blacks and poor whites who either couldn't afford to leave or refused to surrender the ground that their families had grown up on. The church was the one bright spot in the otherwise blighted landscape.

Duncan would lay his father's remains to rest in a massive marble mausoleum less than a hundred yards from where he'd committed murder.

The Catholic Church, as a rule, does not allow for the burial of mobsters or murderers in church cemeteries. But the Bartelli family was given special dispensation. Duncan was sure that the very generous endowment for the maintenance and care of the graveyard in perpetuity had a great deal to do with the Church's decision. But it was also well known that the Bartelli family had done many good deeds for both the Church and the community.

Over the years the exodus of the middle class caused the real estate values to plummet, decimating the town's tax base. In an effort to offset the lost tax revenue, the Bartelli family provided both economic support and protection to its residents.

Long ago, it had been the kind of town where doors were left unlocked. Children had been free to roam the streets under the watchful eyes of the entire community without fear. Crime was virtually nonexistent. No one dared commit a crime for fear of invoking the wrath of Mr. Bartelli Sr.

Times had changed for the worse. Homes now had wrought-iron bars covering their windows and doors. Drug dealers peddled their wares openly on street corners. Such was the backdrop to the funeral of one of the richest and most powerful men in the world.

Duncan had made it clear that no one related to the syndicate was to attend the funeral. Even Carter heeded the order. He wasn't going to let the government use his father's funeral as an opportunity to identify board members or associates of the syndicate.

However, that didn't stop the press from showing up. Since his death, the national press had carried the story. Headlines read, "Suspected Head of the Mob Dies" and "Alleged Criminal Mastermind Dies." The press was out in force for the funeral.

All the major networks had vans and trucks with satellite uplinks to report live. Hordes of reporters from around the state descended on the town like locusts. Media representatives from as far away as Japan and Britain came to cover the story.

The media blitz also aroused the curiosity of hundreds of average people across the country who decided it was worth using a vacation day to get a glimpse of the man reported to be the head of the largest crime family in the world.

It was a regular three-ring circus, with vendors selling everything from candy apples to pins with Mr. Bartelli's likeness on them.

The press was disappointed, along with the FBI, to discover that only a handful of personal friends attended the services. None of Mr. Bartelli's famed underworld associates were anywhere to be found.

The media literally outnumbered the mourners by a factor of twenty to one. They ended up spending most of their time interviewing people who knew Mr. Bartelli about as well as they knew Aristotle.

The major networks were pulling their hair out in frustration. There was no one of any consequence to interview about the man except for Duncan, and he was spirited in and out of town under such tight security that they couldn't even get a good photograph of him.

While it may have appeared from the turnout to be a pauper's funeral, that illusion was dispelled by the thousands of floral arrangements that filled the small church and covered its grounds. Some of them were so large that they had to be stored behind the church. So many arrangements had been purchased that florists in Chicago were forced to have special shipments brought in from neighboring cities just to fill the orders.

To provide some semblance of privacy, Duncan had a ten-foot-high white-cloth screen temporarily erected around the entire graveyard. The shield completely obstructed the media's view of the services. Anticipating that the individuals determined to view the interment services might employ scaffolding, or even helicopters, he also had a massive tent placed over the mausoleum.

It was as if he'd invited the media to the party but wouldn't let them dance. It was the news organizations' worst nightmare.

At his father's request, the service was short and without fanfare. After the few invited guests paid their respects, Duncan knelt alone at his father's coffin for almost an hour before letting it be interred and sealed.

He'd had a father for such a short time. He expected to have another twenty or thirty years to get to know the man. Now he would give everything just to spend one more day—one more hour, one more minute—with his father.

CHAPTER 95

A LOT OF thought had gone into where the meeting of the syndicate's board of directors should take place. It needed to be private and yet have the luxurious accommodations that the members would naturally expect. There was also the issue of how to provide for the large number of assistants and security personnel. Many of the more prominent and powerful associates were also invited to attend the meeting, including Carter, who would be traveling with Duncan.

Upon the recommendation of Señor Rodriguez, the meeting was scheduled to be held in a new resort town called Cabo San Lucas, known by the locals simply as Cabo. It was one of a series of resort towns that had sprung up in the past twenty years along Mexico's beautiful emerald-green coastline. Its residents had migrated primarily from Mexico City in search of work.

Cabo had gained a small degree of prominence as a sport-fishing town. However, it was quickly becoming the destination of choice for whale watchers around the world. Several species of whale—including the largest mammal on earth, the humpback whale—came to Cabo's warm waters to give birth to their pups.

The first hotel built in Cabo (and still one of its best) was the Finisterra. It was built on the edge of a cliff overlooking the ocean. The hotel was situated on the peninsula that separated the Pacific Ocean from the Sea of Cortez. It provided the perfect vantage point for viewing the whale migration.

However, the whales were not due to arrive for several more months. During the whales' absence, the town went into a state of semi-hibernation, relying on its sport-fishing business to tide it over until the whales returned.

Duncan had to exploit his father's connections to rent the entire hotel on only three days' notice. The hotel was only a third full, but it still took a considerable amount of persuasion to get the hotel to force its guests to accept accommodations elsewhere. The owner was convinced to displace his occupants in part by the substantial sum of money paid, and in part by the not-so-subtle pressure applied by several highly placed officials in the Mexican government. Duncan had heard his father say on many occasions, "What I love most about Mexico is its government's unwavering commitment to corruption and graft."

To assist the hotel in the unpleasant task of relocating its guests, the syndicate sent several representatives to make sure every displaced occupant was compensated generously for any inconvenience. Their marching orders were simple: make sure no guest left the hotel unhappy. It helped that they were given a virtually unlimited budget to make that happen.

Although bringing weapons into Mexico is a serious crime punishable by long jail terms, by the time Duncan and Carter arrived in Cabo, the Finisterra was an armed fortress.

As Duncan looked around the hotel grounds, he thought, *The syndicate could take over the country with the arsenal of weapons and the army of security personnel present right here.*

By American standards, the accommodations were above average but not sublime. Given the time restraints, it was the best that could be obtained on such short notice.

CHAPTER 96

DUNCAN DIDN'T WASTE any time in getting the meeting started. Arrangements were made to make sure that all the participants would be at the Finisterra by three o'clock the afternoon he arrived. He scheduled the meeting to take place at seven in a banquet hall that sat atop the hotel's restaurant, leaving just enough time for members to freshen up and eat before the meeting.

It had previously been agreed that due to the importance of the topics to be discussed, only the twenty members of the board and the twelve most senior associates would be permitted to attend the initial meeting. No domestic servants or security personnel would be permitted in the room during the meeting.

The issue of security was in the forefront of everyone's mind. While the board had already appointed Duncan as his father's successor on an interim basis, and it was all but certain that the position would be made permanent, there was still the risk that someone might attempt a coup.

Mr. Bartelli's personal security forces were now under Duncan's control and command. The board agreed that Duncan would have complete control over security. No other security team would be allowed within one hundred yards of the room.

The meeting began as everyone expected. There was nearly a full hour of greetings, words of sympathy, and condolences before they got down to business.

Duncan had asked for, and was granted, an opportunity to address the gathering before they began discussing who would be his father's permanent successor. Almost everyone in the room expected Duncan to make one of those "thank you for being here. I look forward to stepping into my father's shoes if that be the wish of this esteemed and august assemblage, blah, blah, blah" kind of speeches. It was anything but that.

Duncan began by reading a letter written in longhand by his father in anticipation of his own passing. He'd given it to Duncan to hold, instructing him to read it to the board after his death.

If you are reading this letter, then I am either dead or missing. In either event, let me thank you for giving me the opportunity to represent this organization all these many years.

It was always my desire that the board would someday give its blessing that my son, Duncan Gabrelli, assume my role with the organization. I am confident that he has the wisdom to guide this organization to even greater profitability than either my father or I could have imagined during our tenure.

I have discussed this serious and important matter with my son on many occasions. However, he's made it clear to me that he does not desire to assume that level of responsibility within the organization.

Duncan's reading of the letter was temporarily interrupted by the gasps of several members, but Duncan continued reading the letter without comment.

I respect his decision in that regard, and ask that you do the same. If, however, he should change his mind before reading this letter, then I put my full support behind him and request that the board also give its blessing.

However, if it is not to be my son, then I would recommend to the board that it select Benjamin Carter to take over my responsibilities for the organization.

Again, I thank you for your confidence and support over the years and wish you all continued success and prosperity.

The letter was signed, "Your humble servant."

Most interesting about the letter was how completely innocuous the writing was. Had it been turned over to the FBI, it would have been of little use to them. It could just as easily have been referring to his position on the board of any legitimate business.

A wave of nervous anticipation swept over the room, waiting for Duncan to address the gathering.

"It is a great honor that the board finds me worthy for consideration. My father spent his life in its service, and I know that it was his dream that I step into his shoes. But, as William T. Sherman once said, 'If nominated, I will not run, if elected, I will not serve.' I regret to tell you that I, too, will not serve if elected."

Because everyone in the room had expected the meeting to be more of a coronation than an election, no one quite knew how to respond. Several of the board members felt as if they had been intentionally misled. That feeling was correct.

Mr. Bartelli knew that if anyone had known that Duncan wasn't going to succeed his father, there would have been factional infighting within the syndicate. Mr. Bartelli was smart enough to realize that the only way to avoid potentially bloody infighting, and perhaps even a splintering of the organization itself, was to conceal the truth until the last minute. Mr. Bartelli believed the board would be compelled to accept his recommendation, if not out of respect for him, then to avoid a power struggle that could last for months, or even years.

While the board members may have felt that they had been duped, in truth they knew that Mr. Bartelli had done what was best for the syndicate. Most of the board members were loyal to him and would have been equally loyal to whomever he recommended. Therefore, it was almost a certainty that his recommendation would have been followed.

Carter was beaming.

Then Duncan pulled a second letter from his jacket. "Before Mr. Carter gets what he so richly deserves, let me add that before my father passed away, he wrote a second letter to the board. He asked me to read it after killing Mr. Carter."

Before the look of shock had completely covered Carter's face, Victor, Duncan's guard, slipped a cord around Carter's neck, and began choking him to death in front of the entire assemblage.

Carter kicked and flailed wildly. In vain, he pulled and tugged at the hands of his assassin.

This was not a room filled with fearful men. Even so, the anxiety and apprehension was nearly suffocating. Several board members instinctively jumped from their seats and headed for the doors, only to be stopped by Duncan's men, who were guarding the exits.

Duncan raised his voice to be heard over the din. "Please. Please gentlemen. Please take your seats." By the time the room settled down, Mr. Carter had stopped kicking and slumped forward onto the table in front of him. "This is what my father wanted you to see, before I read this letter. Please just be calm, and let me read this letter."

Seeing that there was no escape, everyone finally resolved themselves to find their seats and hear Duncan out.

"Let me read my father's words."

Please accept my sincere apology. I know you must all be questioning my judgment. But, for the good of the organization, this had to be handled this way. Mr. Carter betrayed us all by conspiring with others to seize control of the syndicate. The penalty for betraying this organization has never changed. Let no man in this room forget that. By now, you know my son will not be stepping into my shoes. That is a regrettable reality, but a reality just the same. I therefore respectfully nominate Santino Balleto to run the day-to-day operations. These are my wishes, and I hope that, out of respect for me and all that my family has meant to this organization, you will abide by those wishes. I have spent my life in defense of this organization. I assure you all that this nomination is made for the good of the syndicate and no other.

Sincerely,
Vincenzo Bartelli

Mr. Balleto was the perfect choice to be the successor to Mr. Bartelli. Mr. Bartelli and Mr. Balleto had been friends since they were boys playing in the streets of Chicago. He was well liked and respected by the entire board. Mr. Balleto, while enormously influential, had kept a low profile over the years. Mr. Bartelli had employed his services as a peacemaker and deal broker for many years. More importantly, he was the only person Mr. Bartelli trusted to protect his son. Mr. Bartelli had secretly been grooming Mr. Balleto to take over the syndicate since first learning that Duncan did not plan to follow in his footsteps. To the end, Mr. Bartelli had been one step ahead of everyone, including Duncan.

Mr. Bartelli's scheme worked exactly as planned. While there was a little grumbling during the meeting, not one board member was prepared to reject his recommendation. Three hours after the meeting started, the board gave unanimous approval to Santino Balleto's appointment.

Balleto was now the head of the syndicate, and Duncan was well on his way to creating the separation between it and himself that he had long desired. Mr. Bartelli was much smarter than even his most ardent supporters gave him credit for. He knew that his son wanted to distance himself from the syndicate. While that may have been a personal disappointment to him, it also posed a problem. A person with Duncan's knowledge of the inner workings of the syndicate doesn't just quit. Therefore, he conspired to appoint his own successor. As payment for arranging the turnover of control to his dear friend, Santino Balleto, he extracted two promises.

First, Mr. Balleto pledged an oath, on the souls of his grandchildren, to never let harm come to Duncan. Second, he pledged to make sure Duncan would eventually be permitted to completely sever his ties to the syndicate.

Mr. Balleto would keep those vows for as long as he lived. He was a man of his word. Within six months of the meeting in Cabo, Duncan had severed all ties with the syndicate. It left Duncan feeling surprisingly empty inside. Stranger still was leaving the employ of WB&H.

But to truly put the syndicate behind him, he couldn't stay part of the firm.

He left the firm but not the law. He took with him a substantial number of high-profile clients, his secretary, Stella, and a reputation as one of the best criminal attorneys in the United States.

If it ever was about money, it no longer would be an issue. He didn't need to go into private practice. His personal wealth would have been enough to retire on even before his father's death. As the sole heir to his father's vast estate, he acquired large land holdings and more money than he could ever spend in *ten* lifetimes. In the final tally, the estate was valued at over a billion dollars.

The reason for going into private practice had everything to do with providing cover for his crimes and nothing to do with money. His outrageously high fees were just a way to keep score.

CHAPTER 97

TIME. DUNCAN WAS a man with far too much time on his hands.

No longer having—or even wanting—control over his lust for murder, he used every ounce of his time to search for new victims. He would find one in a small town in Vermont only two weeks after burying his father.

Something had changed inside him after his father's death. The loss sent him into a downward-spiraling state of depression. He found himself constantly fighting bouts of deep depression and guilt. Stella noticed it immediately. Quick to anger, he would become moody, disappearing for days at a time without contacting his office.

For the first time in his life, sleep was filled with nightmares. They would cause him to wake in the middle of the night, soaked in his own sweat, his sheets tied in knots as if there had been a violent struggle. Most nights, they filled his head with fear.

On good nights, Christina came to him and calmed his restless soul. At first they were about how much he loved her and longed to be with her. Gradually they began to change. Over and over he would be witness to her murder. Sometimes she died in auto crashes and other times at the hand of another. After a while *he* became her murderer, ravaging her beautiful body beyond recognition, killing her in every imaginable manner.

Soon his father, mother, and other familiar faces began to appear. No matter how he tried, he couldn't drive them from his subconscious thoughts. Once he closed his eyes they would appear, each waiting their turn to die in some horribly gruesome fashion. At night he became the executioner of everyone and everything he'd ever cared about.

He dreaded falling asleep. He would stay awake for days at a time just to delay the inevitable rendezvous with his murderous dreams. He considered seeking psychiatric help. But with his understanding of the law; how could he? He knew that confessions to future crimes during therapy were not privileged communications. The therapist would be compelled to report him to the authorities.

He was far too brilliant a man not to see what was happening. *I'm sick—mentally ill, possibly insane.*

Trying to self-diagnose, he concluded guilt was destroying him. If he could stop killing, he might be able to pull himself back off the ledge.

The killing did stop for exactly three months and then, without any planning or research, he stumbled upon the perfect location and victim while visiting a client in Salt Lake City. Hiding behind the weak justification that it was just too good to pass up, he murdered a cheerleader from the Brigham Young pep squad.

Early one afternoon, he'd witnessed her having a heated discussion with a rather large and angry-looking man in a parking lot outside a Tastee-Freez. That evening, he went for a drive just to clear his head. Unfamiliar with the area, he ended up on a desolate one-lane road headed toward Provo. As he drove along, he saw a car stranded by the side of the road. Its emergency flashers were blinking dimly. He pulled over just to see if he could lend a hand.

As he put his car in park, he subconsciously began to evaluate the situation. *Hell, I haven't seen another vehicle for the entire half hour I've been driving.*

The car battery was so weak that it was barely providing enough charge to faintly illuminate the flashers.

That car must've been out here for hours. Utah! You got to love those Mormons; they pretty much roll up the sidewalks at nine o'clock. It's not likely there's going to be much traffic on this road at this hour of the night.

The young female occupant had fallen asleep in the driver's seat waiting for someone to discover her disabled vehicle. She was only slightly startled when awakened by the penlight Duncan had used to look inside the vehicle. She instantly became annoyingly bright and bubbly; she tilted her seat forward and opened the door.

"I'm so glad to see you. I thought I was going to have to spend the night out here. You're a godsend," she said in a squeaky little cheerleader voice. "I got this stupid flat tire, and my spare is flat. Oh my God, I'm so happy you found me."

To Duncan's amazement, it was the same girl he'd seen arguing with her boyfriend earlier in the day. *This must be fate,* he thought.

"My spare might fit your car. Do you have a jack?" he said, counting on her youth not to know that the odds that his spare would fit her car were about the same as the odds of her living through the night.

"Yes, sir. I'll get it. It's in the trunk."

Duncan looked up and down the long road for cars and then followed her to the back of her car. She was leaning over deeply into the trunk, and her short skirt had raised up high enough for Duncan to see her lacy white panties. But he was so immersed in the kill that he barely noticed her beautiful form.

"So, young lady, what are you doing out here by yourself?" he asked, still checking to make sure no cars were coming.

"It's this stupid boyfriend of mine. We go to BYU together. He didn't want to go back to Provo until tomorrow. So I just decided to go by myself. Let him find his own way back to campus, if he's going to be that way. Can I borrow your light? I'm having a little trouble finding the handle thingy." She leaned deeper into the trunk trying to locate all the pieces of the jack.

Rather than hand her the light, he shone his light on it inside the trunk, careful not to get her fingerprints on his light, or worse, to inadvertently leave the light behind.

"Why use this road? Wouldn't the freeway be faster?"

"Yes, but nobody uses this old road anymore. On a bright night, like tonight, it's so pretty. You can see all the stars shining. Can't see 'em if there are too many car lights. Besides, I don't like driving in traffic; there are some crazy drivers out there."

He pulled a handkerchief from his back pocket and picked up a large rock.

"There, I got it."

Just as she found the jack handle, the rock came crashing down on the back of her head. He could hear a cracking noise as it collided with her skull. She fell face first into the trunk of her car. Her body convulsed for a moment and then went still.

Using the handkerchief to protect his hands, he lifted her legs and folded her body into the trunk. After hurling the rock as far as he could into the desert, he casually got back in his car and drove back to town.

CHAPTER 98

THE THREE-MONTH hiatus had been yielding small but noticeable results. On the night before he killed the girl in Utah, he'd slept for five hours without a single bad dream. It had been the first time since his father died that he'd been able to close his eyes without the dreams reappearing.

Not that he needed it, but the murder in Utah was proof that he was no longer controlling the murders, the murders were controlling him. All the things that had once excited him about committing murder were now fodder for his nightmares.

Once having believed himself to be a god, it was painful to realize that he was the slave to his illness. It was his destiny being controlled, and not by him, but by the voices that cried out in his head, calling for him to kill.

He intensified his efforts to resist the temptation to kill. At first he could fight the unseen forces for a month at a time. But always, in the back of his mind, he was searching for his next victim.

He finally lost the will to fight altogether. Once more, he was bouncing around the country killing as frequently as the opportunity presented itself. He'd become a murder machine.

Unable to use his logical mind to control himself, he resorted to prayer. *God, send someone to stop this. How can you let this go on?*

When the prayers went unanswered, he resorted to more drastic measures. When he would succumb to his addiction he'd punish himself, first by lashing himself on his back with a belt and later self-mutilation. Disgusted by his inability to gain control of his life, he would carve deep slices into his chest and arms after every murder.

He'd become a man with everything except a reason to live. The nightmares were again visiting him every night. When he was awake, he suffered from constant migraines. The deepening state of depression had him longing for the courage to take his own life.

It had been three weeks since he'd murdered Debra Barns in her small apartment in the Boston suburbs. He could still hear the drops of blood beating rhythmically on the tile floor. The vision of her beautiful body draped over the edge of the kitchen table still haunted his thoughts.

Today was his birthday. The gift he gave himself that night was the vow to kill himself before he killed another. That vow played over and over in his head like a broken record, as he reached for his favorite instrument of death, the .22 pistol, on the night stand.

He'd not found pleasure in killing for years. It had come down to a test of wills, his versus the voices in his head. Until now the voices had always won. But he was determined to stand his ground or die trying.

As he played with the cylinder of the gun, spinning it round and round, he considered his options.

Is there a middle ground? His logical mind pondered the question as he took his finger off the trigger.

It would take a major change in my life to take control.

It should have been obvious, but he just started to understand that everything about his life facilitated his desire to kill. *I need to limit my access to victims. I'll shut down my practice. No more traveling.*

Closing his office would prove to be a relatively easy task, particularly in light of the fact that he'd been ignoring it for almost a year. Stella had been single-handedly keeping it alive.

Stella was his only connection to reality. Keeping her in his life was the most important decision he had ever made. She was more like family than a secretary. In fact, she was the only family he had left. There was no question in his mind that her loyalty and devotion entitled her to reap the rewards of her new job as his personal assistant. *More money, less responsibility. It's time I let her know how much she means to me.*

Closing his practice was just part of the solution. *I need something to occupy my time, to occupy my mind.*

It wasn't in his nature to sit around watching CNN or *60 Minutes*. He needed to do something that would keep him in one place and tax his mind at the same time.

Having been offered teaching positions by several prominent law schools, he decided to inquire if the positions were still available to him. While he'd represented many high-profile individuals over the years, he'd been off the front pages for a long time. There was the distinct possibility that his withdrawal from the limelight had diminished his appeal to the academic community.

As it turned out, he'd underestimated the esteem in which his peers held him. Every law school he contacted offered him a full-time position on staff. Two of the schools that didn't have teaching positions open offered to make him an associate dean. Most of the schools were surprised to hear that he was interested in becoming a law school professor. After all, the vastness of his wealth was well known.

It had been some time since a smile had come to his face, but the overwhelming welcome from the academic community helped combat his depression, if only for a little while.

He'd moved into his father's palatial estate. It made him feel closer to his dad. There was no way he'd ever consider leaving the Los Angeles area. UCLA was his law school *alma mater* and was only minutes from his house. It was an easy choice.

There was little time to consider the effects of his decision. The semester was scheduled to start in just a few short months. He needed to immediately begin preparing an outline for his course.

Stella was not going to have reduced responsibilities after all, which suited her just fine. She enjoyed taking care of Duncan, whether as an attorney or as a professor. She'd suffered silently alongside her boss, not completely understanding why he was in so much pain. It made her feel good to see him smile again. She'd missed the soft southern tone that began to slowly reappear in his voice.

The transition from lawyer to professor was much more seamless than Duncan imagined that it would be. As was true with all of his endeavors, Duncan immersed himself in the job, trying to fight back the evil he knew was lurking inside the depths of his heart. The changes in his life were helping. As weeks turned into months, the dreams became less frequent and decidedly less grotesque and violent. His depression was also waning, as were the headaches, which had all but disappeared. Watching the young minds under his care blossom was giving his life a sense of meaning and purpose.

One day, after subjecting his class to a particularly difficult examination, one of his students complained, "That test was brutal, man. Why don't you just kill me right now and get it over with?"

Duncan smiled and jokingly replied, "No thanks. But I'll take a rain check."

At least he *thought* he was joking.

CHAPTER 99

I T WAS NOT as if someone had turned a switch off inside his head. Every night he went to bed with murder on his mind, and each morning he was compelled to fight back against his lust to kill. He had resolved himself to wage that battle for the rest of his life.

Even so, with each day that went by the idea of killing became more and more repugnant to him. The demons still frequently visited his thoughts, but they were losing their grip on his soul.

Professor Duncan Gabrelli was in many respects a changed man. He was truly content for the first time in many years. Teaching was not a job, it was a calling.

Stella also found the atmosphere on campus rejuvenating. Each morning, he and Stella would meet in the professors' lounge to discuss the day's events and projects.

His students were some of the brightest in the country. It was more than just his responsibility to keep abreast of every change in the law, it was a necessity. His students spent their evenings looking for ways to challenge the brilliant Professor Gabrelli.

He pushed his students to prepare themselves to be the best lawyers they could be. In fact, he demanded it from them. He also turned that challenge inward, and he avidly read every published criminal law case in search of any nuance that he could share with his students.

That same challenge was evidenced in his lectures and even more dramatically in his written examinations. He was dedicated to making his classes and tests reflect more than just hornbook law. As often as not, they included analysis of legal issues pending before the courts.

The first semester was drawing to an end. As he put the final touches on the semester examinations, Stella buzzed him over the intercom.

"Sir, there is an Agent Zachary Davis on line one for you. He says he's with the FBI. I told him you were busy."

Her words seemed to echo off the walls of his office. Sitting there in stunned silence, Duncan couldn't find the breath to respond.

"Sir, should I take a message?"

"No, no, I'll take the call. Just have him hold."

Taking a moment to compose himself, he walked over to the table to pour himself a glass of water. Then he picked up the phone and said, "Yes, this is Professor Gabrelli. How can I help you?"

"Hello, Professor, this is Agent Davis. Thank you for taking my call. I have a matter I would like to discuss with you. Would it be possible to meet with you this week? Your help would be greatly appreciated."

He thought about inquiring specifically what the agent wanted to discuss, but he didn't want to appear defensive or uncooperative. "It's the end of the semester, Agent Davis. I have a very busy sched—"

Before he could finish his thought, Agent Davis cut in. "It should only take a few minutes of your time."

Seeing he wasn't going to just take a simple no for an answer, Duncan replied, "If it's that important, I'm sure I can find some time for you this week. In fact, I have an hour tomorrow afternoon if you'd like to meet at three here in my office."

"That would be very helpful, sir. I will see you tomorrow at three o'clock."

Why Duncan suggested that they meet so soon wasn't clear. Maybe he was trying to appear nonchalant. Maybe he just wanted to get it over with. That night he had his first sleepless night in many weeks.

The next day, the clock seemed to visibly slow down as the hour grew nearer to three o'clock. Agent Davis shuffled into his office right on time. He was dressed in an awkward Sears-quality suit. He looked like a little boy. He couldn't have been older than twenty-five.

Duncan's pulse rate began to slow back to normal at the sight of his youth. *They certainly wouldn't have sent a boy to interview one of the most prolific mass murderers in the nation's history,* he thought.

"Have a seat, young man. How can I be of service to the FBI?" he said with an almost comical lilt in his voice.

"Well, sir, for a number of years the central office of the FBI has been developing a theory that a large number of unsolved murders are linked. It may be that they were committed by the same person, or group of persons."

The intellectual part of his brain was thinking, *Why is it that all government agents speak in tones and phrases that sounded more robotic than human?* The practical side was suddenly scared shitless.

He began to feel a little nauseated. Reaching across his desk, he took a drink from his glass of water to clear his throat.

"Are you okay, sir? You don't look well."

"No, I'm fine, just needed a sip of water." *My God, they* did *send this boy, this snot-nosed boy, to interrogate me.* He felt a little insulted by the thought.

"Well, sir, the main office has all but given up on these cases. However, I have spent the last year reviewing them. There is just something about these cases that makes me believe that they're connected."

There was a brief pause in the conversation. It was as if Agent Davis thought he'd posed a question and was waiting for an answer. Duncan sat patiently, looking at the agent, waiting for him to complete his thought.

"Well, sir, Dean Price tells me that you are one of the foremost authorities on criminal behavior. I was hoping that you might be willing to take a look at these files. Perhaps, with your expertise, you will see something we're missing, if there are any clues that might connect these murders."

The color slowly returned to Duncan's face. He could tell from the tone of the agent's voice that he was nervous, and perhaps a little in awe of the law school professor, who no doubt came highly touted by the dean of UCLA.

"Son, how long have you been an agent for the FBI?" he asked in an intentionally condescending tone.

"Just over a year, sir."

One of those hard-charging types, probably looking to impress his boss with a little independent research. Reminds me of me.

"How many cases do you believe are connected?" Duncan questioned.

"At least thirty-five, but I believe that a thorough search of our files will reveal that there are more. Many more."

"And just what makes you believe that the cases may be connected?" This was the first question that he really wanted to know the answer to since the young agent walked into his office. *What did I do wrong? What clues did I leave behind?*

"It's a little complicated," the agent replied.

Being too young and naive to realize that he'd just insulted the world's foremost authority on criminal behavior, he continued without thought of an apology. "There is this computer in our Washington, DC, office. Its only job is to look for similarities and patterns in crimes. It also calculates murder rates, picking up even small changes and aberrations. In these cases, the computer found only a few similarities. First, the murders were all committed in very cold temperatures. Second, they were always committed at night, between the hours of six and midnight. Last, they were committed in small towns all across the country, but always within an hour of a major city."

"And just what is so complicated about that?" Duncan replied sarcastically.

"I'm sorry, sir. What was strange about *these* cases is that the computer singled them out as being so completely different. With the exception of what I have told you, there are *no* commonalities. That in and of itself is an anomaly. It suggests that maybe the murders were committed with the intention of making them look different to avoid detection."

Duncan thought about what the young agent was saying for a moment before responding. It was not only clear that he was not a suspect, but it also dawned on him that the agent had no idea whom he was talking to. The only thing the agent knew about him was that the dean had declared him an authority on the subject.

"Son, do you know who I am?"

Thinking at first that the question might be rhetorical, but not wanting to sound impolite, he responded, "Yes, sir. You are the professor of criminal law here at the university."

"Is it safe to assume that you haven't received authority to show those files to me?"

"I have authority to show these files to the professor of criminal law here at UCLA. Inasmuch as you hold that position, I *do* in fact have that authority."

"I'm going to help your career, young man. What I want you to do is go to your superior and tell him that you have asked Duncan Gabrelli, the son of Vincenzo Bartelli, to assist the FBI in reviewing its files. If he gives you authority to show me those files, then I would be glad to assist you."

It sounded like a strange request, but the agent felt confident that his boss would give his okay, no matter who this Vincenzo Bartelli turned out to be. "I will do that first thing tomorrow morning and get back to you right away."

As he stood to say goodbye, Agent Davis couldn't resist the temptation to ask if Duncan thought that there was a chance that the murders might be connected. "I know you haven't looked at the files, but have you ever encountered a case where a serial killer attempted to make his crimes look like random acts?"

Responding after taking a second to consider the question, "No, I think not. You see, serial murderers are always caught. If the vast resources at the FBI's disposal—not to mention its computer in Washington—can't find a solid connection between the murders, then a connection most likely doesn't exist. Besides, thirty-five murders over the course of more than a decade? That's fewer than three murders a year. No. The reason you can't see a connection is because they are random acts."

Agent Davis gave Duncan a puzzled look. "These files involve murders that took place over the last *four* years. That is as far back as our database goes on murder cases. That's why I'm sure that a manual search would reveal more cases."

A nervous silence filled the room. At least, it felt that way to Duncan. When he could stand the feeling no more, he said, "Perhaps, after you have spoken to your supervisor, we will have an opportunity to discuss this matter further."

For a brief moment, Agent Davis wondered what made Professor Gabrelli think that the cases went back over a decade. However, his desire to run back and obtain authority to turn the files over to the renowned professor caused the question to fade away without inquiry.

The two men shook hands and said their goodbyes.

EPILOGUE

TWO WEEKS LATER

STELLA LOVED DUNCAN more than he could possibly know. His highs were her highs, and his lows were her lows. Duncan was too self-absorbed to see it, but she was completely committed to him, in every way that a woman could be committed to a man.

In his own way, Duncan loved her, too. Not in the way that Stella may have wanted, but still he had no closer friend and confidante than Stella.

She was particularly happy with how Duncan had taken to his new position as a law professor at UCLA. The pressures of his high-profile law firm were gone. He had not been practicing law, at least not full time, for just over a year. Even so, it seemed like a distant memory for both of them. Duncan would still take on the occasional pro bono case, just to keep his head in the game, but in truth he had put that part of his life behind him.

Stella, like Duncan, had no other family to speak of, so they frequently dined and occasionally had a few drinks in the pubs and taverns that lined the streets of Westwood, near the law school campus. Most of the students hung out in Westwood, drinking and discussing the pearls of wisdom that they had acquired during their lectures earlier in the day.

Duncan had become a very popular professor in a very short period of time. Popular might not be the correct word; everyone dreaded his tests. He demanded excellence from his students, and his classes were hard. As tough as his classes were, it was even tougher to get into one of his lectures. There were already waiting lists for students trying to get into classes he taught.

Rumors of his possible connection to the mob and aloof nature made him seem dark and mysterious. Most students were too afraid to approach Duncan outside the campus, but he always could feel the cold stares and hear his name among the whispers.

Stella was hard at work filing away last semester's binders when she heard Duncan's voice over the intercom. "Stella, come into my office when you get a minute."

As was always her way, she dropped what she was doing and headed directly into his office. "What's up, boss?" she said in a playful tone, as if she were one of his peppy students. There had been a transition in the way they spoke to each other since leaving the practice of law. They had always had a kind of sarcastic banter between them, but it had become much less biting.

Duncan liked the change, but he tried not to let Stella know. "Christ, Stella, you sound like a giddy schoolgirl. 'What's up, boss?' You must be...what? A hundred years old? Act your age." He was smiling as he said it, and Stella knew he was kidding, but it stung a little when he made fun of her age. But as usual, she ignored his snide remarks.

"What you need, boss man?"

Duncan just shook his head and smiled again. "I was wondering if we ever heard back from that FBI agent, what was his name?"

Sometimes Duncan completely underestimated Stella. She knew he had a photographic memory. He had no more forgotten the agent's name than he might forget his own. Even so, she played along. "Davis, FBI Agent Zachary Davis," Stella interjected.

"Yes, Agent Davis. Any word from him?" Duncan inquired, trying not to sound like he really cared too much.

"Nope! Not a peep, boss man." She was really trying to annoy Duncan at this point with her childlike responses.

Duncan knew what she was doing, and he fought back a smile. "Thank you, my love; that was all I needed," he said sarcastically. *Two can play at this game.* He looked down at the papers on his desk as if to say, *Go away.*

"As you wish boss man."

Stella, with a bounce in her step, turned to leave, giving him a little wiggle of her fanny on the way to the door.

Just as she reached the door she turned and said, "You did get a call from Mr. Balleto today. You were out so I put the message on your desk." Stella pointed to the message sitting on the corner of his keyboard.

Duncan stared intently at the single yellow Post-It. He had not spoken to Mr. Balleto since leaving his position with the syndicate. There was no reason why Mr. Balleto would call him. It was made clear that all of his connections to the syndicate had been severed, permanently and absolutely. Duncan's mind searched frantically for answers.

"Did he leave a message?" Duncan tried to hide the near-panic in his voice.

"Just that he would like to speak to you about Agent Dav--"

She paused as she spoke the agent's name. All the color had drained from Duncan's face, giving him a distressed look that Stella had never seen before.

"Are you okay, sir? You look a little flush."

Duncan didn't respond.

"Sir, are you--"

"Yes, I'm fine. Just shut the door behind you."

How did Mr. Balleto know about the agent's visit? How could he know? Only Stella and I--

Duncan paused mid-thought, his mouth agape.

Stella had just sat down at her desk when Duncan's voice came over the intercom. "Stella, come back in here."

Duncan was still wearing that distressed look as she sat down in the chair across from him.

"Stella." A long pause, and then, "Did you tell anyone outside this office about Agent Davis' visit?"

"I don't think so. Why? Was I not supposed to tell anyone?"

Duncan was not at all pleased with the question. Stella knew that she was never to discuss anything that happened in his office. The fact that they had switched from a law office to a professor's office made no difference to him.

"Damn it, Stella, you know damn well the answer to that question!"

Stella looked down at the floor to avoid his condemning glare. It had been a long time since Duncan has spoken to her in such an angry tone.

"Yes sir, I know."

Duncan tried to calm the rage in his voice. He paused, took a deep breath, held it for a moment.

"Stella, I want you to think very hard. Is it possible that you told anyone about Agent Davis' visit?"

She opened her mouth to speak, but then hesitated. She dropped her eyes back to her lap as she said, "No sir, I did not discuss that with anyone. I swear, no one." She looked up and met Duncan's gaze once more. "Is there a problem, sir?"

"No, that was all I needed to know, just let me have some time to think. Sorry for raising my voice. You're excused now. I just need to think."

As she headed for the door, she asked, "Sir, do you want me to get Mr. Balleto on the phone?"

"No, Stella, I will call him myself."

Stella was so anxious to leave his office that she was already back at her desk before he could finish his reply. Tears were beginning to roll slowly down her cheeks. But not because Duncan had screamed at her.

She had lied to him. She had disclosed the agent's visit to someone. In truth, she had been lying to him for a long time. Stella had secrets of her own. She was too afraid to tell him what she had done, or how deep the deception went.

In her effort to protect the man she loved, she had unwittingly unleashed evil forces beyond her comprehension. Both of their lives we now in grave peril.

Had Duncan not been so preoccupied, perhaps he would have noticed the desperate look in Stella's eyes, or he would have given greater consideration to his own question. *How did Mr. Balleto know about the agent's visit?*

Duncan rested his hand on the telephone receiver for at least a minute before lifting it from the cradle. The receiver felt too heavy in his hand, as if to portend the ominous nature of the call to come. This was not a call he wanted to make, but Mr. Balleto was not a man you kept waiting.

He glanced out the window of his office and sighed. Life as a college professor suited him. But he feared it would be short-lived.